ROAD
OF
BONES

ROAD OF BONES

A Billy Boyle World War II Mystery

James R. Benn

Published by Soho Press, Inc.
227 W 17th Street
New York, NY 10011

Library of Congress Cataloging-in-Publication Data

Names: Benn, James R., author.
Title: Road of bones : a Billy Boyle World War II mystery / James R. Benn.
Description: New York, NY : Soho Crime, [2021]
Series: The Billy Boyle mysteries ; [16]
Identifiers: LCCN 2021016213

ISBN 978-1-64129-200-9
eISBN 978-1-64129-201-6

Subjects: GSAFD: War stories. | Mystery fiction.
Classification: LCC PS3602.E6644 R63 2021 | DDC 813/.6—dc23
LC record available at https://lccn.loc.gov/2021016213

Printed in the United States of America

10 9 8 7 6 5 4 3 2 1

Dedicated to two men who helped form my view
of the world as a young man:

Thomas Dulack, novelist, playwright, and professor of English
literature at the University of Connecticut, who brought literature
to life in the classroom.

Arvis Averette, my supervisor when I was a VISTA Volunteer in
Portage County, Ohio, who taught by how he lived his life and
opened my eyes to issues of race and poverty.

Half a century later, I remember.

Death is the solution to all problems.

No man—no problem.

—Joseph Stalin

CHAPTER ONE

"NUMBER FOUR'S ON fire!"

"Jesus, Jesus, Jesus."

"God dammit, shut up!"

"Keep her straight, Skipper. IP coming up."

"Jesus, Jesus, Jesus."

An explosion burst outside the plexiglass, a flash of black and fire that sent shrapnel spitting against the metal frame of the aircraft as the concussion from the blast sent me sprawling against the bombardier. I strained to see engine number four, but from my position all I could make out was the spinning prop. I searched for flak damage, but didn't spot any holes in the fuselage or in me.

"Keep her straight! Fuck!" That was the bombardier, leaning over his bombsight, readying for the final run in to the target as we approached the initial point. Even though he was within arm's length, I could only hear him through the intercom, along with the other nine aircrew.

The bombardier sat forward in the nose compartment of the B-17, working either the bombsight or the controls for the twin machine guns in the front turret directly below him. To his left rear, the navigator had a small table where he kept track of our position. He was also responsible for two machine guns, one on the left cheek of the nose right above him, and one on the right. The skipper had put me on the right cheek gun, where I had to stand pressed against the side of the compartment, watching my assigned patch of sky.

"Shutting down number four."

"Extinguishing fire."

That was from the pilot and copilot, calm and businesslike.

"It's still smoking. Shit!"

"Jesus, Jesus, Jesus."

That was from the gunners who had a view of number four belching flame and smoke. It wasn't a vision that inspired calmness.

"Two 109s, ten o'clock high!"

"Heading low!"

The navigator manned the left cheek machine gun in the cramped nose compartment. He strained to get a bead on the two Messerschmitt 109 fighters diving toward the formation, but it was the top turret gunner who cut loose, the shattering bursts from his twin .50 guns echoing throughout the fuselage. I gripped the right cheek machine gun and searched for something to shoot at. Everything was happening too quickly, too loudly, too deadly sharp. The Fortress ahead of us was hit, bright sparks dancing along its wing as the fighters flew through the formation and banked away, tracers tagging after them.

"Fighters breaking off."

"Petey, you see anything back there?"

"No more fighters. How's number four?"

Petey was the tail gunner, and he had reason to be worried. If the order came to bail, he would take the longest to get out, hook a parachute to his harness, and exit the rear emergency hatch.

"How's number four, dammit?"

"Relax, Petey, she's fine."

"Relax, Skipper? That's a good one." The crew gave Petey and the skipper a razzing, blowing off steam as the bomb run drew closer.

"IP in five seconds." Navigator's update. That was Carter, whose freckles and red hair made him look eighteen, tops. Maybe he was twenty, although I doubted it.

"Turning," the skipper announced. The intercom went quiet.

I scanned the ice-blue sky decorated with streaming white contrails trailing the Flying Fortresses. The absence of fighters meant we were entering a zone of concentrated antiaircraft fire. The Luftwaffe would be waiting for us to emerge on the other side.

The sky ahead was crowded with angry black puffs, cherry red bursts at the core. Flak. We were approaching the target area, and, from the initial bombing point, the entire formation would fly straight and true for the target. The oil refineries in the German city of Chemnitz.

"Jesus, Jesus, Jesus," the ball turret gunner repeated.

Straight and true, which meant we'd be flying into the thickly defended ring around the city where the 88mm antiaircraft guns were situated, filling the air with explosions calculated to bring down as many bombers as possible. We were following the lead aircraft with the lead bombardier, presenting the Fritzes below with a nice steady stream of targets. Over seventy-five B-17 Flying Fortresses, each carrying five thousand pounds of bombs.

We'd been lucky so far. Although, if I'd truly been a lucky guy, I'd be having a beer back in London right now, not flying through the frigid, flak-filled air twenty-five thousand feet over Germany. But I didn't have time to dwell on what had brought me here. From my view over the bombardier's shoulder, I could see more than I wanted to of what lay ahead. The leading edge of the fuselage was a clear plexiglass nose, allowing the bombardier a dizzying view of the ground and the target ahead.

Flak so thick you could walk on it. I always thought the flyboys were kidding, but that's what it looked like.

"Jesus." That was the ball turret gunner. He was running out of Jesuses.

The air began to rumble, as if we were flying into a thunderstorm. Cracking explosions of flak darkened the sky around us, the concussive blasts shaking the aircraft, tossing me against the machine gun, then sending me crashing into the ceiling. Each burst seemed louder than the last, until the roar of the engines and the detonating flak merged into a single, all-encompassing tidal wave of sound, penetrating my bones and boring into my skull.

The Fortress ahead and above us took a hit above its tail assembly, the flak sending debris spinning off the plane and showering our nose with metal. I raised my arm to shield my eyes as the fragments struck, but the bombardier didn't flinch. Hunched over his Norden bombsight, he was flying the airplane now, guiding us to the target.

The wounded Fortress ahead and above us lost altitude and swayed side to side as the pilot struggled to stay in formation with a hunk of tail section gone. Except for his drift, the stream of bombers held steady.

So far.

Flak exploded low in front of us, the black oily puffs working their way higher as the gunners below adjusted their aim.

A Fort low and to the left took a burst under the wing, which broke apart at the fuselage and folded up like a book slammed shut, the spinning props ripping into the other wing and ensnaring it in a final, terrible embrace. The plane twirled downward, almost lazily, but I knew that any crew left alive were pinned by the centrifugal force, unable to act, unable to escape.

Robbed of its forward motion, the doomed Fortress dropped through the formation, other bombers taking evasive action to avoid a collision, then reforming as it passed, carrying ten men down to the hard German ground.

"No parachutes," the ball turret gunner reported. "Jesus, Jesus."

He'd found the Lord again.

"Okay, eyes front. Watch for fighters," the skipper ordered, not because there were any fighters in sight but to draw the crew's vision away from their dying pals.

"Lead bomber has dropped," the radioman reported.

"Opening bomb bay doors."

It wouldn't be long now. If this was area bombing, the entire formation would have released at once. But the assignment was to hit an oil refinery on the outskirts of the city, and that required a pinpoint approach. I could see the explosions on the ground below, and I prayed for the bombardier to release our load quickly so we could escape the growing flak.

Two bursts bracketed the aircraft, sending me tumbling forward.

The intercom went loud, live with frantic crewmen checking in as the skipper asked for a damage report. More flak exploded around us, rocking the ship like a cradle in a windstorm.

"Bombs away," the navigator announced, calmly giving a thumbs up. "Get us the hell outta here." The aircraft jolted, rising as it shed its heavy load of ordnance. I didn't care about the bombs exploding below or whether they hit the oil refinery. I cared about escaping into the vivid blue above.

"Boyle," the skipper called out.

"Here," I said, keying my throat mic.

"Make yourself useful and get to the tail. Petey didn't respond. And hurry, the fighters will be back once we clear the flak."

I unhooked from the intercom and oxygen system, grabbed a portable canister, and plugged in. Without oxygen, I'd be unconscious in no time and never know what hit me. Maybe Petey got disconnected by accident, or maybe there was intercom trouble. Either way, someone had to check, and as the least useful man aboard, I was elected.

I struggled to get through the narrow compartment, clumsy in my thick, insulated flight suit. But it was the flight engineer, Mick Heller, who sent me reeling. Pushing past me as he climbed down from the top turret, he slammed to a halt at the bomb bay.

Cold winds hurled against us as he shouted into my ear.

"Bomb's hung up!"

He pointed to a single five-hundred pounder hanging in the rack, the tail fin stuck and the warhead slanting downwards. If flak hit anywhere near that thing, or if we took fire from a fighter, it would blow us all to hell and gone.

Heller gripped a stanchion and stepped out onto the narrow metal catwalk that spanned the open bomb bay. The wind blast was so fierce, I could see the exposed skin around his oxygen mask blown back. Holding on, with no parachute and five miles of air beneath him, he kicked at the bomb, again and again.

It didn't budge.

He pointed at my feet, jabbing his finger at a box secured to the fuselage and making a squeezing motion. I spotted a tube of grease and got the message. I grabbed it, took hold of a stanchion, and eased my way onto the catwalk, shocked at the frigid wind pushing at me. I looked down and decided that hadn't been a good idea. I felt dizzy, frozen, and shaky.

Heller pulled me closer, closer than I needed to be just to hand him the tube. He took it and greased the rack, then raised his leg to kick again. But this time he hesitated, waiting for me to join in.

Hell no, I wanted to say. I wanted to tell him I was afraid of heights and afraid of jumping on armed high-explosive bombs.

But instead we kicked. One, twice, then a third time. At the third kick, the bomb gave out a high-pitched squeal against the rack. The fourth kick did it. The bomb fell away, descending to whatever German real estate was unlucky enough to receive it. A flak gun, I sincerely hoped, but the truth was, I didn't give a damn. That was the enemy below, the enemy that had been trying to kill us all damn morning.

We inched our way off the catwalk as the bomb bay doors began to close. I was shaking when we got on what passed for solid ground. Fear and arctic cold are a lousy combo for keeping your hands steady.

Not that my right hand hadn't been shaky as all hell at sea level either. But that was different. Shell shock. Combat fatigue. Nervous in the service, whichever way you sliced it, I'd needed a rest. But instead, here I was dodging lead five miles above Nazi Germany, and these shakes were from the frigid temperature and wind chill.

Heller thumped me on the shoulder and removed his oxygen mask. He whacked it against his arm, sending shards of ice flying. Then he pointed at me and put it back on. I followed suit, dislodging the ice crystals that had condensed from my breath. It felt better, if better is possible at forty degrees below zero.

Petey. I still had to check on Petey.

I plugged into the intercom and keyed my throat mic again.

"Skipper, I didn't get past the bomb bay."

"Petey's okay, I sent one of the waist gunners. Comm is knocked out. Get back to your position. Hey guys, Boyle's now an honorary bombardier."

That earned a few choice comments. The navigator gave me a

thumbs up as I squeezed back into the nose section, and the bombardier sent a grin my way from behind his mask. I marveled at how good it felt. Only a few hours ago these men were none too happy at having a passenger along for the ride. Now we were pals, all crewmen of the *Banshee Bandit*, veteran of fourteen missions. They were almost halfway through their thirty-mission tour.

I couldn't imagine flying thirty of these missions. But then again, most crews never made it to thirty. And I thought I'd had it hard in this war.

I craned my neck to pick out the *Sweet Lorraine*, flying off our starboard wing, about five hundred feet up. No signs of damage. I hoped their passenger was safe, from the Germans and their crew. They hadn't exactly been glad to see him.

CHAPTER TWO

I'D BEEN ENJOYING what I considered to be a well-earned rest when the summons had come. I was sitting in the bar at the Dorchester Hotel, sipping an Irish whiskey and watching the world go by. Most of the world was in uniform, and, from my perch, I looked out over an array of khakis, browns, and blues in various shades, along with the occasional evening gown to brighten up the joint.

"Billy, we got orders," Big Mike said, tossing an envelope on the table and heaving his muscular frame into the chair, which gave out a creak. Staff Sergeant Mike Miecznikowski, better known as Big Mike for obvious reasons, signaled the barman for a pint.

"To do what?" I asked, trying to sound unworried. Our boss, Colonel Sam Harding, had promised a few days off. Not that the brass at SHAEF—Supreme Headquarters, Allied Expeditionary Forces—were above pulling the rug out from under their juniors. "And when?"

"You ain't gonna believe it," Big Mike said, watching the progress as his pint was pulled. "We gotta leave right away for Thorpe Abbotts airbase."

"That's three hours away at least," I said. "What's the rush?"

"Two guys are dead," Big Mike said. "Sam wants us on the case."

Big Mike and me were two-thirds of the SHAEF Office of Special Investigations. The other third was Lieutenant Piotr Kazimierz of the Polish Armed Forces in the West. He was also an aristocrat, a baron of the Augustus clan, one of the few of the Polish nobility left standing after the Nazis and the Russians had overrun his nation.

But to us, he was simply Kaz.

Big Mike was Polish too, but he was a working-stiff Pole from Michigan. A flatfoot with the Detroit cops, he still carried his shield wherever he went, a bluecoat through and through.

Right now, Kaz was finishing up medical leave and tending to his long-lost sister Angelika, whom he'd thought dead in Nazi-occupied Poland. She'd managed to get out but was in bad shape. Kaz had taken her to the country, to Seaton Manor, where Sir Richard Seaton had offered his hospitality to aid her recovery.

Diana was there as well. Diana Seaton, the woman I loved. She was with SOE, the Special Operations Executive, the group the Brits had put together to operate behind enemy lines. Diana had been captured by the Gestapo, but she'd evaded the worst of what they could have done to her.

Long story. But she needed time to rest and recuperate too, so Sir Richard brought in a nurse for Angelika and let Kaz stay on as long as he wished. I'd hoped to get up there for at least a weekend, but now we had two stiffs that needed our attention.

"Murdered at the airbase?" I asked. Dead men were everywhere in September of 1944, but we specialized in the kind of crime that was frowned on even in peacetime.

"Looks like it. Not at Thorpe Abbotts. Another airbase," Big Mike said, his eyes tracking the pint as it was delivered to our table. He smacked his lips and gulped a good portion of it.

"What the hell are you not telling me?" I asked, eyeing the thick envelope containing our orders. It seemed like more than the usual paperwork. Big Mike took another drink.

"The airbase is in Russia. That's where we're going," he said. And drank again.

"What do two dead Russians have to do with us?" I said, as I leaned forward in my chair and tried to take in the reality of what Big Mike had told me.

"One dead Russian, one dead American," he said. "You remember Bull Dawson?"

"Sure. Army Air Force colonel. Helped me out in Northern Ireland,

and we met up with him again a few months ago at air force headquarters in High Wycombe," I said. Big Mike nodded and waited for
me to make the connection. It didn't take long. "Shuttle bombing. He
was working on a plan for shuttle bombing missions. Take off from
England, land and refuel in Russia, then hit the Germans again on the
way back. Keep 'em guessing."

"Right. Except now Bull's a general, and he's stationed at one of
those bases. Poltava, in the Ukraine. He has an international incident
on his hands and got in touch with Sam."

"Who volunteered our services. Nice of him," I said, and downed
the last of my whiskey.

"He didn't have much choice," Big Mike said. "Our ambassador in
Moscow was already calling for help. The Russkies are blaming us and
demanding we hand over the guilty party. They finally agreed to allow
a team to be sent in to work with their investigators."

"Russia," I said, hardly able to take in what Big Mike was telling
me about diplomats and dead men. "We're going to Russia. How the
hell do we get there?"

"You might want another drink," he said.

WE HAD A driver to take us to Thorpe Abbotts. We tried to sleep
in the back seat, which was easy for Big Mike. Me, I tended to dwell
on what was coming next. A briefing at 0430 hours, which was army
talk for way the hell before the sun came up. Then a long flight over
Nazi Germany. Swell.

I'd had to pack my Class A uniform, because the brass wanted us
to look spiffy for our Russian allies. I had no idea how we were going to
conduct a joint investigation, but at least I'd impress the Soviet coppers
with my shiny buttons.

I managed to doze for a while. After the driver got us to the base,
we were directed to a tent with a couple of cots and lots of scratchy
blankets. Big Mike sawed logs while I worried. About what was
coming. About Kaz, recovering from his medical procedure and caring
for his kid sister, who'd been through a brutal ordeal.

About how Diana was doing. She hadn't been in Gestapo custody long, thank God, but any amount of time in the clutches of those Nazi bastards was too long. I wanted to be by her side, not flying off into the wild blue. Yeah, I wanted to be with her, to make sure she healed up well in mind and body, but also to make sure to she didn't get any crazy ideas about going on another SOE mission.

Of course, I was hardly the one to talk.

I must have slept, because the next thing I knew a guy was shining a flashlight in our faces and hollering for us to get up. We followed the line of grumbling, yawning aircrew to the latrines, washed up, and made for the mess hall. It was a damp, chilly morning. In our army fatigues, we stood out like two left thumbs, surrounded by men in leather jackets and flight suits.

No one talked to us as we wolfed down powdered eggs and sausage, accompanied by steaming hot joe. Men leaned over their food, their voices a low, steady murmur. A few guys just sipped at their coffee, eyes focused on the far wall, their thoughts straying from the eggs and sausage congealing on their plates.

Home. Death. Dismemberment. Survival. Fear. I'd seen that searching look on muddy battlegrounds, but on these clean-shaven faces it was a first. Didn't do much for my appetite.

Somebody called out for officers to assemble in fifteen minutes for their briefing. That meant pilots, copilots, navigators, and bombardiers. Enlisted men, all sergeants, were to head to their aircraft. Nobody acknowledged the guy, but men began to drift off, leaving the room half empty in a minute.

That made it easy to spot Colonel Harding. Tall, stiff-necked, and steely-eyed, Sam Harding commanded attention. And me, which often led to a whole lot of trouble for Mrs. Boyle's eldest boy.

"Sam!" Big Mike shouted, waving him to our table. The colonel drew himself a cup of coffee at the urn before heading our way. Big Mike was a staff sergeant who often disregarded the niceties of rank. He was on first-name basis with more generals than I cared to count. I couldn't carry it off, but, then again, with those shoulders, Big Mike could carry off an ox. He also had a scrounger's magical ability to come up with whatever was needed without reams of army paperwork. Most officers loved that, especially when it worked to their benefit. But with Sam Harding, it was different. They'd become real pals since Big Mike joined us in July of last year after giving me a hand when I needed it in Sicily.

As far as Harding and I went, let's just say we respected each other. I don't think I'd ever called him Sam, and right now, I had a few other choice names for him, but I kept them to myself.

"Colonel, tell me this is a big joke," I said, as soon as he sat down.

"No joke," Harding said, glancing around to see who was listening. No one had sat near us, and more guys were headed out, so we weren't about to be overheard. "We've got a dead Soviet and a dead American in strange circumstances. Moscow is raising hell and demanding we turn over the killer."

"Who must be a Yank, of course," I said.

"That's their take. Crime is a symptom of capitalist decay, after all," Harding said.

"I didn't take you for an expert on Marxist ideology, Colonel," I said.

"I've picked up a few things from their communiques," Harding said. "That's the most flattering one. I need you two there, Johnnies-on-the-spot."

"Why?" Big Mike asked, gulping the last of his grub. "Gotta be a safer way of getting there than on a bombing run."

"Safer, yes, but slow. What worries Ike is the possibility of the Russians grabbing one of our guys and charging him with the killings. Then we'd have to react, and before long there could be a standoff."

"And since the airbase is surrounded by a whole lotta Russia, they'd win the standoff," I offered.

"Right," Harding said, pausing to have another go at his joe. "Which could get nasty. We have three airbases over there. Poltava, where you're headed. That's designated as Station 559, and it's where the heavy bombers are based, along with a smaller field at Mirgorod. The third, Pyriatyn, is for Mustang long-range fighters."

"Nasty enough for them to grab our hardware?" Big Mike said.

"It's a possibility. If we fly them all out, then the Soviets could accuse us of reneging on our deal with them. If we leave everything in place, they could snap it all up. Either way it would be a political nightmare and interfere with the war effort," Harding said, his coffee forgotten.

"So we're supposed to uncover the murderer," I said. "With help from some Russian cop?"

"That's the idea. A joint investigation. The American Military Mission in Moscow got the Russians to agree to that much," Harding said. "Here's the thing, though. If the killer turns out to be a Russian, good luck with ever bringing him to justice. If he's American, get him out of there as soon as possible. We'll put him on trial, but not where the Soviets control things. Your first priority is to contain this thing. Make your best case, and protect any Americans involved."

"You think the Russians will really cooperate?" I asked.

"No. They're not known for playing nice. But they have assigned an English-speaking officer to the case, so at least you can talk to him."

"But what about talking with other Russians?" Big Mike asked. "We can't depend on him for speaking with witnesses or suspects."

"No. But you can depend on Lieutenant Kazimierz. He'll arrive several days after you do. With his language skills, he'll be a big help," Harding said.

"You sure, Sam?" Big Mike asked. "He hasn't been out of the hospital that long."

"But he's healthier than before," Harding said. Kaz had some repair work on his ticker, which had been giving him trouble. Bad trouble. But Harding was right, Kaz had healed up just fine.

"But not healthy enough for this trip," I said, jerking my thumb in the direction of the officers making for the briefing.

"Listen, I know this is a tough assignment, but I didn't see any reason for Lieutenant Kazimierz to undergo the stress of a long and unpressurized flight at high altitudes. He'll go by Sunderland flying boat. It's a hotel compared to the B-17. It'll take him via Cairo and Tehran, then up to Poltava on a regular C-47 resupply flight."

"No, I'm glad," I said. "We can handle it until Kaz gets there, right Big Mike?"

"Sure. If Sam says we gotta get there PDQ, then we'll take the express. It is important, isn't it, Sam?" It wasn't exactly insubordinate, but Big Mike had made his point. He wanted to know if this mission was on the level.

"It's very important," Harding said, fixing Big Mike with a stare. "So important that the orders came from high up. I had all I could do to get Lieutenant Kazimierz on that slower flight."

"By high up, you mean Uncle Ike?"

"The general himself," Harding said. General Dwight David Eisenhower, commander of SHAEF, was a distant relation. A second cousin or something along those lines, but I'd always called him Uncle Ike on account of how old he was. He was the reason I was here, on his staff. My dad and uncle, both detectives on the Boston police force, cooked up a scheme for me to stay safe and sound during this war. They got me appointed to Uncle Ike's staff in Washington DC, where he was pushing paper as an unknown colonel. What we didn't know was that he was about to be tapped as head of US Army forces in Europe. He got a promotion to general and me to take along as his special investigator.

Now what Uncle Ike couldn't have known was that for the Boston Irish, the police department is sort of like a family business. It gets handed down, which usually involves someone being compensated for the favor. But enough gossip about the good old Boston PD. The upshot was although I'd just made detective grade right about the time Pearl Harbor took a shellacking, I didn't really have the experience needed. What I had was an uncle on the promotions board and a father on the homicide squad, and they were both teaching me the ropes. When I paid attention.

More times than I can count, I'd wished I had focused more on what they were telling me. But I didn't want to fail Uncle Ike, and I also didn't want to be sent off to the infantry to take a chance on the average life expectancy of platoon leader. So I worked at remembering what they'd tried to drum into my head, and Uncle Ike was never the wiser. I think.

Anyway, I'd managed to get myself promoted to captain, which was nice. But as I thought about this mission, a foxhole on the front lines became strangely appealing.

"Let's get to the briefing," Harding said. "I'll introduce you to your crews. I've split you up."

"In case one doesn't make it?" Big Mike said. "That's cheery."

"No. Weight requirements. Besides, you both could get shot down," Harding said, his face twisting itself into an attempted smile as he stood. It took me a second to realize he was joking. Harding was career Army, a West Point graduate. Humor hadn't been issued to him, so it was strange to hear him attempt it.

"Comforting, Colonel," I said as we made for the door. "Are you sure you've told us everything about this case? It still seems to me that something's missing."

"What?" Harding asked, his voice slightly higher than normal. That was his tell.

"A lot of Russians have died in this war. Joe Stalin doesn't seem like the kind of leader to care much about one more corpse. What makes this Russian so special?"

"He's NKVD," Harding said. "The People's Commissariat for Internal Affairs."

"The Russian version of Hitler's Gestapo," Big Mike said.

"Essentially, yes. But don't say that when you're their guest. It might turn into a permanent stay," Harding said, opening the door to the Quonset hut where the briefing was about to start.

"You've got to be kidding, Colonel," a first lieutenant said, striding forward toward us. He wore a crush cap and a pencil thin mustache that probably looked great on a movie star from his youth. Which wasn't all that far in the rearview mirror. "This guy's too big. We'll have to leave a two-hundred-and-fifty-pound bomb behind."

"Seriously, Colonel," another officer said. "There isn't enough room on a B-17 for an extra guy his size. Where we gonna put him? Why can't we have the skinny one?"

"Lieutenant Franks, Sergeant Miecznikowski has been assigned to your aircraft," Harding said. "I will leave the details to you. Carry on."

"I hope *Sweet Lorraine* gets off the ground," Franks said. "And I hope we have a parachute in your size, Sergeant. Come with me."

Harding and I shook hands with Big Mike and wished him luck.

Franks told his copilot to bring Big Mike to the rest of the crew assembling to check the aircraft, then hustle back.

"Don't worry, there's only one size parachute, Captain," another first lieutenant said, extending his hand. "I'm Bert Willis, skipper of the *Banshee Bandit*. We'll be giving you a lift."

"Call me Billy," I said, appreciating his welcome. "I'll try not to get in the way. What's with Franks?"

"Your sergeant is a big fellow," Willis said. "Can't blame Franks for wondering where he's going to stash him. I figure I can squeeze you in the nose and you'll man one of the cheek machine guns. The navigator switches back and forth as needed, but if you stay pasted to the wall, you won't be in anyone's way. Can you hit a barn door?"

"Pretty sure I can, long as it's not flying."

"Okay, just don't shoot at the *Sweet Lorraine*. They'll be off our starboard wing. Now let's listen up. The show's about to start," Willis said.

"Looks like Big Mike drew the short straw," I whispered to Harding as we took our seats.

"Franks and his crew have completed twenty missions," he said. "They know what they're doing. You have to admit, making room for Big Mike is a challenge."

"Speaking of challenges, any more details you haven't shared?" I asked as a bird colonel took to the stage, where a curtain covered a large map board where the mission would be laid out.

"Only one. The OSS is involved. They have men on the ground at Station 559."

Great. The Office of Strategic Services, our own spy outfit. That could complicate things.

"Gentlemen, the mission for today," the colonel intoned, pulling back the curtain. "The oil refineries at Chemnitz."

A groan rippled through the room. It was a long way to Chemnitz, over the Netherlands and into the heart of Germany. After hitting the target, it was an even longer trip to Poltava.

We'd have fighter escort all the way, long-range P-51s with drop tanks. That was the good news. The bad news?

Everything else.

CHAPTER THREE

"LITTLE FRIENDS JOINING up, three o'clock high." That was Heller in the top turret. Our fighter escort had gone high during the bombing run and flak barrage. Now they were back as the bomber stream reformed into the box pattern, maximizing the defensive fire of all those .50 machine guns.

"Watch for enemy fighters, they'll be back too."

I could make out the P-51 Mustangs above us, sunlight glinting off their gleaming, nimble airframes. They were little friends indeed, the only friends we had for hundreds of miles. We still had nine hundred to go to get to Poltava, almost half of that over enemy territory. If it wasn't for the Mustangs, the Luftwaffe would have plenty of time to chew us up.

"Here they come, twelve o'clock low," the skipper announced. I could barely make out a series of black specks in the distance, climbing to intercept the formation. Four Mustangs zoomed down on them, sending the line of German aircraft into a sprawling, circling dogfight, breaking up their frontal assault even as the bulk of our escort kept pace above us.

"Keep your eyes peeled, that was just the opening act," Willis said.

Things were quiet for a while. Then I noticed a B-17 ahead of us slowly losing altitude, smoke sputtering out of an inboard engine. Flak damage, maybe. Whatever the cause, the Fort was headed lower and slower, not a healthy combination in these parts.

"That's *Mad Mary*," Heller said. "O'Brien's crew. They're new."

"How far to the Russian lines?" Willis asked.

"Checking," Carter replied, and came back on the intercom in a minute. "Two hundred and eighty miles, assuming our info is accurate."

Nobody spoke. I watched as *Mad Mary* fought to maintain airspeed and altitude. It was a slow but steady process, and as the Fort faded from view beneath our wing, I fixed my gaze on the sky ahead, trying not to think about the fate of the crew. Even if a couple of P-51s stayed with her, they wouldn't be able to hold off the German fighters who were sure to swarm any damaged bomber trailing the main formation. In the terrible calculation of death at twenty-five thousand feet, *Mad Mary* was on her own. Even if the crew managed to get her across the Russian lines, it was a long way to any airbase. The Luftwaffe was still strong on the Eastern Front, and their range would extend deep into Russia.

Mad Mary's best bet was to make it out of Nazi territory and crash land in a nicely plowed field. What was more likely was they'd be shot down before they got twenty miles, once they lost the protective fire-power of the box formation and the escort fighters.

It wouldn't be long. Maybe they'd decide to bail out and settle for a long stretch as POWs. From all reports, the food was lousy, but the Luftwaffe didn't treat American *kriegies* all that badly. *Kriegsgefangener* was the mouthful for prisoner of war in German. *Kriegie* made it sound almost friendly and welcoming. After all, no one was trying to blow you out of the sky in a POW cage.

"Bandits! Nine o'clock!"

"Closing fast. Mick?"

"I see 'em."

Heller's twin fifties blasted away, along with the waist gunner and Carter on his left cheek gun. I saw tracers flash across our bow and in a split second two Me 109s sped by, one after the other. The bombardier fired at them with his two guns in the chin turret as I cut loose, too late to hit the leading plane, but I swear I hit his wingman, sparks lighting up his fuselage.

It was exhilarating, I gotta admit.

"Four more!"

"Where, dammit?"

"Ten o'clock high!"

Machine guns let loose all around us as the Me 109s dove into the formation, twisting and turning, darting between bombers, and scoring hits as they weaved their way in and out of the bomber stream, putting on one helluva show. These guys were good.

But so were our fighter jockeys, who were too smart to follow the Fritzes into the maelstrom of fire that greeted them. Above us, they circled, waiting to pounce as soon as the Messerschmitts got clear.

"I think I hit one!" I said, keying my mic and unable to rein in my enthusiasm.

"We all think we hit 'em. Keep your eyes open. Petey, you okay back there?" That was Heller, the flight engineer and basically the top dog among the enlisted men.

"Havin' the time of my life, Mick," Petey answered. "Here they come again, pair on our six!"

Guns shattered the air, Petey in the tail position and Mick in the top turret getting a bead on the two fighters. For all the silence you'd expect five miles up, it was blisteringly noisy.

"I got him, the fucking Nazi bastard, I got him!" Petey was whooping and hollering over the intercom.

"Jesus, Jesus, Jesus."

"He's smoking," Carter reported.

"Spiraling down," Willis said. "Confirmed kill, Petey."

There was a lot of chatter over Petey's victory, but Willis told the crew to knock it off and stay alert. Good advice. It should have been easy to stay alert between the sharp wind, frigid temps, and Germans trying to kill me, but I felt exhausted. Drained. I leaned against the cold metal, hunched over my weapon, and scanned the sky for more fighters.

I tried to rub my eyes, but my cheeks were numb, and all I managed to do was knock ice crystals off my eyelids. I caught sight of *Sweet Lorraine*, sunlight glinting off the aluminum frame. B-17s were arriving unpainted these days, no need for camouflage paint which added unnecessary weight. With contrails streaming behind us, and reflected light from the sun brightly flashing off airframes, we were signaling our presence to anyone within miles.

There were so many Allied aircraft over Europe these days that stealth was not deemed necessary. But up here, with several of our original number gone, it felt like unnecessary bravado to me.

I leaned over to Carter and shouted, asking if we were still over Germany.

"Poland," he answered, pointing to a smudge on the distant horizon. "Krakow."

Kaz had a cousin in Krakow, I think. I'd have to remember to tell him I'd seen the city. And to give him a hard time about his comfortable first-class ride, while Big Mike and I froze our tails off. As the formation droned on, I began to think about all the things I wanted to do once we were on the ground in one piece. Like get warm. Sample some Russian vodka. Catch a killer.

Simple stuff.

Enemy fighters left us alone for a while. Carter announced that the Russian front lines should be coming up soon. We were down to twenty thousand feet now, and it was a little easier to make out landmarks below, including the Vistula River, which the Soviet forces were approaching. I spotted several thin plumes of smoke marking the clash of armies. Not much to see at this distance, but if we could spot if from four miles up, there had to be a lot of death and destruction going on at ground level.

"Friendly territory below," Carter said over the intercom a few minutes later. Good news too, since we were swarmed by a dozen fighters right away. But they never got close to our ship and scattered as soon as the P-51s engaged.

"Look alive, boys," Willis said. "We may have company soon."

I shrugged in Carter's direction. He grabbed my arm and leaned in, pulling down his oxygen mask. "Those guys might be too low on fuel to hit us hard. But they might tail us and radio other squadrons to join in, then attack. Sometimes they follow us right to the base."

"Don't the Russians escort you in?" I shouted.

"Hell, we'll be lucky if they don't fire on us. Trigger-happy bastards."

With that reassuring notion, I went back to my gun. We left the smoke-shrouded front lines behind, and soon Carter told us the

Soviet border was coming up. Now we were over the Ukraine, one of the many republics of the USSR. All I really knew about it was that it was a big place filled with dead bodies, two of which got us sent here.

"Bandits dead ahead!"

"One o'clock high!"

"Here they come, diving low."

I saw the German fighters. There were a lot of them, and they seemed to be coming straight at me.

Silver Mustangs chased the fighters, a mix of Me 109s and Focke-Wulf 190s. Some of the Germans broke away and got tangled in dogfights with the P-51s, but the bulk of them kept coming in a frontal attack.

A dangerous tactic, but one that paid dividends if they took out the pilot and copilot. Then there was nothing to do but bail out. I watched the tracers zipping ahead of the fighters, hitting Forts as the fighters dove and darted to not give us a steady target.

A burst of flame, and a Fort fell from formation, trailing fire and smoke. The fighters were on us. I aimed at the closest one, but he dove and rolled, coming up beneath my gun's arc, firing as he turned away from our aircraft, his wingman following.

I sprayed the air with fire, hoping to at least distract their aim. I sighed with relief as they passed to our right, then shook it off and readied myself for another attack. A pair of Fw 190s swooped from above, hammering away with their 20mm cannon. I followed the two of them, hoping to score a hit, but my tracers fell short.

They broke right, headed straight for *Sweet Lorraine*. I saw she'd already been hit, the nose cone shattered and the chin turret silent. Cannon fire raked the cockpit before the Fw 190s pulled up and raced away, leaving the Fortress shattered and wobbling in midair.

Big Mike.

Where was he? If they'd stashed him up front, he was a dead man.

"*Sweet Lorraine* is going down," Heller said. "They got Franks and Schwarz for sure."

No pilot, no copilot, no hope.

The Fortress slowed and lost altitude, heading nose down. It vanished beneath our wing, and I keyed my microphone.

"Parachutes. Do you see 'chutes? How many?"

"None."

"Wait, here they come." That was the ball turret gunner, who'd have the best view. "One. Two. Three and four. One more. Oh shit. Jesus, Jesus, Jesus."

"She's going into a spin," Petey said. "No one else is getting out."

Five parachutes. A ten-man crew plus Big Mike. I didn't like the odds, not one damn bit.

I felt sick.

I slumped against the gun, resting my head against the chilled plexiglass.

"What's our position?" I managed to croak into the throat mic.

"Thirty miles northwest of Kozova, Ukraine," Carter answered.

"We'll radio the coordinates, Boyle," Willis said.

"Will our people send out aircraft?" I asked. "Or ask the Russians to send out a patrol?"

"No. It doesn't work that way out here," Willis said. "God help them, they're on their own. Now keep your eyes peeled, dammit. This is no time to slack off."

I tried to focus, tried to watch for tiny specks in the sky ready to turn deadly. It was all a blur of contrails and memories. Meeting Big Mike in Sicily. All the times he got me out of a tough jam. His Detroit cop stories. How he could wind senior brass around his oversized pinky and scrounge whatever was needed to keep them happy.

Could he really be dead?

I couldn't imagine it. He was Big Mike.

Larger than life.

He wasn't dead.

Jesus, Jesus, Jesus.

CHAPTER FOUR

"HOLD YOUR FIRE! Hold your fire!"

"Yaks, two o'clock low."

"Skipper, maybe we oughta give 'em a warning shot, uh?"

"Hold your fire and shut up."

"What the hell is happening?" I asked.

"Russian fighters," Willis said. "They're known to shoot first and not answer any questions later."

Three Yak-9 fighters swooped through the formation, big red stars clear and bright against their dull green camouflaged fuselages. They didn't shoot, but they did seem reckless, flying too damn close to our wing and diving under the B-17 in front of us.

The formation had descended, those Forts with wounded aboard given priority for landing. My priority was to get to Bull Dawson and make sure he mounted a rescue mission to bring in Big Mike. He knew him and was a general to boot. He was sure to have some leverage around here. The Bull I'd known got things done.

Finally, it was the *Banshee Bandit*'s turn to land. We thumped down on the steel matting laid out over a dirt runway, and I got my first close look at the Union of Soviet Socialist Republics. All I saw was a muddy field and a row of bombed out buildings on the far side. We taxied and followed the directions from ground crew in jeeps, a mix of Americans and Russians, as far as I could tell from the dirty uniforms. We passed rows of B-17s and B-24 Liberators, along with a few C-47 transport aircraft. They all seemed crammed together with no attempt at camouflage. Aircraft were usually dispersed and at least draped with netting to hide them.

"What gives?" I said, finally able to speak normally without the oxygen mask strapped to my face.

"Rules," Carter said. "The Russkies love their rules. We have to stay close to the assigned runway. Makes no sense to bunch up all those aircraft, but that's how things work here. Meaning mainly, they don't."

We clambered down from the Fort, shedding wool-lined jackets, gloves, and heavy pants. Jeeps pulled up to the Fortresses lined up in a row, and crews began to pile in for the debriefing, toting their duffels. A few yards away, Russian soldiers were in a line, rifles sporting two-foot bayonets on their shoulders and their faces draped with scowls.

I savored the solid ground, even though it didn't seem like friendly territory. It was earth and I was upright, which was enough to be thankful for. I prayed Big Mike was on his feet as well.

Another jeep drove up, this one at high speed, with a Russian at the wheel. A lady Russian attired in an olive green uniform. She slammed on the brakes and jumped out. Up close I noticed her light blue shoulder boards matched her eyes.

"Captain William Boyle!" she shouted. I raised my hand and she gave me a snappy salute. "I am Lieutenant Maiya Akilina. Leave your bag, our men will take care of it. You are to come with me."

"Where to?" I asked, returned her salute.

"Don't waste your breath asking questions," Willis said as he got into a jeep. "Maiya's one of General Ilia Belov's interpreters. He's the base commander, for the Russians, anyway. He's a man of many demands and few answers."

"Captain Boyle, please hurry," she said. I tossed the rest of my cold-weather gear into Willis's jeep and got in next to Maiya.

"Your English is very good," I said.

"I have had much practice here, Captain, since no Americans have bothered to learn Russian," she said, gunning the engine and executing a turn that sent ground crew scattering. "A very big mistake, if you do not mind my saying."

"Well, I never thought I'd pay your country a visit," I said, holding onto my forage cap as she accelerated. Sandy-colored hair flew back from under her service cap, and she smiled, her cheekbones riding high.

"And I never thought I would be able to practice my English with you Americans. It is so different from the English I learned at school. What's buzzin', cuzzin?"

"What's cozy, Rosie?" I answered, and she laughed.

"I do not know what all the phrases mean, but I do enjoy Mister Cab Calloway," Maiya said. "They play his records in the officers' club."

"Where are you taking me?" I asked.

"General Belov wishes to greet you," she said. "It is an honor."

"Coffee would also be an honor," I said. "It's been a tough day. Tell me, how do I go about organizing a search party? Some of our guys had to bail out near Kozova."

"The Red Army will find them, do not worry," she said, taking a turn onto a road that once had been lined with buildings, some four stories high. All ruined now, bombed, burned, and blackened. "This was a major air base before the Germans came. A city unto itself. They destroyed everything when they left."

"Yeah, they're big on destruction. But shouldn't we alert the troops in the Kozova area?"

"You may ask General Belov," she said. "But foreigners are not allowed to roam about the country. The Red Army will apprehend them."

"You mean rescue," I said, as she took a corner without slowing.

"You may ask General Belov," she repeated. "There are spies everywhere. Germans in our uniforms. Polish bandits, fascist Ukrainians. It is dangerous."

She pulled up in front of a row of wooden buildings. Recently built, some of them with the planks still unpainted, they ran along a road facing a tall apartment building with soot-stained gaping windows and a caved-in roof, blackened timbers jutting out at odd angles.

"Your barracks are at the end of the street," Maiya said as she got out of the jeep, smoothing down the folds of her uniform and taking a deep breath. "This is the joint US-Soviet operations center."

"Is Belov a tough boss?"

"You may ask General Belov," she said. She took the four steps onto a wide porch and opened the door, holding it for me. I had to admit, that was a pretty useful line.

I went in, Maiya on my heels. She guided me past a nest of desks where Russian and American clerks sat, working telephones and typewriters. Then to an office with General Dawson on the nameplate. She knocked and ushered me in.

"I will inform General Belov you are here," she said, turning on the heel of her black boot.

"Billy, it's good to see you," Bull Dawson said, stepping out from behind his desk to shake my hand. "Welcome to Station 559."

"Not exactly pleased to be here, General, but at least I arrived in one piece. Can't say the same for Big Mike. His plane was shot down. Five parachutes." The room felt hot. Sweat soaked my back and I reached for a chair to steady myself. Then I shivered, as if the ice-cold sky was still with me.

"Christ," Bull said, guiding me to the chair. "Have a seat. You sure you're not hurt?"

"I'm okay," I said. "Just bone tired. What can we do about Big Mike? We gotta find him."

"Hang on," Bull said, and grabbed the phone. He ordered sandwiches and coffee to be brought in, along with a Major Black. "Let's get some grub into you first."

"Who's Black, General?"

"OSS. He's here as part of joint operations between the OSS and the NKVD. He understands how they think better than most. I figured he could help. So, you don't know for sure if Big Mike was one of the five?"

"He was," I said, avoiding the other possibility. "But the question is, what are you going to do about our five guys lost out there?"

"Where, exactly?"

"Northwest of Kozova. Carter, the navigator on the *Banshee Bandit*, said he'd radioed in the coordinates."

"That's almost five hundred miles west of here," Bull said, leaning back in his chair and pointing to a map on the wall. "There's a lot of Soviet ground out there. The good news is they didn't bail out over German-held territory."

"That's what passes for good news around here," said a US Army major holding the door open for a corporal bearing a plate of sandwiches and a pot of coffee.

"Billy, this is Preston Black. He's with the OSS Mission. He works closely with the NKVD and I thought he could give you advice on working with them," Bull said.

"I'm working with the NKVD?" I said, nodding my thanks to the corporal and grabbing a bacon sandwich.

"It's inescapable," Black said. "Assume every Russian you speak with will report the conversation back to an NKVD officer. They're the ones with the blue bands on their caps. But their influence is everywhere."

"What about the Russian cop I'm working with?" I asked, getting the words out around a mouthful.

"Whatever uniform he shows up in, assume he's NKVD, and that his primary goal is to pin these murders on an American and extract something from us as well. It could be propaganda points, war materials, or control over the targets we bomb," Black said.

"He's not here yet? Christ, I made it here from England in record time and lost Big Mike along the way. I thought this was a rush job," I said. I was mad, but not mad enough to spill the coffee, hot, strong, and bitter, just like the news I was getting.

"Welcome to the Soviet Union," Bull said. "These people can be generous, fun-loving, and helpful. Until they're not. It's hot and cold with them."

"It all comes down to Moscow and the NKVD. If your average Russian knows that Joe Stalin and his boys approve of something, they'll move heaven and earth to make it happen. If they're uncertain about it, they'll promise the moon while they stall and do nothing."

"And if Stalin objects?" I asked, watching Black over the rim of my cup as I savored another gulp.

"You're a dead man if you push it," Black said.

"Even Americans?" I asked.

"Bull said there was a lot of Russian ground out there," Black said, gesturing with one hand toward the window and the ruined buildings across the street. "He's right. Good farmland, soft earth, easy for digging shallow graves."

"These guys are our allies, right?" I asked.

"Paranoid allies," Black said. "But their paranoia is based on real fears. The Communists have long memories. They remember that after the First World War, America sent over thirteen thousand soldiers to fight against them, along with a lot of British, French, and other troops."

"I never heard of that," I said.

"That's because we have short memories, and the whole attempt to intervene in the Russian Civil War was a massive failure. It was a quarter century ago, which is yesterday in this country. You might not know about it, but every good Marxist is well aware America tried to defeat their glorious revolution, and given another chance, would try again."

"So what the hell are you doing here, working with the NKVD?" I asked.

"The enemy of my enemy is my friend," Black said, giving an apologetic shrug. "We're coordinating activities and exchanging information. Our networks in Eastern Europe need to be aware of what each agency is up to, otherwise we could end up working at cross purposes."

"Sounds logical," I said, going for another sandwich, trying to fuel my body. I was exhausted. The massive adrenaline rush from the bombing raid across occupied Europe was crashing down on me, but I needed to stay focused. I needed to find a way to navigate this strange place and get the hell out of Station 559 and search for Big Mike.

"Major Black is our resident specialist on Russia," Bull said. "He speaks the language, so he'll be with you when you meet with Belov. Strictly a courtesy visit, but it will be good to have him confirm what Maiya translates."

"I'm not fluent," Black said, "but I can tell if she's translating you correctly."

"Why wouldn't she?" I asked, feeling there was more going on here than I could grasp.

"If she feels you're going off into uncharted waters, she'll muddy them," Black said. "It's easier that way, see? Then Belov isn't forced to concern himself with things that might upset Moscow."

"Or the local NKVD," I said.

"Right. You're getting the hang of how things work," Black said.

"How'd you get to be such an expert on the Russians?" I asked, washing down the last of the sandwich with coffee. Bacon grease and caffeine were my best friends right now.

"I majored in Russian literature at Yale," Black said, beaming at his academic prowess. "You?"

"Last time I was in a college classroom it was Cambridge, 1939, arresting some Harvard punk for dealing cocaine," I said. "You?"

"Sorry," Black said, sounding sorrier that I wasn't a college boy than for assuming I was.

"Let me guess," I said to him, leaning in close. "Your old man works on Wall Street and was pals with Wild Bill Donovan. One of his anointed recruited you and you got your commission without going through basic training. Am I close?"

"My father doesn't work on Wall Street. It's Philadelphia, and he's the head of a medical supply firm. Mister Donovan is a family friend, so you got the rest right," Black said. "No wonder you were a cop."

"Doesn't take a cop to know Donovan recruited from the cream of high society," I said. "That's why they say OSS stands for *Oh-So-Social*."

"Okay, fellows, you can stand down now," Bull said. "Cut the crap, and that's an order."

Black and I made up as he handed me a wad of rubles for anything I might need to buy or anyone I might need to bribe. Cash has a way of sealing friendships.

There was a knock at the door, and Maiya entered. General Belov was ready for me.

"Captain William Boyle, reporting as ordered, sir," I said, standing tall and issuing a snappy salute to General Belov. He rose from behind a paper-strewn desk and flicked back a salute. His face was like a slab of granite with five o'clock shadow. His uniform was slathered with medals that clinked quietly as he strode forward and spoke in Russian.

"The general does not like your appearance," Maiya said. "He says other Americans wear their dress uniforms well, but you come to him like rumpled enlisted man. The general is quite particular about this." That last bit was whispered for my benefit.

"I apologize to the General," I said. "Tell him I have just come from dropping bombs on Germany and have shot down a fascist fighter plane. There was no time to change uniforms."

Belov laughed when she translated that. I glanced at Black, who gave an approving nod.

"Good, the general says. But he also says to find the murdering hooligan who killed Lieutenant Ivan Kopelev, and to wear the proper uniform as you do so," Maiya explained.

"And the American victim," I said. I waited a few seconds then gave her a nod. She finally spoke up and Belov responded with an angry growl.

"That is your concern. His concern is justice for Kopelev. You must find his killer. No excuses will be tolerated."

"When will the Russian investigator arrive?" I asked.

When Maiya finished, Belov looked to another officer seated at a desk in the corner of his office, a service cap with a blue band lying in front of him. NKVD. His face was pinched and thin, his cheekbones high and decorated with a scattering of scars. He had startlingly icy blue eyes that drilled me from beneath dark brows. They exchanged a few sentences, and Belov nodded to Maiya.

"He is coming a long distance," she said. "He will arrive early tomorrow."

"I have also come a long distance. My sergeant's bomber was shot down," I said. "Thirty miles northwest of Kozova. Parachutes were seen. Can the general organize a search effort? I need my sergeant to assist in the apprehension of Lieutenant Kopelev's killer."

"The Red Army will search for the men," Maiya said, her eyes glancing at the NKVD man who lit a cigarette. "We are diligent in searching out foreigners who wander near the front lines."

"Five parachutes," I said. "That means five men. Alive."

"The general thanks you for your information," Maiya said. "Now we go."

She hadn't translated that last bit. But by the flicker in the NKVD man's eyes, he'd understood. And he didn't like it one bit.

"Who's the spook in the corner?" I asked Black out in the hallway.

"Major of State Security Pavel Drozdov. My counterpart in the joint OSS-NKVD Mission. He's charged with overseeing the investigation," Black said. "Come on, I'll walk you to your barracks."

"Wait, I thought the guy coming tomorrow was their investigator," I said, following Black out the front door.

"He is. Drozdov is the overseer. He handles the politics," Black said.

"Drozdov is the guy who makes sure everything comes out okay," I said.

"The Soviets like happy endings," Black said. "The brave Communist who prevails over fascist invaders and reactionary Westerners. Think of Drozdov and his NKVD pals as storytellers. The guys in the red hats always win. Come on, your room is in that next building."

"Never mind that, show me the crime scene," I said.

"You sure? You've had a rough day," Black said.

"I'm sure. Just you and me, no Maiya and no Drozdov," I said.

"You Cambridge boys work fast," he said.

"Boston," I corrected him. "The only reason I ever went to Cambridge was to arrest people."

"Okay, if you insist. Sure you don't want to clean up first? It's almost chow time," Black said, stopping and glancing at his watch.

"I'm not hungry, and I have no idea what time it is," I said. "We left England at dawn and must have gone through two or three time zones."

"It's 1735 hours," Black said.

I adjusted my watch, setting it ahead. I was already losing time on this case.

CHAPTER FIVE

"THIS PLACE IS huge," I said, as Black drove the jeep to the warehouse where the murders had taken place. We passed rows of tents pitched next to ruined brick buildings, then more new one-story wooden buildings and open-sided hangars where Soviet aircraft, including biplanes, were being repaired.

"Yeah, the Luftwaffe used it for a regional headquarters, then did their best to destroy it when they retreated. The warehouse is one of the few places they didn't get. It had two five-hundred-pound bombs hidden under it, ready to be set off by radio waves, but something must've gone wrong. It's sturdy, so that's why we use it to store valuable supplies."

"How valuable?" I asked, as Black stopped for two Russian trucks to cross at an intersection. I watched as one of the biplanes started, its engine spouting blue exhaust smoke. It coughed, then conked out.

"Hard to figure in this country," Black said, crossing the intersection. He stopped in front of a two-story brick building. "I mean, there's a lot of bartering. Cigarettes, liquor, prophylactics, Spam, all those things have value. But there's no money in it. What are you going to buy with rubles, anyway? They're no good outside the USSR and there's damn little you'd want to buy in any Soviet store. If you could find one."

"Then what are they guarding?" I asked, nodding in the direction of two guards at the warehouse door.

"The barn door. After the horse bolted," he said. Black led the way, a key ring dangling from one hand as he returned the salutes of the Russian guards with the other. He unlocked the heavy metal door which creaked on its hinges as he opened it.

"Wait a second," I said, studying the lock. "How many people have keys to this place?"

"I do. General Dawson does, and the American commander's office has a spare. Far as I know, that's it for us. The Russians? I have no idea. I know Drozdov has one," Black said.

"The NKVD guy?"

"Yeah. We're both responsible for a section of this warehouse."

"This lock is new," I said, studying the shiny mechanism.

"Right. Barn door once again," Black said. "Come on."

Inside, he switched on lights. Bare bulbs hung from the ceiling illuminating shelves of supplies and pallets groaning under the weight of crates stacked to the ceiling.

"What's all this?" I asked.

"The usual military supplies, Russian and American. Foodstuffs, spare parts, ammunition, blankets, that sort of thing. Everything needed for home away from home for our boys. Upstairs is where we found the bodies."

"Who's *we*?" I asked as I followed Black up the wooden steps.

"Drozdov and me. Inventory," he said, by way of explanation. He flicked a switch at the top of the stairs.

Up here, the ceiling was lower and the shelves less well stocked. A wall divided the room, with a solid metal door that matched the one downstairs. Black opened it up and gestured for me to enter.

"The bodies were found in here?" I asked. He nodded.

Inside, there were signs in English saying NO SMOKING and DANGER—EXPLOSIVES, next to signs in Cyrillic lettering which I figured said the same.

"Right there," he said, pointing to a stretch of flooring between the doorway and the rows of wooden shelves. Dark stains had soaked into the floorboards.

"Where are the bodies now?"

"They took away Lieutenant Kopelev for burial, I don't know

where. Sergeant Jack Morris's body was shipped home via C-47 to Tehran. We don't maintain an American cemetery here," Black said.

"Both bodies are gone?" I couldn't believe it.

"Yeah. There was a flight to Tehran yesterday, so they put him on it," Black said with a shrug. "I mean he was shot dead. What else do you need to know?"

"Just tell me everything you saw when you opened the door," I said, suppressing my anger. Black was as much a suspect as anyone right now, so everything he told me was going down with a grain of salt.

"Well, I opened the door."

"It was unlocked?" I asked.

"No. Okay, I unlocked the door. No, wait, Drozdov unlocked it. We went in and the bodies were on the floor. Kopelev on the left, Morris on the right. There was a lot of blood."

"How did Drozdov react?"

"He stopped in his tracks. Said something in Russian, I think it was a curse," Black said. "Then he checked them for a pulse. But they were dead for sure." He looked away from the stains, his gaze settling on the shelves, wishing he could forget what he'd seen. Probably not too many blood-drenched corpses at Yale.

"Where were they shot?" I asked.

"In the back of the neck," Black said, rubbing his eyes, as if he might rid himself of that vision. Or was it an act?

"Favorite method of the NKVD. The Gestapo too, for that matter," I said. "Doesn't tell us much. You probably knew that, right?"

"Me? Yeah, we've been briefed on the Soviet security methods. You're saying it could have been a Yank?"

"A Yank with the right keys," I said. "This door took a different key than the main entrance?"

"Right."

"Who has keys to this room?" I asked.

"Me and General Dawson. Drozdov has one, and like I said, I don't know who else on the Russian side. They keep things pretty close to the vest," he said.

"You need to find out, and fast," I said. "Otherwise you're going to be a prime suspect."

"I didn't shoot anybody," Black said. "You can't let that happen."

"Never in the line of duty? You're an OSS agent, aren't you?"

"I'm a specialist in Soviet affairs, and I can speak some Russian. That's why I'm here, not for cloak and dagger work."

"You're working on a joint OSS and NKVD mission, Major. Both are spy outfits, and two men have been murdered. This isn't an academic exercise, and you need to wake up to that," I said. I was putting the pressure on Black to see how he took it. Maybe he was just in over his head and had no clue about how dangerous this was. Or maybe he was playing the hapless professor for my benefit.

"Okay, okay," Black said, holding up his hands as if to push back on the dose of reality I'd unleashed on him. "I did wonder about Drozdov. I mean, it's possible he did it, right? He's got access, and I get the feeling he's no stranger to a well-placed bullet or two."

"If he is the killer, then maybe he was acting on orders, have you thought about that? In which case you're the perfect patsy. A capitalist American spy, it's made to order," I said. "And if this was an off-the-books hit, he still needs someone in the frame for it. But we're getting ahead of ourselves. There's no reason to suspect Drozdov, or you, Major. I'm just tossing out ideas. There's a lot more I need to know before I get close to figuring this out."

"Like what?" Black asked.

"Was anything missing? And what's so special about the stuff in here? Why the extra security?"

"No, nothing was taken," Black said. "I did a full inventory with Drozdov, and we submitted a joint report. It's all here."

"All what?"

"Everything from gold to explosives," he said, stepping around the bloodstains and giving me a tour of the shelves. "American Double Eagles and British sovereigns, sewn into money belts. Plastic explosives and detonators, right next to medical supplies. Pep pills and morphine syrettes."

"Tempting," I said, reaching into a box and feeling the heft of the fabric belt. Gold and drugs. Very tempting.

"True enough," Black said. "Which is why they're useful for bribes and payments to underground groups. We're working with anti-German groups in Bulgaria right now, and that's where most of this is going."

"What are the suitcases for?" I asked, spotting a dozen worn suitcases on one shelf, looking like the lost and found at a railway station.

"Suitcase radios, the latest design," he said. "We're way ahead of the Russians on designing small and powerful radios. Not that they'd admit it, of course. These are perfect for smuggling radios to resistance groups. Here we have crates of plastic explosives and detonators. Hence the no smoking signs."

"These are weapons?" I asked, patting one of the large wooden crates.

"Yes. Everything from silenced pistols to submachine guns. Also, compact crossbows for silent killing," Black said, warming to his subject.

"Did anyone report hearing shots?" I asked.

"No. There was a guard on the door, but he didn't hear a thing," Black said.

"Did you check the silenced weapons to see if any had been used?" I asked.

"No. We were told to wait for the official investigation," he said.

"Okay. I'll need to talk to the guard tomorrow," I said. "After the Russian cop shows up."

"The guard's not here," Black said, moving on to another shelf. "These crates contain the latest version of the SCR-300 backpack radio, along with the handheld SCR-536."

"Wait a minute," I said. "What happened to the guard?"

"He and his whole platoon were transferred to the front," Black said, as if a potential witness disappearing was totally normal. Which might be the case in the USSR, after all. "There's a big push toward Krakow, in southern Poland, Drozdov told me."

"He wasn't concerned?"

"Should he be?" Black asked. Now, Major Black was a smart guy, having gone to Yale and then recruited to the OSS. It took him less than five seconds to tumble to the implications. "Oh. Maybe he saw something?"

"Yeah. And maybe he told his pals about it or reported to an officer. So he gets shipped off to the front. That could be the end of him," I said. Now, I don't consider myself a slouch in the brains department, even though I never went to college. As a matter of fact, it took me about one second to see this as an opportunity. "I need a map."

"Um, they're hard to come by," Black said. "They don't like Westerners wandering around the countryside. What do you need it for?"

"How far away is the front near Krakow?" I asked. "I want to find that guard."

"Seven hundred miles, something like that. You'd have to ask Drozdov for travel authorization, then General Belov for a flight. They might approve if they thought it was important."

It was important all right. A flight sounded good, but it would have to make a stop.

Kozova was between us and the front. Now I had a reason to head in that direction. All I needed to do was convince a bunch of suspicious Russians to let me go there.

And then rescue Big Mike.

CHAPTER SIX

I WAS FADING fast. I'd started out my day in London, something like seventeen hundred miles away. I was hungry but too tired to do anything about it. Black had pointed out the officers' club when he dropped me off at the barracks and invited me to join him there. I'd declined, more interested in falling into bed than carousing with a bunch of flyboys.

Third room on the left, he told me. I saw a light on and heard someone whistling as I walked down the hall. I stopped in the doorway and watched a guy in a crumpled Russian army uniform brushing out my Class-As.

"Who the hell are you?" I said, unsure if he'd understand.

"Private Maxim Bogomozov, boss," he said, snapping to attention. "I help you, yes? Shine boots. Clean clothes, see?" He indicated an ancient armoire where my shirts were hung. Two beds and a small table by the window completed the décor. A few well-worn towels were folded up on the bed, and my sheepskin flight jacket was draped over a chair.

"Private Bogomozov, have you been assigned to me?"

"Max. Is easier. Call me Max, *Kapitan* Boy-el. Yes, General Belov himself tells me to help you. Because good English I speak," Max said, beaming at the mention of Belov's name and his implied approval. Max had crooked teeth and a gap in his lower row. Tattoos peeked out from his shirt collar and sleeves. His close-cropped hair was flecked with gray, and wrinkles crowded the corners of his eyes. He was one old guy for a private.

"It is good English, Max. And it's Boyle. Billy Boyle."

"Good. I learn better, Captain Billy. You no go to officers' club? Good booze they have."

"I'm tired, Max. Could you get me something to eat and drink? Is that part of your duties?"

"What you need is my duty, Captain Billy. Max will be back in two shake."

"Two shakes, Max."

"Ah, good, two shakes," Max said. "*Vannaya* is down hall." He made a washing motion, rubbing his hands under his armpits.

"Bathroom? Showers?"

"*Da*. Clean. I come back."

I took a shower and put on clean skivvies. By the time I got back to the room, Max was there. A bowl of stew and a plate of black bread was on the table, along with a bottle of clear liquid. I couldn't make heads or tails out of the Russian script on the label.

"Is this water, Max?"

"Ha! Good joke, Captain Billy. Russian water, yes?"

"Yeah, I'm a funny guy," I said, tossing my clothes onto the bed and rummaging through my duffel. I came up with a couple of packs of Lucky Strikes and a bar of chocolate. I didn't smoke, but it paid to travel with goods that were highly valued in a wartime economy. "Here you go, Max. Thanks."

"Captain Billy, you are good Yankee," Max said, grinning as the items disappeared into his uniform pockets. "Anything you need, you tell Max, okay?"

"How about a jeep?"

"Sure, no problem. General Dawson, he get you one. I ask."

"And some extra gas jerricans. Then you and me go for a drive," I said.

"General Belov gives papers, then we go," Max said. "Jeep from Dawson, papers from Belov. Then we go. Max is mechanic, can fix jeep. But one thing Max cannot do is travel without papers. With American."

"It's dangerous?"

"You are spy if no papers. Max is deserter and counterrevolutionary.

Maybe they put you in prison. Maybe they send you back. Max, they shoot. Then Max dead and you no find man who killed in warehouse. No papers, no good."

"You're right, Max. Don't worry about it," I said, sitting down to the stew. "Thanks for the grub. The food."

"Yes, and water!" Max went off laughing. He enjoyed a joke, but he'd been dead serious about traveling without papers. That would be the first item on my agenda tomorrow. Right now, the stew had my full attention. It wasn't heavy on the meat, but it was full of carrots, potatoes, onions, and a good measure of garlic. The vodka went down easy.

So did I.

I FELT RIGHT at home in the morning, wolfing down powdered eggs in the officers' mess along with Willis, skipper of the *Banshee Bandit*, and Carter, the navigator.

"Not flying today?" I asked as I sipped my hot coffee.

"Nope," Willis said. "Ground crew are patching up the aircraft. If the weather clears over Romania, we'll probably make a run at the oil fields, then land in Italy. Then back across Germany to England. The grand tour."

"Either of you guys know Jack Morris? The sergeant who was shot in the warehouse?"

"No," Carter said, after he and Willis gave a shrug. "Mick Heller might know him. I think he was a crew chief for one of the C-47s. They have their own area off the south runway."

"They do the Tehran flights, don't they?" I asked.

"Yeah. Supply runs, personnel, that sort of thing," Willis said. "Once in a while the Russkies allow a flight to Moscow so the brass can meet with the Military Mission."

"No rescue flights for downed aircrew?"

"Not a priority with them. The official line I've heard is that front line commanders can't be burdened with Westerners unfamiliar with the territory. Sooner or later they scoop up our guys and deliver them here," Willis said. "Mostly later. Good luck, Captain."

"Not what you wanted to hear, Captain," Carter said as he lingered over his coffee. "We've gotten used to the way Russians run things here. They can be really friendly one to one, but when it comes to the chain of command, it's another whole story. They can't take a crap without wondering if Joe Stalin is constipated."

"Lieutenant, you've just about spoiled my breakfast," I said. "But you can make it up to me. As navigator, you must have maps showing this part of the country."

"Sure I do."

"Like the area between Kozova and here," I said.

"Yes, and they're my responsibility. Maps keep us alive and get us home, Captain," Carter said.

"Hey, call me Billy. They must show rail lines, right? As navigation aids," I said. "I just want to look at it and get a sense of the route Big Mike and the others might take to make it here."

"That's your sergeant? Good name for him. How can you be sure he's alive?"

"How could I assume he's dead?"

"Okay. I'm in barrack number four. Come by later this morning and I'll go over them with you. Glad to help if I can, Billy," he said.

"Hey, you ever run into the Russian who was killed along with Morris?" I asked as we left the mess. "Lieutenant Kopelev, NKVD."

"Saw him around, yeah. Always brown-nosing Drozdov, snooping into everything. I got the impression not many Russians liked him. A real stickler. I mean, I bet nobody likes the NKVD, but Kopelev was unlikable all on his own."

"You ever have a run-in with him?"

"No. But ask Mick. He's knows what's what around here."

I didn't like hearing that about Kopelev. It only widened the pool of suspects. But maybe I could parlay that into an advantage with Belov. With so many people on Kopelev's bad side, it made it more vital to interview the men who might have witnessed anyone near the warehouse.

Yeah, I could work with that. Question was, had they been transferred out on purpose and were they already being sent straight into German machine guns?

CHAPTER SEVEN

I TOOK THE steps two at time and returned a salute to the Russian guards who snapped to attention outside General Belov's office. Thanks to Max's ministrations, my dress uniform was wrinkle-free and my buttons were polished. Having a Communist butler was working out a lot better than I'd expected.

Maiya was in the outer office. She told me to wait while she checked to see if the general had time for me. I cooled my heels in the hallway, my eyes drawn to a map posted on the wall. Everything was in the Cyrillic script, so it was hard to make out place names. I was pretty sure about Poltava, and there was a rail line from the city running northwest to Kiev. That was as far west as the map went.

I figured Big Mike would do the same as I would; hitch a ride on a freight train going east. If he'd run into Russian troops in a friendly mood, we'd have heard about it, or would soon. The longer there was no information, the greater the chance he was working his way here. If he caught an empty boxcar on the fly, it could be a safe place and a fast ride. Unless the bulls caught him. Railyard guards were one thing. Russian security troops checking for deserters were another.

"Captain Boyle?" It was Maiya, beckoning me to enter Belov's office.

We went in. Belov was leafing through a file on his desk. He frowned, his bushy eyebrows coming together in worried unison as he rubbed his chin. In the corner, Major Drozdov stood huddled with another officer, this one wearing the uniform of the Red Air Force.

Drozdov glanced at me as he whispered to the other officer. Belov ignored me, shaking out a Chesterfield from a new pack and lighting up. Apparently, I wasn't the only Yank handing out smokes. Belov blew smoke and gave Maiya a quick nod.

"Captain Boyle, your colleague in this investigation," she said. "Captain Kiril Sidorov."

"Who?" I couldn't believe what I was hearing. It couldn't be the same man.

It didn't look like him.

Did it?

"Ah, it is Captain Boyle now? Congratulations," Sidorov said, stepping forward and extending his hand. "I am still a captain, but that is good. We are on equal footing in this sad business."

"I'm sorry, Captain Sidorov," I said, clasping his hand and wishing I didn't have to. "I didn't expect to meet you again. How are you?"

He looked terrible, a rail-thin version of the suave military attaché from the Soviet embassy in London I'd encountered almost a year ago. His face was shrunken, pale skin stretched over high cheekbones. A knot of scar tissue decorated one eyebrow, raising it to a look of permanent surprise.

"Pleased to be here," Sidorov said, a faint smile flashing across his face.

I bet. I thought he'd be dead by now.

"I'm eager to begin, Captain. But first, Maiya, please ask the general if there is any news of my sergeant and his fellow airmen," I said. Her eyes darted to Drozdov, then she translated for Belov.

"The general says there have been no reports of Americans in the rear areas," Maiya said.

"Has he asked for a search to be conducted?" I asked.

"If I may," Sidorov said, holding up a hand to halt Maiya, and spoke to the general. Belov glanced at Drozdov, then barked at Sidorov. Everybody in the room was checking in with Major Pavel Drozdov. Hey, I'd be worried about offending a high-ranking NKVD officer myself.

"The general will ask for a report from the area commander," Maiya said. "That is all."

"I am here at the direct order of General Eisenhower," I said, veering close enough to the truth. "He will be very disappointed if our brave Soviet allies do not rescue these men after they have bombed the fascist homeland."

I was pretty proud of myself for sounding like one of Joe Stalin's mouthpieces. But I didn't get a chance to hear how my comradely words sounded in Russian. Sidorov shook his head, a signal to Maiya who opened the door and ushered us out. Sidorov gave out what sounded like pleasantries as he grabbed me by the arm and dragged me along. I looked back as Belov glared at me and puffed on his American cigarette like a locomotive building up a head of steam.

Outside, Major Preston Black skidded his jeep to a halt in front of us and vaulted out.

"Sorry I'm late," he said, walking up to our little group. Maiya looked worried, which only made me worry about what Sidorov had said to the general.

"That's okay, we had plenty of translators. All Russian, of course," I said. It would have been nice to have Black's take on things, not that he'd been much help so far. "Have you met Captain Sidorov?"

Sidorov was already busy throwing a salute Black's way and telling him what a pleasure it was to meet him, and how surprised he was to see me here, since we had known each other when he'd served in London.

Which was one way of putting it.

"Your English is excellent, Captain," Black said. "I can hear the BBC accent. Where were you stationed before they brought you here?"

"I was in the Far East. Quite a different assignment," Sidorov said. "Now, how shall we proceed? Ah, my dear Maiya, we have little need of an interpreter. Perhaps you have other duties to attend to?"

"I will remain," she replied. "Captain Boyle may have need of me. Major Black's Russian is fair, but far from perfect. Wouldn't you agree, Major?"

"Quite accurate, Maiya," Black said. "Boyle, there's a jeep here at your disposal. Gentlemen, how do you propose to begin?"

"Billy, what have you learned?" Sidorov said, then turned to Maiya. "We knew each other well in London. It is a beautiful city." Sidorov had the charm turned up all the way. I thought I detected a glance here and a shift in posture there which signaled a closeness between Maiya and Black. Sometimes when you try to hide these things too hard it shows. Or was Maiya only there to keep track of us and report back to the general?

"Not much, Kiril," I said, maintaining the fiction that we were old pals. "I got in yesterday the hard way, in a B-17 from England. Major Black showed me the crime scene. That was it. Why don't we start there?"

"Very well," Sidorov said. "If we have two vehicles, perhaps you could brief me on the way there. Maiya and Major Black can take the other jeep. Is that satisfactory?"

It was. Maiya was happy to sit next to Black, which supported my lovestruck theory. And she was equally happy to be bird-dogging us, which led me to believe she was reporting back to Belov. Or Drozdov.

"I didn't recognize you at first," I said, as soon as we were alone. The last time I'd seen him he'd been wearing a tailored uniform, his blue eyes sparkling with confidence and power. This was a changed man.

"My homecoming was not as I expected," Sidorov said, a sigh escaping between his lips. "I have been in a labor camp in Kolyma."

"Where is that?"

"Where it is very cold. A few days ago, I was working on the road of bones," Sidorov said as I pulled out and followed Maiya and Black. Whatever they were chatting about was probably a lot cheerier.

"What's that?" I really didn't care what his fate had been, but when someone hits you with *road of bones*, a natural curiosity arises.

"A road, from the interior to the Sea of Okhotsk. It is being built by prisoners on permafrost, with only the simplest tools. Little food, very cold, long hours. Many prisoners die there. Because of the frozen ground, the authorities decreed that interments be made in the roadbed as it is dug. Much more practical. Hence, road of bones."

"Why did they send you there?" I asked. I had a pretty good idea, but it seemed like Sidorov wasn't aware of the role I'd played. Otherwise, he'd be at my windpipe right now.

"I was never told, other than the usual talk of counterrevolutionary activities," he said, craning his neck as we passed a row of B-17s being serviced. "They are beautiful machines."

"They're even more beautiful when you land in one alive and breathing," I said. "Did they pull you out of the camp because you know me?"

"The authorities are practical, as I said. Once your name was brought up, files were searched, and my name was found. Or my number, I should say. There is something I must tell you, Billy. Pull over."

I did. Black kept driving away in front of us.

"I will never go back. I will find this killer and it will be an American, you may be certain of that," Sidorov said, turning sideways in his seat.

"They've made that clear?"

"I am making it clear to you, that is all that matters. It will be an American. Failure will be a disaster for all," Sidorov said. "And watch yourself around Maiya. She reports to Drozdov. Everything. Now drive, before she notices."

I shifted into first gear and lurched out into the lane.

"How do you know about Maiya? You just got here," I said.

"I can tell. Remember, I used to be NKVD," Sidorov said. When I first met him, he wore the uniform of an air force major, but that turned out to be a cover for his secret activities.

"Used to be?" I said, unsure of what to believe.

"I am nothing now," he said. "When I returned home, I was stripped of my rank and put on trial. I had been denounced as an enemy of the people and a spy for the English."

"Do you have any idea by whom?" If he knew who'd sent that message from London, I'd know who the Soviet spy was within British intelligence.

"No, but it matters little. Anyone who came into contact with the West is tainted, so I was not surprised. What did surprise me is being brought out for this investigation."

"And a chance at freedom," I said.

"Life, yes. Freedom, in the sense you understand it, I will never know," Sidorov said, his voice low and wistful. "But after what I have seen, that will be enough."

"How many died on the road?" I asked.

"I saw hundreds buried," he said. "There must be thousands. Tens of thousands. It is a very long road."

Sidorov had given me fair warning. I couldn't blame him for not wanting to be sent back. It looked like Siberia had aged him a decade in ten months. His pale skin was withered, his posture stooped, his hands raw and rough.

But there was still a spark there. A dangerous spark, if anyone got in his way. I knew that much from England. Kiril Sidorov had blood on his hands. He'd committed murder. Not your routine NKVD killing in the line of duty—if such brutality could be called duty—but cold-blooded and personal. For his own gain.

For all that, he did show some honor at the end. He confessed in order to spare a woman he loved. We had him dead to rights, or close enough, but when he saw a chance to spare her, he talked and shouldered all the blame. So he wasn't the worst human being in the world, except if you'd been one of his victims.

The British government had been about to request that the Soviets allow him to be arrested. Because of the nature of his crimes, there was a chance they'd waive diplomatic immunity. But Winston Churchill intervened directly. For the sake of the war effort and allied unity, Sidorov was let go, returned to Red Mother Russia with a cover story about being injured during a Luftwaffe attack.

I wasn't too happy with that, but who disobeys Winston?

As a matter of fact, I had driven Sidorov to the airfield and seen him off. In his mind, we parted on decent terms. Perhaps not friends, but opponents who understood each other. Grudging respect and all that bullshit.

He didn't suspect a thing.

I knew there was a Soviet spy somewhere within MI-5, Great Britain's counterintelligence service. Sidorov had dropped a lot of hints which pointed in that direction. I just didn't know who it was. But that didn't matter. When I'd returned to London, I informed the MI-5 committee involved in the case that Sidorov had agreed to spy for us. I gave them a recognition codename and told them he wanted a lot of money.

I had hoped someone in that room was the mole, and that they'd taken the bait.

Today was the first time I knew they did.

Glancing at Sidorov, I had to remember his victims, because he damn sure looked like one himself. Justice isn't always pretty.

CHAPTER EIGHT

I GAVE SIDOROV the nickel tour of the crime scene. Black and Maiya hovered about, avoiding the bloodstains and paying more attention to each other than to us.

"Major Black," Sidorov said, raising his voice to get Black's attention. "Nothing is missing, you are quite sure?"

"Nothing," Black said. "We did a full inventory."

"Very odd," Sidorov said, giving me a sideways glance. "Two men are murdered here, in front of gold and other valuables. A small fortune on the black market. If such a degenerate form of capitalism existed within the Soviet Union."

"What does that tell us?" I said, opening one box and checking the packs of morphine syrettes. SOLUTION OF MORPHINE TARTRATE, 1.5CC. "Not even the morphine was touched. It would have been simple to slip some of these into a pocket and slap on one of those money belts. Why didn't the killer take advantage?"

"Perhaps we need to check paperwork," Sidorov whispered. "Compare the previous inventory with Major Black's and calculate in any recent deliveries."

"Put that back," Black said, grabbing the kit from my hands and returning it to storage. "You can check all you want, but you'll find everything's in order. Major Drozdov won't be happy about your lack of trust, I'm sure."

"He will applaud it, I am certain," Sidorov said. "The only way to truly trust is to be constantly suspicious. Otherwise you invite deception. You have nothing to be concerned with, do you, Major Black?"

Black didn't say anything, except to order us out of the room. He locked the doors and stormed off, Maiya a few paces behind him. He jumped into his jeep and started the engine, looking expectantly at her. Sidorov said something in Russian and she nodded, reluctantly, and got in with Black, who drove off without a word.

"I told her Black was a possible suspect and she should spend time with him, then report back to me," Sidorov said. "To us, I mean. Now, what next?"

"Let's find out if anyone did an autopsy," I said. "Ask the guards where the medical unit is." Sidorov spoke to a soldier and we got in the jeep. There was a base hospital near the main entrance, a solid mile away.

"You are handling it all wrong, you know," Sidorov said, settling back in the passenger seat. "Your request to search for your sergeant. Is it the same large fellow from London?"

"Yeah, Sergeant Michael Miecznikowski. Big Mike."

"Ah. A Pole. That complicates things."

"He's an American," I said, deciding to keep mum about Kaz coming to us the long way 'round. "What's the right way to do it?"

"General Belov can do very little," Sidorov said, watching as a pair of Soviet Yak-9 fighters lifted off from a grass runway. "He is an air force general who commands this base, but he has no control over rear-area troops. It is the NKVD that maintains rear-area security. Their internal troops guard factories, railway lines, bridges, any important installation."

"I should ask Major Drozdov then?"

"Not yet. Let us come up with something to offer him. A clue, to symbolize our progress," Sidorov said.

"I forgot to mention it when Black stormed off, but the officer in charge of guarding the warehouse was transferred to the front near Krakow, along with his entire platoon," I said. "Big Mike and the others bailed out near Kozova."

"You would pass close to Kozova on the way to the Krakow front,"

Sidorov said as I pulled over in front of a large wooden building marked with a red cross. "Let us hope the doctors can tell us something useful."

I knew that meant digging up some dirt on an American. Half of me kept my fingers crossed for just that while the other half felt like a traitor.

Sidorov asked around and we finally found our way down a corridor to a ward where a dozen beds lined each side of the room. Most of them were filled, a few with injured or wounded men who looked like they'd be up and about soon. Other patients were swathed in bandages, tended to by nurses as their groans and moans filled the room.

"*Doktor* Mametova?" Sidorov said, standing back as a woman spoke in hushed tones with a nurse. She was stout and gray-haired, with bags under her eyes, and a splash of blood across her white coat. She held up a hand. When she was done speaking to the nurse, she motioned for us to follow into the next corridor, a scream from one patient sending us on our way.

Her office was spartan, shelves filled with paperwork and files. A window looked out onto bombed-out buildings with scorched door-ways. We sat and she began speaking with Sidorov.

"*Doktor* Mametova heard of our investigation," he told me. "She has been waiting for someone to come by. She did the autopsies."

"Are the bodies in the morgue?" I asked, even though Black had told me otherwise. He could have gotten that wrong or been lying.

"No, they were taken away," Sidorov said after a back-and-forth. "But she does have something to show us."

Doctor Mametova dug through a desk drawer and came up with two small envelopes, a handwritten note scrawled on each. She opened them and two misshapen slugs tumbled out.

"This is Kopelev," Sidorov said, holding up one bullet. "From a Tokarev automatic, 7.62mm."

"And this must be from Sergeant Morris," I said, fingering the remnants of a .45 caliber round. "Were they wearing their personal weapons when she saw the bodies?"

"Yes," Sidorov said. "She does not know what happened to them.

Both bodies were taken away the next day." He said he'd ask about exact cause of death.

She got up and walked behind us. She pushed my head forward and pressed the tips of her fingers against the back of my neck, then said something that sounded like Russian for bang.

"No other marks or wounds," Sidorov said. "There is nothing else she can tell us."

I watched as Doctor Mametova walked back around her desk and sat down with a heavy sigh. She looked exhausted. So exhausted I couldn't tell if she was holding anything back.

"How many doctors are there here?" I asked, keeping my eyes on her.

"Four," Sidorov said after she'd answered. "The base hospital treats both Russians and Americans, although Americans are sent for further treatment to Tehran as soon as they are able. They also provide medical care for any Soviet forces in the area. Quite overworked, in her opinion."

"What are all the injuries in that ward? The patients seemed to be in a lot of pain," I said.

"The usual," Sidorov reported. "A fuel tank exploded. Several have burns. Accidents, on the ground and in the air. One pilot with shrapnel in his legs. All Russians."

"Russians in pain," I said, nodding for him to ask about that.

"Morphine is in short supply," he said, as the doctor shook her head sadly. "Her patients suffer as a result."

Sidorov and I looked at each other. There was a stock of morphine under lock and key down the road. Did the shortage have anything to do with the killings?

I tried to flash a thank-you smile at the doctor, but she was too tired to notice. Usually it worked wonders, but maybe something was lost in translation, or drowned out by the shouts coming from the ward. Doctor Mametova shot out of her chair, shoving Sidorov aside as she spoke.

"Changing bandages on the burn victims, she said," Sidorov told me, wincing at the terrible sounds.

"I have an idea," I said. "An experiment."

Sidorov thought a moment, listening to the cries from the ward. Then his eyes brightened. "You wish to see how easy it would be to steal a set of keys for the warehouse. Purely as an exercise to assist in our investigation."

"*Da*," I said, tossing out the one word of Russian I was sure of. "Then we talk to Drozdov about a road trip."

"Perhaps," Sidorov said. "If we are not shot first."

As we left, I had to remind myself that Sidorov was a killer himself and not to be trusted. I was beginning to like the guy, now that we were on the same team, sort of.

And that was dangerous.

CHAPTER NINE

"MAJOR BLACK," I said, knocking on his office door at the operations center. I half expected to see Maiya sitting on his desk, legs crossed and eyelids fluttering. But he was alone with a stack of files. It was hardly the image of a dashing OSS secret agent.

"Enter."

"I wanted to apologize, sir. I didn't mean any disrespect about the morphine supplies," I said, as contritely as I could manage.

"It is a sad fact of investigations, Major," Sidorov added. "One must question everything, even the most mundane of matters and the most trusted of men." He was laying it on nice and thick, which was fine. It was hard to go too far when lavishing praise to get what you wanted out of a guy.

"Well, okay," I guess that does make sense," Black said. He was sounding magnanimous, which was something I'd found people enjoyed. Give them an inch of repentance and they'll give you a mile of permission. "What do you need? I have all the supply reports here." He hooked a thumb in the direction of a couple of file cabinets behind him. It looked like a full day's work right there.

"Well, actually we have another question, sir. Something's come up about the keys, and we need to understand where all the duplicates are kept, and who has access," I said.

"You have a lead?" Black asked.

"It is too soon to tell, Major. But you will be the first to know, yes?"

Sidorov said, giving Black a wink and a hint that we'd come to him before Drozdov. I could tell he liked that.

"Glad to see you're already making progress," Black said, lapping up the subservience. "How can I help?"

"Please show us where you keep your keys to the warehouse and the storage room," I said. "Then we'll move on to Bull. General Dawson, I mean."

"Sure. I carry the key to my desk everywhere. It's the only one," Black said. He took out a key from his pocket and unlocked the top drawer. Inside was a set of keys on a ring. He took that and unlocked the file cabinet behind him, withdrawing two keys on a chain from a file folder. "I only take these out when I need them. I checked as soon as the bodies were found, and they were right here."

"Layers of security," I said, glancing at the lock on the desk drawer. "Smart."

"Major Black, one other question," Sidorov said. "Were both victims found with their sidearms?"

"Yes," Black said. "Morris always wore his. Too bad he didn't get a chance to use it."

"I don't think he ever saw it coming, Major," I said. "Where is his weapon now?"

"Check in with Transport Command over at the south runway, where all the C-47s are. Lieutenant Reed was his CO and should have his gear. Morris's personal effects went back with his body, of course."

We thanked Black for his cooperation and walked down the hall to Bull's office.

"It would be simple to pick the lock on that desk," Sidorov whispered.

"Right. But there were no scratches on the lock. A professional lock picker wouldn't leave a mark, but anyone else probably would," I said.

"Which leaves us with the possibility of a skilled criminal," Sidorov said, "or the weak link."

"The key he keeps with him at all times," I said. "Which isn't possible. What with showering and sleeping, it probably sits out in plain sight in his quarters."

"And accessible to any visitor he may entertain," Sidorov said.

"Speak of the devil," I said, as Maiya walked out of an office down the hall. "Why don't you speak with her and I'll talk with Bull." Sidorov agreed and went off to catch Maiya while I went to see Bull.

"Billy, take a load off and tell me what you've been up to," Bull said, leaning back in his chair and setting down a magnifying glass. Photographs littered his desk. Bomb damage and reconnaissance shots.

"Checking into who has access to warehouse keys," I said. "You keep yours secure, I assume?"

"Right here," Bull said, kicking something under his desk. "Cast iron floor safe. Small, but weighs a ton. My boss, General Hampton, has one as well."

"Combination?"

"Yep. Only Hampton and I know them. The safes were brought in via Tehran, in case you're wondering. They're not Russian."

"Major Black has less secure storage," I said.

"Well, the OSS doesn't necessarily think things through," Bull said. "Like cooperating with the NKVD. I wouldn't trust those bastards with a plug nickel."

"Bull, you're cooperating with the Russians too," I said, smiling so he wouldn't take offense.

"There's a difference between strategy and working directly with the NKVD. They slaughter their own people on the slightest pretext. Watch your back, Billy. Kiril Sidorov is ex-NKVD."

"Yeah. I'm being careful," I said. Bull wasn't in the know about what had transpired in London, and I left it that way. "What do you know about a shortage of morphine at the base hospital?"

"I've heard that," he said. "Belov told me it was due to counter-revolutionary forces disrupting the flow of supplies. *Disorganizers of the rear and the enemy's ally* is the exact phrase he used. Their supply of morphine comes from the Kyrgyz province on the Chinese border, and a lot can happen between there and here. It could be a poor poppy harvest, sabotage, or theft, who knows? Anything that goes bad is always because of reactionaries or counterrevolutionaries, so it's never actually anyone's fault. Or the fault of the Soviet system, God forbid. Why do you ask?"

"I'm just trying to find some sort of motive or purpose behind the murders. You've seen the morphine in the storage room where the two men were killed?"

"Yes, and I've checked the inventory reports. Nothing's missing," Bull said.

"That's the oddest thing of all, so far at least. All those valuables, and nothing was taken," I said. "It's like that dog in the Sherlock Holmes story."

"What dog?" Bull asked.

"In 'The Adventure of Silver Blaze' Holmes investigates the abduction of a famous racehorse taken from his stall in the middle of the night. Holmes draws the police inspector's attention to 'the curious incident of the dog in the night-time.' The inspector doesn't see the importance, because the dog was quiet all night."

"And that's the curious incident?" Bull said.

"Exactly. I want to know who got in there and if the killer went in with someone or alone. But the important thing is to understand what anyone was doing in the warehouse at all. There's plenty of secluded spots to shoot people around here and leave their bodies. Why do it in such a high-profile area? They were guaranteed to be discovered pretty quickly."

"I'm not so sure about that," Bull said, rubbing the stubble on his chin. "Only Drozdov and Black have keys to that storage room. If they had no need to go in, it would have been days before the smell would have leaked out."

"Why would have Kopelev and Morris even gone up there?" I said, to myself as well as to Bull.

"Well, Captain Boyle, that's why you received this all-expenses paid trip to the workers' paradise," Bull said. "You figure it out. We need answers, and fast. The US Military Mission in Moscow is breathing down my neck. They want answers, and so do I."

"The only answer I have so far is how they were killed. Looks like they each took a slug from their own pistol. You didn't happen to check Sergeant Morris's automatic, did you?"

"No, didn't think to," Bull said. "It was in his holster. You sure about that?"

"The doc took a .45 caliber round out of Morris and a 7.62mm round out of Kopelev. She told us the shots were to the back of the neck. Standard NKVD execution. Means they were probably on their knees," I said.

"Keep that dope to yourself and tell Sidorov to do the same. If anything points to the NKVD, we need to be one hundred percent certain before we say anything," Bull said. "Any other cheery news?"

"The hospital ain't the cheeriest of places, Bull. They got burn victims and they're low on morphine. What's Black saving his supply for?"

"It's a joint operation, Billy. OSS and NKVD. Supposedly it's for a mission to Bulgaria, although so far, it's been nothing but talk. If Drozdov wanted to release it to Doctor Mametova he'd only have to ask. Besides, it wouldn't be enough to make a difference."

Tell that to the guy screaming his lungs out, I wanted to say.

But I kept my mouth shut. When it came to generals, even a decent guy like Bull, his ignorance was my bliss.

CHAPTER TEN

SIDOROV AND I were comparing notes over fried Spam and egg sandwiches in the mess hall. Served on Russian black bread, it wasn't half bad. I'd heard that the Russians loved Spam as much as they loved the jeeps and tanks we sent them on Lend-Lease, which didn't say much for the cuisine in the Soviet Union.

"General Belov also has a safe for storing top secret materials," Sidorov said, finishing his sandwich. He wet a finger and ran it around his plate, gathering crumbs. He looked up at me, his face flushing. He quickly brushed the crumbs from his finger. "I don't really need to do that, do I?"

"You can have another sandwich," I said softly. He closed his eyes, his forehead wrinkling. Whatever I thought about the guy, right now he had painful memories playing around in his head. "Want me to get you one?"

"No, no, it is not a matter of hunger," Sidorov said, waving his hand dismissively. "Not now. It is difficult to shake off the fear of starvation. Of not enough. Not enough food, warmth, rest, or decency."

"You survived," I said.

"Yes. And now the thought of being sent back there paralyzes me. I was ready to die, Billy, and then they came to the road one day and took me. I thought they were going to shoot me, finally. I was glad. Instead, I was brought here. A miracle. But I do not deserve miracles. You know this."

"I do, Kiril," I said. "Tell me, how bad was it? The camp?"

"Prisoners died every day," Sidorov said, his voice hushed. "In their sleep. Working on the road. In the assembly area. Death was every-where. Work was everywhere. It is impossible to describe."

"Sorry, I shouldn't have asked," I said.

"I should have the words to tell you, but it is difficult. You have been in battle? You have seen horrible things?"

"I have."

"Multiply that by one hundred, and then consider there is no rhyme nor reason why people have to endure it. No logic, no clear reason, no guilt, no innocence. There is only the camp and the cold," Sidorov said, and he shivered, as if his memories had carried the frigid air in with them.

I took Sidorov's cup and filled it with tea. I brought it back and put it in front of him, the steam drifting up before his faraway eyes.

"There were families in the camp," he said in a hoarse whisper. "Whole families were punished for the crimes, real or not, of the parents. There was a section for children, some who had been born in the camp. Their eyes were vacant. The camp has nothing to offer a child, no love, no warmth, no brightness. But the guards—some of them—tried to be kind to the children. One fellow was in charge of the guard dogs, and one of the animals had a litter. He gave the children two puppies to raise and told them to name the dogs."

Sidorov clasped his hands around the cup, absorbing the warmth.

"It took them two days to think of names for them. They had nothing to draw on, no memories of pets or anything beloved. In the end, they named the pups Ladle and Pail. And that, Billy, is what the camps are like."

He drank his tea. I said nothing.

"As to the safe," Sidorov said a few minutes later, bringing himself back to the present, "Belov and Drozdov both keep their keys in it. I spoke to Maiya, and she said they are the only two who know the combination."

I told him about Black finding the bodies during his search for Kopelev. "It looks like we should ask Comrade Drozdov if he gave Kopelev the key for any reason," I said. "He was Kopelev's boss, after all. He might have given orders to do something in the storage room."

"What does not make sense is the fact Major Drozdov never

mentioned it. That means it either did not happen or he wishes it not to be known," Sidorov said. "The former is unhelpful and the latter is dangerous."

"Okay, so we hold off for now," I said. "What about Black's key?"

"The one to his desk drawer? I think your idea is a good one. An experiment, strictly to assist in our investigation," Sidorov said. The idea seemed to perk him up.

"It's risky," I said. "If we're caught, we could be arrested for grand larceny."

"Perhaps you would, Billy, but not I. As you must know, there is no such theft in the Soviet Union. There is no need in our classless society. All I would be doing is redistributing wealth held by Western capitalists." Sidorov laughed. I joined in, just to be polite, but he found it a whole lot funnier than I did.

We drove over to Transport Command, which was housed in the buildings and hangars near the south runway. The twin-engine C-47 transport aircraft were drawn up in rows, a few being worked on by aircrew. One was being fueled as we pulled to a halt in front of the operations building. We found Lieutenant Reed in his office, signing forms.

Lots of them.

"Whaddya need, Captain?" Reed said, barely taking note of us as he wrote out his name and handed a corporal standing nearby paperwork to stamp. "I got to get these requisitions on that bird out there before she flies. Otherwise we'll be short a lot of spare parts."

"And bourbon, Lieutenant," the corporal said. "Don't forget the bourbon. Here ya go."

"We can see you're busy, Lieutenant. But I need to talk to you about Sergeant Morris," I said.

"The late Sergeant Morris," Sidorov added. Reed looked up, seemingly surprised a Russian was in the room. The lieutenant was thin and wiry, curly-haired with oil stains on his cuffs and grease beneath his fingernails. An officer who actually worked.

"Get me a cup of coffee, willya?" Reed said to his corporal, who scooted out of the small office. "What about Morris?"

"Anything you can tell us about him," I said. "Like who'd want to kill him."

"Everyone liked Boris," Reed said. "Swell guy."

"I thought his name was Jack," Sidorov said. "Was he Russian?"

"No, it was a nickname. Since he got along so well with you guys. He spoke a few words here and there. Said his grandparents came from the old country. So Boris Morris. A joke, ya see?"

"Amusing," Sidorov said. "He had no enemies, then?"

"He had a competitor," Reed said. "He's probably the guy who knew him best. But it was nothing to kill a guy over, if that's what you're thinking."

"Who? And what were they competing for?" I asked.

"Technical Sergeant Marty Craven," Reed said. "He maintains our supply of spare parts. Most of these requisitions are from him. He's good at what he does, from scavenging parts out of damaged aircraft to getting the most out of the supply chain, if you know what I mean."

"He's an operator," I said.

"An expert scrounger and a creative businessman," Reed said. "He hasn't crossed me, and he hasn't screwed up on the job, so what he does with our aircrew and our Russian friends is none of my business. Not as long as he keeps these birds flying."

"He and Morris were in the same line?" Sidorov asked.

"Yeah. Competition is good for business, Boris always claimed. But don't bother trying to pin anything on Craven. His was on a supply flight to Mirgorod when Morris was killed," Reed said. "He was gone thirty-six hours. No way he could have done it. Hell, I don't know how anyone got into Fort Knox anyway."

Sidorov shot me a look. Apparently, he hadn't heard of it.

"Where American capitalists keep their gold," I explained.

"Ah," Sidorov said. "Lieutenant, perhaps you can tell us where to find Sergeant Craven? He may be able to tell us more about his comrade."

"Two buildings over," Reed said as the corporal returned with his joe. "There's Maintenance, then Supply."

Supply was housed in a low, one-story concrete structure. It had new windows and a sheet-metal roof, but the rest of it looked like it had a new coat of whitewash splashed on to cover the scorch marks.

"The Germans left little standing when they left," Sidorov said as we approached the door. "I look forward to returning the favor when we reach Berlin. If I live to see the day. It would be something to see."

"We knocked a few down for you on the way here," I said. "Not a trip I'd want to make on a regular basis." Inside, a wide counter separated the entryway from shelves filled with a jumble of equipment. Engine parts on pallets, propeller blades stacked against the wall, radio sets next to drums of oil and cans of grease. Tool kits and tires formed a low barrier, behind which sat a sergeant sporting two rockers under a T beneath his stripes.

"Technical Sergeant Craven?" I asked, even though it was evident, not only from his stripes but by the crates of scotch and bourbon behind him. A wheeler dealer.

"Yes, Captain, what can I do for you?" Craven looked up from the pistol he was cleaning, a .45 automatic in pieces on the desk in front of him. He had a heavy five o'clock shadow and dark eyes which flitted between Sidorov and me. "And *Kapitan*, I should say."

"We're here investigating the death of Boris Morris," I said. "But you probably know that already, given your connections."

"Captain Boyle and *Kapitan* Sidorov," Craven said. "I hope you guys find the bastard who killed him. And Kopelev, too, not that anybody cared for the guy. Sorry, *Kapitan*, if he was a pal of yours."

"I did not know him," Sidorov said. "But you did. Why do you think they both were killed?"

"Listen," Craven said, wiping his hands on a rag. "Me and Boris were kinda in the same line. Helping spread the virtues of the free marketplace, if you don't mind me mentionin' it, *Kapitan*. But it was Boris who knew the lingo, enough to get by, leastways. He was always hanging around with the Russian groundcrews, trading for stuff. It wasn't big business for him, he just enjoyed it. He actually liked it here. Said he felt at home, crazy as that sounds. I mean, this ain't St. Louis, not by a long shot. Again, no offense, *Kapitan* Sidorov."

"I understand," Sidorov said, waving his hand as if batting away the slight. "But you have not answered the question."

"I got no idea. What I'm tryin' to say is that I wasn't privy to a lot of his deals. I work more with our guys. There's only so much you can barter for here. Vodka, sure, but not much else. And you can't take rubles out of the country, so this is one place where cash ain't king."

"What is?" I asked.

"Scotch, rubbers, and nylons," Craven said without missing a beat. "There's a shortage of all three. Vodka takes the sting out of no scotch or bourbon, but they ain't got nylons at all, so nylon or silk stockings are gold. Condoms are practically nonexistent. Guys bring rubbers in on every flight and trade for whatever they can get. Officers like Kopelev are desperate for them. I heard that if they knock up a dame, they get demoted or sent to the front. You know what NKVD really stands for, *Kapitan*?"

Craven gave me a wink as he grinned. Sidorov didn't take the bait.

"No ketch venereal disease," Craven said, chuckling at his joke.

"You are a clever fellow," Sidorov said, moving to the side of Craven's desk and standing over him, his head inclined like a vulture eyeing dead meat. "You must have gotten something of value from Lieutenant Kopelev. What was it?"

"Hey, I wasn't anywhere near the place," Craven said, leaning back in his chair to escape Sidorov's gaze. "And me and Boris were pals, no matter what anyone says."

"Fine. But what did you get out of Kopelev?" I asked, circling around the other side of the desk.

"Favors, you know. It ain't hard to get a pass from Reed, but we need permission from the Russians to go anywhere. The town of Poltava ain't much, but it's a change of pace. They even got a hotel with a restaurant and a band. Dancing, you know? And you can buy Kraut souvenirs. Nazi daggers, Lugers, that sort of thing. That's where the rubles come in handy. Guys back in England will shell out real cash for that stuff."

"Now I get it," I said. "That's how you do business. Bring in stuff the Russians want and use the rubles to buy what GIs want."

"Yeah. Free enterprise they call it," Craven said. "It don't interfere with my duties. Just ask Reed. Everybody's happy."

"What happened to Morris's stock?" I asked. "His rubles and whatever he was trading."

"His personal effects went with him, minus anything embarrassing," Craven said. "His crew chief divvied up his booze with Boris's section. They were pretty close. Far as the rubles go, I have no idea. All I ended up with was his .45. Lieutenant Reed let me have it on account of we were friends. And since I lost mine. Stolen by a Russian, I think."

"Which means you sold it, but never mind. That's it?" I asked, pointing to the weapon he was cleaning. Craven nodded. "Had it been fired?"

"Yeah. One round. Looks like he got off a shot, huh?"

"No, Sergeant. He was murdered with his own pistol. Which means the killer got the drop on him," I said.

"Which also means it was someone he trusted," Sidorov said. "A pal, as you say."

"Hey, I was nowhere near the place," Craven said, folding his arms across his chest. "Now what else can I do for you? Need some booze? Hitler Youth dagger? A couple of ladies at the Cosmos Hotel?"

"Prostitution is illegal in the Soviet Union," Sidorov said. "So is procuring. What do you call such a man, Billy?"

"A pimp," I said. "And that's in polite society. We have laws against that too, but I'm not sure what the army calls it."

"Hey fellas, it was just a friendly offer to introduce you to some ladies. They ain't hookers, nothin' like that," Craven said, his quavering voice betraying his nerves for the first time.

"Don't worry about it, Sarge," I said, now that Craven was getting worried. That's exactly how I wanted him. Off balance and unsure. "We're just kidding around. No harm in a little black-market work on the side, right Kiril?"

"I am sure it is quite illegal in both our armies," Sidorov said. "But as you say, where is the harm? I cannot see any. Then again, I have not looked very hard."

"Hey, fellas, I mean captains, I got nothing to do with those killings, I swear," Craven said. He stood up, as if looking at us eye-to-eye might improve his chances of being believed. "Tell ya the truth, they made me real nervous. That's why I wanted Boris's piece. It cost me six bottles of bourbon."

"Reed sold it to you?"

"Nah. The booze just greased the skids," Craven said. "Reed was ticked off that I lost my pistol. He wouldn't sign off on a replacement. But a few bottles of his favorite hooch convinced him to let me keep Boris's .45. The guy took real good care of it." Craven traced his finger along the grip of the automatic and let out half a laugh. "We really was pals, ya know."

"Okay," I said. "Tell me this. When you got the pistol, it definitely had been fired?"

"Yeah. Recent, too. That's why I thought Boris had maybe put a slug into Kopelev and then took one in return," Craven said.

"Not unless they managed to shoot each other in the back of the head," Sidorov said.

"They went in there with someone they trusted," I said. "Now maybe you weren't within miles of the place, but somebody, a pal Boris trusted, might have told them to meet a guy at the warehouse. The guy who plugged them."

"Captain, I didn't tell Boris to go anywhere," Craven said. "Plus, they got that place locked and guarded. Ain't they?"

"Have you heard otherwise?" Sidorov said, cocking his head as he studied Craven's face.

"Everyone knows that kid got himself and his men transferred to the front," Craven said. "But no one seems to know why. Or won't say, on account of the NKVD boys."

"What kid?" I asked.

"Lieutenant Vanya Nikolin. Freshly minted junior officer," Craven said. "Looks like he hasn't started to shave yet. I hear his men like him 'cause he's not mean and looks out for them. Unusual in an officer in any army, wouldn't ya say?"

"I wonder if they think that now, facing the fascists instead of guarding a warehouse," Sidorov said. "You know nothing else about this?"

"Zip. And I'd be happy to spill if I knew anything else, just to get you two lookin' in another direction. Snoopy officers make me real nervous. You got any other questions?"

"No," I said, taking a last look at the disassembled pistol. If there had been any fingerprints on it, Craven's cleaning had eliminated them. "I hope you've been straight with us, Sarge."

"I do believe Sergeant Craven has been truthful in response to our questions," Sidorov said as I began to walk to the door. "But there is the unspoken truth, and that is often more difficult to grasp. So, Sergeant, what is it you are not telling us? There is something you know, I can smell it on your breath. Secrets have an odor all their own, subtle, but detectable. Yours are like bile wrapped around gun oil."

"Look, *Kapitan*, I don't know what you're talking about," Craven said, sitting down heavily as if he'd been hit by an iron hand. "You're sniffin' gun oil right here, that's all. I told you all I know, honest."

I stood back, watching Sidorov drill Craven with those steady eyes of his. It wasn't a hot day, but I watched as beads of sweat broke out on Craven's temples. He looked away from Sidorov, unable to withstand his gaze, then warily back again. Sidorov rested his hand on his holster, as if the weight of it was too much to bear. But the threat was unmistakable.

"Okay, okay, there is one thing," Craven said. "It might mean nothing, you unnerstand?"

"Everything means something," I said. "Spill."

"A few days before Boris and Kopelev bought it, there was a rumor about a guy goin' toes up with a needle in his arm," Craven said. "Major Drozdov and his NKVD boys were workin' overtime trying to make it look like everything was normal. But they were tense. Real tense."

"This guy," I said. "Russian?"

"Can't say for sure, it was just scuttlebutt. But everyone was talkin' about it. I was gettin' ready for a fire sale, I'll tell ya."

"Fire sale?" Sidorov spoke perfect English, but this stumped him.

"Going out of business," I said. "Everything is for sale, cheap."

"Yep. I'd already started to unload my merchandise. I had a crate of Kraut souvenirs on the next flight to Tehran, where I got a buddy at the airbase. A partner."

"But why?" Sidorov asked. "You have a successful business here."

"Listen, it's a racket. You know it and I know it. I like making a few bucks free and clear off hooch, Lugers, and condoms. But I'm small time. I got nothing to do with drugs. If someone's sellin' horse on this base, all it's gonna do is put everyone on the spot and grind business to a halt. I was ready to hunker down and keep a low profile."

"Who would sell horses on the base?" Sidorov asked.

"That's slang for heroin," I explained. "Easy enough to make from morphine if you have the right chemicals."

"Yeah, and more potent, too," Craven said. "If you're selling to users, you make more rubles with heroin."

"So what happened to the low profile?" I asked. "You obviously changed your mind."

"Nothin' happened. That's the point," Craven said. "The rumors stopped. Drozdov went back to his usual cheery self. The NKVD guards at the gate actually smiled when I went into town. I expected the base to be turned upside down looking for the Cadillac. But nada."

"What Cadillac? And nada means what, exactly?" Sidorov was beginning to lose track of the conversation.

"A Cadillac is an ounce of heroin," I said. "Nada means zilch. Nothing."

"That is very interesting. Thank you, Sergeant. You have been most helpful. I think we are done here, Billy."

CHAPTER ELEVEN

"How did you know he was holding back?" I asked Sidorov as we left the supply building. The sun was bright, but there was a bite in the air, a reminder that the wind blowing across the steppe came all the way from Siberia. It held the scent of frost and decay as if it had crossed the road of bones and borne its icy misery thousands of miles, right to where we stood.

"They always hold back," Sidorov said, buttoning up his jacket as if he felt the deathly chill enveloping him. "Minor criminals such as Sergeant Craven are never willing to provide anything for free if it may be of value later. Or if it may put them in danger."

"It was a bluff?" This wasn't my first interrogation by a long shot, but Sidorov had seen deeper into Craven than I had.

"You may call it that, but it has never failed me," Sidorov said. "The information is not always useful, but the subject does provide it. Petty criminals such as Craven are clever about holding back what they have. He would not provide information for free any more than he would hand out hosiery gratis."

"How can you trust a person you're interrogating when you threaten them? Especially back when you were with the NKVD," I said, scanning the hangar across from us, where ground crew were busy around a C-47 transport. "Wouldn't people say anything to make the pain stop?"

"By the time the Soviet security forces begin inflicting pain, all hope is lost," Sidorov said. "Pain and terror are the purpose. They have already decided what the truth is, so there is no need of extracting it from any one person. Believe me, I know. But what is necessary is for the subject to confess everything. This includes both the truth he knows and the truth his interrogators reveal to him. The Soviet truth."

"How much truth was revealed to you?" I asked, wondering if Sidorov had ever guessed at his betrayer.

"A great deal," he said with a sharp laugh, as if he was spitting out something foul. "I was an agent for British intelligence. A reactionary, a counterrevolutionary. An enemy of the people. I agreed, of course, not that it helped."

"Pain is the purpose," I said, reminding myself that Kiril Sidorov was a murderer.

"Precisely," he said. "Now, what is our next step?"

"Let's find Morris's crew and see what they have to say. Or what they're hiding."

We made our way across the runway, a solid stretch of Marston Mat, one of those testaments to Yankee ingenuity that had found its way even to this desolate patch of land. The mats were pierced steel planks that came in huge rolls, ready to lay down over cleared runways, and our bootheels clanged against the metal as we approached the C-47. We explained what we were doing to a small group of ground crew clustered around the aircraft.

"Yeah, Boris was in our section," one of the mechanics told us. "Damn good communications man. Any problem with a radio, pilots would ask for Boris Morris. He was a good guy. You gonna find who plugged him, Captain?"

"Hope so. Did Sergeant Morris have a beef with anyone? Any trouble over his business ventures?"

"Nah, Boris was easygoing. He traded with the Russians a bit. Just ask around," he said, nodding to Sidorov. "He got along with everyone."

"Even Craven?" I asked, hooking a thumb over my shoulder in the direction of the supply building.

"Even Craven. Between them, they cornered the market for souvenirs. That's where the money is, getting SS daggers, Nazi flags, and all that crap back to Italy or England," he said.

"No bad blood between them?" I asked.

"Captain, if anyone thought Craven had killed Boris, he woulda met with a terrible accident by now. Walked into a prop, maybe." He grinned, letting us know he was kidding. Sort of.

"What about Lieutenant Kopelev?" Sidorov asked.

"No one shed a tear, not that I noticed."

"No, I mean did Sergeant Morris and Lieutenant Kopelev get along? Were they often seen together?" Sidorov clarified.

"I saw Boris sell him condoms once, but that's nuthin' special. Your stores ain't exactly well stocked, Captain. Lots of your comrades buy raincoats any chance they get. Gettin' posted here is like guarding a Sears, Roebuck and Company and havin' the keys."

"Yes, yes," Sidorov said. "I assume that is one of your famous American department stores. We have them also. The Ukraine is not the most progressive area within the Soviet Union. If you ever get to Moscow, you will see many stores."

"Sorry, Captain, no offense. If they ever let me travel, I'll be glad to see Moscow. Gotta be a damn sight nicer than Poltava. Anyway, Boris and Kopelev knew each other, alright. But Kopelev wasn't the chummy type. He was always yelling at his men and refusing to help approve anything. Travel, buying local food, manifests, that sort of thing."

"A loud officer is uncommon in your army?" Sidorov asked, offering a friendly smile.

"Captain, there are people who just ain't happy less they're makin' someone else miserable. That was Lieutenant Kopelev in a nutshell," the mechanic said. "Now I gotta get back to work, this baby's gotta be ready to fly to Tehran tonight."

"Hey, just one last quick question," I said. "What did you mean about Kopelev approving manifests?"

"NKVD checks crew and passengers departing the base," he said. "They don't like their own people gettin' out. Coupla months ago, three guys tried to take a Polish refugee out. They'd bailed out over Polish territory and he'd helped them get back. They'd smuggled him in, dressed him up as one of ours, and put him on a Tehran flight. Kopelev spotted something fishy, pulled the Pole off, and raised holy hell. General Dawson got our men out as fast as he could."

"What happened to the Pole?" Sidorov said.

"You know what happened to him, Captain," the mechanic said, his demeanor changing as he narrowed his eyes and stared down Sidorov. "You damn well know."

We left.

"Dead?" I said as we got into the jeep.

"The Pole? Yes, probably shot not far from here, out in the grassland, after digging his own grave," Sidorov said. "It would have been an embarrassment for Kopelev. A quick execution was better for everyone, the Pole included. Less suffering that way, and perhaps Drozdov never found out. Nothing to do with our case, I'm afraid."

"No, just a poor guy taking a chance on freedom. As you did. Without the killings, of course."

"Please, Billy, spare me your bourgeois preaching," Sidorov said. "You come from the land of riches, with a Sears Roebuck on every corner. You cannot criticize me for trying for the same thing in the only way I could manage. The Pole tried. I tried. He is dead and I have been to hell. Perhaps freedom is overrated, after all. What would you sacrifice to attain it?"

"I'd like to think the lives of innocent people wouldn't top my list," I said as I started the jeep. "But listen, I'm sorry I brought it up. We need to focus on the present, not the past. What's next?"

"For my part, it seems Sergeant Craven is an excellent candidate. He is a criminal, probably habitual. Who would miss him?" Sidorov said.

"What about his actual guilt or innocence?" I asked. I pulled the jeep out into the road as one of the C-47 engines kicked over, spouted blue exhaust, and snarled into life.

"A trivial matter. You don't think they will allow us to actually investigate, do you? There is too great a chance that someone important will be implicated. We need a quick solution."

"*You* need a quick solution," I said. "I'm not the one with the threat of Siberia hanging over me. We need more evidence. Like why the warehouse guard detail was transferred out of here."

"Good luck with that," Sidorov said. "We would need something to offer General Belov and Major Drozdov, something they want."

"Condoms?" I asked. "Nylons?"

"Who doesn't want those things? No, I mean something they are desperate for. An American suspect. Technical Sergeant Craven, as I have been saying."

"I'm not fingering Craven as the killer, Kiril. Not without evidence, and there's nothing to pin on him."

"You misunderstand," Sidorov said as I came to a halt at an intersection, waiting for a couple of Russian trucks to lumber by. "We could simply indicate that he is a potential suspect. If Belov and Drozdov see that we are in agreement on this, they will take that as good news. That would be the moment to request travel to question the officer in charge of the warehouse detail. With time to search for your big sergeant, if Drozdov is in a good mood."

"Sounds good," I said, shifting into first. "But what happens to Craven?"

"Perhaps General Dawson would see fit to transfer Sergeant Craven. I'm sure your airbase in Tehran could use a skilled supply specialist," Sidorov said. "If the general acts quickly, he could get the paperwork approved before Drozdov notices. After all, checking manifests was Kopelev's job. There may be a new officer assigned, or Drozdov is managing that in addition to his other duties and may not take note."

"Tricky timing," I said. "But what's the worst that can happen? Craven loses his bid to corner the condom market?"

"What is the expression? A silver lining in the cloud?"

"Close enough," I said, thinking mostly about Big Mike. This was a long shot, but every day that Big Mike and his surviving crewmates didn't show up made a long shot look like easy money.

We drove by six Soviet fighters, Yak-9s, scrambling to take off from a grass runway. They taxied at high speed, racing one another to get into the air without regard to formation or altitude.

"Are we under attack?" I said, looking at the sky and expecting to see enemy bombers.

"Not that I can tell. Russian pilots can be enthusiastic with their machines. Not so that one," Sidorov said, pointing to the biplane we had seen being worked on earlier. It rolled along at a sedate pace, its wheels bouncing on the grasses until it slowly climbed into the air. The biplane's engine chugged along like a sewing machine, unlike the snarling growls of the Yak-9s.

We decided a search of Kopelev's and Morris's quarters would be our next stop. I was all for going to Drozdov right away, but Sidorov said searching their rooms was such an elementary step that we couldn't skip it. He was right, so I pulled up in front of the barracks, looking for Max. He'd be the guy to ask, rather than the brass. Less saluting and fewer questions.

Sidorov went down the hall to look for his gear. He'd been brought straight to Belov this morning and hadn't seen his accommodations, nor had he any belongings to bring. He seemed excited, which made sense for a guy who probably hadn't seen new underwear or socks anytime during the year.

"Max!" I hollered, checking the room across from mine.

"Here, boss!" Max answered, scurrying from the washroom. "You need me?"

"Yeah. Tell me, where were Kopelev's quarters? And Sergeant Morris. We want to do a search," I said.

"Sure, sure. I show you," Max said, bobbing his head eagerly.

"Who is this?" Sidorov said, strapping a holstered Tokarev automatic to his belt. Apparently Drozdov trusted him with more than new skivvies.

"Max, the guy I was telling you about. He's been assigned to me," I said.

Sidorov and Max studied each other. Max stiffened and took one step back. Wariness and worry flitted across his face under Sidorov's scrutiny, and I wondered what the hell was going on between them.

"*Zasuchi rukava*," Sidorov snapped, one hand resting on his leather holster.

"*Da, Kapitan*," Max answered, and rolled up his sleeves, revealing a display of tattoos. On one forearm, a rose was ensnared in barbed wire. On the other, a skull with bared fangs instead of teeth sat above a star.

"Open your tunic," Sidorov ordered. Max grinned and unbuttoned. On his thin, white chest was a large elephant, done in fine detail. The groveling Max, eager to please, was nowhere to be seen. This Max was clearly proud of his tattoos and showed no deference to Sidorov's rank. Or his pistol.

"You are a *kat*, Kapitan," Max said, buttoning up. "I see it in your eyes. And hands. Rough, like a dockhand."

"Cat?" I asked.

"*Kat*," Sidorov said, glancing at his callused hands. "*Katorzhnik*, a hard labor convict. It describes either a political prisoner or a professional criminal. Max is clearly not political."

"You're a jailbird?" I asked Max, who wrinkled his brow in confusion. That bit of English was too much for him. "*Kat?*"

"Yes, boss. No worry, Max no steal from you," he said.

"He was sent to the camps when he was very young," Sidorov said. "A juvenile. That is what the rose behind barbed wire means. And the fangs on the skull symbolize defiance of authority. I am surprised you are in uniform, Max."

"I was young man. Foolish. Now I only want to fight fascists and have freedom. No more jailbird, yes?"

"Yes, I must agree," Sidorov said. "Admirable goals. What were you charged with?"

"I worked on docks. Loading ships. Yalta, Sevastopol, Odessa. I was very young, alone. *No mat', no otets.* Police say I take things, send me to prison. Very hard. Young boy must fight, you understand?"

I understood. A kid in the company of adult criminals would be nothing but prey. From the little I knew about Soviet prisons, it had to be a hundred times tougher than any stateside penitentiary. Max had a hard face, sinewy arms, and suspicious eyes, but for all that I could see he was younger than he'd appeared to be. A few years older than me, but not much more.

"It is difficult to be an orphan, even in the Soviet Union," Sidorov said. "I congratulate you on your rehabilitation, as well as your command of English. Where did you learn it?"

"From work on docks and ships. I learn fast. English crews teach me. I also know French. *Est-ce que tu parles français?*"

"*Un peu.* Now show us to Lieutenant Kopelev's quarters, Max."

"Okay," Max said. "I drive, yes?"

"No," I said, remembering the Russian pilots and their crazy take-offs. "Just show us the way."

We drove off, and Max pointed out a two-story building topped with corrugated metal roofing, housing for the permanent ground staff. It was another repair job, the roof slapped on along with a few windows boarded up. Morris had bunked in there, along with a non-com. That would be our next stop.

On the main road, leading to the gate, we came upon a block-long three-story building, looking a lot like an apartment building you'd find in any city. Except that one end had been blown off, leaving one set of rooms exposed to the elements.

"Nice place, yes?" Max said. "General Belov and NKVD officers live here. All fixed up. *Vannaya.* Hot water." It was a nice enough place that two guards patrolled the sidewalk in front of the entrance.

I told Max to wait with the jeep. I didn't think it needed to be guarded, but I didn't want him getting in the way. Sidorov flashed papers in front of the sentries, who saluted and stood aside as we entered.

"It must feel good to have guards do what you tell them," I said, as we entered the central hallway.

"And to have a pistol at my side," he said. "But these things can be fleeting, so let us hope we find something. And by the way, do not trust Max. Not at all."

"Because he's been in a prison camp? That's where you just came from."

"I will explain later. Now, let us focus on the search. Although after several days, I doubt anything of value is left," Sidorov said.

We went to the second floor and Sidorov led the way to a door with a notice tacked up. He told me it said no entry permitted. We entered.

It was a nice room for a lieutenant. Curtains on the window

overlooking the main road. A bed with a soft quilt. A table and chair with a small bookcase. An armoire with a uniform and shirt on hangers. I went through the pockets and found nothing.

"The books are mostly political," Sidorov said. "Marx and Engels. Some by Comrade Stalin himself. They actually look well-read. He's even made notations in the margins. He was a diligent Marxist indeed. These tomes are dreadfully dull."

I turned over the mattress, looking for anything Kopelev wanted hidden from sight.

Nothing.

"Letters," Sidorov said, leafing through papers held between the pages of a book with a red star on the cover. "From his parents in Novgorod. The usual blather about Stalin and the great struggle, intermingled with family sentimentality."

"No evidence of a girlfriend?"

"None. Ivan Kopelev was a serious young Communist, according to all here and from what I can glean from these letters. Of course, as an NKVD officer posted here, he would have to be. Only the most trusted Party members are allowed contact with Westerners."

"Well, as we know, that doesn't always work out well," I said, thinking back to Sidorov's assignment with the Soviet embassy in London.

"Ivan had an earnestness to him that I could have never claimed," Sidorov said, looking behind the bookcase. "There is nothing here to tell us he was anything but what he appeared to be."

"Which likely got him killed," I said.

"Why do you say that?" Sidorov asked.

"Kopelev went by the rules. He was the kind of guy who would never give anyone a break, right? Other than that, I don't see any defining characteristic. Chances are, he discovered something he shouldn't have."

"That makes sense. But if we don't come up with anything credible, Moscow will decide what he stumbled upon, and it likely will be a Yankee imperialist plot," Sidorov said.

"What are those other books," I said, pointing to the small stack next to Marx and his pals.

"A volume of poetry," Sidorov said. "Alexander Pushkin, the greatest of the Russian poets. Stalin approves of him, so he is a safe choice for a rising NKVD man. This one is by your Mark Twain. *The Yankee in King Arthur's Court*. A good choice. The hero is an engineer, which fits well with the view of the ideal Soviet man. And the modern devices he introduces to medieval society is akin to Marxism leading the masses to a better life."

"It's *A Connecticut Yankee in King Arthur's Court*," I said. "I've read it."

"No one in Russia knows where or what Connecticut is, so the translators likely dropped it. This last one is less interesting. An atlas of the Soviet Union, with articles on each of the autonomous republics. Laudatory comments abound," Sidorov said, leafing through the oversized book.

"Let me see it," I said. I'd hoped the maps might prove useful if I ever got out of here to look for Big Mike. But the writing was all in Cyrillic script and was indecipherable. As I flipped through the pages, a slip of paper fell out. It marked a two-page spread of the Black Sea, with Turkey recognizable to the south. Some of the ports on the Black Sea were circled. Batumi and Poti in Russia, near the Turkish border. Samsun and Trabzon in Turkey itself.

"This is a receipt," Sidorov said. "From the *Goskomizdat* bookstore in Poltava. The State Committee for Publishing, that is."

"Looks like a second-hand book," I said, which made sense in the midst of war. "Are we on this map?"

"No," Sidorov said, tracing his finger along the top of the page. "Poltava is north of here, directly above Sevastopol, see?"

"That's in the Crimea, isn't it? It's one of the places Max told us he worked."

"Max never worked a day in his life. That star beneath the skull tattoo on his arm? That signifies he is a *vor*. A professional thief. *Vor v zakone*, a thief in law. They disdain labor of any sort and dedicate themselves to supporting fellow thieves and resisting the government. The star tattoo is significant. The higher the rank, the higher on your body the star rises. Max is young, but he is part of the thieves' world."

"It is like the mafia?"

"Somewhat. But the primary purpose is not to make money. It is to live the life of the *vor*, free of state interference, and to help your fellow thieves. They trust each other completely, and distrust everyone else."

"Are you sure about Max? Maybe he got those tattoos just to impress the other prisoners," I said.

"Billy, I knew a fellow on my labor detail who did that. He made his own ink by burning his boot heel and mixing the ash with his urine. He put those stars on his knees, which is the sign of a high-ranking *vor* since it symbolizes his refusal to kneel before any authority. But he was found out quickly. He was beaten and raped, then left with a piece of broken glass and a brick. He was given two days to remove the tattoos, which he did. Then he was forcibly tattooed, with a teardrop beneath one eye. The message of the teardrop is that the prisoner has been raped and is not to be respected. So, no, I do not think Max adorned himself with false tattoos," Sidorov said, going to the window.

I joined him and watched Max talking with the sentries, lighting cigarettes for them, laughing and clowning it up. He looked harmless, which might just make him dangerous.

"What's with the elephant tattoo?" I asked.

"That is perplexing. You see, the Russian word for elephant is *slon*. Those letters, or the picture of an elephant, is a recent development. They stand for *suki lyubyat ostry nozh. Slon*," Sidorov said, rubbing his chin, his eyes fixed on Max. "Bitches love a sharp knife."

"What does it mean?"

"When the fascists invaded, prisoners were offered the chance to serve in the armed forces. We had lost so many soldiers in the first months that it was critical to fill the ranks with whoever would fight," Sidorov said. "This apparently split the *vor* community. Those who volunteered to gain their freedom were seen as traitors. They had broken the sacred vow to never serve the state or obey its orders. They are the Bitches."

"Max is one of them?"

"I cannot be sure. A *vor* with his tattoos has a stature which makes it doubtful in my mind. He must have a vendetta against one of the volunteer prisoners to have the *slon* tattoo already," Sidorov said.

"I don't get it. What do you mean, 'already'?"

"A number of volunteers from the camps have already been convicted of crimes and re-sentenced. Some have fought well, but others were likely looking to desert at the first opportunity or succumbed to the temptation to steal. They were greeted with predictable violence by the *vor* when they were returned. In the camps they call it the Bitch War."

"You have to wonder, then, what is Max doing in uniform? Maybe he offended a high-ranking *vor* in the camp and had to get out in a hurry. What other choice would he have?"

"Thieves in law have their own courts, their own process for dealing with disputes. Fairer than Soviet justice, in their own way. Still, you could be right," Sidorov said, in a way that told me he didn't think it likely.

"Could Max be involved in the killings?"

"We should determine if he has an alibi," Sidorov said. "However, an execution within a military base is not their style. It brings too much attention. A thief would gain a great deal of stature if he stole supplies from that storeroom. But to kill two men for no profit? He would be seen as a fool."

"I see that. But someone had a motive to murder those two. And we're nowhere near finding it. Let's go talk to Bull before it's too late to get Craven on that flight."

"You do that, and I will request a meeting with Drozdov and Belov. Your Major Black should be there as well," Sidorov said. "I think we are done here."

I agreed. But I took the atlas. You never know when a map might come in handy.

CHAPTER TWELVE

MAX TALKED THE whole way back, asking about what we'd found and who we thought killed the lieutenant and the Yankee. I told him Uncle Joe Stalin had told me to keep it zipped, and he laughed, asking why Comrade Stalin wanted me to keep my trousers zipped. Even Sidorov chuckled. Max was a charmer, and smart enough to make a joke in spite of his fractured English. He would bear watching.

After we'd dropped Max off at the barracks, we made for the Operations building. Sidorov went off to find Drozdov and I headed for Bull's office. He was in, but Major Black was with him. They were seated at a table, maps and files spread out before them. I tried to back out, but Bull waved me in.

"Any news, Billy?" he asked.

"Well, I do have a favor to ask," I said, shooting a glance at Black. "It's a bit unusual."

"Shut the door and ask away," Bull said. "We're all friends here. The air force has nothing to hide from the OSS."

"Major Black may not want to know, sir," I said, pulling up a chair.

"This investigation does concern me, Captain, so if the general doesn't mind, I'll stay," Black said. "I must admit, you've got me curious."

"Do either of you know Technical Sergeant Marty Craven? He's with the C-47 transport squadron."

"Sure," Black said. "Everyone knows Marty. He's an operator."

"I know he trades a lot with the locals," Bull said. "Never had a complaint about him from his CO. Why?"

"There's a C-47 headed to Tehran pretty soon. Can you put him on it?"

"That's the favor? What the hell for?" Bull asked.

"I need some leverage with Drozdov. I want to tell him Craven is a possible suspect, since all Drozdov seems to care about is pinning the murders on an American," I said. "If you get Craven out of here fast enough, he won't be in any trouble."

"But you might be, if Drozdov thinks you tipped Craven off," Black said.

"I'm not worried about that. I want Drozdov to approve travel for me to question Lieutenant Vanya Nikolin. Pointing the finger at a Yank might put him in a good enough mood to do it. He doesn't have to know about this little chat, and we can explain away the transfer as nothing but routine."

"Now I can see why you didn't want me in the room, Captain. Fewer witnesses," Black said.

"Nikolin is the NKVD officer who was assigned to guard the ware-house, right?" Bull said.

"Yeah, he and his men were transferred out to the front east of Krakow, far as I know. I'd like to question him before the Krauts fill him full of holes."

"Speaking of NKVD, they have to approve the manifest for all transport flights," Black said. "They may not appreciate a last-minute change, especially if any of them have traded with Marty. Every Russian within ten miles knows he's always ready with a fistful of rubles."

"I wouldn't worry about that," Bull said. "Kopelev's replacement is playing catch-up. He was just transferred in and he's probably never heard of Craven. As it happens, I have the final manifest right here, ready to go."

"You sure it's a good idea?" Black asked, addressing the question to Bull, not me.

"It is," I said. "We need a break, and this could help. If nothing comes of it, there'll be another guy ready to take Craven's place. The army's full of them."

"Okay," Bull said. "Major Black, you never heard this conversation. I'll get the paperwork going and send someone to get Craven on board. Wheels up in one hour, Billy. Good luck."

I found Sidorov, who said Belov and Drozdov would see us in fifteen minutes. I took the time to hustle over to the barracks and find Carter, the navigator on the *Banshee Bandit*. He'd offered to go over his maps with me, and I was glad I took the time to find him. The weather over the Romanian oil fields had cleared, and they were scheduled to take off on a mission before dawn.

He showed me Kozova, where Big Mike's B-17 had gone down. There was a rail line leading to Kiev, about two hundred and eighty miles to the east. After that, it was another couple of hundred miles farther east to Poltava. If I were Big Mike, I'd watch for a train headed in that direction. The farther from the front they got, the less danger they'd be in. In theory.

Or maybe he was already in custody, rounded up by the NKVD internal troops. I was getting a good sense of how paranoid the Russians were about outsiders, so I knew our downed aircrew wouldn't get a hero's welcome. But sooner or later, even the most suspicious NKVD office would have to recognize these Americans as allies.

They had to. And Big Mike had to be alive.

Carter gave me a couple of small-scale maps. Spares, he said. One was of the Ukraine region and the other showed part of the Ukraine at the top and northern Iran at the bottom. He had that one in case they ever flew out of Russia via the Persian Corridor, the Lend-Lease supply route to our south.

"No such luck," Carter said. "It's sunny Italy for us."

I wished him luck, since that meant tangling with the Luftwaffe and thick flak again, then hoofed it back to Operations. I wondered why the Poltava airbase was so far behind the lines. The front was now five hundred miles to the west and moving farther away toward Poland and Germany. Maybe the location was logical when Operation Frantic was first planned, but it wasn't now that the Red army had advanced so far to the west. Why make our aircraft fly hundreds of miles farther than they needed to? Moving nearer the front would put us closer to targets, closer to any aircrew who had to bail out, and save fuel. Relocating the airfield would make sense, but good sense was often in short supply when it came to army decision-making, Yank or Red.

"This way," Sidorov said from the doorway of the Operations building. "We are meeting in the briefing room around back. Maiya will translate. I have the impression Drozdov does not trust me to do it. Or perhaps he trusts her to leave out anything he doesn't want Belov to hear."

"There's no politics like army politics," I said, following Sidorov to the Quonset hut behind Operations. Long shadows trailed us as the sun began to disappear beyond the horizon.

"An NKVD posting like this is an important step for a career officer," Sidorov said. "It demonstrates how much he is trusted by the Party to be put in charge. I imagine Drozdov has his sights set on Moscow, but he knows that any failure here, especially one involving Westerners, will be the end of him."

"Of him or his career?"

"The Communist Party is Stalin. Anyone who makes the Party look bad makes Stalin look bad. That means either a bullet or a shovel on the road of bones. I plan on neither, myself," Sidorov said, opening the door to the Quonset hut as I glanced at my watch. By now, I hoped Craven was stowed safely aboard the C-47 along with as much loot as he could carry.

Inside, Belov and Drozdov sat at a table in front of a large map of the Ukraine and points west. Maiya stood at their side, hands folded behind her back. Major Black sat facing them, and I hoped he had a good memory for forgetting things. A con job always worked better if people believed what they were being told. Even though Black wasn't the intended mark, I didn't want his expression giving anything away.

General Belov spoke first, and Maiya conveyed his wish for a speedy conclusion to this terrible tragedy. Then Drozdov began, his tone as menacing as his cold blue eyes and pock-marked face. He tapped the table with his forefinger a few times, finally calming down and nodding to Maiya to begin.

"Major Drozdov demands that you reveal what you have discovered," she said. "It is unacceptable that the murderer of Lieutenant Kopelev has not been found. He says you must not care about your dead sergeant very much either. What have you accomplished so far, and when do you plan to apprehend the killer?"

"I understand the major's concern for both victims," I said, buying myself a little time to figure out the best way to respond. Back on the Boston PD and in the army, I'd been on the receiving end of a wagonload of shit rolling downhill, so it wasn't a new experience. First time in Russian, though. "Since Captain Sidorov arrived this morning, we have been busy surveying the crime scene, questioning people who knew the deceased, speaking with Doctor Mametova, and searching the lieutenant's quarters."

I stopped there, waiting for Maiya to translate and for Drozdov to get back on his high horse. I figured it was better to let the major exhaust himself before mentioning Craven. Not to mention giving his C-47 more time to roll down the runway.

"Major Drozdov wishes to know for what purpose you searched Lieutenant Kopelev's room," Maiya said. "He was a victim, not a suspect."

"Of course not," I said. "We looked for clues about anyone who may have had a strong dislike for the lieutenant. We saw nothing to indicate he was other than a very diligent officer. He had recently purchased an atlas of the Soviet Union and appeared to be studying Black Sea ports. He also had numerous books written by Joseph Stalin. Very studious."

I figured the mention of Stalin's name might calm Drozdov, or at least direct his anger to a new subject. He spoke, flicked his hand, and Maiya told me to continue.

"There is one person we wish to investigate further," I said.

"A potential suspect," Sidorov said, speaking in English for my benefit. "It is too early to say, but further interrogation may bear fruit." He was smart not to mention who it was or his nationality. That got Drozdov's attention.

"Who is it, the major wants to know?" Maiya said.

"Technical Sergeant Martin Craven," I said. "He is with the C-47 transport squadron."

"Sergeant Craven is active in the black market, bartering goods for war souvenirs which he transports to Italy and England to sell at a profit," Sidorov said. "A capitalist of the lowest order."

After Maiya finished translating, Drozdov and Belov put their heads together and whispered for a minute. Then Belov spoke.

"When will you arrest this man?" Maiya said.

"When we have sufficient evidence," I said. "We still need to gather facts so he can be court-martialed." Drozdov wanted to know what else we had, which surprised me. I thought there was already enough red meat on the bone we'd tossed him. I needed something else.

"I believe there may be a connection between the murders and the recent drug overdose," I said. "One of your soldiers was found dead with a hypodermic needle in his arm, I understand."

Maiya faltered for a moment, then launched into the translation. Drozdov and Belov kibitzed again, and then she asked what other information we planned on gathering. I told her the closest thing we had to a witness was Lieutenant Vanya Nikolin, who was somewhere near the front lines east of Krakow.

"It would be helpful to understand why Nikolin and his men were transferred out, so soon after the murders," I said. Sidorov caught my eye, flashing me a warning with a slight nod. "While I am sure they were questioned properly, an investigating officer always prefers to speak to potential witnesses directly."

Maiya went on in a tone that suggested she softened the seeming criticism in my question. Drozdov drummed his fingers on the table, whispered to Belov, who sat rigidly and gave no response. Drozdov finally spoke.

"Comrade Major Drozdov questioned each man," Maiya said. "They all stated no one entered or left the building while they were on duty. It was the custom before this crime to guard the warehouse only at night. The comrade major concluded the killer departed after the guards left. Even so, Lieutenant Nikolin requested transfer, feeling that he had lost the trust of his commanding officers. The transfer was granted."

"Still, we would like to speak to the lieutenant ourselves, if permission would be granted," I said. "Perhaps he has information about Sergeant Craven's involvement, information he did not realize was important at the time."

When Maiya translated that, Belov bobbed his head, seeming to like the idea. He and Drozdov came to a quick agreement.

"General Belov will decide if he can grant your request," she said. "Soon."

"How soon?" I asked.

"We trust the general will make the decision as he feels best," Sidorov said, cutting me off before I antagonized the old boy. "If he decides to allow us to travel, perhaps Captain Boyle could also be authorized to contact NKVD officers in the rear areas for information about his sergeant. Perhaps the local Railway Protection Regiment would know of any American airmen seeking transport."

That took a bit of back and forth, with no clear answer from the comrades, then Maiya told us we were dismissed. Drozdov remained at the table with General Belov, who listened intently as the major whispered and slapped his hand on the table. Neither guy looked happy, but not many generals in my army would be happy with a major talking to them like that, no matter how quietly.

"It is time to eat, sirs," Maiya said, ushering us out of the Quonset hut. Black held the door for her, and they walked side by side to the mess hall.

"Major, why didn't you tell us about the warehouse being guarded only at night?" I asked. "I've been wracking my brains trying to figure out how anyone could have gotten in there while it was guarded."

"Sorry, I didn't think to mention it," Black said. "It was a routine procedure, Captain. Didn't seem to make much difference. Locked or guarded, it's all the same."

"Murder is never routine," I said. "Anything else we should know?"

"No, I'm certain," Black said, then quickened his step to stay by Maiya's side. He apparently had his own priorities.

"There is something else you should know," Sidorov said quietly as we walked behind them. "Maiya did not translate anything about the *narkoman*."

"Who?"

Sidorov mimed shooting a needle into his arm.

"And I think Drozdov understood what you said. His eyes widened when you mentioned the needle and he stared at Maiya," Sidorov said. "She understood and did not translate anything about it."

"Was it an NKVD man who overdosed?"

"Sergeant Craven never said. And if everything worked as we planned, you would have to go to Tehran to ask him."

"What do you think our chances are?" I said. "Think Belov will let us go?"

"I do not think General Belov makes any decisions regarding state security. He can order his airmen about and consult with your General Dawson about targets and flight paths, but nothing else. If it serves the state for us to go, we will go."

"And here, Comrade Major Drozdov is the state," I said, slowing my pace so Maiya wouldn't overhear. Not that she was likely to anyway, with Black whispering into her ear.

"Yes. You understand the Soviet system perfectly," Sidorov said. "Drozdov has the power, but any hint of drug use by the comrade major and he would soon be denounced as a social parasite and enemy of the workers. Then the only way he'd make it to NKVD headquarters in Moscow would be via the basement of the Lubyanka prison."

"No wonder he kept it hush-hush," I said, buttoning up my field jacket against the evening chill. As we walked past the jeep, I noticed the atlas was gone. I'd left it on the rear seat and now there was no sign of it. "Looks like somebody wanted a book with pictures."

"Shall we add petty theft to the list of crimes we are investigating?" Sidorov said.

"Right now, all I want to do is eat," I said. "But if we don't get travel authorization, maybe Drozdov would let us go into town. Might be worth visiting that bookstore to see if anyone remembers what other books Kopelev was interested in."

"Why?"

"Because somebody was interested enough in the atlas to swipe it. Might mean nothing, might mean something," I said.

"A soldier who wishes to improve his knowledge of the Union of Soviet Socialist Republics, just like the dedicated Lieutenant Kopelev," Sidorov said. "Is that not possible?"

"Anything's possible," I said as we neared the entrance to the officers' mess. "Even a girl like Maiya falling for Major Black."

"But unlikely," Sidorov said. "I told you not to trust her."

"Okay. I shouldn't trust Max or Maiya, and the secret police run the joint. I need to be careful around Black because whatever he knows Maiya will too. What have I missed?"

"Not a thing. Welcome to the workers' paradise."

CHAPTER THIRTEEN

WE SAT NEXT to Bert Willis, skipper of the *Banshee Bandit*, at one of the long tables in the officers' mess. Sidorov had loaded his plate with ham, macaroni, a mixture of cabbage and carrots, along with pickles, and a slab of black bread. I did the same, just not in the same weight class.

"Hungry, Captain?" Willis said, eyeing the mound of food.

"One never knows when the next meal may come," Sidorov said.

"Well, I'm hoping my next dinner is Italian," Willis said. "Weather's cleared, so we're taking off at dawn. You coming along for the ride, Billy?"

"Not this time," I said. "Good luck."

"The *Bandit* will get us through, don't you worry," Willis said, pouring himself a healthy slug of vodka. Bottles of water and vodka were set out on the tables, and with a mission in the morning, the hard stuff was getting a workout.

"You hear anything about the *Sweet Lorraine*?" I asked.

"Zilch. No word from the Russians. Those five guys have to be out there somewhere," Willis said, gulping his drink. "Belov tell you anything?"

"Besides the runaround? No. But we're hoping to get a search organized," I said.

"Hard to understand these Russians, if you don't mind my saying so, Captain," Willis said, his eyes fixed on Sidorov. "We fly all this way and bomb targets for them, and they won't lift a finger to help our crews. What gives?" Willis asked, finishing off the booze and pouring himself another.

"Oh, they will help, Lieutenant," Sidorov answered, taking the bottle and topping off his drink. "The military simply doesn't want you to know about it. Because if they fail, they will appear weak and ineffectual. If they succeed, then it appears they are helping the decadent Western capitalists, and that could be used to denounce them. But believe me, the Russian people will help your men."

"That sort of makes sense, Captain. Thanks," Willis said.

"*Za vashe zdarovje*," Sidorov said, raising his glass. "To our health, gentlemen."

"To long life," I said as we clinked glasses.

"No argument there," Willis said. "Bottoms up."

We had another round and Sidorov taught us a few Russian toasts. Carter joined us, and that brought on a round or two. Willis wanted to call it a night, telling us that hangovers at 25,000 feet were worse than flak. Sidorov offered one last toast.

"*Chtoby stoly lomalis ot izobiliya, a krovati ot lyubvi*," he said. "To tables breaking of abundant food and beds breaking from much love." Everybody liked that one.

Willis and Carter left, along with the other officers flying out in the morning. Major Black left, Maiya in tow. It looked that way, but my money was on Maiya pulling the strings.

"Shall we discuss our plans for the night?" Sidorov whispered across the table. "The experiment with the key?"

"I've got nothing else to do," I said, perhaps emboldened by the vodka. It wasn't often that a scheme which sounded sensible in the bright light of day still seemed like a good idea after dark, but the glow in my gut banished whatever caution I would've normally mustered.

"Perhaps a stroll, to watch where Major Black goes?"

"Sure," I said, getting up from the table. "I have a feeling he won't have that key on his body much longer." As we headed for the door, I spotted Major Drozdov, carrying a sheaf of papers, strolling in with Bull Dawson and General Belov.

"Good evening, *Kapitans*," Drozdov said. "I have come from a most interesting discussion with General Dawson. Apparently, your suspect was transferred to Tehran and left this afternoon. A pity." He was unable to suppress a smirk as he surprised us with English leavened with a clipped Oxford accent.

"It seems like a lot of people get transferred out of here at the most inconvenient times," I said, recovering as quickly as I could and watching as Drozdov's eyes darted to Sidorov.

"Your English is quite good, Major," Sidorov said. "I detect the accent of my instructor at the Lenin Military Institute of Foreign Languages."

"Quite," Drozdov said with an exaggerated British accent. "Our academic comrades from Great Britain never lose their affectations and pass them onto us. Obviously, I felt no need to announce my fluency until today. You noticed, *Kapitan* Sidorov, did you not, that I understood what Maiya failed to translate?"

"Yes, Major," Sidorov said, his voice low and his eyes wary. He didn't know where this was going, and neither did I. Belov stood with his hands clenched behind his back, his dark eyes beneath bushy eyebrows focused on Sidorov.

"Well, no matter. As I am sure you know from your previous association with state security, secrets are often kept from other agencies. That is the case here. It has nothing to do with your investigation, of course," Drozdov said.

"Of course, Major," Sidorov said, his face pale. I wondered if he was afraid that had been his last decent meal.

"Now, as to the substance of your report today. General Belov and I agree that you may travel to question Lieutenant Nikolin. I have made all necessary arrangements. I hope you have better luck with him than I had with Sergeant Craven," Drozdov said, with a sly glance at Bull, who kept a poker face.

"Thank you, Major Drozdov," I said. Sidorov let out a long breath, as if he'd been ready for a firing squad. "When do we leave?"

"You misunderstand," Drozdov said. "Only you will be traveling, Captain Boyle. Alone. Your colleague will remain here. The investigation must continue, yes?"

"Of course, Comrade Major," Sidorov said, giving Drozdov a reluctant nod of agreement. The major looked at him, his gaze full of contempt. He gave no response.

"These are your travel documents, Captain Boyle. The flight plan has been approved by General Belov. The documents allow you to travel within designated areas and instructs NKVD officers to provide you with support. I have radioed for them to gather information about American flyers who have been taken into custody, since you will be traveling in the same locale in which they came down. I hope you find your sergeant."

"So do I, Major. What is my destination?"

"Zolynia, a small town about one hundred kilometers outside of Lwow. An NKVD regiment is assembling there as we prepare for an offensive. You will be taken to an airstrip outside of Zolynia, where Lieutenant Nikolin has been instructed to meet you," Drozdov said. "Private Bogomozov will awaken you and take you to the aircraft at 0500. Do you have any questions?"

"No sir," I said, hardly believing his change in attitude. I nearly asked if he'd received new orders from Moscow but thought better of it. Why antagonize the guy when he finally got around to being helpful?

"Here's some more good news, Billy," Bull said as Drozdov headed for the food. "Lieutenant Kazimierz is due in on a flight from Tehran tomorrow afternoon. I'll have Major Black and Captain Sidorov brief him while you're gone. Good luck and bring those men back."

"Wait, General. Can't we wait for Kaz to get here? I could really use a translator."

"*Nyet*, according to Drozdov. It's tomorrow or nothing. Besides, I understand the lieutenant is recovering from surgery. It's probably not the best idea to get him off one aircraft and put him on another so quickly. Besides, Drozdov's orders should get you an English speaker pronto. He may be only a major, but he's definitely got clout."

"Okay. Better not to wait another day anyway. Big Mike is counting on me, I can feel it."

"I bet he is. I am, too. And keep your eyes open for other Americans out there. We've had reports of prisoners escaping as the Germans move POW camps farther to the west. The Russians are moving fast in places, and we know that some POWs slipped away as the Krauts marched them away from the front. I'd like to think our Soviet allies are taking care of them, but you never know."

"Understood, General. But do me a favor," I whispered. "Tell Kaz to trust no one."

Bull nodded and followed Drozdov to the table, leaving Sidorov and me to wonder what the hell had just happened.

"It is no surprise he was taught such good English," Sidorov said. "I was, after all, for my assignment in England. It is the sign of a man on his way up. And it stands to reason Moscow would put an English-speaking NKVD officer in place here."

"And he was smart enough to keep it to himself," I said as we walked outside. "It gave him an advantage. He looked angry at the end of the conversation. Think he blames you for revealing his secret?"

"No," Sidorov said. "It is because I called him comrade. I did it out of habit, but prisoners are forbidden the use of the honorific, since we have betrayed the revolution."

"It's just a word," I said, heading back to the jeep.

"No. Not in the Soviet Union. It is a magical incantation, casting a spell of equality where there is none, justice where there is only brutality, and idealism where there is nothing left but disillusion. *Kats* can see through all that, like the child in the story. The one where the emperor has no clothes. So, the word is reserved for those who convince themselves that lies are the truth, that the great Stalin loves them and cares about their lives. I have committed a great crime tonight. An offense against thought. An unforgivable one, perhaps."

"It'll be okay," I said, not at all sure it would be. "Drozdov was in a good mood. He'll eat and drink and forget about it. He needs you to run the investigation with Kaz. Is that going to be a problem for you?"

"My escapades in London are behind me," Sidorov said. "I have nothing against Lieutenant Kazimierz, personally. It was simply a convenient ruse to allow him to be charged as a murderer. As soon as I met you, I knew you would exonerate your friend. I simply never thought you would take it farther and disrupt my plans. I underestimated you, Billy. I hope Drozdov has as well."

"What do you mean? Has he got something up his sleeve?" I got into the jeep and started it up.

"There is no such thing as a straightforward NKVD officer, certainly not one at his level. But don't worry, I am perhaps too suspicious. I have betrayed people and have been betrayed. It makes for a nervous imagination. Now, let us find where Major Black and Maiya have gotten to, so we can go through his pockets."

I drove back to the barracks, wondering if it was Sidorov who had something up his sleeve. Was I underestimating him? He'd vowed to never go back to the camps again, and I can't say I blamed him, but I didn't want to be his patsy either.

Sidorov stayed silent on the short drive, and I couldn't think of any comforting words. So I let the quiet settle over us as I thought about who I'd be willing to kill not to have to spend the rest of my life in the USSR.

"Max!" I shouted as we entered the barracks. He materialized, as if he'd been ready to sprint to that spot as soon as I walked in. "You know about tomorrow morning, right?"

"Yes boss. Coffee and black bread. I bring, wake you, we go to runway three. Okay?"

"The same for me, Max," Sidorov said. "I will see Captain Boyle off. Now, tell us where to find Major Black's quarters."

"Not far," Max said. "I take you."

"Max, do you have a bottle of vodka?"

"I am Russian, *Kapitan*," Max said. "Which means answer is yes, but bottle is half empty."

"Perfect," I said. "Get it." I went to my room, stashed the travel orders, and grabbed some of the rubles Black had given me.

"Too much, boss," Max protested, with minimal enthusiasm, as he pocketed the grimy notes and led us to the apartment block which housed the permanent contingent of American officers. In five minutes, we were at the door of a two-story brick building. There were four doorways, each set above a short set of concrete steps.

"Germans burn it, but your engineers, they fix up nice," Max said. "Better than most Russian officers, no kidding. That is Major Black, there." He pointed to a first-floor apartment, a faint light glowing behind drawn curtains.

"What's the layout?" I said. "The rooms?"

"Room with chairs and couch. Sitting room, yes? Small bedroom. No *vannaya*, except at end of hall. Only generals have own *vannaya*."

"Tell us, Max, how long has Maiya been sleeping with Major Black?" Sidorov said.

"Who says that?" Max asked, feigning outrage. "Maiya is good Communist girl."

"Of course," Sidorov said, taking the bottle from me and handing it to Max. "Which is why the major likes her, isn't it? Major Black is sympathetic to our struggles."

"Yes," Max said, taking a slug and eyeing both of us, trying to figure the angles. "He speaks Russian, not too bad, not too good. Tells me about Russian artists, but I do not know the names. The only artists I know make the *taty*."

"Here," I said, forking over more rubles and taking the bottle back. "Tell us more."

"You know how it goes with the *musor*," Max said to Sidorov. "They always want something."

"Who?" I asked.

"The police, the authorities," Sidorov said. "Although it does not mean exactly that."

"What you feed the pigs," Max said. "Waste, garbage. Like those in power."

"You work for them too, Max," I said. "Like Maiya."

"Max is simple private," he said. "Privates obey the bosses, no choice. Maiya, she too. The *musor* wants to know everything. What Americans say, what they think of Stalin, what secrets they have. Max cannot get secrets like Maiya, no."

"Do you think Black knows what she's after?" I asked.

"Black knows what she wants, but like all men, he is blinded by what he wants," Max said. "Now I go. This talk is dangerous. *Spokoynoy nochi*."

"Good night, Max," Sidorov said. "Be careful."

"Was that a warning?" I asked as Max faded into the night.

"I must admit to some sympathy, even though he is a criminal and obviously is telling Drozdov everything we do. He could be sent back for the slightest indiscretion," Sidorov said. "I suspect he may have been released on Drozdov's orders, to have another English-speaking informer. He can't provide women for every American, after all. Max can more easily mix with the enlisted ranks and pick up information that may be useful."

"Think he'll report this stroll to Black's place?"

"Money makes people forgetful, Billy. There is also nothing strange about you visiting a fellow American officer, or my accompanying you. But if there were the slightest chance he would get in trouble with Drozdov for withholding information, he would denounce us immediately."

"Then let's get going, just in case," I said, spilling a bit of vodka into my palm and rubbing it into my cheeks like aftershave. Sidorov just took another slug.

We went inside, slamming the foyer door against the wall and banging on Black's door.

"Black! We're here for a drink, open up," I shouted.

"*Davayte vyp'yem, drug*," Sidorov yelled, which I figured meant much the same.

"What the hell are you doing, Boyle?" Black demanded as soon as he had the door open. Not all the way, I noticed.

"Hey, I'm a long way from home, I just wanted to have a drink with you," I said, working at slurring my lines. "We can talk about old times in Cambridge. You know that bar, the one at the corner of Bow and Linden? Can't remember the name. You know it?"

"Captain Boyle, the last thing you need is another drink. And I went to Yale, remember?" Black said, backing up as we moved into the room, alcohol vapors preceding us. His shoes were off, his field scarf was gone, and his shirt was half unbuttoned. The last thing he wanted was two drunks in his sitting room when he was halfway to paradise.

"Major Black, just one drink," Sidorov said. "It is all we have left in this bottle anyway."

"You got any bourbon, Major?" I said, looking around the room and spotting keys in a small dish on a table by the door. The perfect spot to leave debris from your pockets at the end of a long day. "I'd kill for some bourbon."

"Please leave. Both of you. Captain Boyle, you have an early flight, you should get some sleep," Black said, his face turning red.

"Oh, you already knew," I said, staggering backwards and reaching out for the table to steady myself. "I wanted to surprise you and celebrate with a toast. Let's have a toast, okay?"

"I think Major Black is correct," Sidorov said, having observed my clumsiness. "We should go. *Ya proshu proshcheniya.*"

"Apology accepted," Black said, ushering us out and slamming the door as soon as we dragged our heels across the threshold. I heard high-pitched laughter as we descended the steps.

"The laugh will be on us if we are caught," Sidorov said. "Are you sure you wish to do this?"

"Hell yes," I said. "Too bad he'll never know, long as we get this key back tonight."

"Then let us proceed before we sober up," Sidorov said.

Operations was next. The place was quiet, with night duty personnel at their desks, looking busy and avoiding the eyes of prowling officers who might mean trouble, or a new assignment. We checked Bull's office first to be sure he hadn't come back for some late-night paperwork. An American corporal carrying a cup of coffee told us the general was expected back after dinner, which could be any time now. We moved on to Black's office as a Russian private brushed by us, weighed down with a stack of files. Wandering officers seemed to be taken for granted.

I turned the knob on Black's door. It opened, and I wondered if the Russians kept their offices locked. Maybe not, since that would only make it harder for the NKVD to snoop around. Sidorov slid inside and I closed the door behind us. Not bothering with the lights, I used Black's key to unlock the desk drawer, grabbed the key to the file cabinet, and got that open.

"Easy," I whispered to Sidorov, dangling the keys to the warehouse by a chain. I pocketed it and we walked out like we owned the place.

"The next lock will be more difficult," Sidorov said once we left Operations behind. "It will be guarded."

"Then make it an official inspection," I said. "Tell the guards its part of our investigation, and we're doing a security check of the building. Put a lot of bark into it."

"Excellent," Sidorov said. "For all we know, it was this time at night that the killings occurred. Should Drozdov ask, I will tell him we wanted to observe the scene during darkness."

"And see what the guards' routine is," I said as we walked to the warehouse. "With any luck, I'll be able to compare notes with what Nikolin tells me. If I can find a translator."

"That may be a challenge," Sidorov said. "But Drozdov did say he radioed ahead, and he may have arranged for an NKVD translator."

"I'd rather it was you," I said, realizing how easily we'd worked together. Which brought Kaz to mind. "I want you to extend Lieutenant Kazimierz every courtesy. It will be a shock to hear about Big Mike and to find me gone."

"I will. I understand you are friends. I will endeavor to make up for the past," Sidorov said. It was a tall order, but it sounded like he meant it. Or I was a sap. One or the other.

We approached the warehouse and two sentries snapped to attention. There was no one else around, and the wind had a damp chill to it. It looked like these guys had a long, cold night ahead of them.

Sidorov identified himself and I could hear my name in the flow of rough Russian consonants. He pointed at the door and the second-floor windows, the guards answering his questions as fast as he fired them. His voice softened as he evidently showed his satisfaction with their responses. He nodded. They nodded. Everyone was relaxed. That's when he told me to unlock the door. I pulled out the keychain and the guards stepped aside, relief evident on their faces. These officers weren't going to report them and were about to get out of their hair.

"Well done," I said as we entered.

"I told them not to mention our inspection, since we will be conducting it randomly, and we did not want their comrades to have advance notice," Sidorov said as he flicked on a switch. A faint and gloomy yellow light illuminated the staircase. At the top, I unlocked the door to the storeroom. Sidorov hit the light, and everything was as we last saw it.

Except for the three boxes.

Stacked one on top of another, off to the side, were three stout wooden crates. They were painted with the universal green-pea-soup paint beloved by armies everywhere. A padlock held each one shut tight. They were about four feet by two feet, and two feet high each. Hefty, but not too heavy to be easily carried by the leather handles affixed to each side. I tried Black's keys, but they didn't work.

"More top secret weaponry?" I asked.

"Perhaps," Sidorov said, squinting in the dim light to make out the stenciled Cyrillic letters on the side. "It seems destined for Khazar Brothers Shipping in Tabriz."

"Where the hell is that?"

"In Iran, about six hundred kilometers northwest of Tehran," he said. "There are warnings about tampering with the shipment. State security, that sort of thing. I would not attempt to open them."

"We'd need a crowbar anyway," I said. "If they arrived after the killings, I don't see how it would matter anyway. Who knows what the NKVD and OSS are up to in Iran? Can't say I know much about that part of the world."

"The Soviet Union and Great Britain invaded Iran in 1941," Sidorov said. "The Shah was pro-German, and it was thought necessary to have a more friendly government to secure the oil fields and transport routes for supplies from the Mideast."

"And now we have a friendly government?" I asked, feeling the weight of the top box and trying to guess its contents.

"The son of the old Shah, Mohammad Reza Pahlavi, was installed as the new king. The young Shah has declared war on Germany, and now we have supplies and oil flowing to everyone's satisfaction."

"Okay, that's enough history. Let's help ourselves to some morphine," I said.

Everything was still in place on the shelves. Gold coins, plastic explosives, radio sets, and dozens of weapons. I spotted the silencers and gave them each the sniff test. None of them had been used, or if they had, the killer had taken the time to clean and oil them down.

"One carton," I said. "If they don't take inventory again it might not even be noticed." The stacked cartons were filled with smaller cardboard containers of five morphine syrettes each. Each carton contained sixty of the cardboard boxes. Three hundred syrettes might help tide Doctor Mametova over until her regular shipment of morphine made it through.

"Take it from the bottom," Sidorov said. "Each carton is numbered, and they might notice if the top one is gone."

"You'd make a good thief," I said. "Max would be proud."

"Max would be overcome in here," he said. "A *vor*'s paradise."

Smuggling the carton out past the guards was our next challenge. Sidorov came up with the idea of strapping the box to my back, using the adjustable canvas slings from a couple of Sten guns. As long as I buttoned up my jacket and didn't jump around too much, I'd be okay.

I hoped.

We took the stairs and headed out. The guards jumped to attention as Sidorov locked the door behind us. They saluted. I raised my right arm to return the salute and felt the box shift. One of the straps had loosened and began to slide down my chest. I tucked my arm in to hold it and staggered with the shifting weight.

Sidorov stepped in front of me, saluted the guards, and spoke quickly, in a friendly voice. The guards laughed.

"Turn around and walk, you capitalist tool," Sidorov said, blocking their view. I tucked my hands into my pockets and used my elbows to keep the carton in place.

"Is that how you described me?" I asked.

"That, and more. The rest of what I said was far worse. I told them you couldn't hold your liquor."

Once we reached the hospital, I took off my jacket and Sidorov took the carton in hand. The place was quiet except for the groans and what sounded like murmured curses. Two nurses ran by us, their eyes grim and exhausted.

We found Doctor Mametova in her office, reading medical files by a faint light, a cigarette clamped between her lips. Her eyes went wide as Sidorov set the carton down on top of the paperwork. She might not have been able to understand English, but she knew exactly what these syrettes were.

"She wants to know where we got this," Sidorov said, after they had both spoken. "I told her Bulgaria."

"Tell her not to spread the word around," I said, putting my finger to my lips. "Hush hush."

"*Doktor* Mametova understands," he said. "She wants to know if we will be going back to Bulgaria anytime soon. I told her sadly, no. She still does not know when their regular supply of morphine will resume."

"Ask her about the soldier who overdosed," I said. "Was there a theft of the hospital supply?" Sidorov and the doctor had a bit of back and forth.

"She has not had any drugs to be stolen," he said. "And she wishes to know where the fool got his supply so she could buy some as well. It must have been very pure, because he died instantly, with the needle still in his vein."

"Heroin?" I asked.

"*Da*," Doctor Mametova said, the Russian version evidently close to the English. She exchanged a few sentences with Sidorov, who told me she hadn't tested the residue but thought it was likely heroin. Or poison, she didn't really care how the idiot killed himself.

"Was he an airman or solider?" I asked. "Or NKVD?"

"She says the only thing worse than stealing morphine is stealing morphine and asking about the secret police," Sidorov said. "Come, we have things to do."

But not before Doctor Mametova rose from her desk to hug and kiss us. Then she shoved us out of the small room, patting us on the back like small boys who'd unexpectedly done a good deed.

We went back to Operations and returned the keys to Black's filing cabinet. At his apartment building, the lights were all out. Good news, because that meant he likely hadn't noticed the missing desk drawer key and wasn't tearing the place apart searching for it. Inside the foyer, I took the key out of my pocket and slipped it under the door, flicking it with my finger to shoot it closer to the table where he'd dumped his stuff.

In the morning, he might curse my clumsiness, but I'd be long gone by then. To some spot on the map close to the Polish border. Zolynia. Closer to a potential witness. Closer to the Germans. And with any luck, closer to Big Mike.

CHAPTER FOURTEEN

FIVE O'CLOCK CAME too damn early. I downed hot coffee and dark Russian bread after I'd washed and shaved as Max laid out my flight gear. Helmet, lined jacket, gloves, web belt with my .45 automatic and combat knife, plus a cloth sack with a couple of cheese sandwiches and an apple. It was like going camping with a nice lunch put together by a heavily tattooed mother hen.

"Okay boss, we go," Max said, grabbing my jacket and helmet. "I drive you, yes?"

"No, I will drive," Sidorov said, finishing his cup of coffee. "His flight will be dangerous enough."

"Sure, sure," Max said. "You got to watch out for Messers close to front. *Ublyudki.*"

"I would not worry, Billy," Siborov said. "I am sure General Belov arranged for an escort to fend off those German bastards flying Messerschmitt fighters."

"You don't have to worry, you'll be safe on the ground," I said as we clambered into the jeep, Max hanging on in the back and clutching my gear. As it turned out, Sidorov was an enthusiastic driver himself, and I quickly forgot about German fighters as he took a corner like a getaway driver at a bank heist.

Engines began to roar in the distance, the full-throated sound of snarling Wright Cyclone supercharged engines rising in intensity as we drew closer to the main runway. Sidorov pulled over as the first B-17 rumbled slowly down the runway, its massive wingspan lit by running lights as it passed by, prop wash blasting us with swirls of chill morning air. As a sliver of dawn cracking the eastern horizon, more Forts moved into position. The lead aircraft lifted off, wheels up. Then another, and another, engines howling as each took off, the squadron circling, gaining altitude, individual planes jockeying for position in the faint light.

The last of the Fortresses rose and joined the armada, engine noises merging into one terrible and mighty sound as the full squadron circled the airfield, beginning its journey to the Romanian oil fields, and then safely home to airbases in Italy. Most of them, anyway.

Not all of them, certainly.

We sat in the jeep for a moment, listening to the fading sound, the thundering engines disappearing in a steady drone, until finally, the air was silent. The passage of men and machines left behind a deathly quiet, leaving me in awe of the parade that had filled the air, proclaiming its wrath and fury while carrying steel and flesh into battle hundreds of miles distant.

Sidorov drove on in silence. Even Max was left without words, his eyes on the empty sky and its dawning reddish hue.

Runway Three was quiet in comparison. At the first hangar, a dull yellow light spilled out feebly onto the runway as ground crew pushed out a small biplane. The only other illumination came from General Belov's jeep, with Maiya at the wheel and the general firing up another of his American smokes.

"You're sure it was Runway Three?" I asked Max as Sidorov braked just in time to avoid Belov's jeep. Our own headlights illuminated the biplane as the crew rolled it out. An open cockpit two-seater.

"Yes, boss. Major Drozdov tell me. Runway *tri*. General is here, yes?"

"Yeah, but where's Drozdov?" I asked as I swung my legs out of the jeep and saluted in Belov's direction. He waved his Chesterfield at me and leaned in to whisper to Maiya.

"Major Drozdov was called away," Maiya said, stepping out of the jeep. "The general wishes you luck on your journey. He wanted to see you off personally. It is a great honor."

"Please thank the general, but I'd be more honored to see my aircraft. Is there any problem?" I asked.

"No. No problem," Maiya said. "This is your aircraft. Lieutenant Chechneva will fly you to your destination. Zolynia airbase, as Major Drozdov agreed."

"In that contraption? Where's the major? There's obviously been a mistake," I said, looking to Belov. He avoided my eyes. I glanced at Max, who stifled a grin.

"No, Billy," Sidorov said. "There is no mistake, I am afraid."

"Exactly," Maiya said. "No mistake. Here comes Comrade Lieutenant Chechneva. She is an excellent pilot, Captain. You need not fear."

"She? I'm being flown hundreds of miles to the front in a crop duster by a dame? You gotta be kidding," I said. The lady lieutenant saluted Belov, who had risen from the jeep to greet her.

"You should show respect, Captain Boyle," Maiya said, her voice low and angry. "The lieutenant is a member of the 46th Guards Night Bomber Regiment. Very famous in Russia. She has flown many missions."

"I did not know the Night Witches were based here," Sidorov said.

"Who?" Now I was really confused.

"The Germans called them the Night Witches," Maiya said. "They attack at night, cutting their engines and gliding in to drop their bombs at low altitude. It is very dangerous. And daring."

"I am sorry, Maiya," I said, hearing the awe in her voice. This pilot and her regiment were heroes to her, that much was clear. "I was not expecting such a—basic aircraft."

"Lieutenant Chechneva arrived here last week on a courier run," Maiya said, answering Sidorov's question and ignoring my apology. "Her aircraft needed repairs, which were completed yesterday. She must return to Zolynia today, and Major Drozdov arranged for her to take Captain Boyle. Why send another aircraft when one is already available?"

It seemed pointless to debate that logic. Maiya introduced me to Lieutenant Tatyana Chechneva, who regarded me with the same sense of healthy suspicion as I had for her. She was on the short side, with a pile of curly hair, dark, lively eyes, and a row of medals glinting on her tunic.

"Lieutenant Chechneva will tell you about the aircraft and her mission as she conducts her check," Maiya said. I got the feeling that was a suggestion from Maiya and perhaps General Belov, since Tatyana barely concealed a roll of her eyeballs. But like a good solider, she carried on as she went through the preflight routine, with Maiya translating.

The biplane was a Polikarpov Po-2, and oddly enough it had been used as a crop duster before the war. It flew low and slow, cutting its engine as Maiya had said, producing an eerie whistling sound as the wind hit the wings' bracing wires. German prisoners had reported it sounded like a broomstick waved through the air, and had given the regiment the nickname Night Witches.

Nachthexen.

Their attacks weren't meant primarily to inflict heavy material damage. The bomb load was too small for that. The idea was to use the attacks to inflict psychological damage, denying the Germans sleep and a chance to rest from the stress of combat on the Russian front. It worked particularly well when they could strike a fuel dump or ammunition supply, lighting up the sky with evidence that they could hit anywhere without warning.

Tatyana explained that while there were many pilots and ground crew who were women, the 46th Guards Night Bomber Regiment was the only all-female unit in the Red Air Force. Administrative staff, mechanics, cooks, pilots, navigators, all were women. I didn't need Maiya to translate the obvious pride evident in Tatyana's voice.

"Please tell her I am honored to fly with her," I said. "But isn't the second seat for a navigator?"

"Yes, but flying in daylight over friendly territory does not require navigation," Maiya said. "The lieutenant has flown the route before. She says you should enjoy the scenery, and she will get you to Zolynia safely."

That didn't sound so terrible, so I left Tatyana alone to finish up. I stepped back to get a good look, now that the morning light was filtering in. The tail had a large red star outlined in yellow. Same on the side of the fuselage. The entire plane was painted in green and brown camouflage. It wasn't pretty, but it did look sturdy. By the pilot's seat, a name was painted in Russian letters, along with a vine of yellow flowers. I asked Maiya what that meant.

"Raisa. Her first navigator," she said. "The fascists killed Raisa, so Tatyana named her Po-2 after her. The flowers are a common decoration with the girls. They try to remain as feminine as they can, even as they fly many sorties each night, and live in poor conditions close to the front."

"Have you met them? The Night Witches?"

"No, only Tatyana. But they are my heroes. I wish I could join them. I learned to fly before the war at my *Komsomol* flying club. I have asked for a transfer, but General Belov says he requires me here. It is a disappointment, but I must stay where I am needed," she said, with little conviction.

"You know, as the Americans and British draw closer to Germany from the west, and the Soviets from the east, there will be a need for translators in frontline units. Do you know if the 46th has any English-speaking personnel?"

"No, Captain Boyle, I do not. That is an excellent idea. Thank you. And good luck," Maiya said as a smile spread across her face and she headed for Belov.

"Be careful, Billy," Sidorov said, sidling up to me and making sure Max and Maiya were out of earshot. "They are separating us and sending you off on a long, slow trip. This plane flies at one hundred and fifty kilometers per hour, maximum. Zolynia is some nine hundred kilometers from here. You will have to land and refuel on the way, and you will reach your destination late in the day. It may take you a day to locate a translator and find Nikolin. Then there is the matter of the return trip."

"That's after I get to Kozova and search for Big Mike," I said. "Yeah, I wish I had a faster way to get there, but at least I'm going."

"I hope you return, my friend," Sidorov said, extending his hand. He wasn't much as friends go. Disgraced NKVD operative, murderer, and the kind of guy who would do anything to avoid another trip down the road of bones. But here I was, deep inside the Soviet Union, with no one else I could trust in sight. So I shook.

"I will. Watch your back," I said. "And Kaz will be surprised to see you. Not happily, I'm sure, so take it easy with him."

"We are now on the same side, do not worry," he said. "I need his help, you understand?"

I did. Solving the case was Sidorov's ticket to freedom. Not that there was a whole lot of freedom to be had under Stalin's rule, but at least he'd be free not to have his bones buried in some Siberian roadbed.

"Here, boss," Max said, handing me the sack of food and my helmet. "See you soon, yes?"

"Damn right, Max," I said, stuffing the sandwiches and apple in my pockets. "Did you know about this?"

"Sure, I know. But better not to say. You only worry, right? And you have to go, no choice. Not in Red Army, not in your army," Max said, looking serious for the first time since we met. I nodded my agreement as one of the ground crew snatched my helmet away and thrust a leather flying helmet and goggles at my chest.

"No good," Max translated, pointing at my helmet. "Too heavy. Wear this."

"Okay. What about parachutes?" I said. The ground crew guy laughed as Max translated.

"No *parashyut*," Max said. "You fly too low. No use. And too heavy." Great.

I climbed into the rear seat and pulled on the leather helmet and goggles as Tatyana fired up the engine. I still hoped they were playing a joke on the gullible Yankee imperialist, and someone would come trotting out with parachutes for us, and we'd all laugh.

Nope. Instead, they all waved, led by General Belov himself, a guy I'd never seen smile before this morning. Did the fact that I was flying in an old biplane nearly a thousand kilometers to the front lines have anything to do with that?

Tatyana said something through the interphone and waved her hand in the air. She sounded cheery, so I laughed as I buckled my straps and grasped the edge of the fuselage. She opened up the throttle and I was rewarded with the vision of caps flying, including Belov's, as she turned onto the runway and began taxiing at high speed.

The ground flew away below us. The rising sun cast long shadows across the grass runway as Tatyana pulled up the nose and gained altitude. She made a slow turn and the entire airbase displayed itself sprawled across the Ukrainian steppe. The grasslands went in every direction, a sea of sunbaked brown and green. Tatyana turned and smiled. I couldn't help doing the same. Up here, with the wind whipping my face and a clear morning sky ahead, I felt unaccountably peaceful. Happy to be alive.

We couldn't have been more than a few hundred feet high when she leveled out, following the course of a river and heading northwest. I'd seen a lot of the USSR flying in, but then I was pretty much concentrating on not getting killed. And from five miles up the world looked a whole lot different than from five hundred feet. Here, I could see the land, the dried-up riverbeds, the wreck of machinery strewn over blackened ground. A village of about half a dozen dwellings, not one of them habitable, their charred ruins a monument to the scorched earth policy practiced by both sides. This land had been liberated from the Nazis, but there wasn't much life left in it.

I began to feel less peaceful.

I tried to focus on my next steps. One thing at a time. First, find Nikolin and someone to translate. I hoped Drozdov's orders carried enough weight to make that happen. NKVD directive or not, the closer you got to the front lines, the less interested people were in going out of their way for visiting officers, especially those from another country.

If Nikolin was bivouacked at the airbase, then it shouldn't be too hard to find him, as long as I could say *Leytenant* Vanya Nikolin and be understood. It would have been a helluva lot easier to have Kaz along for the ride, but that wasn't in the cards. There wasn't room, for one thing, and Bull had been right when he mentioned Kaz's recovery. He was in good shape now, had been since the day after his surgery. But it was a long trip traveling by air via Cairo and Tehran, and even Charles Atlas could use a rest after that circuit.

So Nikolin. Then ask the local NKVD officer to try and get word on Big Mike and the rest of the crew. Assuming he was the cooperative type, I'd ask for transport to Kozova so I could begin the search for Big Mike. With a driver who knew the area, and a translator, of course.

Simple.

That was as far ahead as I could think, for this excursion, anyway. It would end with me finding Big Mike and the other guys. We'd head back to Poltava and celebrate. Kaz, Big Mike, and I would be together again, and we'd figure this case out. Find the killer, head back home.

Hey, when you have no idea what's going to happen, you might as well imagine the best.

Tatyana banked left and then evened out. Ahead of us a wide river cut through the grassland. As we drew closer, she pointed to the river.

"*Reka*," she said via the interphone. "*Reka Dnepr.*"

"*Da, da,*" I said, recognizing the words. The Dnieper River. I'd heard of it, one of the major rivers in this huge country. I'd seen it recently in the atlas we'd found in Lieutenant Ivan Kopelev's room. It flowed south, emptying into the Black Sea near Odessa.

How valuable was a used atlas on a Soviet airbase? Someone had swiped it from the jeep, and that still bothered me. Was it just petty theft, or had there been something important about that book? When I got back, I'd pay a visit to the government bookstore in Poltava where Kopelev bought the book. Kaz would enjoy a visit to a bookshop, even a Soviet-style one.

I had too many damn questions and too few answers. I needed Kaz and his brain power to work on this. I could only hope he wouldn't be too outraged at meeting Sidorov after all these months. Not only had the guy tried to railroad him, there was also the matter of the Katyn Forest Massacre. The Russians had executed thousands of Polish officers after they'd captured them in 1939, back when the Nazis and the Soviets worked together to dismember Poland. The mass graves had been discovered when the Germans took Russian territory around Katyn. The Germans made big news of it, always happy to find another government with the blood of innocents on its hands. Stalin, of course, blamed the Germans. But letters and documents found on the bodies revealed the officers had been killed during the period the Russians held them.

They were murdered by the NKVD, which would make for a poor working relationship between Kaz and Sidorov, even though he was now ex-NKVD. It was a distinction likely to matter little to Kaz, Sidorov's tenure on the road of bones notwithstanding.

But maybe Kaz's distrust would be a good thing. Sidorov might be pulling the wool over my eyes. I'd begun to trust him, although he'd done little to earn it other than being good company in a tough situation. Understanding, too. He'd been on my side when it came to my plan to search for Big Mike. Had he really been upset when he found out he wasn't slated to make this trip? Maybe not. Maybe he'd engineered things, so I'd be away while he worked at what he'd tried to accomplish back in London. Pinning an innocent man for a murder.

We crossed the river, flying close to a pontoon bridge loaded down with trucks and troops. Tatyana waggled her wings and I could see men waving at us. Did they know she was a Night Witch? If they did, none of them seemed to have a problem with lady pilots in combat.

It shouldn't have sounded so strange to me, either. After all, Diana Seaton was with the SOE, and the kind of combat they engaged in, behind enemy lines, was just as dangerous as flying low and slow with no parachute.

I tried to focus on the case, wondering what Kopelev and Morris had stumbled into to get themselves killed. But thoughts of Diana kept creeping into my mind, distracting me from any notions of means, motive, and opportunity. All I could envision was Diana, recovering at Seaton Manor, safe and well-cared for. I prayed that she'd have the sense to stay put for once and not volunteer for another assignment as soon as she could walk ten paces unaided.

The good Lord might listen to my prayers, but Diana was less likely to.

It was an hour later when Tatyana banked slightly and leveled off in a slow descent. Dead ahead was a clear patch of green and a row of small buildings. As we approached the grass runway, I spotted the burned-out hulk of a fighter plane and several blackened bomb craters that hadn't yet been filled in. I guess we were getting close to the front.

I saw camouflage netting and a few aircraft hidden underneath. As we touched down and bounced on the soft earth, ground crew came running out to meet us. Tatyana taxied, bringing the Po-2 closer to the buildings. She cut the engine and we both pulled off our googles and helmets and climbed down.

Most of the men were ground crew. Unarmed mechanics, who stopped in their tracks as they took in my uniform. Shouts rose up from their ranks and two soldiers burst from the building behind them, rifles aimed straight at my chest. An officer followed, pushing the soldiers aside as he held his pistol on me. They looked confused and scared, shouting something I couldn't understand while they kept their quivering fingers on their triggers.

I stuck my hands up in the air, which seemed the only sensible thing to do.

"*Amerikanskiy,*" Tatyana yelled, stepping in front of me and gesturing for the men to lower their weapons. "*Ne fashist. Amerikanskiy!*"

"American," I repeated. "Stalin. FDR. Churchill." They lowered their guns, so I lowered my hands.

"*Tovarishch,*" Tatyana said, stepping aside as if presenting me as a newly minted comrade.

"Stalin!" I said again, figuring that was the one word no Russian would argue with.

"*Dokumenty,*" the officer said, his pistol lowered but unholstered. He didn't seem impressed with my love for Uncle Joe or my uniform. He held out his free hand, and I reached inside my jacket for the travel orders. The pistol came back up.

"Documents," I said, slowly. He seemed to grasp the concept and let me take out the paperwork without a shot being fired. It's nice to meet new allies.

He beckoned us to follow him into the nearest building. The two soldiers stayed a pace behind us just in case we got lost. The structure wasn't more than a wood hut with a rough plank floor. A map covered one wall, and a portrait of Stalin hung on the opposite wall. A couple of tables, one with a radio, completed the décor. Through the window I could see men rolling drums of aviation fuel toward Tatyana's aircraft. This must be the planned refueling spot. As soon as they gassed us up and Joe Stalin Junior satisfied his curiosity about my orders, we'd be on our way.

Tatyana forked over her orders, and the lieutenant sat to read them. There wasn't another chair at his makeshift desk, and he seemed fine with leaving us standing. He and Tatyana had the same rank. I could tell by the two stars on their shoulder boards and the light blue piping that they were both Red Air Force lieutenants. I'd noticed at Poltava that captains had four stars.

"*Leytenant*," I said, in a sharp voice that was my best imitation of Sam Harding. That got his attention. "*Kapitan*." I pointed to the silver bars on my collar. Then I leaned forward and tapped the two small stars on his shoulder board and held up four fingers.

"*Kapitan* Boyle," Tatyana said, barely suppressing a grin. She shot off a few sentences in Russian and I picked up Belov's name tossed about. That brought about a sudden change in attitude, and the Russian louie stood up and barked out orders. Tatyana mimed drinking something to let me know what was happening.

The lieutenant offered me the chair, which I declined and offered to Tatyana. She shook her head, refusing as any junior officer should do. So, I took a load off, figuring that was the gentlemanly thing to do in this situation. Right now, she was another junior officer, not my date to the prom. The lieutenant snapped his fingers and one of the soldiers brought in a stool for their visiting Night Witch.

Tatyana's orders were returned to her. The lieutenant read mine carefully, probably looking for evidence that I was a fascist spy or at least some hiccup that would allow him to put me behind bars. Not that this airstrip had anything as fancy as a decent slammer. I doubt it had much of a latrine for that matter.

He finally finished reading and returned my papers, seemingly mollified. Or fearful of offending anyone traveling under NKVD protection. Mugs of hot steaming tea were brought in, and I shared my sandwiches with Tatyana. As we ate, the radio operator was busy writing out a transmission. There was a scurry of activity, and it seemed like the lieutenant was asking the radioman to check again. As he waited, he consulted the map and called Tatyana over. Their fingers traced routes on the map, which was nothing but a jumble of Cyrillic letters to me.

The radioman brought them a report. From their looks I could tell it confirmed whatever had come in earlier. The lieutenant spat out orders and one of his men ran outside.

"What's happening?" I said, before I remembered they couldn't understand me. Not my words, anyway.

"Jedlicze," Tatyana said. "*Ne* Zolynia." She pointed to a spot on the map. Zolynia. She shook her head. Then pointed south, to a small town. Jedlicze.

"Why?" I asked, shrugging my shoulders and raising my eyebrows in a questioning look.

"*Fashisty*," she said, making a thrust with her hand, sweeping in from the west. "*Ataka*."

"The Germans are attacking, so we're going to Jedlicze instead," I said, half to myself. From what I could make out, Jedlicze was about sixty miles south of Zolynia. If Nikolin kept himself alive and they held their ground, we could be there tomorrow. It meant a delay, but it was better than flying directly into a Kraut attack.

Tatyana went outside to check on her aircraft and I followed. Ground crew were pulling two handcarts, each with three bombs. Tatyana spoke with them as they wheeled the carts toward her aircraft, and then I understood. We weren't avoiding the battle.

We were going straight into it.

CHAPTER FIFTEEN

I DIDN'T LIKE this one damn bit. Being ferried like a tourist in the bright sunlight was one thing. Being taken along on a solo night bombing mission in a biplane with six tiny bombs was another thing. Another crazy thing.

What was even crazier was not understanding what everyone was talking about. I watched as Tatyana and the lieutenant—I'd found out his name was Chernov—compared her map with the larger wall map, charting out the course to Jedlicze. They kept pointing to a river east of town, and from what I could figure, there was a German fuel dump near a bridge. Tatyana kept making sounds like the woosh of a giant exploding fireball while jabbing her finger where a road crossed the river, right at the center of a U-shaped bend in the waterway.

I assumed the explosion was intended for the fuel dump, not our little airplane.

Earlier, she'd pointed at me, and I got the impression she was asking Chernov if she could leave me behind. He wasn't having it. I figured there was slim to no chance he'd saddle himself with a Yank traveling under NKVD orders. They had a bit of an argument about that, but Tatyana seemed to resign herself to taking me along.

I worried about what the person who normally sat in my seat was supposed to do, namely navigate. After gesturing at the maps and Tatyana, she pointed to her eyes, then the map. She'd get us there.

But that didn't stop her from giving me an assignment. Which was when I decided I wasn't really cut out to be a Night Witch.

The job involved flares. She showed me one as the ground crew loaded a dozen into the navigator's compartment. Through hand gestures and some engine-noise sound effects, she let me know that the flares had to be tossed out when she cut her motor. Once a cord was pulled, it released a small parachute and lit the fuse. The flares would float down and illuminate the area, helping her to pinpoint the target.

"Stalin," she said, and mimed pulling the cord and throwing the flare. "Stalin." She did the same. I got it. Every time she yelled Uncle Joe's name, I dropped a flare over the side.

It was absolutely insane.

Once we straightened that out, I pointed to the map and held up one finger.

"Jedlicze," I said, then held up two fingers. "Zolynia. Then we go to Zolynia. *Da?*"

"*Nyet*," she said, holding up three fingers. With two fingers she pointed to an empty spot on the map, east of Jedlicze, about halfway to Zolynia. We had a different stop after the attack, if we lived that long. I gave a shrug and pointed to the location, nothing but clear green on the map. What's there?

"*Nochnye Vedmy*," she said, patting her chest, then the map. "*Nachthexen.*"

"Okay," I said, nodding. We'd be joining the rest of the Night Witches at an airfield that wasn't on the map, in the dead of night. If I did manage to find Big Mike, he'd never believe the route I took to get to him.

When I found him. It was beginning to get tough to stay optimistic.

As soon as the sun hit the western horizon it was time for takeoff. Chernov had orders prepared for Tatyana. Maybe it was the way they did things, or maybe he was covering his ass since he was diverting an NKVD transport. She signed two copies and gave one back to him. It looked like a lot of Cyrillic hen scratches to me, but other than that, it seemed like any army paperwork designed to protect officers and keep file clerks busy. Tatyana grinned as she stuffed the orders into her pocket. I got the feeling she agreed.

We got an enthusiastic wave off, even from Chernov. As we left the grass airstrip behind, I caught the glow of the setting sun going down behind the German lines. I was still kicking myself for thinking about *if* I found Big Mike, not *when*. That bad choice of words stayed with me for a while, until it was totally dark, and I had more to worry about than jinxing us with poor phrasing.

Splashes of soft light slid beneath the wings as we passed villages and isolated houses hidden in the forested hills. This was a big country, and maybe some of those folks managed to get through the war without armies rolling up to their doorstep. From a few hundred feet up though, it looked damned empty, like a lot of poor souls hadn't been so lucky.

The sky was mostly cloudy, but the half moon rising gave off enough light to shimmer on a river ahead. Tatyana bore north to follow it. She turned to get my attention and shot out a hand in the direction of the river. That would take us to the target.

She stayed low, which was probably the best protection against being spotted. Time and space seemed to stand still, the darkness blurring the distinction between land and air; the river below shining in the intermittent moonlight; and the sound of the puttering, chugging engine enveloping us in a falsely reassuring cocoon of noise.

Then the real world intruded. Artillery fire lit up the skyline ahead. Whose it was—impossible to tell. Tracer rounds swept the sky and explosions *crumped* dully in the distance, leaving trees, grasses, and God knows what else burning.

Tatyana yelled, her arm signaling downwards. The clouds parted, and the moon lit up the large bend in the river ahead. I could make out a thin line across it; a bridge bisecting the bend just like on the map.

This was it. She lifted up the nose of the little Po-2, gaining altitude, and cut the engine.

Silence.

A frightening silence, as we floated and fell through the air in a fabric and wood coffin. The aircraft dropped, then steadied as Tatyana brought it around in a wide arc, riding the winds as they played on the struts and wires like thrumming guitar strings.

The heavenly music of the Night Witches.

"Stalin! Stalin!" Tatyana shouted, and I fumbled with the first flare, pulling the cord and getting it clear of the plane before it ignited. Then the second, which went more easily. I looked back, saw the small parachutes floating slowly, the incandescent red glow casting itself over the landscape.

"Stalin!"

Another flare. Tatyana banked left as shots rang out from below, random spurts of gunfire searching the sky.

Then I saw it. Camouflage netting, unmistakable in the harsh light, casting shadows from the tall poles used to prop it up. I tapped Tatyana on the shoulder and pointed as the first flare hit the ground and sputtered out. She didn't respond but brought the aircraft around in a tighter circle, lining herself up with the netting as the last flare floated right over it.

The crack of rifles and the chatter of submachine guns picked up, quickly joined by a heavy machine gun, a real antiaircraft weapon that sprayed incendiary tracer rounds in wide arcs, searching for the gliding biplane.

Tatyana yelled something that could have been the Russian version of *bombs away*, and the biplane lifted in the air, relieved of its ordnance. Tracer rounds passed close by, flashes of light just yards to our right.

Red-hot rounds ripped through the lower wing, cutting through the fabric.

Explosions rippled behind us, a series of detonations that sounded small and puny compared to the volume of fire coming up against us. Tatyana started the engine and I looked back as another machine gun sent bursts in our direction.

Our small explosions turned huge, a massive fireball bursting high into the night sky, silencing the machine guns. Flying cans of fuel burned like rockets, cascading flame and certain death over the Germans below.

The gunfire stopped. The sky glowed with carnage as the Po-2 puttered along, Tatyana shaking her fist in fury, repeating the same words I'd heard her say earlier. It wasn't bombs away. It was Raisa, the name of her dead friend, her first navigator.

Raisa, Raisa.

She was a true Night Witch, cursing the fascists, shouting out revenge as her blood enemies burned below.

CHAPTER SIXTEEN

I DIDN'T KNOW where the front line was, exactly, but from the flashes of artillery and small arms fire, we were damn close. Tatyana banked the aircraft, moving away from the clashes below. She flicked on a flashlight and held up a compass, probably to comfort me. It was a nice gesture, but the long ribbon of darkness we flew over was unnerving.

Nothingness. No cozy village lights, no flash of machine guns, no water reflecting moonlight. The cloud cover thickened, making it difficult to discern the horizon. It was like being at sea in a thick fog where your disoriented senses play tricks on you.

As bad as this was, at least it wasn't cold. How did they manage in these open cockpits during the Russian winter?

A throaty, purring sound arose, carried on the wind, coming from somewhere to our rear. Tatyana banked again, then returned to her course, waggling her wings as she did. I craned my neck, trying to see in the inky darkness. Squinting, I managed to catch sight of something. Another biplane, a Po-2 by the engine, sounding like a sewing machine going full tilt.

Then another, and another. A whole flight of Night Witches, six aircraft rendezvousing with Tatyana and overtaking us as she throttled back, letting them pass. Perfect; six navigators to guide us home.

After twenty more minutes, I spotted two fires on the ground, and I could make out the lead aircraft reducing speed and descending. The flames reminded me of landing zones the Resistance laid out for

Lysander aircraft in the deserted French countryside, each fire marking one end of the runway, such as it was.

By the time we bumped to a landing on the grassy field, the other Po-2s were lined up next to the trees that marked the boundary of the wooded hill and the open meadow, and the fires were extinguished. This wasn't an actual airbase. There were no buildings, not even a hut, only four large trucks filled with containers of fuel. Tatyana taxied closer, cutting her engine as the ground crew stood ready to push the biplane into position.

We climbed out of our seats, and I felt the stiffness in my bones after sitting for so long, but I was thankful for the feel of earth beneath my boots. Tatyana stretched as well, shouting out to the others and pointing at me. This time, there were no guns leveled, just a press of flyers and ground crew, all women, inspecting me and my uniform, while Tatyana explained about the *Amerikanskiy* she'd brought them. There was a lot of excited chatter, cut off only when one of the pilots was helped out of her aircraft, her forehead bleeding and one arm held close to her chest. Two of the ground crew ran to her and began unpacking a medical kit. The pilot looked dazed, but not too badly injured.

Suddenly the throng parted for an officer, slightly older than the other women who all seemed to be my age or younger. I couldn't make out the rank insignia on her shoulder boards, but I figured the smart thing to do would be to come to attention.

"Captain Billy Boyle," I said, my salute as crisp as the crease on Colonel Harding's trousers.

"*Mayor* Amosova," she said, returning my salute. That sounded close enough to major for me to quickly hand over my travel orders when she snapped her fingers. She produced a flashlight and read through them, glancing up at me and to Tatyana who kept up a running commentary. When she repeated "Stalin, Stalin," even the major laughed. Major Amosova gave my orders back and snapped out some of her own to her crews.

I don't know what I expected to happen next. My best guess involved sleep. But the Night Witches had other plans. Jerrycans of aviation fuel were unloaded from the trucks and the Po-2s were topped off. Bombs were dragged on wooden sleds to each plane and affixed to the undercarriages. They were going out again.

Well, there was no place to sleep anyway.

Tatyana pointed to the navigator who now didn't have a pilot, telling me she didn't need me along for the ride. I surprised myself by feeling a bit disappointed. She patted me on the arm and went to speak with the wounded pilot, her head swathed in bandages, who was being led to one of the trucks. Tatyana and the other flyers climbed into their cockpits, resting while the crew readied the aircraft.

Feeling like a third wheel, I decided to pitch in and help haul the bombs from the trucks. At first all I got was a salute, but I waved it off and told the kid—she looked about eighteen—I wanted to make myself useful. Maybe she got the tone, because she shrugged, told me her name was Kira, and stood aside as a bomb was rolled to us across the truck bed. We grabbed it and set it down on the sled as gently as possible. One-hundred pounders, I figured. Two was all the sled could hold, and we hauled it back and forth while armorers attached them to racks under the wings.

With bombs loaded and fuel tanks full, we pushed the biplanes into the field. Engines fired up and the small group of us staying behind waved as each Po-2 flew off into the night. Kira went to check on the wounded pilot, and I helped load empty fuel drums onto the trucks. The fumes clung to my clothes, filthy from the hard labor in the field.

"*Kapitan*," Kira said, offering me a canteen. I nodded my thanks and took a gulp. It was warm and metallic, but it went down my parched throat like a cold beer. I went to take another drink and noticed four of the girls sitting on the grass next to the truck with the pilot, passing around a single canteen.

"*Spasibo*," I said, thanking her as I handed it back. Evidently there wasn't a lot of fresh water to be had. With *Mayor* Amosova in the air with her unit, I was the senior officer. I didn't have any clout or responsibility, but one of the things my dad had drummed into my head was that an officer doesn't eat, drink, or rest until his men do. He'd had an officer in the First World War who hadn't abided by that, and it always irked him.

Colonel Harding felt the same way, and I'd seen him live by his words. So even though this was a different part of the world and a different army, not to mention a unit of women instead of men, I did my best to follow their advice.

I still had that apple in my pocket, a little bruised and worse for wear, but so was I. I cut pieces and offered them to the wounded pilot, who smiled bravely and took one. Kira took the rest and passed the pieces around, followed by a small loaf of black bread and the water. I took a small piece, and suddenly thought of holy communion, a strange remembrance here in godless Russia.

I smiled, looking up into the night sky, feeling a part of something greater than me, greater even than my search for Big Mike or a murderer. It was a fight for what was right. I'd been in France and saw what the Nazis did there. From what I could make of Russia, and how Russians felt about the Nazi invaders, it was even worse here. Much worse.

Kira and the others began to sing softly, a low, lonely, mournful song. I didn't understand the words, but they were beautiful, and as they sang, I sat on the grass, closing the circle of bodies gathered by their wounded comrade.

"*Kapitan*," Kira said, as one of the others shook my shoulder. They were all up, heads craned toward the western sky, listening. Someone had draped a blanket over me, and I threw it aside as I joined them, trying to pick up the sound of engines. It was still night, but a thin line of dawning red lit the eastern horizon. I heard the distant, light drone of engines, and everyone burst into action.

Two women ran off to light the signal fires, and in minutes the fuel-soaked wood was burning brightly. Two others grabbed medical kits, while Kira and I scanned the sky, the sound growing louder.

"Look!" I said, spotting a pinprick of light in the sky. Kira pointed at three Po-2s circling the field. If they weren't landing, the pinprick of light following them was bad news.

Fire.

Everyone moved into action. Trucks were started and driven deeper into the cover of the woods. Jerrycans were swiftly carried into the trees as well, minimizing the chance of a crash landing turning into a conflagration. I stayed out of the way as Kira and the others did their jobs, working with practiced efficiency.

I stared, open-mouthed, as the aircraft drew closer, flames lapping the undercarriage, right beneath the pilot. The plane wobbled as it slowed to landing speed, and I wondered about the flares. Were they still on board, or had the navigator tossed them out? If she were dead or unconscious, and the flames reached the flares, it would be all over, real quick.

The biplane hit the ground hard, bounced, and the pilot cut the engine as she steered away from the area where the fuel had been. I ran, sprinting to the plane as flames licked up the side, sending the pilot scrambling out of the cockpit and onto the wing.

The navigator hadn't moved.

The biplane collapsed, one landing gear giving way, the pilot barely hanging on as she tried to pull the navigator out, working to release her harness. Fire reached up the side of the aircraft as if hunting the pilot, punishing her for trying to free her comrade from the grasping flames. I jumped up on the wing next to her and vaulted onto the fuselage, pulling the navigator straight up and sliding her down the side, where the pilot had been joined by Kira.

Smoke swirled up from beneath the navigator's position, then flame broke through.

There were half a dozen flares mounted next to her seat.

"Stalin!" I shouted, jumped down and scrambled across the grass as Kira and the pilot dragged the navigator to safety.

A *woomph* blasted my back as the fuel tank exploded, sending a plume of flame skyward. I fell and rolled away, shielding my eyes as the flares ignited, creating a hot white glow that consumed the cockpit and the rest of the wood and fabric construction.

I scurried over to where Kira was kneeling over the navigator, opening her leather jacket, as two other girls pulled bandages from their medical kits. But by the clear light of the burning wreckage, it was all too plain to see. She was dead. Shells had hit her in the side and gone straight through. Blood oozed from her wounds where the tightly belted leather coat had acted as a compress. It soaked the earth beneath her ruined body as red as the flames which consumed her aircraft.

Tatyana landed shortly after that, with *Mayor* Amosova the last to touch down. As the navigator's body was wrapped in a shroud, the officers had a huddle. Kira joined them, pointing to me at one point and talking about the *Kapitan*.

Amosova nodded. Kira came over, stood at attention, and saluted. I returned it, giving it my best. She darted off, helping the others carry jerrycans to fuel the aircraft. No bombs this time.

The *Mayor* came over and removed a decoration from her tunic. She pulled my coat open and pinned it above my pocket. It was a five-pointed star, red, with a hammer and sickle at the center. She stepped back to admire it, smiled, and stuck out her hand. We shook, and she quickly left to check on the wounded pilot.

Tatyana patted her chest, then mine. We both had the same medal. She tapped it and said something that must have been its name. She turned and pointed at the wrecked Po-2, its metal struts now glowing red-hot.

"This medal is for that?" I said, mirroring her gestures. Seemed like it was. We gazed at the fire, unable to look away.

"Zolynia," she said, after a moment of silence.

After more gestures and pointing again at the burning aircraft, I got the message that we had to move out, since the flames could be seen for miles. Everyone else was going back to their regular airbase, forty kilometers east. But not me. Tatyana had been given the job of taking me to Zolynia.

Then, I'd be on my own.

The Po-2s took off, one by one. The trucks rumbled away on a dirt track through the woods. Tatyana lifted off last, turning north as the others vectored to the east. The flames, dying away at last, still lit the meadow like Scollay Square on a Saturday night.

Tatyana turned and pointed to her eyes and to the sky above. I gave her a thumbs up, message received. Focus on the sky. The Messers might be out hunting, drawn by the bonfire light like deadly moths.

CHAPTER SEVENTEEN

IT WAS LIGHT as we neared Zolynia airfield. Coming in low over a camouflaged hangar, I spotted Yak-9 fighters, twin-engine bombers, and a scattering of transport aircraft. An antiaircraft gun tracked us as Tatyana brought the Po-2 in for a smooth landing on the tarmac. Not surprising, since she was making an unannounced visit. One of the many features the simple biplane lacked was a radio.

Simple, but it got the job done.

A jeep rolled out to meet us, and I could see the officer in the rear seat eyeing me. He vaulted out as soon as the jeep braked to a halt, his hand resting on his holster. Tatyana saluted, giving her name and unleashing a few fast sentences. The officer returned the salute, and she nodded in my direction, probably relating the story of my circuitous route here.

"*Kapitan* Boyle," she said. "*Kapitan* Kolesnikov."

A fellow captain. Good, that cut down on a lot of saluting. I gave him my orders, but he seemed more interested in my medal. He pointed to it and spoke to Tatyana, suspicion weighing heavy on his words. She answered him, and he responded by shaking my hand, then gesturing to the jeep.

"You?" I asked Tatyana, doing the same. She shook her head. No, she was going back to the Night Witches. She smiled, kissed my cheek, and stepped back, offering her own salute.

"Good luck," I said as I snapped one back. She seemed to understand.

I got in the jeep with Kolesnikov and watched over my shoulder as we drove away. The little Po-2 roared into life and carried Tatyana off, disappearing over the treetops as I waved, even though she could not see.

The blue piping and wings on his shoulder boards marked Kolesnikov as an air force officer. He seemed friendly enough, keeping his gun hand away from his holster now that Tatyana had vouched for me. He was tall, dark-haired, and thin, sitting erect in the seat next to me, smelling of cigarette smoke and gasoline, the standard-issue fumes of any airbase.

He led the way inside a two-story building that had to be the operations center, since everyone looked busy or at least working at looking busy. The main room was a wide-open space, centered around a radio operator and three clerks pushing paper. Kolesnikov escorted me to a room down a hallway. It held a table and two chairs. The words *interrogation room* flitted through my mind, but he kept the door open after he called out to an enlisted man.

As we sat, he offered me a cigarette, which I waved off. It was one of those Russian brands with the tobacco inside a cardboard tube. He compressed the hollow end, stuck it in his mouth, and lit up. It smelled like burnt cabbage. Kolesnikov unfolded the orders I'd been given and settled in for a good read, puffing away and filling the small room with a god-awful stench. If he was a chain smoker, I wouldn't last long.

A few minutes later a private came in with a mug of tea along with a slab of black bread slathered in butter. I sipped as Kolesnikov read the orders line by line. He pointed to one line and asked me a question, and all I could do was shrug.

"Sorry, *Kapitan*, I can't read a line of it."

He stood to leave, motioning me to remain. The private who'd brought in the food was waiting in the hallway, and Kolesnikov had a conversation with him, bringing the soldier into the room and sounding pleasant about it. I got the impression he was more of a guide than a guard and tested that by asking for the *vannaya* after Kolesnikov left. I was escorted to the back of the building and allowed to use the bathroom. I washed up as best I could, wishing I had a change of clothes. It seemed days ago that I'd left Poltava.

I drank the tea as I ate, hoping it would wake my exhausted mind. Questioning a potential witness is demanding work. It pays to appear confident and informed, even when you're not close to either. The most effective interrogation is disguised as a conversation, my dad always told me. Nobody likes being peppered with questions, but they do like talking about themselves and the things they care about, or the wrongs done to them. Everybody has a life story, Dad said. Get them to tell you theirs, and the truth will be easier to tease out of them.

That was solid advice, but how would it work here, via a translator? I hoped I'd find out. For all I knew, Kolesnikov had gone to fetch Lieutenant Nikolin and would be bringing him back here for questioning. I'd gotten good at pantomiming words and making myself understood, but this wasn't a game of charades. I needed someone who knew how to say *murder* in Russian.

Kolesnikov returned with a soldier in tow. A soldier who could have served in the last war, or maybe even in the czar's army. Solidly built, the aged private had a thick gray mustache and straw-like hair peppered black and white. He walked with a limp, favoring his right leg. Heavy bags pulled down his eyes, putting red-rimmed lids and a suspicious gaze on full display.

Kolesnikov gestured for him to sit, speaking gently to him.

"American?" the private asked me.

"Yes. You speak English?"

"It has been," he said, huffing up a heavy sigh, "a long time."

"Are you all right?" I asked, as he looked at the open door behind him.

"Yes," he finally said. "I am not punished? Being punished, I mean."

"No. The *kapitan* brought you here to help me. I'm Captain Billy Boyle, and I need a translator. Can you do that for me?"

"Certainly," he said, straightening his shoulders. A bit of life came into his eyes as he seemed to realize nothing terrible was about to happen. He was no stranger to bad things, that was for sure. "Fedor Popov, at your service, Captain."

I glanced at Kolesnikov, who smiled, pleased with Popov's responsiveness.

"Your English is good, Private," I said.

"I am out of practice," he said, speaking slowly and deliberately. "But the words feel familiar in my mouth."

"Please thank *Kapitan* Kolesnikov for me," I said. "Tell him I appreciate his help, and I hope you can remain with me while I am here."

Popov spoke with the captain, then turned to me.

"Lieutenant Tatyana Chechneva told Captain Kolesnikov of your journey here, and how you helped rescue her comrade from the burning airplane. He is grateful and gives you his personal thanks. His wife is a pilot with the 586th Fighter Aviation Regiment. She flies the Yak-9 fighter, as he does." Popov seemed a bit bored with communicating this personal information and gave a quick eye roll to show his displeasure.

"That explains his interest in helping me," I said, nodding my understanding to Kolesnikov. "Now tell me about yourself. Where did you learn such good English?" What I really wanted to know was what kind of duress he was under. I needed to depend on this guy, and he looked a bit flaky.

"At university in Moscow," Popov said. "Years ago. I graduated and taught history. Then I said something wrong. I was denounced. I lost my position, spent five years in Siberia. Internal exile, not the camps, thank God. Thank goodness, rather. There is no God, only Stalin."

"Then you joined the army?"

"Of course. Russia needs all her sons, even those who lack understanding of the glories of Marxism," Popov said, his eyes darting around the room. Looking for hidden microphones was my guess. He understood plenty.

Another private entered, handing Kolesnikov a folder. He read it and spoke to Popov.

"The *kapitan* wishes you to know that the man you are seeking, Vanya Nikolin, is not at this base," Popov told me. "His unit passed through here on the way to the front yesterday."

"I was told he would be here by an NKVD officer. Lieutenant Nikolin is also NKVD and was given permission to transfer from Poltava airbase to a frontline unit."

"Given permission?" Popov laughed, then he and Kolesnikov had a back-and-forth. "You are amusing, Captain Boyle. No one seeks permission to be in that unit."

"Which unit?" I asked, not getting what was so funny.

"The 18th Detached Penal Company," he said. "I barely survived it myself." He rubbed his eyes as if vanquishing a memory.

"I don't understand," I said, looking to Kolesnikov, hoping I was just too tired to grasp what was being said. "Where's Lieutenant Nikolin?"

"There is no Lieutenant Nikolin, do you not understand?" Popov said, his voice trembling as he slammed his fist on the table. "He is nothing. A private. A *shtrafniki*."

It took a while to piece things together. What I got out of Popov was that he, too, had been sentenced to three months in a punishment company. Known as *shtrafbat* units, they were for soldiers who had retreated or disobeyed any one of Stalin's many orders. Popov had been in a unit that was surrounded. The order came to stand and fight to the last man, since Stalin had issued a decree about not taking one step backwards.

Popov, deciding it was foolish to die for a piece of ground the Germans would take anyway, took a whole bunch of steps back, and snuck out of the encirclement. He made it back to the Russian lines. Instead of being congratulated for rejoining the fight, he was sent to the 18th Detached Penal and became a *shtrafniki*. Most men didn't survive. Popov was wounded close to the end of his term, which saved him. He was declared rehabilitated by his own blood, discharged from the *shtrafbat*, and sent to the hospital at this air-base. Due to his age, he was assigned here as a medical orderly after he recovered.

"I see there's been a misunderstanding," I said. "I didn't know that Nikolin was sent to a punishment detachment. Two people were murdered while he was on guard duty, so I guess someone decided he deserved to take the fall."

"The fall?" Popov asked.

"The blame," I said. "Tell me, do the *shtrafbat* units get the most dangerous assignments? I need to get to Nikolin before the next attack."

Popov spoke to Kolesnikov, a bitter laugh escaping his lips. The lieutenant shook his head sadly, gesturing for Popov to go on.

"Captain Boyle, you do not understand. You see before you a ghost, a man who should be dead. Yet here I am, alive against all odds. The main function of the 18th Detached Penal Company is the clearing of mines."

"That must be very dangerous," I said. "Mine-clearing can be treacherous."

"Treacherous? Yes, it is very treacherous to clear a mine field by walking through it. That is all the *shtrafniki* are good for, to clear mines by blowing themselves up. Do you know what saved me and put me in this hospital, Captain? Not German bullets, not even a German mine. No, it was the bone from my friend's leg. He stepped on a mine and it blew his leg into my hip. They were picking out bone fragments for days."

Popov buried his face in his hands. Kolesnikov called for vodka. Popov needed it. I needed it.

"Tramplers, they call us," Popov said, rubbing his hand across his face. "Each day in the minefields was a horror, knowing that each step could be your last. Some men died quickly. Others bled to death, their limbs torn apart. More than a few went mad. Perhaps I have gone mad too. It is sometimes hard to tell."

The vodka arrived, thank God. Or Stalin.

CHAPTER EIGHTEEN

IT WAS A subdued round of drinking, especially for Russians. Kolesnikov capped the bottle after pouring a last glass for Popov.

"Please ask the *kapitan* if Nikolin can be recalled and brought here for questioning," I said.

No. The penal detachment was an NKVD unit, and they would not let one of their men be recalled for any purpose, especially not by an air force officer.

"Ask if I can travel to the penal company, and if the NKVD commander would allow me to talk to Nikolin."

"No, it would not be allowed," Popov said, without translating. "No. never."

"Don't worry, Fedor, you won't have to be a trampler again," I said, sensing what he was afraid of. "Fedor, that's Russian for Theodore, isn't it?"

"Yes," he said, refusing to look me in the eye.

"Okay, Teddy, now please ask *Kapitan* Kolesnikov. He seems like a decent man, right? He'll protect you."

"Yes, he is a good man," Popov admitted, and talked with Kolesnikov. It went on for a while.

"Yes, it could be arranged," Popov said. "But Nikolin may or may not be alive. The company commander may or may not allow you to speak with him, even with the orders you carry. The unit at the front. It will be dangerous. Very dangerous."

"What does he mean? I have orders signed by an NKVD major.

Ask him. Major of State Security Pavel Drozdov, assigned to the Soviet airbase at Poltava."

As Popov spoke, Kolesnikov shook his head, checking the orders once again, line by line.

"No Drozdov, no NKVD," Popov reported. "The orders are all signed by General Ilia Belov, Red Air Force. See?"

Kolesnikov showed me the signature lines. The handwritten scribbles were impossible to decipher, and the Cyrillic typewritten symbols didn't tell me a damn thing.

But while they didn't tell me anything, they did suggest a hell of a lot.

First, I didn't have any NKVD clout to back me up. Sure, orders from any Soviet general carried weight, but there was nothing like the long arm of the secret police to put the fear of God—or Stalin, in this case—into any officer who stood in my way. Now that I thought back on my conversation with Drozdov, I was pretty sure he never actually said he'd signed the orders. He did give me the impression he was responsible for them, but maybe he'd had them drafted for Belov's signature.

Or maybe not. Because the second thing this suggested was that Belov was the one behind everything that had happened. My cop's suspicious mind thought back to him at the Poltava airfield seeing me off. Was he there because he was a fan of the Night Witches? Or did he want to be sure his plan to get rid of me went off without a hitch?

"Teddy, is there anything in those orders about looking for American flyers? Crewmen who bailed out of their aircraft over Soviet territory?"

"What Americans?" Teddy asked. "Here, in the Soviet Union?"

"Yes, there are three airbases, the largest in Poltava. I flew here on a B-17 bombing run from England, and saw a friend's plane shot down, near Kozova. I'm hoping your people have found them," I said.

"I have never heard of Americans in Russia, but I will ask," Teddy said. He and Kolesnikov huddled, going over the paperwork. Kolesnikov tapped his finger on one page triumphantly. "Here. All security forces are directed to report and detain any foreign nationals within our rear areas. A list is to be compiled and sent to General Belov."

"That sounds like an arrest warrant," I said.

"The *kapitan* says this is normal procedure," Teddy explained. "Except for a list to be sent to General Belov. He offered to find out if any Americans have been reported in our area. But Kozova is some two hundred and fifty kilometers to the east. He doubts they would move in our direction, toward the front. But he will check."

"Yes, please do that," I said, nodding my head to Kolesnikov. "But ask him what would happen to any foreigners found nearby and brought to this airbase. Would they be kept here or passed on to another headquarters?"

The two men had a quick conversation and Kolesnikov left to investigate reports of downed flyers. Teddy watched him leave, then rose to shut the door.

"I did not ask the good *Kapitan* your question," Teddy said. "I did not wish to embarrass him in front of an American, since he is a decent man, as you pointed out."

"About foreigners?"

"Yes. Because the truth is, foreigners in our rear areas are not tolerated. Last week two Poles were found hiding in the woods nearby. Half dead. They had escaped from a German camp during a retreat. Since the Germans left them only half dead, our men finished the job," he said, making a pistol with his fingers.

"Why?"

"Ha! You do not understand Russia then, or Comrade Stalin, for that matter. Everything foreign is a threat, you see? Better to eliminate the threat. Or deny it exists. You tell me there are three bases in the Soviet Union with American aircraft, helping us to fight the fascists. Very well, I believe you. But no one will hear of it, since Mother Russia needs no help."

"Would they kill Americans?"

"Stalin murders his own people. What do you think a few American lives mean to him? But he would not do it if it put at risk all the materials you send us. I read English, so I see the markings on the trucks, jeeps, and crates of supplies brought to the front. They stencil over them with Russian, and few can read the English words anyway. But I can. I know which trucks are Studebakers and which tanks Shermans. The average *frontoviki*, he believes all these machines come to us from our factories beyond the Ural Mountains."

"*Frontoviki?*" I asked, as my mind scrambled to figure out what all this paranoia meant for Big Mike's chances at survival.

"The front line troops. The men who do the fighting and dying, the average solider," Teddy said.

"I see. Tell me, Teddy, do you think Nikolin is still alive?"

"Perhaps. I have not heard of a large attack, so they may be holding them back. But who can say? Tell me, what is so important about this poor soul?"

"Two men were murdered, one Russian and one American," I said. "I'm investigating the killings and need to find out if he saw anything. He's a witness, a very important one."

"Oh, Capitan Boyle, are all Americans like you? You fly here in your B-17, dropping bombs on the Germans while the Hitlerites kill millions and Stalin washes the blood of his own people from his hands. And you seek a witness to two deaths? Oh, we are all witnesses here, witnesses to many deaths. Thousands. Tens of thousands. Two? Most amusing," Teddy said, as he buried his head in his hands once again.

"Yeah, we're real amateurs at this killing business," I said, wondering how dependable Teddy would be if I got to take him along on a visit to his *shtrafniki* buddies. He had a good point but making it had nearly shattered him.

While Teddy collected himself, I went back to Belov.

With all the other aircraft at his disposal, what was really behind his dispatching me in the Po-2 biplane? And who made the change in orders to Tatyana? How many people even knew which airfield she'd land at to refuel? It would be a simple matter for a Red Air Force general to set the wheels in motion for her to be sent from there on a mission all alone. What were the odds of survival? Who would even question the regrettable loss of a Night Witch and her American passenger?

There was also the question of Nikolin. He'd gone from soft duty at an airbase in the rear area to suicidal duty with a short life expectancy, clearing minefields the hard way. Pretty easy way to eliminate inconvenient witnesses. I had no idea if it took a court martial to get sent to a penal company, or if any senior officer could make that happen with the stroke of a pen. Given what I'd seen and heard, it was my guess a denunciation by a general would do the trick.

Had Drozdov spoken up for Nikolin? After all he was a fellow NKVD officer. Or was it better all-around to place the blame, and the punishment, on the most junior officer. The shit slid in the same direction here as it did everywhere else. Downhill.

Right now, Nikolin was the key to understanding all this. What had he seen? What did he know? And when the hell could I be done with him and get on to Kozova and start looking for Big Mike?

I leaned back in my chair, trying to think through all the possibilities. Maybe Belov was the guy cleaning up loose ends by setting up suicide missions for both Nikolin and me, but who actually pulled the trigger on Kopelev and Morris? Why those two victims? What did a straitlaced NKVD lieutenant and a stand-up Army Air Force sergeant have in common, and what did they stumble into that meant a death sentence?

The next thing I knew, Teddy was shaking my shoulder.

"Wake up, Captain Boyle," he said. "It seems as if you've earned me a return to the front. The good news is, we don't have to travel far. That is also the bad news."

"Sorry," I said, looking at my watch. I'd been out for an hour. "I mean, I am sorry you have to go back. But just to translate for me, right?"

"Yes," Teddy said as Kolesnikov came in, paper clutched in his hand. More orders. "The *kapitan* has prepared orders and travel documents. I will drive you to the *shtrafbat* and translate. On the way we must take six men. That way Kapitan Kolesnikov cannot be criticized for wasting fuel while aiding a foreigner."

"I'm an ally, Teddy, but I get it. Are the six men going to the penal company?"

"No, they were wounded and have been discharged from the hospital. Regular *frontoviki*. Otherwise I could not do it. Who could deliver men to such hell?"

Kolesnikov explained the orders via Teddy. The men were to be delivered to a regimental headquarters about forty kilometers west of here in the small village of Bratkowice. The 18th Detached Penal Company was bivouacked not far from there. Teddy and I were both named in the orders, traveling on official business per the orders of General Ilia Belov, commander of the Poltava airbase. True enough. No need to mention he probably wanted me dead.

The document requested that the commander of the penal detachment make Vanya Nikolin available for questioning. Kolesnikov apologized, saying a request is all he could realistically manage, having no authority to order the NKVD to do anything.

I told him I understood, and that I liked the last part of what he'd written. Private Fedor Popov was ordered to return with the truck and me no later than 2100 hours tonight. That meant anyone who wanted to detain us might be held liable for preventing Popov from executing his orders. It might not impress the NKVD, but it could tip the scales in our favor with suspicious sentries at a roadblock.

Teddy explained that he'd also written I'd been presented with the Order of the Patriotic War, which was the red star medal *Mayor* Amosova had given me. While she had presented it to me, I doubted it was official. Still, it was nice to have a cover story in case the wearing of Red Army medals by foreigners was a shooting offense.

I complimented Kolesnikov on his use of military language, and he grinned, lighting up another cardboard cigarette. I asked how he could manage to smoke those things, and the answer came via Teddy.

"Life is short, you might as well get the most out of everything. Including Belomorkanals," Teddy said, pointing to the name on the package. "The strongest cigarette in Russia. The world, perhaps."

Life is short. The *shtrafniki* were sure to agree.

CHAPTER NINETEEN

KOLESNIKOV TOLD POPOV to take me to the mess hall while he organized the truck and six men. Long wooden tables ran the length of the room, with a portrait of Stalin at one end and a red hammer and sickle banner at the other. Patriotic posters of workers and farmers graced the walls, all of them looking heroic and well-fed. We each had a plate of potatoes, fried Spam, and carrots. My American uniform attracted a lot of attention, and Teddy spent most of his time explaining who I was. At one point, a round of backslapping and applause broke out.

"I told them you Americans brought us Spam," Teddy said. "Some did not believe me, but others knew it to be true. You see, many of the cans are relabeled with Russian words. But enough come through with American labels that *frontoviki* learn the truth. So, they are glad. At the beginning of the war, I did not have meat for two years. Then the first meat I had was Spam."

I was about to make a wisecrack about Spam not really being meat, but I thought better of it. It wasn't a joke to Popov and his *frontoviki* pals. It was sustenance, precious nourishment sent all the way from America. I cut a big piece, ate it, and grinned.

I washed up, shaved, and tried to make myself as presentable as possible. I combed my hair and put on my fore and aft cap, trying to look chipper and wide awake. The bags under my eyes told another story.

A US Dodge three-quarter ton open-topped truck with a big red star on the door panel was waiting outside the mess hall. Six men, who looked like they believed they'd just eaten their last meal, were climbing into the back. Teddy kept up a line of chatter as he tossed them a pack of cigarettes and hoisted himself into the driver's seat, wincing as he swung his gimpy leg into the cab.

"I can drive if your leg bothers you," I said as I climbed in.

"No, Captain. If I am a passenger, then they might keep me at the front," he said. "No, I have a job to do. Drive this truck there and back again."

"And translate for me," I said.

"Of course. Then drive right back here," Teddy replied as he shifted into first and the truck lurched toward the gate. "Unlike these poor souls. The rumors say a new offensive is coming. It must be true, since they let these boys go. Some still are bandaged under their uniforms. But they can walk and carry a rifle, which is their bad fortune."

We drove a few miles, the softly rolling landscape of untended fields and overgrown grasses giving way to forested hills, blasted in places by artillery, some of the shattered trees fresher than others. The Germans came through here in 1941 and got chased back out not too long ago. It was the more recent blackened craters I worried about. Were we within shelling distance, or had this road been bombed?

As if thought gave birth to reality, the snarl of aircraft rose from the horizon. This wasn't the soft sputtering of the Po-2, this was the aggressive sound of high-performance engines, fighter aircraft coming in low and fast.

Teddy pulled off the dirt road, sheltering under the canopy of leaves between two oak trees. The planes roared overhead, their prop blast sucking branches upward as they passed. I could spot the bombs mounted under their wings along with the black iron cross markings.

"Messers," Teddy growled as the *frontoviki* huddled in the back, heads down.

"At least a dozen," I said. "Low level attack on the airbase, probably."

"I hope someone radioed the base," Teddy said, backing the truck out onto the road. "They had to fly right over the front lines moments ago, the *ublyduki*. Bastards."

"Keep your speed down," I said. "We don't want to kick up a lot of dust. Dust means death, we said in Normandy."

"It means the same here," Teddy said. "But then, most things mean death here."

Teddy drove slowly, proving that even fatalists understand common sense. The rutted lane curved and spilled out into a downhill slope, leaving the forest behind. Below, a burned-out tank sat off the road, its red star barely noticeable under the scorched exterior. Wrecked trucks had been pushed off the road, which curved around another hill and brought us to the cover of fir trees. Open ground was dangerous ground.

"Messers!" one of the guys in back shouted, pointing skyward as the sound of droning engines could be heard. The Messerschmitts were returning from their treetop raid, much higher on their journey home. Low altitude was fine for a fast and stealthy attack, but now that Russian fighters had been scrambled, they needed the advantage of height in case they got jumped.

"Easy," I said, as Teddy craned his neck to look at the planes, his knuckles tightening on the steering wheel. I knew he wanted to floor it. Hell, I wanted him to, but I knew they'd be sure to spot the plume of dust, even at that height. Slow and easy, we had a chance.

"Easy is hard," Teddy muttered, his eyes now fixed upon the cover of the trees ahead. He managed not to speed up, even as the excited chatter from the back of the truck urged him to hurry.

We were almost there.

A lone fighter flew in from the east, just over the tree line behind us. He was trailing smoke, maybe too damaged to gain altitude. But not too damaged to point his nose at us and squeeze off a burst that chewed up the road. Rounds lashed the side of the truck as Teddy punched the accelerator and the Dodge spit gravel, swerving into the field, then back onto the track and into the woods.

When he stopped to inspect the damage, the men in back were huddled together, close to the cab. Five of them. The sixth man sat in his position at the end of the truck, one hand clutching the wooden slate on the side, the other gripping his rifle.

His head was gone. His body was drenched in blood, but otherwise intact. It looked to me like he'd been hit with a 20mm cannon shell, an explosive round that could make short work of a human skull.

His pals weren't taking it well, especially the one with blood and gray matter splattered all over him. Teddy got out and spoke to them, his tone soothing but firm. He held up his hand to stop them as they began to climb over the side. I didn't blame them a bit, but Teddy had other ideas. He got them to lay the body out in the back, covering it with a rain poncho and laying the rifle on top.

"We could have left him here," I said. "Those boys are pretty shook up."

"No," he said, shaking his head for emphasis. "I am to deliver six men. No matter that one is dead. If I show up with only five, I will become the sixth. No."

His logic was solid, for an illogical world.

We came to a checkpoint at an intersection. The sentry called over his lieutenant and pointed to my fore and aft cap with the silver captain's bars. Teddy handed over our orders and the officer returned a nice salute, more interested in a live American than the headless corpse in the back. He gave Teddy directions and me a big grin. Maybe he thought the second front had come to him.

We drove through rows of camouflage netting draped over supplies and vehicles. I spotted a couple of antiaircraft positions and a field kitchen on wheels serving up food. Blackened craters dotted the fields, splintered trees scattered like toothpicks. The distant *crump* of artillery and the faint *rat-tat-tat* of sporadic machine-gun fire told me we were almost to the front lines. Of course, to the men here, this was the front, where a sudden barrage could destroy your entire world. But to the *frontoviki* in the forward positions, this was the comfy rear area, where you could walk upright without fear of a sniper's bullet.

Teddy took a right, following a narrow dirt track along a stream, pulling over at what was left of a farmhouse. The low-lying land was wet, and the men's boots squelched mud as they reluctantly dragged their dead comrade along with them.

Teddy gave his paperwork to a sergeant. Six soldiers delivered, as ordered.

"Now we go to the *shtrafbat*," Teddy said. "And I hope we leave as easily."

The penal company was even closer to the front line.

Artillery shells whistled overhead, cratering in the field behind us. More crashed into the woods on our left as we drove over a small stream, rough pine logs serving as a bridge.

"Fritz is firing blind, hoping to spot our artillery when we return fire," Teddy said. "An old trick. There, look." He pointed to tents set up in a clearing. Men sat in the field, about a hundred of them, eating from their mess kits.

"At least they're fed," I said.

"Of course," Teddy answered as he parked the truck. "They must be strong enough to walk, after all."

"What are the civilians doing here?" I said as we got out. I'd noticed about a third of the men weren't in uniform.

"They are from the recently liberated villages," he said. "If they have been under German occupation for the last three years, they are obviously traitors. Otherwise they would have committed suicide or fought the invaders to the death."

"You have got to be kidding," I said, stopping to look at the gaunt faces staring at me.

"Comrade Stalin does not kid. Nothing he says is to be laughed at, I promise you. These men are lucky. Usually they would be sent to labor camps in Siberia, where they would die a slow, miserable death. Now they will die more quickly, or if by chance they live through three months of this, they are rehabilitated, and may go home."

If that was Russian luck, I'd take the luck of the Irish any day.

One man spoke to Teddy, a look of surprise on his face. Apparently, they knew each other, and I could guess the guy's question. *What the hell are you doing here?*

A couple of officers strode out of the tent, quickly followed by two soldiers toting submachine guns. Teddy stood to attention, saluting smartly as if to demonstrate he was once again a regular soldier, not a

mere *shtrafniki*. I stood by his side, saluting when I made out the rank
of major on one of the officers' shoulder boards.

He didn't bother returning the salute. Instead, he snapped his fingers and barked an order, and in no time, I had two Russian submachine
guns pointed at my belly. Teddy let loose with a volley of Russian,
gesturing to me and handing over his orders. I was glad he had them.
If I'd reached into my pocket one of those things might have gone off.

As Teddy and the major spoke, I spotted one man get up and walk
slowly toward us. He shuffled, slack-jawed and confused, focused
on me.

On my uniform. He recognized an American, and the closest
Americans were at the Poltava airbase. That had to be our man.

"*Kapitan* Boyle," Teddy said, pulling on my sleeve. "You may talk
with Nikolin, the major says."

"Is that him?" The guy had stopped ten feet away, his eyes warily
watching the officers. And the guns. He had blond hair, a long chin,
and blue eyes. He was maybe twenty-five, tops, and shaky, like someone
who'd had his legs knocked out from under him. The ground under
his feet wasn't about to get any firmer, especially not after he found
out I wasn't here to spring him.

"Yes, the major says that is Vanya Nikolin. We can use this tent,
come."

Teddy motioned for Nikolin to come, and when he hesitated,
one of the soldiers got him moving with the butt of his weapon.
Once the three of us were inside the tent, the soldier tied back the
front flaps and stood guard, his eyes following our every move.
There were a couple of cots in the rear, boxes and rucksacks piled
along either side. Teddy pulled three wooden crates out of the stack
and gestured for Nikolin to sit. He looked at both of us, hollow-
eyed and frightened. Teddy spoke to him, calmly and patiently.
Nikolin's eyes fluttered, as if he was having a hard time taking in
what he was being told.

"I told him who you are, and that you've come from Poltava to ask
him some questions," Teddy said. "I stressed that it was not within
your power to get him released. Best to get that out of the way."

"Good," I said. Nikolin's gaunt face looked about to crumble. Outside, another submachine-gun-toting soldier, a non-com, whispered to our guard, then left. Nikolin's eyes widened, following the man as he moved among the *shtrafniki*, waving his arms. "Ask him if he knows about the murders in the warehouse. Lieutenant Kopelev and Sergeant Morris."

"No, he does not," Teddy said, after their back and forth. "He is shocked to hear that Sergeant Morris is dead. He was a decent man, very kind." I could see the pained look on Nikolin's face. Surprise and sadness, mixed with confusion.

"You don't seem upset about Lieutenant Kopelev," I said, speaking directly to Nikolin and letting Teddy work the translation.

"I am sad to hear of any death, but Kopelev was a difficult man to like," Teddy said, picking up on how I was working the conversation. I needed to hear Nikolin's own words, to the extent I could. "He loved rules and regulations as much as he loved Mother Russia, but more than the people in it."

"But Sergeant Morris was different?" I asked.

"Yes. Jack was friendly. He liked Russians and was curious about our country. He could speak a little Russian and wanted to learn more. What happened? Were they killed in an attack?" Teddy raised his eyebrows as he finished translating. Outside, the men began to mill about, their non-coms moving them into line.

"You mean you don't know what happened?" He didn't. "Before you were sent here, you'd been on guard duty at the warehouse. What happened that night?"

"I was ordered to report to General Belov. That little fellow Max came running up and said the general wanted to see me immediately. He had a note with Belov's signature. I didn't wish to leave my post, but I had little choice. I had two men with me and thought that would be a sufficient guard. I went to the Operations building and then to the general's office."

Artillery thundered from beyond the next hill. It was outgoing, the measured volley of a dozen or so cannon. Nikolin flinched, then rubbed his temples.

"What time was this, Vanya?" I asked, leaning forward and trying to look him in the eye. Another volley of cannon fire sounded, and Nikolin took a deep breath.

"An hour or so after midnight. There was no one in his office, although a few people were on night duty. Then Major Drozdov walked in. He demanded to know why I had left my post. I told him about Max and the written order but that only made him angrier. I tried to show him the note, but he threw it back at me, called me a counterrevolutionary, and said my shoulder boards were obviously too heavy a burden for me. He ripped them off." Nikolin fingered the torn threads of his shirt, his eyes all the while on the *shtrafniki* moving slowly into formation. His breathing quickened. I could smell his fear and despair.

Shouts came from the soldiers gathering the *shtrafniki*, the curses of those who drive others to their deaths. Angry, demanding, in a hurry to get it over with.

"What happened then?" I asked. I could see the major watching us. I got the sense we didn't have a lot of time. Now Nikolin was frozen. I told Teddy to ask again.

"What?" Nikolin said, unable to focus as the officer drew closer. Then he rallied, as if he knew this might be his last chance to tell his story. "Yes, Drozdov had me disarmed and put under guard. Within the hour I was in a truck headed here. I have no idea of what crime I committed. I had orders to leave the warehouse, orders from a general! I don't understand what is happening. What have I done wrong? I am a Party member!" Nikolin's voice broke, and he struggled to regain control.

"Lieutenant Kopelev and Sergeant Morris were killed," I said, leaning in to grab him by the arm and shake it. "Murdered in the warehouse, in the upstairs NKVD section where the OSS supplies are kept. They were shot in the back of the head on the night you received that note. Do you still have it?"

"No. They took everything," Nikolin said, staring in horror at the major standing not ten feet away.

"Him? This major?" I asked.

Yes, it had been the major. He took everyone's personal effects upon arrival. I asked Teddy if he had had anything returned when he was released.

"No, but I had nothing to begin with," he said. Machine guns opened fire, maybe a hundred yards ahead. An assault was brewing.

Nikolin asked if I knew who killed the two men, and why, as his eyes flitted between the guard, Teddy, and me. There was a desperation in his voice, a plea for a delay, any small thing to postpone what he knew was coming.

"That's what I'm trying to find out. Is there anything you remember, anything unusual you saw that night, or even before that? Anything out of the ordinary?"

"I saw General Belov arguing with Major Drozdov earlier that evening. At one point the general pushed him."

"A general throwing his weight around is not so unusual," I said.

"No. But the major pushed him back. A hard push. And the general did nothing. He looked afraid."

The major whispered to the guard, who gestured with the barrel of his weapon. It was time. Nikolin spoke to Teddy, grasping him by the arms, begging, pleading, tears glistening on his cheeks. Once an NKVD man, now he was nothing. A *shtrafniki*, good for only detonating a mine and clearing a path for the true Soviet *frontoviki*.

CHAPTER TWENTY

GUARDS ON THEIR flanks and at their backs, the *shtrafniki* marched into the woods to the tune of Stalin's organ. That's what the Germans called the Russian Katyusha artillery, rocket launchers mounted on trucks. The array looked like a pipe organ, and the screeching sound they made sounded like a song from the devil's own hymnal. I watched the rockets blazing across the sky, heading for the German lines, just as Nikolin was.

The major wasn't going with his men. He stood outside his tent, smoking and watching the rockets along with Teddy and me. He came over and spoke to Teddy in a friendly tone, as if the brutal departure of tramplers had all been a charade.

"He remembers me," Teddy said. "He told me he was glad to see me alive."

"Really?" I asked, giving the major a quick but respectful nod.

"Perhaps. But what he really wants to know is why you spoke with Nikolin. I think he is worried it may affect him in some way, since Nikolin was NKVD," Teddy said.

"Tell him the young man was simply a witness. Another NKVD officer and an American were murdered, and he may have seen something," I said. As Teddy translated, I could see the major relax. It wasn't something political that would come back and bite him. He wouldn't be denounced as a counterrevolutionary, at least not for having Nikolin under his command.

"He says he hopes Nikolin survives his sentence," Teddy explained.

Apparently, the major had a soft spot for the former NKVD man, as opposed to the other deserters and criminal scum who filled his ranks.

"Does he recall the paper he confiscated from Nikolin? The order from Belov?" I asked.

"He does," Teddy said, and we followed the major as he beckoned us into his tent. He rummaged through a worn and bulging briefcase, pulling out a file which I assumed was about Nikolin. He withdrew a crumpled piece of paper, a half sheet with a couple of sentences typed in Cyrillic letters. At the bottom was a scrawl.

"The name is Belov," Teddy said, after consulting with his former commander. "And it does say report to the Operations center immediately." The major nodded and spoke to Teddy.

"He wants to know if this will help Nikolin," he said.

"Hell, it can't hurt him," I said. "I can take this back to Poltava and see if I can get Drozdov to change his mind."

The major handed me the order as he spoke to Teddy.

"He knows Drozdov. An ambitious man. He warns you to be careful," Teddy said.

We didn't hang around long. Teddy didn't want to reminisce, and I wanted to get the hell out before the Germans returned the favor and started their own artillery barrage. I stuffed the order in my pocket and held on as Teddy drove as fast as he could without kicking up a cloud of dust. Somewhere, on a ridgeline not too far away, some Fritz was watching with binoculars for just that.

The boom and slam of artillery melded with the rapid fire of machine guns until the sound of battle washed over us in a single incoherent melody. Maybe a quarter mile away, no more than that, men were advancing against the German positions. Nikolin and his fellow tramplers might be in the middle of a large minefield, or perhaps it was just a grassy meadow, untouched by war until today.

"Who do you think killed those two men?" Teddy asked me, perhaps to take his mind off the memories of what he'd gone through with the penal company.

"My guess is either General Belov or Major Drozdov pulled the strings," I said, holding onto my seat as Teddy skirted a muddy patch and drove up on the wet grass. "But I have no idea who pulled the trigger or why."

"To steal something?"

The whistling sound of incoming artillery shrieked in fast, explosions shattering the woods to our right. Teddy floored it, all worries of dust vanishing as debris cascaded over us. We got back on the road and barreled by rear area positions with *frontoviki* diving for the trenches.

The road veered through the woods again, giving us some cover. We hit a checkpoint and our papers withstood a thorough inspection. Teddy breathed a heavy sigh of relief after we cleared that final hurdle.

"You still worried about being sent back?" I asked.

"Less with every kilometer I put between me and those *ublyudki*," he said. "Now, who stood to gain from the murders?"

"There were a lot of valuables in the storehouse," I said. "Weapons, drugs, gold. But nothing was stolen."

"Weapons are not hard to come by," he said. "And who can use gold in the Soviet Union? A few extra rubles are nice, but what is there to buy with gold? Nothing. In a state with no private property, what use is gold? It would mark you as a capitalist or in their employ. Not a good thing, my friend."

"There was morphine. I did manage to steal a carton of morphine, but only as a test, to see if the warehouse could be broken into," I said. "I gave it to the base hospital, where they needed it. I don't want you to think I'm a *vor v zakone*."

"A *vor* would have slit my throat by now and stolen my boots and the truck," Teddy said with a laugh. "That was a good thing you did, giving the morphia to the hospital. We could use some as well."

"Your hospital is running low?"

"It is very bad. There is only a small amount for the very worst cases. I had no idea there was a shortage. But why was a supply locked away in the warehouse at Poltava?"

"It wasn't a lot, and it was destined for some joint NKVD and OSS mission to Bulgaria," I said, watching Teddy's quizzical expression. "The OSS is our NKVD, only a lot nicer."

"That would not be difficult," Teddy said, as we drove past the burned-out tank where the Messers had attacked us this morning. "Do you think they were killed where they were for a reason?"

"It was a secure area. Quiet, no one around to ask questions," I said.

"That describes much of the Motherland," Teddy said, down-shifting to climb the hill as he scanned the sky for airborne threats. "But I mean near the drugs, when there is such a shortage."

I hadn't thought of that angle.

I should have.

The warehouse was chosen to send a message. Teddy was on to something. They could have been killed anywhere. But their bodies had been left next to the only supply of morphine in the area. It wasn't much, but it was a new way to look at this case, at least.

"That could mean something, Teddy," I said. "Did you hear anything about a shortage of morphine anywhere else?"

"No, but I did not think to ask. I will talk to the head of the hospital when we return. He is not a bad officer and has been asking the high command for more drugs," Teddy said. "Vodka only goes so far."

As we both searched the sky, I wondered about the five live soldiers we'd delivered, and how many of them would survive their first fight.

"Do you have any idea where the morphine comes from?" I asked. "Has the war interrupted the poppy harvest?"

"All I know is that the poppy is a crop grown in the Kirghiz Soviet Socialist Republic," Teddy said. "It is a region far to the east of the Caspian Sea, on the border with China. The war has not reached that far, I am certain."

"What did you say you taught at college?" I asked.

"History. Well, Soviet history. It is sometimes complicated," Teddy said. "It can change, and change is dangerous if you are not aware of it."

"You know, you'd make a good policeman," I said, as we drew closer to the gate at the airbase. "You've got an interesting way of looking at things. You'd make a good investigator."

"No, not an investigator. In the Soviet system, there is only one way to look at things," Teddy said, shaking his head as he laughed. "That is, the way the Party looks at things, which changes like the seasons. Men are sent to labor camps simply because they have not kept up with the latest ideological fashions and favors. No, I am quite happy as an orderly. Hospital bedpans never change."

The Messerschmitts had scored some hits, based on the smoldering wreckage of two aircraft and a collapsed hangar. Men were already at work filling in bomb craters as Teddy entered the Operations center to report on his successful mission. Six replacements delivered to the front, as ordered, the fact that one arrived minus his skull not worth a mention. No reason to create tedious paperwork.

We found *Kapitan* Kolesnikov in the mess hall, goggles and leather flying helmet on the table, his hands wrapped around a mug of steaming tea. Lines from his goggles still showed beneath his eyes and across his forehead. He ran one hand through his thick blond hair and leaned back in his chair, speaking in a strained voice, emotion stuck in his throat.

"His wingman was shot down, behind the German lines," Teddy told me. "He shot down two Messers, but it was a bad trade."

"I'm sorry," I said, sliding into a seat across from Kolesnikov. He nodded grimly. No translation needed.

"He has good news for you," Teddy said, after another exchange. "A group of Americans are at a Military Medical Directorate hospital in Kozova. Some are slightly injured, but it seems the local NKVD security troops do not know what to do with them, so they are kept under guard at the hospital. There are twelve, maybe fifteen, according to what he hears. Perhaps your friend is among them."

"That's great news," I said, tempering the excitement in my voice. It didn't feel right to rejoice while Kolesnikov was mourning his own friend. "I need to find a way to get there. Is there a convoy going east, or a train?" Kolesnikov and Teddy whispered for a while, glancing around the room for any obvious snoops.

"You must get there faster than that," Teddy said, whispering even though no one could understand. "We know the ways of the NKVD. The Americans are kept under guard in a hospital so they can be released and speak well of their treatment by their Soviet allies. Also so that if they are declared a threat as foreigners, they can be easily eliminated."

"How do I get there?" I said. "Fast."

"There is a medical transport flight leaving shortly," Teddy said. "I am to go along to assist, and there is room for you. We have four patients who are being transferred to the Directorate hospital. I will attempt to get you on the transport to the hospital from the airfield, but that is all I can do. The *kapitan* orders me to return immediately with the aircraft."

"That's fine, Teddy. I appreciate the help. Are you sure you won't get into trouble?"

"Not if I come back here. The Military Medical Directorate is a very correct facility. Very political, many high-ranking officers. I prefer being close to the front. But not too close, mind you. *Kapitan* Kolesnikov also offers to radio your base at Poltava, in case you wish assistance from the Americans or Russians there."

"No, I think I will decline his offer," I said, nodding to Kolesnikov. "They may think I'm already dead. It may be easier to let them think so a while longer."

Kolesnikov and Teddy had a laugh over that one.

"Now you are thinking like a Russian!" Teddy said. "There is an old saying. 'Close to the Tsar, close to death.'"

It made perfect sense, God help me.

CHAPTER TWENTY-ONE

I WAS EXHAUSTED. As they loaded patients into the Lend-Lease C-47 transport, I found a spot in the back and curled up on a couple of scratchy wool blankets. The plane took off, and even though the twin engines droned loudly, and the fuselage vibrated in the high winds, I fell into a deep sleep. I dreamed of home, my mother's kitchen, then somehow Big Mike was there, but then he was gone, and I was alone.

Sort of like now, I thought, as the plane touched down, rolling to a halt on the side of the runway where two ambulances and a truck were waiting. I felt more tired than when I'd closed my eyes, but I roused myself as medics clambered aboard.

"Show them all your orders," Teddy said as the last patient was carried off in a stretcher. "Everything. It will impress them, or perhaps frighten them. Even better."

We approached an officer standing by the truck, overseeing the men loading the ambulances. Teddy saluted and launched into a long speech, gesturing for me to show my orders. I gave the guy everything, even Kolesnikov's statement about my medal. He actually read through everything, handed them back, and spoke to Teddy. They exchanged a few more words and Teddy ended with another salute as the guy clambered into his truck. Officers love salutes, and you couldn't go wrong piling it on in any army.

"You are to go with the Comrade Doctor. I told him you were a very important American who has come to take charge of your countrymen and deliver them to Poltava," Teddy said. "He seems agreeable."

"Thanks, Teddy. I wish I could repay you," I said, shaking his hand.

"Please repay me by saying something harsh and insulting. I don't want anyone to see me consorting with a Westerner. It could be dangerous for my health," Teddy said. "But before you do, I will tell you I asked if he could spare any morphia for our hospital. He said no, his own supplies are low."

I did as Teddy asked. I gave him my gruffest voice, telling him to get back to his bedpans and to stay safe, in a tone that announced to all who could hear what a jerk this capitalist American was and how lucky Fedor Popov was to be rid of him.

The ride to the Military Medical Directorate—which sounded much more sinister than Military Hospital or some version of the same—was uneventful. The Comrade Doctor was quiet, stealing an occasional glance at his very important American passenger. The streets of Kozova were subdued, nothing but military traffic on the roads and civilians on the sidewalks, skirting piles of bricks and timber still clogging the roadways. But there was a sense of normalcy this far from the front. People went about their business calmly, their clothes threadbare but neat and presentable. After battles flowing over their city and years of Nazi occupation, this had to be heaven. Soviet heaven, anyway.

The hospital was a large three-story building, miraculously intact. The small convoy went around the back and through an archway, where more medical staff waited to unload their new patients. My comrade doctor driver signaled me to follow him. He issued a few sharp orders to his men, turned on his heel, and took me inside.

The place smelled like carbolic soap and all the other hospital odors you'd associate with bodily fluids and bad food. Wards were filled with patients, the badly wounded who required treatment at a major rear area facility. There were a lot of them, walls of flaking paint looming over rows of beds where men lay, bandaged in every conceivable manner.

At the end of a corridor, two guards stood in front of double doors. Their rifles had long bayonets fixed, and they looked ready to add to the patient population at any moment. They came to attention, opened the doors, and a rush of excited babble burst out from the room as we entered.

It was English. American English.

"When are we gettin' outta here?"

"You can't keep us cooped up in here, you got no right!"

"Ain't we supposed to be allies, dammit?"

A crowd of Yanks stood facing three Russians. One wore the distinctive blue cap of the NKVD. Another had the same medical insignia as my escort, and the third was an air force officer and the most unfortunate of the lot. He was speaking English, and everyone's fury was directed at him. Including the other two Russians, who scowled in his direction as he tried to calm the Yanks down.

"Please, we are awaiting instructions from Moscow," he said, his hands up as if in surrender.

"I've got your instructions right here," I said, in my most authoritative voice.

"Jesus, Billy, is that you?" It was Big Mike's voice, booming up from behind the scrum of airmen.

"Big Mike!" I yelled, pushing through the Russians with no thought of military courtesies. Or common sense. "I've been looking everywhere for you."

"I'm right here," he said, and as the crowd stood aside, I found him stretched out on a bed, one leg up on a pillow.

"You okay?" I said, taking his outstretched hand and pumping it like a politician at a county fair.

"Yeah, I'm fine," he said. "Twisted my ankle when I landed, that's all. What's happening? You springing us?"

Other guys chimed in with the same question. I counted ten of them standing and four others in beds. I recognized a couple of guys from the *Sweet Lorraine*, the B-17 Big Mike flew in on.

"I understand you have orders, *Kapitan* Boyle?" The Russian air force officer said. "I would be pleased if you could take these men off our hands. Without authorization, I cannot release them."

"Here," I said, handing over a wad of crumpled paperwork. "Do you know General Belov? He ordered me personally to find these men and escort them to Poltava for repatriation."

"I know who the general is," he said, flipping through the orders and glancing at my medal. "This instructs the NKVD to assist you. Very helpful."

"You'll let them go?" I asked, moderating my tone. He wasn't giving me a hard time and I didn't want to antagonize him. I wanted to be the solution to his problem.

"Please understand, this is a delicate matter," he said, pulling me away from the others and speaking in low tones. "The Military Medical Directorate needs these beds. None of your injured men require the level of treatment given here. As a fellow flyer, I wish to help them rejoin the fight against the fascists. But the security troops are always worried about Westerners traveling within our rear areas. And we have received no guidance from Moscow. None."

"I understand, sir. You are in a difficult position. Are my orders good enough to get them out of here? That would help everybody, it seems."

"Perhaps. I will speak with my comrades," he said, and they went off into a huddle.

I waited by Big Mike's bed as the Russians talked things over. The American aircrew were a problem waiting to be solved, and the way things went in the USSR, it might be solved either with violence or vodka. It looked to me like the NKVD guy wasn't too happy, which meant the other two officers were pitching a solution that kept us upright and the guards' bayonets sparkling clean.

"What's been happening?" Big Mike asked. "And how did you know where to find us?"

"It's a long story," I said. "I've been away from Poltava for the last couple of days, looking for a witness, which was mainly a way to get out and look for you. Kaz should have gotten in yesterday, so pretty soon we'll be together again."

"You hope," Big Mike said. "These Russkies are paranoid about foreigners. They took us prisoner at gunpoint, like we were saboteurs. Hell, you could see the smoke where *Sweet Lorraine* went down from where we landed."

"We saw five 'chutes. I didn't know if you were one of them," I said.

"Yeah. They had me manning a waist gun after one of the guys was hit. Otherwise I wouldn't have made it out. One of the guys broke his neck when he landed, so there's four of us left."

"I didn't know if you were one of them," I said again, kneeling by the side of his bed. "One of the five who got out." There was a catch in my voice which I hoped no one heard.

"I'm sorry, Billy," he whispered, laying a hand on my shoulder. "That had to be tough to watch."

"It was, for everybody in that squadron. Those guys all knew someone on the *Sweet Lorraine*."

"I don't know how they do it," Big Mike said. "Thirty missions? I'd rather walk home than get into one of those things again. And I'm fine, really, other than going stir-crazy in this joint."

"Maybe they'll send us back via Tehran, the way Kaz came in," I said, eyeing the Russian confab. Voices were raised, and the NKVD fellow was doing a lot of pointing at the other two. Which meant it was two against one. Good news, unless the third was threatening to shoot the other two.

"I knew you'd find us," Big Mike said, giving my arm a shake to get my attention. "I knew it."

"You're hard to miss," I said, giving his beefy arm a punch. I stood before I hugged the poor guy and embarrassed him in front of his flyboy pals. The three surviving crewmen from the *Sweet Lorraine* came by to shake my hand and kibitz with Big Mike as we waited. The resentment they'd displayed toward Big Mike back in England had disappeared, replaced by the camaraderie of survival.

As the talk swirled around me, I felt dizzy and tired. Unaccountably weary, like an old man. I sat on a cot and watched Big Mike laugh and carry on with the other guys. The Russians continued to talk, their argumentative tones easing, the tenor more appropriate to an agreement fraught with difficulty, but not impossibility.

I looked back to Big Mike. He'd gotten up, using a crutch to stagger around, and moved closer to the knot of Russians, the flyers sensing, hoping, for good news. I should have felt relief, but grief and loss

weighed me down. I'd almost lost Diana recently, and now she was
safe. Same with Kaz. And now, here was Big Mike, alive and well,
when I'd feared him dead.

It was too much. Too much good luck. Which meant bad luck was
just around the corner. I should have been happy, but it wasn't in the
cards. Instead, I rose and put on a false smile, burying the thought of
Big Mike, or any of the others I loved, dead and gone.

"*Kapitan*, we have a plan," the air force officer said as he
approached me, the two other Russians in tow. He took a deep
breath and began by counting off on his fingers. "One, the Military
Medical Directorate requires this ward to treat those badly wounded
in the fight against the fascist invaders and demands the immediate
removal of foreigners. Two, the Soviet Air Force agrees to provide
immediate transport to Poltava so that these men may return to
the fight against the Hitlerites. Three, the People's Commissariat
for Internal Affairs will provide security as we remove this group
and transport them directly to the airfield, in complete secrecy.
Truck flaps will be tied down, and no one may look outside as we
drive. This is for their own safety, of course." He gave a nod to the
other two men, telling them he'd delivered the message they'd
agreed upon.

"Of course, thank you very much," I said. "Everyone gets something,
no one can be blamed."

"Yes. The hospital gets its beds, General Belov gets these men, the
security people keep foreigners under cover, and the fascists are
bombed. Very good all-around. We leave immediately, *Kapitan*."

No one argued with the man. We gathered up the walking wounded,
and I counted off fourteen men under the watchful eye of the NKVD
guards. We were warned not to speak to anyone and to obey all orders.
Anyone not complying would be labeled a provocateur and kept for
questioning, which quickly quieted down the crowd.

We marched through the corridors and out the rear door, Big Mike
limping along with his crutch. Two trucks and two jeeps were idling,
with more NKVD guards to oversee the transfer. I went into one
truck with Big Mike and the wounded men, while the rest got into

the other. The truck flaps were tied down and we sat in darkness as the convoy lurched forward, guards following us in the jeeps.

"Think this is on the up and up?" Big Mike whispered, even though the Russians couldn't hear. The slightest thought of being left behind was enough to mute our conversation.

"I do. Not that we have a lot of choices. But this way, everyone can report they did their duty," I said. "And none of them will talk it up too much, in case some bigwig takes exception."

"I guess the Russkies ain't so different," Big Mike said.

I kept my reservations to myself, until I heard the sound of aircraft engines. When the truck finally stopped, and the flaps were untied, a beautiful sight awaited us. A C-47 with a big red star painted on the tail.

Guards hustled us to the rear door, shouting in Russian. It wasn't the fondest of farewells, but that was mutual. It was probably best no one understood each other. I tried to help Big Mike up the steps, but he shook me off and hopped his way up. Once we were settled, he bombarded me with questions about the investigation.

"How about I fill you and Kaz in at the same time?" I said. "Except there's one thing I should warn you about. Remember Kiril Sidorov from London?"

"Not likely to forget that bastard," Big Mike said. "He tried to railroad Kaz. Didn't you say he was probably dead?"

"He's been resurrected. I've learned that Stalin has miraculous powers."

CHAPTER TWENTY-TWO

CHEERS ERUPTED AS we came in for a landing and guys spotted a row of P-51 fighters lined up at the end of the runway. The C-47 rolled to a stop next to a hangar with the American flag flying atop it, and that brought about another round of cheers.

"Feels like home already," Big Mike said, watching as American and Russian personnel came out to greet the aircraft. "There's Kaz."

I looked out the window. Kaz was walking with General Dawson, their heads close together as they talked. Sidorov and Major Black trailed them, their eyes on the aircraft. Kaz and Sidorov stood apart from each other. Happenstance, or bad blood?

"Kaz don't look too happy with that Russian bastard," Big Mike said. "Can't blame him. Sidorov had it in for all Poles, not just Kaz. Can't say I look forward to working with him myself."

"Remember General Eisenhower, Big Mike. Allied unity."

"Yeah, but he means unity with the Brits. At least we have something in common with them," Big Mike said. I couldn't agree more, but I held my tongue. I needed to make this partnership work, hard feelings and all.

I followed Big Mike as he hobbled down the steps and took a few giant steps with his crutch, nearly bowling Kaz over and burying him in a bear hug. Belov and Drozdov pulled up in a jeep, and quite a crowd began to gather.

"Fourteen airmen, General," I said, giving Bull a salute. "Courtesy of our comrades in the Red air force."

"Well done, Boyle," the general said. "Big Mike, good to see you again."

"Same here, Bull. Now, when do we eat?"

"Soon. I want the doctors to check out everyone first," Bull said as he moved off to talk to each of the returning aircrew.

"Billy," Kaz said, moving through the press of men milling around him. "We were growing worried."

"Me too," I said, grabbing him by the shoulders. "It's good to see you, Kaz. Sorry I wasn't here when you got in."

"Captain Sidorov explained it to me," Kaz said as Sidorov sidled over. "I was quite surprised to see him, as you can imagine." I watched Kaz for any sign of trouble, but his face was unreadable.

"Major Black was gracious enough to meet Lieutenant Kazimierz when his plane landed and explain the circumstances," Sidorov said. "I have apologized for the situation in London, and the lieutenant was gracious enough to accept it."

"Oh yeah?" Big Mike said, balancing himself with one hand on my shoulder.

"Sergeant," Sidorov said, acknowledging Big Mike's presence with a nod. "I am glad you are well."

"Did you discover who the killer was while Billy was gone?" Big Mike asked. "I seem to remember you were pretty good at putting the finger on a guy, guilty or not."

"Enough," Kaz said, cutting through the tension with a sharp glance at Big Mike. "We must work together here, however strange that may seem. I suggest we put the past behind us and move on."

"Everything okay here?" Bull asked, returning to our group. "We're going to give everyone a quick medical check and then off to the mess hall."

"Fine, Bull," Big Mike said. "Just talkin' over old times."

"Welcome back, *Kapitan*," Drozdov said, as he and Belov joined us. "The general gives you his compliments on finding your men."

"Please tell the general it was all due to his excellent orders," I said, watching the two of them for any reaction. Belov beamed as Drozdov translated. His excellent orders had nearly gotten me killed, but he showed no trace of guile or surprise. Drozdov was neutral, his face betraying nothing.

"General Belov wishes to hear of your experiences, once you have rested," Drozdov said. "Perhaps in the morning." I agreed to see them first thing tomorrow, and they left after some backslapping with Bull and Major Black. Everybody was in a good mood.

The wounded men were taken away in ambulances and the rest of the airmen piled into a truck. Bull helped Big Mike into his jeep, and Kaz and I took the back, with Sidorov and Black following in their vehicle.

"Did Bull give you my message?" I said to Kaz. He nodded.

"It was good advice," Kaz said. "But quite unnecessary. I would not trust Sidorov for a second."

"That's natural, after what he did in London," I said.

"True," Kaz said, glancing back at Sidorov. "But this is not England. Here in Russia, I trust him even less."

"Hey, where's your Poland patch?" I asked, noticing Kaz's uniform and the absence of his red shoulder flash as he turned in his seat.

"It was decided at SHAEF that it would be a provocation if I were to arrive wearing the markings of the London government-in-exile. As you know, the Soviets have their own Polish government already organized. In the interest of Allied unity, I was ordered to divest myself of it."

"Sorry, Kaz," I said. He stared straight ahead.

"I have no desire to be here," he said. "I have no desire to work with that man. But I must do both, for a false unity that in the end will once again betray my nation."

There was nothing I could say to that. We finished the ride in silence.

Doctor Mametova checked out the wounded men and pronounced them all in good shape. Besides Big Mike's bum ankle, there were various lacerations, a broken arm, and two shrapnel wounds, all healing nicely. She told Big Mike his ligaments were torn and to not walk on that foot for a couple of weeks, Sidorov doing the translating. When she was done re-taping Big Mike's ankle, she spoke directly to Sidorov.

"She says the situation is still the same," Sidorov said in a low voice, his eyes darting around the room. "In regard to the medicine."

"What medicine?" Kaz asked.

"I'll fill you in later," I said and helped Big Mike get up, wondering if Black had noticed his missing carton of morphine yet.

The mess hall was busy, the rescued airmen having moved on to vodka toasts with their hosts, the language barrier fading further away with each belt. We took the end of a long table where Big Mike could sit with his leg propped up. Sidorov came with me to get food while Major Black and Kaz settled in on either side of Big Mike.

"You getting along with Kaz?" I asked as I gestured for the cook to top off the bowl I held out. Meat stew with vegetables, or at least that's what it looked like.

"Yes, remarkably well," Sidorov said. "Lieutenant Kazimierz was very kind, once he got over his surprise. I got the distinct impression he'd thought me dead."

"He probably wished it at one point," I said, handing Sidorov Big Mike's bowl and getting a normal portion for myself. It took Sidorov a second, but then he chuckled.

"Of course," he said as we headed to the table. "I do not think I could have been so gracious." A bottle of vodka had appeared, and drinks were poured. Big Mike went to work on his food, and I sat down next to Sidorov, wondering how this little dinner party would end up.

"Have you seen the scene of the crime?" I asked Kaz as I tasted the stew.

"Yes, Captain Sidorov showed me the warehouse, in the company of Major Black. Quite odd, wouldn't you say?"

"Which part?" I asked.

"The part where a fortune in drugs, gold coins, and equipment was left untouched," Kaz said. "Two dead bodies are commonplace these days. But next to undisturbed riches? Most unusual."

"Lay it out for me," Big Mike said, not missing a beat between spoonfuls of stew.

Kaz reviewed the layout of the warehouse, the guards at the door and the locked room upstairs. He checked with Sidorov a few times, and the two of them gave a perfect description of the crime scene. They chatted back and forth like a couple of old friends, and I caught a look of surprise on Big Mike's face. This was all new to him, and I could tell he was having a hard time with Sidorov. So was Kaz, but he did a much better job of hiding it.

"Apparently, the officer in charge of guarding the warehouse was transferred immediately after the killings," Sidorov said. "Billy was given permission to travel to interview him as a witness."

"Not you?" Big Mike said, pointedly not looking at Sidorov. "Why not?"

"I do not pretend to understand how my superiors come to their decisions," Sidorov said. "I was ordered to remain and continue the investigation with Lieutenant Kazimierz, which I did."

"We uncovered no new evidence," Kaz said. "It took me a day to recover after my long journey here. This is my first assignment since my surgery, and the flight was exhausting."

What that meant to me was Kaz had been enraged to find Sidorov waiting to greet him, and it took a day to get his emotions in check. I believed him that the trip here was rough. What I didn't believe was that he'd ever admit it unless he needed an excuse to avoid Sidorov.

"What did Lieutenant Nikolin have to say?" Sidorov asked. "Did you have any trouble finding him?"

"A bit of trouble, yes," I said. "When we stopped to refuel, my pilot received orders to bomb a German fuel depot. Then she went on to land at a temporary airfield. It was a while before I got to Zolynia."

"You flew in an attack with the Night Witches?" Sidorov said. "Not many men can claim that privilege." He went on to explain about the all-female unit to Kaz and Big Mike.

"And I lived to tell the tale," I said. "Although I did wonder where that order originated from."

"What do you mean?" Major Black asked.

"I'm not sure," I admitted. "But sending a single biplane with an American in place of the usual navigator into an attack was risky business. Risky enough that we might not have survived."

"Who issued the order?" Kaz asked.

"I don't know. It came in over the radio, and nobody spoke English," I said, going over how I'd learned about it and the signal we'd come up with for me to drop flares.

"Stalin! Perfect," Sidorov said. "Stalin solves all problems."

I described my time with the Night Witches and showed off my Order of the Patriotic War. "I was finally flown to Zolynia where I found out the truth about Lieutenant Vanya Nikolin. He wasn't transferred. He was sentenced to a penal unit. Tramplers, they call them."

"What's a trampler?" Big Mike asked.

"They clear minefields. The hard way," I said. "Nikolin told me he'd received a note while on guard duty to report to General Belov. When he got there, the general was gone and Major Drozdov of the NKVD, found him and put him on charges for leaving his post. Nikolin lost his commission and ended up in the penal company."

"Do you have any proof of what he says?" Black asked. The proof was folded neatly in my shirt pocket, but something told me to hold back.

"No, it's the story he told. He had no idea what happened while he was gone, or why Belov sent the note, if he really did. We can ask Max. He delivered it."

"And Max is who?" Big Mike asked, gulping down the last of his stew.

"Our factotum," Kaz said. "A conscript of dubious loyalties who has been assigned to attend to our needs."

"A gofer, got it," Big Mike said. "And he never offered up this tidbit to you? Major Drozdov neither?"

"No, not a mention," I said. "We'll have to talk to them about it. Tomorrow."

"Drozdov might have done it to protect Nikolin," Black said. "I mean, the alternative might have been a firing squad for deserting his post or dereliction of duty."

"A quick death would have been merciful," Sidorov said. "Did you learn anything else?"

"Wait," Kaz said, holding up his hand. "You think someone deliberately sent you on a bombing run, and that Nikolin was set up and sent to the front to a near-certain death?"

"I don't know how deliberate the rerouting of my flight was, but somebody made it happen, and it sure felt like a suicide mission to me. The orders I'd been given had only one name authorizing the trip. General Belov. And yes, it seems as if Nikolin was ordered to leave the warehouse under false pretenses. He may well be dead by now."

"Sounds like you were supposed to join him," Black said, his eyes darting to Sidorov and then back to Kaz. Did he sense tension?

"It's possible. If I were paranoid, which it's hard not to be when people are shooting at you, I'd think it was all a plot. But then again, maybe that fuel depot needed to be bombed and Tatyana's aircraft was the only one available. Maybe it's routine to send NKVD officers to penal companies when murder happens on their watch. What do you think, Kiril?" I caught a glimpse of Kaz's eyes widening at my use of Sidorov's first name.

"It would ruin his career, certainly," Sidorov said. "No one wants to be associated with failure, even if it was not his fault. But a penal company clearing mines? It is rather excessive."

"They send them through minefields, really?" Big Mike asked.

"Yes," Sidorov said. "It is usually a three-month sentence, and a man can be reinstated if he survives. Few do."

"I met one. He was assigned as my translator at the Zolynia airbase. He drove me to the front to talk to Nikolin at the 18th Detached Penal Company," I said. "He wasn't too happy to return to his old unit. He was petrified they'd keep him."

"We should try and get this Nikolin guy back here," Big Mike said, eyeing Sidorov. "You got any clout?"

"Very little," Sidorov said. "It may please you to know that I have been in a labor camp in Siberia since I left England. I am here only because I am acquainted with Captain Boyle and the two of you. That is the only clout I carry." Big Mike kept a poker face. I'd never let on about the trap I'd laid for Sidorov, and if he and Kaz ever suspected, they hadn't said a word.

"I'll see if Bull can request it through Belov, officially," I said. "We have determined Nikolin possesses vital information, so at least we can make the case."

"You come up with anything else?" Black asked, filling his glass and passing the vodka around.

"Well, I got to talking with my translator, Fedor Popov, and told him about the murders. He came up with an angle I hadn't considered. It had to do with the location of the murders. I'd been thinking it was done in that locked room because it was secluded. But Teddy—Fedor—suggested the location might have been a signal. Like you said, Kaz, it doesn't make sense that nothing was taken. But what if the bodies were left there as a warning, or a threat?"

"Maybe Morris and Kopelev didn't go along with some scheme and got plugged for it," Big Mike offered, gulping his vodka and smacking his lips.

"A message, perhaps?" Sidorov suggested.

"A message intended for whom?" Kaz asked. "To what purpose?"

Damn good question.

"Major Black, anything new on your Bulgarian mission? Any new supplies come in for it?" I asked.

"Captain Boyle, that is a matter of some secrecy," he said. "Please don't mention it again, not in such a public place."

"Come, Major," Sidorov said. "Everyone seems to know of it. We are all friends here, are we not?" He said it with a smile, and a quick glance at Kaz, who sat stone-faced.

"Okay, but don't spread this around," Black said, leaning forward and whispering loud enough to let me know he'd been hitting the vodka pretty hard. "Still no go-ahead from Moscow. Drozdov is champing at the bit to kick it off, but he needs approval. From the highest level, if you know what I mean."

Comrade Stalin. Everything seemed to lead back to him. Everything except the double murder, which didn't lead anywhere.

"Too bad all that morphine is just sitting there," I said. "They're short of the stuff everywhere."

"I'm sure our Russian allies will straighten that all out," Black said. "Right, Capitan Sidorov?"

"Certainly," Sidorov said with a straight face. "The Communist Party will not fail the people. It is impossible."

No one else could tell, but Kaz was simmering in anger. He raised his glass to me, and I did the same, downing my vodka. We set our glasses on the wooden table with a thump and my gaze fell upon his uniform jacket, barely able to make out the line of holes where his shoulder flash had been sewn on, like the faint traces of an old boundary on a map, erased by war and treachery.

CHAPTER TWENTY-THREE

THE PARTY HAD gone on way too long. Most of the liberated airmen had made the mistake of trying to keep up with their Russian counterparts in vodka consumption, and I didn't envy them their morning after. Sidorov and Black had left us to have a drink with some of the other American officers, and we'd found ourselves alone in a room of cheerful drunks.

"Do you trust your friend Kiril?" Kaz had asked.

"He's not my friend," I'd said. "But I did have to depend on him the first few days I was here. And he did do one good thing." I filled Big Mike and Kaz in on our morphine heist and the widespread shortage of the stuff.

"Is that why you asked Major Black about the Bulgarian mission?" Kaz asked.

"Yes, I wanted to get a sense of whether he'd noticed anything missing from his stocks," I said. "Listen, I know working with Sidorov is strange. It was a shock to me too. But let's make the best of it and wrap this thing up. I've already had enough of the Eastern Front."

With that, we called it a night. We drove Big Mike to the barracks, where he and Kaz had a room next to mine. Fresh clothes had been left on the bed for Big Mike, and I hoped Max had gone for the largest size in everything.

I was half asleep when Sidorov came in and hit the sack. How bizarre were the twists and turns of this war to have the four of us bunking and working a case together? If indeed we all were working toward the same result.

I pulled the wool blanket over my head and tried not to think about minefields, morphine, and murder, letting the weariness in my body drive those images from my mind.

Unfortunately, they ended up in my dreams.

IN THE MORNING, fortified by coffee, powdered eggs, and Spam, Kaz, Sidorov, and I approached Bull Dawson about asking General Belov to officially request Nikolin's return to the Poltava airbase. I'd ordered Big Mike to take it easy and left him with his leg up on a pillow and a two-week old copy of *Life* magazine.

The request for Nikolin was a long shot, but mainly I wanted to see Belov's reaction and if he would lie again about Nikolin's punishment. The same went for Drozdov.

Bull agreed and had Major Black call Belov's office to arrange a meeting. Ten minutes later, the five of us trooped in to find Belov at his desk, Drozdov seated at his side, and Maiya standing next to him. I checked the knot on my field scarf and brushed down my Ike jacket, wondering if I should have worn my Soviet medal. I'd thought about it, but it didn't seem right on a Class A uniform.

Translating through Maiya, I gave a quick account of my flight with Tatyana, including the refueling stop. I asked if the general was aware his written orders had been superseded by the radioed order to attack the German depot.

"General Belov was not aware of and did not countenance any such order," Maiya said, following up breathlessly with a request for details of the attack. I gave them the full story, Stalin and all, including the crash of the burning Po-2 and the medal on my jacket. Maiya seemed entranced at the exploits of the vaunted Night Witches. Belov nodded his quiet approval, while Drozdov watched me with hooded eyes. No one gave anything away.

Finally, I came to Zolynia and finding out that Vanya Nikolin was not there, but at the front with a penal company. Belov looked surprised. He and Drozdov exchanged glances that might have displayed guilt or perhaps real astonishment.

"Is Lieutenant Nikolin alive?" Maiya asked, translating the general's urgent question.

"He was when I spoke with him," I said. "He said that on the night of the murders, he was sent a note signed by General Belov, ordering him to report to this very office. He left his post as ordered but found no one here. He told me Major Drozdov found him and placed him under arrest, demoting him on the spot."

Belov and Drozdov exchanged a few quick words. Sidorov raised his eyebrows and Kaz gave me a look as they wrapped up. I didn't understand what was said, but neither of them was in the best of moods.

"General Belov did not order the lieutenant to leave his post at any time," Maiya said, boiling down the conversation to basics. "Major Drozdov did transfer Lieutenant Nikolin that night, but it was not to a penal detachment."

"That is true," Drozdov said, looking to Belov for permission to speak, which was granted by a curt nod. "I did order his transfer, but to an NKVD regiment, not a penal unit. I thought it best to get Nikolin away from here. You see, his father is an important official within the Kremlin. I did not wish to embarrass him by his son's involvement in this affair."

"But he's not in a regular regiment. I saw him with the 18th Penal Detachment Company at the front," I said.

"I do not know what happened," Drozdov said. "A mistake, some clerical error? Or perhaps his father is no longer a favored member of the *nomenklatura*."

I must have wrinkled my brow because Kaz broke in to explain the *nomenklatura* was the name given to the administrators who ran things in the Soviet Union, under the watchful eye of the Communist Party.

"General Belov, I would like to officially request that Vanya Nikolin be returned to your jurisdiction here so he can aid in our joint investigation," Bull said. "I am sure that between you and your NKVD comrade this can be accomplished." Belov and Drozdov put their heads together, called Maiya over, and gave her the party line.

"The general agrees," she said. "General Belov wishes you to know that personnel transfers are normally the business of the Soviet state and no one else. But in this case, because of an unfortunate mistake obviously due to allies of the enemy and disorganizers of the rear, he will relent and order Lieutenant Nikolin reinstated to his rank and returned here. Major Drozdov will issue the paperwork immediately."

"If Nikolin is still alive," I said.

"The general relents," she answered. "No further discussion on this topic is called for. Now, Captain Boyle, you must return the travel orders you were given. It is standard procedure."

I handed the folded papers to Maiya, wondering if it was a normal thing. Or was there something in those orders Belov didn't want revealed?

"Thank you, General. I'm sure you must be busy, so we'll take our leave. Unless there is anything else, Captain Boyle?" Bull said, in a way that told me it was time to shut up and get out.

"Only one thing, sir. Unless Captain Sidorov has already requested it, may we have permission to visit the *Goskomizdat* bookstore in Poltava today?"

"What for?" Drozdov broke in, forgetting about the translation. Maiya filled in Belov quickly.

"A small matter concerning a book Lieutenant Kopelev had in his room. Probably nothing," I said.

"You will have a pass within the hour," Maiya said, gesturing for us to take our leave. As she ushered us out, she and Black exchanged the briefest of smiles. They were the only two happy about anything.

"Let's check on Big Mike before we leave," I said to Kaz, eager to get clear of the Operations building and think about what was going on. "I want to find Max and have him bring Big Mike lunch, so he stays put."

"I've got a couple of *Stars and Stripes* that aren't too old," Bull said. "Come on, I'll see what else I have to keep him entertained."

"I will wait for Major Drozdov to draft the orders to release Nikolin," Sidorov said. "It may go faster that way."

"Good idea," I said, checking my watch. "We'll meet out front at ten o'clock."

Bull came up with the newspapers and a couple of paperbacks. *The Adventures of Tom Sawyer* by Mark Twain and a Rex Stout, *Not Quite Dead Enough*. Both were Armed Services Editions, well-worn paperbacks that fit neatly into a pocket. He also had a collection of short stories by Ernest Hemingway. I told him to leave that one behind. We'd encountered Hemingway in France not too long ago, and that had been enough of the guy.

"I always enjoy a visit to a bookstore," Kaz said as we walked to the barracks. "But why are we really going to a government store? I doubt they will have anything for Big Mike."

"One thing I forgot to mention. When we searched Kopelev's room, we went through the books he had. Some Mark Twain, and a lot of Marx and Engels and stuff by Stalin. But he also had an atlas of the Soviet Union."

"You found that suspicious? The atlas, I mean."

"It was second-hand, purchased recently at the bookstore in Poltava. It had one section on the Black Sea marked up. Some of the ports along the Turkish border were circled. I kept the book because something didn't seem right. I had a feeling Kopelev bought it for some specific purpose. Then it was stolen out of my jeep."

"That is a very thin thread, my friend," Kaz said. "A Communist ideologue who also reads Mark Twain buys an atlas. A conclusion as to why he was murdered does not jump to mind. Perhaps he simply liked maps."

"Sidorov didn't mention the book?" I asked.

"No. He did recount your search of Kopelev's quarters, but said you found nothing of interest. This one time, I will choose to believe he is telling the truth," Kaz said.

"I know, it's not much to go on. But there isn't much else to do until Nikolin gets back," I said. "And one other thing. I do have the order Nikolin was given." I patted my shirt pocket.

"Interesting," Kaz said. "Who else have you told?"

"No one. Just you."

"Even more interesting. You do not trust Sidorov either, it seems."

"I didn't feel like blabbing it to the whole mess hall last night, that's all. I figured it would be worth holding this piece of information back," I said. "But you're right. The advice I left for you with Bull still holds. Trust no one."

We found Big Mike snoozing in his bunk, the plate I'd brought him from the mess on his bedstand, hardly a crumb left on it.

"Hey guys," he said, propping himself up. "What's the news?"

"Old news," I said, setting down the newspapers along with the paperbacks. "We're headed to town to check on a bookstore."

"Don't bring Kaz with you, for crying out loud. He takes forever in a bookstore. Why you goin', anyway?" I gave him the lowdown on Kopelev's atlas.

"Do not worry, a Soviet state bookstore will have little to interest me, or any Pole, for that matter," Kaz said. "Where is Max? We wanted to be sure he brought you food."

"I haven't seen the guy at all," Big Mike said.

"Little wiry fellow, jailbird look, lot of tattoos?" I said. Big Mike shook his head.

I checked in Max's room. The bed was stripped and there was no trace of him. It was as if Max had never been there at all.

"Max brought the order to Nikolin telling him to leave his post," Kaz said as soon as I returned and gave them the news. "Now that General Belov has agreed to recall Nikolin, Max disappears. Most convenient."

"Here, keep this hidden," I said to Big Mike, giving him the crumpled paper with Belov's order to Nikolin and explaining what it was.

"Ah, you kept an ace up your sleeve," he said, stashing it inside *Tom Sawyer*.

"Yeah, and I compared the signature to the ones on my travel orders. They match, or they're a well-practiced forgery," I said.

"Okay, enjoy your sightseeing. I'll be spending time with Archie and Nero Wolfe," Big Mike said. "But before you go, any other dope you're holding back on?"

"No. I think you have everything now," I said. "Oh wait, I do have some maps. Got 'em from the navigator on my B-17. See if you can piece together what these locations have in common, if anything."

I grabbed the two maps from my room and marked the places that were important. Poltava, Zolynia, Jedlicze, Kozova. Then the ports that I remembered from Kopelev's atlas. Batumi and Poti plus Samsun and Trabzon in Turkey. Also, Tabriz in Iran. I'd seen that on the shipping crates in the warehouse. Maybe it meant something, maybe it didn't. Maybe Nero Wolfe could figure it out.

We made arrangements at the mess hall to have lunch delivered to Big Mike. Kaz made sure the guy in the kitchen understood we needed two meals delivered, figuring that would hold Big Mike for a while.

At the Operations building, I found Sidorov in Major Drozdov's office.

"The order has been radioed to the 18th Detached Penal Company," Sidorov announced with a smile. "We are awaiting word on Lieutenant Nikolin now."

"Great. But where's Max? His room is cleared out."

"Please be calm, Captain Boyle," Drozdov said, signing a sheet of paper. "Private Maxim Bogomozov has been reassigned to other duties. I will provide you with another orderly soon."

"Will Max be joining the tramplers?" Kaz asked.

"That is an insult!" Drozdov yelled, jumping to his feet. "Private Bogomozov has been officially reassigned to where his language skills can be best put to use. And it is an air force matter. It has nothing to do with the NKVD. Only cowards and traitors are sent to the penal detachments."

"Except for Nikolin," I said.

"An obvious mistake," Drozdov said. "But that does not entitle foreigners wearing the English uniform to slander our government. I know you are one of the London Poles, Lieutenant Kazimierz. And an aristocrat as well."

"Well, you certainly avoided making any mistake about my identity," Kaz said. "It is a shame you were not that careful with Lieutenant Nikolin's destination. Or were you?"

"Get out," Drozdov said, thrusting the paper at Sidorov. "Now."

"You can be such a charming fellow, Baron, when you wish to be," Sidorov said as we walked down the main corridor. "Apparently you felt otherwise this morning. Did you wish to provoke the major?"

"Yes. It is an investigative technique I learned from Billy when we first began to work together," Kaz said, taking the passenger's seat in the jeep. "It involves turning over a rock and seeing what lurks beneath. Or was it poking a sleeping dog? I get those confused."

"Let's hope you didn't poke a sleeping bear," I said. "I would have liked to know where they sent Max. If Drozdov was telling the truth, it sounds like he was sent someplace where there are Americans. Maybe one of the other airbases?"

"Let us ask Maiya," Sidorov suggested, spotting her outside of Black's office, not surprisingly. We did.

"Yes, Max left last night, Captain," Maiya told us. "I am sorry he did not have a chance to say goodbye, but a spot opened up on a flight to Tehran."

"Why Tehran?" I asked.

"The airbase, I should have said. Tehran and the nearby airfield are within the Soviet northern occupation zone, as I am sure you know. Private Bogomozov was assigned there due to a need for English speaking personnel."

"Max is hardly a translator," Sidorov said. "His English is eccentric, at best."

"No, he will not be an official translator, but very few Americans speak Russian, so it will help to have Max to work with them. He has been assigned to your railway service. Much of the supplies coming in through Iran are brought to us by rail, only a small amount by air."

"Can we get in touch with Max if we need to?" Kaz asked.

"We can send a message," Maiya said. "But he may be on the trains at any time. The railway goes from Tehran to Tabriz and then north into the USSR through Armenia. I have no idea where he may be today or tomorrow. Or any day."

"We'll let you know if we need anything," I said. "Was he glad to go?"

"He obeyed his orders, as all good Red army soldiers do. Now, I must get back to work," Maiya said, clutching a stack of files and walking off, giving a nod to Black at his desk.

"What do you think, Major Black," I asked. "Was Max all that happy to get sent to Tehran?"

"I wouldn't know, Captain," Black said, barely looking up from a map he'd spread out over his desk. "Enjoy your trip to the bookstore. And close the door, will you?"

"Nobody's in a very good mood today," I said as we exited the building.

"Someone is," Sidorov said. "Our friend Max. Trains full of supplies are a *vor*'s paradise. He may pass out when he sees the mountains of supplies coming through the Persian Corridor."

"*Vor* means thief," I said to Kaz.

"*Vor v zakone*, a thief in law, to be exact," Kaz said. I should have known. "His prison tattoos were quite interesting. I had not heard of the Bitch War before. From what Capitan Sidorov told me, Max could expect retaliation if he is sent back. He should be careful."

"A *vor* cannot be careful," Sidorov said as we got into the jeep. "It is in his nature to steal. Max will take what he can and then suffer the consequences."

"Maybe he'll run," I said, starting the jeep and heading to the main gate.

"What would a Russian do in Iran?" Sidorov asked. "After the war, I mean. It is a thief's dream now with mountains of riches flowing in from the West. But once the war is over, Iran will be left poor again. With no vodka. Hardly home for a *vor*."

"Regardless of what Max is stuffing his pockets with right now, do you think the story of his transfer is real? Right when we need him to confirm Nikolin's claim about the order, he vanishes," I said.

"It makes sense," Sidorov said as we neared the gate. "There is probably a greater need for language skills with all the Americans and British in Iran. Having Max work with your enlisted personnel would help things run smoothly."

"I can see that, Billy," Kaz said. "I know you feel you were sent away under false pretenses, and Lieutenant Nikolin's case is certainly cause for concern, but that does not mean every military transfer is part of a plot."

"You're starting to think like a Russian," Sidorov said. "Or perhaps like Comrade Stalin, who sees conspiracies at every turn."

"Speaking of conspiracies, was it true what Maiya told us about turning in orders? That it's standard procedure?"

"Yes, since travel orders could be altered. It is especially worrisome when it comes to Westerners who possess them," Sidorov said. "You may be trusted to carry orders for a specific task, but you will never really be trusted."

I stopped at the gate. Guards surrounded us, their PPSh-41 submachine guns trained on our chests. Sidorov handed over our travel papers, and the lieutenant in charge gave them a careful read. Finally, he nodded and handed them back to Sidorov as they exchanged a few words. His men lowered their weapons and raised the gate.

"Whew," I said, as we left the base behind. "They didn't act friendly at all. Did they think we were kidnapping you?"

"That is exactly what the officer asked," Sidorov said. "He apologized but said you can never be too careful around foreigners. He also said his daddy was ready to protect a fellow Russian from these Westerners."

"Daddy?" I asked.

"The Russian nickname for the PPSh-41 is *papasha*," Kaz said. "Daddy."

"We Russians stick together," Sidorov said, although coming from him it lacked a certain punch. After all, he'd betrayed his country and then it threw him to the wolves, almost literally. But, here he was, back in the Communist fold, at least for now.

CHAPTER TWENTY-FOUR

POLTAVA WAS A small city with big piles of rubble. Red brick cascaded from two-story piles, spilling out into the street despite the efforts of workers to carry away and stack the bricks that could be salvaged. As we drove closer, I saw they weren't exactly workers. They were German POWs, their uniforms tattered and caked with dust. Russians stood guard, each with their daddy at the ready.

"It is all the fascists are good for," Sidorov said, practically spitting the words out.

"They should remain after the war until every town and village is rebuilt."

"Yes, I agree," Kaz said. "An invading army should rebuild the nation it conquers. And then leave."

"Ha, yes, I see what you mean," Sidorov said. "But this time we are liberating Poland, not invading it."

"Whatever you call it, the question is, will you leave?" Kaz said.

"You would have to ask Comrade Stalin," Sidorov said, since we all knew the answer. Invading and liberating were one and the same to Uncle Joe. "Go left at this next intersection."

I drove down a wide street that hadn't seen as much destruction as the neighborhood we'd just been through. A few large three-story buildings were faced in pink stone, and one granite structure sported double columns on either side of the entrance. A few shops were open, and people walked the streets dressed in clothing that was worn but only slightly shabby. The neighborhood almost looked normal, except for the military vehicles that were the only transportation in sight. Sidorov pointed to a storefront ahead, and I pulled over.

"Billy, what is it we are after, exactly?" Kaz asked as we got out. The windows of the shop were boarded up, but the sign over the door had a fresh coat of paint.

"Let's just see if anyone remembers Kopelev," I said. "I'd like to know what else he was interested in. Other than the collected wisdom of Joseph Stalin."

"I doubt we will learn anything," Sidorov said. "But it is better than sitting and waiting for word on Nikolin."

"And perhaps I will pick up a good book," Kaz said. "Do they stock any Polish titles, Captain Sidorov?"

"Please do not make a scene, Lieutenant," Sidorov said, as he opened the door for us to enter. "Even if you come across a rock or a stick."

The bookshop was one big room, the walls filled with bookshelves, some of them no more than rough cut wooden planks. Most had books, some of the shelves almost full. Tables in the middle of the room held stacks of used books, missing covers or otherwise damaged. A dozen people milled around, perusing the shelves and flipping through books on the tables. Without a Cyrillic decoder ring, I didn't have a clue what any of them were about.

We caught some curious glances as the customers and staff took in our uniforms, but Sidorov quickly introduced himself to the man in charge. He was bald with a fluff of white hair sticking out from behind his ears, where his hairline was making its last stand.

Kaz drifted off, lured by the thought of a book he hadn't yet met.

Sidorov introduced me to the fellow and a younger woman who stood beside him behind the counter. They looked nervous, maybe wondering if the government had come to check on what they were selling. But no, this was a government bookstore, so they were all comrades. Maybe it was the two foreigners in strange uniforms. I'd bet any Yanks who got a pass into town didn't put the bookstore high on their list.

"I've described Lieutenant Kopelev and asked if they remembered him," Sidorov said as the two workers put their heads together. After a quick talk with Sidorov, he said they did.

"They remembered his uniform, and his blue NKVD cap and shoulder boards," Sidorov reported. "They say he was very earnest and read deeply. Mainly Marxist-Leninist theory. Some fiction, but not much."

"What about maps and atlases? Did he ask about what they had?" They shook their heads *nyet*.

"Do they have a section for atlases and maps?" I asked.

The woman led us to a table filled with children's books. Brightly illustrated pictures of children in the fields, in factories, marching with red banners.

"What's this?" I asked. Sidorov opened a picture book with outlines of the various Soviet republics and the little comrades you'd find in each one. Heart-warming.

"We do not publish maps of Soviet territory to be sold," Sidorov said. "All she had to offer is this type of book for children. Kopelev certainly did buy the book here, but it was likely a used volume, not part of their standard stock."

"What's the problem with maps?" I asked.

"Fear of the foreigner again," Sidorov said with a heavy sigh. "Fear that good maps may be used to plan bombings or for spies to make their way around. I will let you in on a secret, Billy. Civil city maps and road maps are printed with deliberate mistakes, to confuse the enemy, whoever that may be."

"The army must need real maps," I said.

"Of course," Sidorov said, tossing the book back onto the table. "The NKVD administers mapmaking and distribution, to give you an idea of how closely cartographic information is guarded. Military maps are under their jurisdiction, and all maps must be turned in after an operation. Even fragments, if the map is destroyed."

"Do you think they're afraid to admit they sold him the atlas? It wasn't the kind of thing that could help you get from one city to another, after all," I said.

"No, I do not think so. It would not be an offense to resell such a book. I doubt these comrades even know of the errors introduced into our maps. They simply may not recall one book among all those Kopelev purchased."

"Okay. Well, it was worth a try. Know of any good places to eat in town?"

"I hear the Cosmos Hotel is passable," Sidorov said. "Remember, your Sergeant Craven recommended it?"

"He said it was a good place to find hookers," I said. "But hey, they gotta eat too."

"Yes," Sidorov said. "I will ask for directions. And speaking of Sergeant Craven, he was suddenly transferred as well, if you recall. It is not just a Soviet practice."

I gave a sharp laugh, acknowledging Sidorov's point, even though it had been he and I who cooked up Craven's transfer. I told Kaz what the plan was, and he said he'd like to browse around for a few minutes more. I told him to knock himself out, and Sidorov and I went outside to wait in the jeep.

"What do we do if Nikolin doesn't come back?" I said, drumming my fingers on the steering wheel. "He could have been killed ten minutes after I left him."

"I do not know," Sidorov said, shoving his hands into his jacket pockets. There was a chill in the air, and the clouds overhead shrouded the city street in dull grayness. "We can try to question Belov about forcing you into that bombing mission. It seems he is the one who could have most easily pulled those strings. It was an air force matter, after all."

"Right. Pressure the Russian general who's been put in charge of a joint American and Soviet airbase," I said. "Belov has to be pretty well-connected to be given a job like this."

"True," Sidorov said. "Only a man trusted by Moscow would be given this responsibility. It may work in our favor though, since Belov must be seen to be like Caesar's wife."

"Beyond reproach," I said, trying to recall the saying.

"Above suspicion," Kaz said, hopping in the rear seat. "Why is General Belov like Pompeia?"

"Because any hint of wrongdoing, even unproven, could cause his superiors to lose faith in him," Sidorov said. "Didn't Caesar divorce his wife because another Roman tried to seduce her?"

"Yes, even though the fellow was not successful, Caesar divorced her and coined the saying, Caesar's wife must be above suspicion," Kaz said. "Which, as you point out, now applies to all those in sensitive positions. Do you suspect Belov is behind the killings?"

"I find it hard to see how all this could occur without his knowledge," Sidorov said.

"I have to admit, having been sent up in that biplane to attack a German position didn't endear the guy to me," I said. "But I can't figure what's in it for him, or anyone."

"And I am reluctant to accuse the general, or even suggest his guilt, without actual proof," Sidorov said. "Airing suspicions will accomplish nothing, except for my return to Siberia."

"Well then, on to lunch," Kaz said. "In case it is your last decent meal." Sidorov almost laughed.

We found the Cosmos Hotel only a few blocks away, following the directions Sidorov had been given at the bookstore. The building hadn't been damaged. Even the windows were intact. Maybe the Germans had counted on a return visit and liked the accommodations.

The restaurant was clean, the wood polished, and the black and white tile floor gleaming. After we were seated, Sidorov ordered. Pea soup to start, goulash over boiled potatoes for the main course.

"It is what the bookstore manager suggested," Sidorov said. "And from the looks of the menu, there isn't much else to choose from. Supplies are scarce. Peas and potatoes at least are in ample supply. Thank goodness we are in farm country, not that much could be planted this spring with all the fighting."

"The war disrupts everything," Kaz said. "Billy mentioned how even the supply of morphine is quite limited. The two of you provided the hospital on base with some relief, but he reported that the hospitals at Kozova and Zolynia were also running low."

"Sadly, yes," Sidorov said. "We are fortunate that we have our own source of opium from the Kyrgyz province to the east. But it is a long way away, four thousand kilometers, some of the terrain mountainous. As you say, the war disrupts everything, including badly needed medical supplies."

Our waitress brought tea, and we sat silently as she poured.

We sipped the tea in silence. We'd talked about Nikolin, how bad the war was, Caesar's wife, and potatoes. That about did it for subjects we had in common. Sidorov and Kaz acted politely, but this wasn't going to be a luncheon filled with chuckles. There was still tension between them, and I felt torn. There was my loyalty to Kaz, which was unshakable. But in the few days I'd spent alone with Sidorov, I'd seen a decent side of him. I knew it wasn't his only side, but it was more than I'd seen before, and I had to admit, I felt a glimmer of guilt at what I'd done to him.

He'd deserved it, but that sentiment was easier to support with a few thousand miles and a continent between us.

Food arrived and we kept the chitchat easy as we slurped our way through the thick soup. As we waited for the second course, I tried to come up with something to talk about that wouldn't upset Kaz. I remembered that Sidorov had a wife. He'd mentioned her back in England, and that her father was some sort of high Communist Party official.

"Have you had any contact with your wife?" I asked. "Didn't you tell me once she worked in the Propaganda Ministry in Moscow?"

"I have no wife," Sidorov said. "Which is better for her career in Moscow. We were divorced months ago. Her father is an official with the People's Commissariat for Justice, and he moved the paperwork through channels quietly. It seems a husband must also be above suspicion, especially where high-ranking Party members are concerned. Divorce is frowned upon, especially now that Mother Russia needs sons and daughters to replace those killed by the fascists. But for those in the *nomenklatura*, all things are possible."

The goulash arrived, and Sidorov seemed sufficiently over his divorce to enjoy it.

The food was good, and the surroundings passed for elegant on what had recently been the cutting edge of the Eastern Front. Kaz seemed relaxed and kept his subtly barbed comments to himself. Our waitress left the bill and Sidorov tossed a pile of rubles on top of it, then excused himself.

"*Vannaya* break," I said to Kaz. "I'm beginning to pick up a few words. *Morify*, that's morphine."

"Excellent," Kaz said, his eyes following Sidorov as he walked to the rear of the restaurant and went downstairs. "Tell me, Billy, what did we learn today?"

"Not much," I said. "Russians don't like atlases. Poltava is dreary. That's about it."

"There's something else," Kaz said, turning to watch for Sidorov's return. "Think about it. Actually, two things, but you've observed only one. When it comes to you, I'll tell you the other."

"I take it we're keeping this a secret from Sidorov," I said.

"I think that best."

CHAPTER TWENTY-FIVE

SIDOROV INSISTED ON driving back, which didn't leave much time to think about what Kaz had meant. I was too busy hanging onto my seat and the windscreen, not to mention closing my eyes whenever he took a corner and fishtailed the jeep.

As Sidorov thankfully slowed for the gate, I caught the sound of engines in the distance, the steady drone of B-17 Pratt & Whitney engines churning through the air.

"There," I said, pointing to the western sky as we drove onto the base. The lead formation emerged from the clouds, descending as they neared the field. We joined the flow of people and vehicles headed for the main runway to watch this latest shuttle bombing mission land.

A couple of ancient fire trucks were parked by the hangars, along with ambulances and jeeps. The wounded aircrew would be rushed to the hospital, the rest of them taken to debriefing. The dead? I didn't know where they'd end up. In body bags, on the next flight to Tehran? The first four Fortresses landed smoothly, even the one decorated with holes in its tail assembly. Then the flares started dropping. That meant wounded aboard the next ships. Other aircraft circled the field, giving the stricken ships priority.

The next Fort came in low, trailing smoke from two engines, wings wobbling as the pilot struggled to keep it straight. It landed, bounced hard, and kept rolling, past the end of the runway and into the grassy field. Ambulances and jeeps sped out, along with one of the fire engines. Smoke choked the air around the B-17, enveloping the res-cuers and rendering them invisible.

The first Fortresses to land taxied to the hangar and cut their engines. An ambulance raced to the plane with the shot-up tail, the rear gunner's position stitched with bullet holes. As the crew climbed out, they wearily waved off the ambulance. Other parts of the fuselage were shredded, the tell-tale marks of 20mm cannon shells all too evident. The tail gunner, and maybe others, must've been dead.

More flares.

Flames erupted from the Fortress that ran off the runway. Crew-members ran, getting clear of the flames that began to lick at the fuselage. A fireball blossomed, sending inky black smoke and bright yellow flame into the sky. The only good thing was that at the end of the long run from England, there wasn't that much fuel left in the tanks.

"This was my first mission."

I turned to see a lieutenant, still in his flight gear, watching the landings. He must have been on one of the first Forts to land. He was young, but by the vacant look in his eyes, he'd aged some in the last few hours.

His trousers were soaked in blood.

"Lieutenant, are you all right?" I said, laying my hand on his shoulder and checking him out. He was standing just fine, no sign of a wound anywhere.

"It's Anderson's," he said, speaking with a hypnotic drone. "Ander-son's blood. Waist gunner. I tried to stop the bleeding. I did."

"Was that your Fort, the one with the tail section all shot up?"

"Skipper said I should check on them," he said. "I never saw any-thing like it."

"Come on, let's get out of here," I said. I wanted to get him into the jeep, but he stood rock solid, watching the flow of bombers circling and landing.

"I saw guys bail out and get hit by flak," he said. "Guys from the *Frisco Gal*. Friends of mine. Anderson all ripped up. Tommy, the other waist gunner, his arm was shot off. Completely gone. But it's the strangest thing. You know the only thing I can think of?"

"No, pal. What?" I let go of his arm and tried to make eye contact, but he was seeing something far beyond his range of vision.

"Back home—my folks live in the Bronx—I used to watch the place across the street when I got home from school. It was a big apartment building that the army took over. They had guys going to NYU for some special courses, and they put them up there. I'd watch them when they came back after class every day. I was waiting for my eighteenth birthday so I could sign up too. I couldn't wait. The building was huge, two big wings and a courtyard in the middle. There were two main entrances, but these guys didn't bother with that. They'd gather by the fire escapes, then they'd jump up, real high, and pull down the ladders. They'd climb up the fire escapes, doing all sorts of crazy daredevil stuff, and get into their apartments through the windows. It was like a free aerobatic show every day. They were so full of life, so sure of themselves, nimble and quick, like nothing could hurt them. Nothing."

The last bomber landed. The lieutenant walked away.

I watched the Fortress burn.

"THAT WAS A rough mission," Bull said a while later as Kaz and I stopped in his office. "The Luftwaffe harassed them all the way across Germany after they hit their target."

"We saw one crash and burn," I said, still thinking about all those athletic young men. Boys.

"Yeah, we have aircrew to send back via Tehran. I'm organizing a flight for the wounded," Bull said. "Which reminds me. I went over to see Big Mike while you were gone. He's already a bit stir crazy, especially after the time he spent locked up in that hospital ward."

"It is not in his nature to sit still for long," Kaz said. "But he must."

"I think he feels useless," Bull said. "So try this idea on. I can get him on a medical flight to Tehran. We have a hospital at the airbase. They can check him out and he can ask around about that Max character you wanted to talk to. Maybe even find him."

"It would help to have someone there," I said, glancing at Kaz.

"There's not much he can help with here. We're doing nothing just fine ourselves."

"I agree, as long as he takes care of his leg," Kaz said.

"Okay. I'll make sure the doctors give him a thorough checkup, and that he has clearance to send me radio messages," Bull said. "I'll add his name to the manifest. Any news on Nikolin?"

"Sidorov is checking with Drozdov," I said. "We should have known one way or the other by now."

"I have good news," Sidorov said, entering the office with Maiya at his heels. "Nikolin is alive and is being recalled. He will be at the Zolynia airbase within the hour."

"And General Belov has approved me to fly as copilot and pick him up," Maiya said, beaming. "It is wonderful."

"I am sure Lieutenant Nikolin thinks so too," Kaz said. "When do you depart?"

"Now," Maiya said. "The aircraft is being fueled. We will return this evening. I must get ready. Runway three, in case you should wish to see us off."

Maiya left in a rushed state of excitement. It was the only good news we'd gotten, and her joy at being able to fly on a transport mission was infectious. Kaz, Sidorov, and I decided to watch her take off, then head over to Big Mike and talk about his jaunt to Tehran.

"See, gentlemen, we have found Nikolin and will bring him home," Drozdov said when we found him already at the runway, standing by the Yak-6 twin engine transport. "The prodigal child. You doubted, did you not?"

"Let's just say we're all glad he's alive," I said, with a sharp glance at Kaz.

"As am I, Captain," Drozdov said. He did seem pretty chipper about it, and I began to wonder if it really had been a clerical screwup, or if Nikolin had simply been shanghaied into filling a quota for the penal unit. "When I sent Vanya away, I did so for his own good. I never imagined he'd end up with the tramplers. Ah, here is Maiya. One of the new Soviet women, accomplished in all spheres of life!"

"Please, Major Drozdov, you embarrass me," Maiya said. She tried to suppress a grin as she went through the preflight check with the pilot.

"The Yak-6 is a useful aircraft," Drozdov said. "Good for courier flights, transporting wounded, or resupplying partisans behind the lines. It can land in a small field." He gave a quick tour of the compact aircraft, pointing out the space for four passengers in the rear compartment. By the time he was done, Maiya and the pilot were ready. She waved as the engines started and the aircraft taxied out of the hangar and rumbled down the grass runway.

"By this evening, you will have some answers," Drozdov said. "I hope you make something of it." With that, he stalked off.

"His good mood didn't last long," I said.

"I was surprised it lasted as long as it did," Sidorov said. "I heard a clerk talking in Operations earlier. An NKVD colonel is coming in for an inspection tomorrow. Apparently concerning the death of the *narkoman*. He said Drozdov was quite angry when he heard."

"Of course," I said. "The top NKVD man at a sensitive installation must be above suspicion."

"What *narkoman*?" Kaz asked. Sidorov filled him in on the drug overdose of a NKVD lieutenant.

"Sorry, I forgot to mention that incident," Sidorov said.

"It is odd that with a shortage of morphine, this officer found enough to kill himself with," Kaz said as we headed back to the jeep.

"Doctor Mametova thought it was heroin, but she said she couldn't be sure," Sidorov said. "Either way, it is trouble for Drozdov to have one of his men involved in drugs. Very decadent."

"We're sending Big Mike to Tehran," I told Sidorov as I started the jeep. "He can try to track down Max. He's not doing us much good here."

"I will be surprised if Max is where the army thinks he should be," Sidorov said. "People have a habit of disappearing at the most inopportune times, don't they?"

"Or getting themselves killed," I said. "I wish we'd found something useful at the bookstore, something that would give us some insight into what Kopelev was up to." I realized I hadn't had a moment to give any thought to Kaz's cryptic comment in the restaurant and tried to focus on that as I made the short drive.

"Only the killer knows," Sidorov said.

"Wait," I said, slowing down as a flatbed truck with a mounted .50 machine gun careened down the road in the other lane. "Not necessarily. Remember what Teddy—Fedor—told me? That the killings could have been staged as a threat, a message. What better way to deliver a threat than in person?"

"That would explain why they were shot with their own pistols," Kaz said. "The killer could then make a chilling threat; cooperate or die by your own weapon."

"You do have a clarity about what makes a productive threat, Baron," Sidorov said. "Quite an imagination."

"You don't want to know the kind of things I imagine, comrade," Kaz said, his tone as icy as the Siberian snow.

Big Mike was in his room, leg stretched out on the bed, paperback in hand.

"You guys think you can manage without me?" he said. "I'm going a little crazy here. Wouldn't mind a change of scenery."

"Bull told us," I said. "It is a good idea to locate Max, if you can do it on one foot."

"Check with the military police," Sidorov said. "He may already have gotten himself into trouble, if he didn't desert immediately."

"Think he would?" Big Mike asked.

"Max strikes me as the resourceful type," Sidorov said. "He has some status in the criminal world, but he may have lost that due to his cooperation with the authorities. The mere fact that he is in uniform is proof of that. But he managed to get out of the prison system and secure a posting here, rather than as a *frontoviki*. Then be sent to Tehran. Most fortunate."

"Which is to say suspicious," I said. "So be careful. When do you leave?"

"Bull's picking me up in ten," Big Mike said, checking his watch. "I'm glad you came by, didn't want to miss saying goodbye."

"Safe travels, my friend," Kaz said, clasping his hand. "We will wait to hear from you."

"Hey, you guys ought to be able to solve this thing toot sweet, now that you're not wasting time searching for me or carting over reading material," Big Mike said. "Here's the maps you left me. I couldn't come up with anything. And the book you wanted, Billy." *Tom Sawyer*, where I'd stashed Nikolin's order.

"I know you'll track him down," I said. I didn't bother telling Big Mike to rest up or take it easy. It was more important that he feel part of the team. And he wouldn't listen anyway.

Bull showed up a few minutes later. The paperwork was done, and Big Mike was approved on the manifest along with the other downed aircrew.

"It's been easier, now that General Belov assigned an air force officer to approve the manifests and check the cargo. Drozdov still hasn't gotten a replacement for Kopelev, otherwise it might have taken days," Bull told us.

"If there is an NKVD colonel coming for an inspection, he may bring his own man as a replacement, to report on Major Drozdov," Sidorov said. "It is how things are done."

"No wonder Drozdov's been on the touchy side," Bull said. "His boss is coming, and Belov is intruding into his domain. Military politics are bad enough, but NKVD politics are something else."

"Brutal," was all Sidorov had to say.

Big Mike hobbled out to the jeep with Bull, and we waved him off. Seeing him go should have made me glad. He'd been through a lot, and I'd rest easier knowing he'd been treated in an American hospital. But it felt like a bit of home went with him. Still, I was glad he was going back without a bombload over the Third Reich.

CHAPTER TWENTY-SIX

"WHAT SHALL WE do next?" Sidorov asked as we went back inside. "It will be some time before we hear of Maiya reaching Zolynia. Shall we look at those maps?"

"Why not?" I said. I unfolded the two maps and laid them out on my bunk.

"You did not get these at a Soviet bookstore," Sidorov said. "They look quite accurate."

"They're from the navigator on my B-17," I said. "This one is a spare. Here we are. Poltava, in Ukraine. To the west is the Dnieper River, which I crossed in the Po-2 on our way to bomb the Germans here, in Jedlicze."

"Almost a thousand kilometers east," Sidorov said.

"Right. Then about one hundred kilometers back west, here's Zolynia, where Nikolin was supposed to be. The front lines weren't far from there. Then to Kozova, where Big Mike and the others were held in the Military Medical Directorate. They'd bailed out about thirty miles north of there."

"What of the other map?" Kaz asked.

"Carter had this when he thought they might return via Tehran, but that wasn't in the cards. It shows this part of Russia all the way down to northern Iran," I said, tapping my finger on Tehran. "It even shows the rail lines headed north out of Iran into Ukraine. Probably a navigation aid."

"There is Tabriz," Kaz said, pointing to a spot near the Russian and Turkish borders. "I recall that was the destination for the crates in the warehouse. Khazar Brothers Shipping, I think." He looked to Sidorov for confirmation.

"Yes, that's correct. What could the OSS and the NKVD be shipping to Iran? Weapons, perhaps," Sidorov said.

"I figure those crates would be flown into Tehran," I said. "Then, what would be the most direct route to get them to Tabriz?"

"On a train," Kaz said. "The same train Max is on."

"Once a thief, always a *vor*," Sidorov said. "What could he have stolen?"

"Wait," I said. "Max didn't have access. How could he have packed those crates and got himself assigned to the railroad in Iran? It's too much."

"Unless he had help," Kaz said.

"Or, if he were forced into it," Sidorov said. "Or maybe he did the forcing. We have nothing but more questions."

"Let's take another look at the warehouse," I said. "Maybe we missed something on those crates."

It was a long shot in a case that was filled with long shots. Kaz and Sidorov agreed, so we went back to Operations and knocked on Black's door and asked him for the key.

"Sure, sure," he said, jumping up from his desk and hastily closing a file. "I just heard, the Bulgarian mission is on. Drozdov got the approval from Moscow."

"Congratulations," I said. "Who else is going besides you and Drozdov?"

"Hey, I said too much already. After all this time, I just couldn't believe it," Black said as he unlocked his file cabinet.

"We will not be interrupting the removal of your supplies?" Sidorov said. "I would hate to interfere with your preparations." He glanced at me, and we both wondered if Black would blow a fuse when he discovered he was missing a case of morphine.

"No, that hasn't started yet, don't worry," he said, handing over the keys. "But bring these right back, okay? I'd hate to lose them at this point."

"Don't worry Major, you haven't yet," I said. Sidorov coughed, and I didn't dare look at him.

Outside Black's office, I looked around for a *vannaya*. I asked Sidorov if he knew which way it was, and he pointed to the end of the corridor and said it was the last door on the right. I told them I'd be right back and headed down the hall.

It came to me as I opened the door. The thing Kaz had noticed in the restaurant.

Sidorov had gotten up from the table and walked straight to the stairway and went down to the restroom. He didn't look around, didn't ask, and from what I remembered, there was no sign.

He'd been there before. When? Unless everyone was lying about his stretch in the labor camps, it had to have been recently. It must have been the day Kaz had arrived, the day he'd spent recovering from his flight, or from the shock of seeing Sidorov. Okay, that answered *when*.

What about *why*?

I thought about that on the way back to the jeep. Unfortunately, Sidorov had commandeered the driver's seat again, and all further thoughts were of survival. It was only when he slammed on the brakes and swerved to a stop in front of the warehouse that I had a chance to whisper to Kaz, *I got it*.

Men were unloading supplies from a truck at the front door, a lot with American labels. Spools of telephone cable, cans of ham, salt, flour, radios, all of it just a fraction of what flowed from American factories and traveled halfway around the world to help defeat the Nazis. Boxes were marked with red crosses, but they all contained medical instruments. No morphine.

Upstairs, I unlocked the interior room, and switched on the lights.

Everything was there, just as it had been. Except for the crates bound for the Khazar Brothers. They were gone.

"I will check the truck," Sidorov said. "They may have already taken them."

"Go ahead, but they would have unloaded first, then loaded the crates," I said. "Ask them if they've taken anything out of here in the last few days."

"Damn," I said, setting my hands on my hips. "Now we don't even know when they were taken or what's in them."

"If they were flown out, there would be a manifest," Kaz said. "We can check with General Dawson. Tell me, what did you conclude about Sidorov?"

"That he'd been to the restaurant before," I said. "He was familiar with the layout. But what else did you come up with?"

"I did not speak Russian when I was in the bookstore, so I assume the staff thought I would not understand them," Kaz said. "After Sidorov left, the woman asked the manager if he thought the captain was satisfied. He replied that he hoped so, and that he didn't look forward to a third visit."

"What's his game?" I said.

"There seems to be only one possibility," Kaz said. "That he took it upon himself to follow up on your hunch about the bookstore and discovered useful information there. He then hid what he knew with a return trip under false pretenses. He'd obviously warned the manager to play along."

"Why not just tell you he'd gone and found nothing?"

"He can tell I don't trust him," Kaz said. "This way he proves to both of us that the bookstore is a dead end. And gets himself a second decent meal. The soup was very good."

"Nothing in the truck," Sidorov said, entering the room. "Anything new in here?"

"No," I said, walking around as if we'd been surveying the place. "Same number of morphine cases and all the other stuff looks untouched."

"Based on where the bodies were found, there does seem to be ample room for four people," Kaz said, moving around to the front of the shelves and aiming his hand downward. "The two victims were made to kneel, after being relieved of their pistols. Two shots." His hand jerked twice, simulating the handgun's recoil. Then he turned and looked at Sidorov, his hand aimed at his chest. "Wouldn't you agree, Captain?"

"Yes, I would," Sidorov said. He locked eyes with Kaz as he walked past him and knelt where the bodies had been. "I would have made the accomplice holster the pistols on the dead men. It would cement the relationship."

"Very good," Kaz said. He took a step and handed over two imaginary pistols. Then he drew his Webley.

"Wait a minute, Kaz," I said.

"No, no," Sidorov said. "This is excellent. We must recreate the crime. Of course, this would be a tricky moment. The witness is stunned at what he saw and accepts the weapons meekly. But the killer must maintain control and momentum, while keeping his subject compliant. So, with a gun at my head, I replace each victim's pistol." He waited a second, daring Kaz to do just that.

He did. He placed his thumb on the hammer as if to cock it.

Sidorov raised an eyebrow. He mimed placing two pistols on the imaginary corpses and then slowly rose, his hands out at his sides.

"I am in your power," he said, Kaz's Webley not a foot from his head.

I wondered what would happen next. Kaz's revolver did not waver.

"You are now complicit," Kaz said, finally holstering his Webley. "The unknown subject, I mean."

"Of course," Sidorov said. "That was an impressive demonstration. The killer fired the shots, but his companion was likely the one with blood on his hands." He made a washing motion with his hands, turning away from Kaz.

"That bound him to the killer," I said. "It explains a lot."

"We may assume Lieutenant Kopelev stumbled across something he was not meant to see," Sidorov said.

"And Sergeant Morris?" I asked.

"Perhaps he refused to go along with the scheme Kopelev discovered," Kaz said, his hand still resting on the butt of his revolver.

"Morris also spoke some Russian," Sidorov said, walking along a shelf stacked high with explosives. "He could have overheard something incriminating. Something that cost him his life. Eavesdropping can be dangerous."

"Or the killer wanted something from him," I said, wondering if Sidorov was dropping a heavy-handed hint. "Something he didn't want to do. Or a trade he didn't want to make. He was in the souvenir business, small-time black market stuff."

"Morris was part of the air transport ground crew, was he not?" Kaz said. "He may have been pressured to smuggle something aboard one of the C-47s."

"But the manifests and the actual aircraft are checked by NKVD," Sidorov said. "At least they were until recently. It would be quite difficult. Remember, it was Kopelev who discovered the smuggled Polish refugee aboard one of the transport aircraft."

"What happened to him?" Kaz asked.

"He was removed and taken away. You can guess what came next," Sidorov said. "Now, are we done with our playacting here?"

"I'm done," I said. "Let's see if we can track down the manifest."

We locked up and left in silence, the spaces between us filled with coiled tension and the hint of ready violence. I knew Kaz was on edge, unhappy with this forced arrangement. But this was the first time I'd seen Sidorov's mask crack and reveal anything other than his cooperative and collegial persona.

I had to remember Sidorov was only here to place the guilt on an American, or, at a minimum, deflect any blame away from a Russian. His life depended on it.

"Kiril, would you mind checking with Doctor Mametova at the hospital?" I asked as we got into the jeep. "I'm curious if she's gotten any morphine shipments in yet."

"I will ask," Sidorov said as we started the short drive to Operations. At the end of the runway sat two trucks, more of the flatbeds with .50 machine guns. I hadn't seen any real antiaircraft weapons, only machine guns manned by Russians. Every other airbase I'd been on had heavy stuff in sandbagged emplacements. "Any reason why you think she would?"

"No shortage lasts forever," I said. "Meet us in Bull's office, and we'll let you know what we found out about the manifest. And we can check on Nikolin's flight back."

"Do you think we should split up?" Kaz asked as I pulled in at Operations. "I wouldn't want Captain Sidorov to shoulder the burden alone."

"Do not worry on my account, Baron," Sidorov said, swinging his legs out of the jeep. "As sure as I am that you've kept no secrets from me, I shall keep none from you."

"Jesus, Kaz," I whispered as we took the steps into the building. "I thought for a minute back there you were going to plug him. What's got into you?"

"I am poking a stick and enjoying the response. Soon we will have to put Sidorov to the test and see what side he is on," Kaz said.

"He's on the side that will keep him out of the labor camp," I said. "Did he tell you about the road of bones?"

"Yes, in some detail. He is an enemy of my people as well as a man who tried to do me harm. His masters will enslave Poland just as the Germans did. I shed no tears over his Siberian sojourn."

"You don't know that's true," I said. "The Brits and Americans can't let that happen, not after your people have fought so hard."

"Billy, there was a time when your naivete was charming," Kaz said, stopping outside Bull's door. "But after more than two years of war and all we have endured, surely it is time to leave it behind. I am a realist. Soviet tanks are now crossing into Poland. They will not leave. This I know. You should as well."

"You're right, Kaz, I should. I'm sorry Harding sent you here," I said.

"He told me I could decline," Kaz said. "Perhaps I should have. I wanted to learn more about my next enemy, but for the most part, he is much like my old enemy. I suppose it was a trip for biscuits, yes?"

I smiled. It was one of the first bits of American slang I'd taught Kaz. A meaningless journey.

"Come on, let's check on the manifests," I said. It was hard to keep a grin on my face, but I did my best.

"I've got duplicates on file," Bull said when we explained what we were after. "Months of them."

"I'd say the last four days, including Big Mike's flight," I said. He handed over today's manifest and pulled a thick file from his desk drawer. It included a diplomatic pouch from Moscow, nothing else in terms of cargo.

"That was a scheduled flight from our Military Mission in Moscow,"

Bull said. "It refueled here, carrying mostly officers being rotated out. Big Mike should be over the Caucasus Mountains right about now."

"Here," Kaz said. "Yesterday, the manifest shows mostly cargo. Including five cases, measuring four feet by two by two, destined for Khazar Brothers Shipping in Tabriz, Iran. Designated as classified."

"Right," Bull said, checking the sheets. "Yesterday afternoon, that flight was mainly cargo. Engine parts for repair in our shops at the Tehran airbase. A couple of men who had been injured and sent out for treatment. Plus these cases."

"Signed for by Major Preston Black of the OSS," I said.

"Five cases," Kaz said. "Billy, you said there were three."

"Right," I said. "We need to talk to Black."

"You can talk to him, but it won't do any good," Bull said. "He's got top secret security clearance for this mission, whatever it is."

"Bulgaria? Everybody knows about that. He told us it was just approved by Drozdov's bosses," I said.

"He's been flapping his gums about Bulgaria for a while, complaining that Moscow was withholding the go-ahead," Bull said. "If they've given him the green light, it is news to me. If this shipment has anything to do with Bulgaria, it's news to me. OSS operates in its own world, just like the NKVD. Black doesn't report to me any more than Drozdov reports to Belov."

"Has Major Black shipped other items to Tehran?" Kaz asked, taking a seat in front of Bull's desk and crossing his legs, shaking out a crease in his finely tailored trousers.

"He's gotten plenty in from Tehran," Bull said. "He sent back a couple of defective radios about a month ago, I remember that. But I wouldn't know what else he's sent."

"You're saying you don't know what Black sends to Iran?" I asked.

"Correct. He has clearance from the top to conduct his mission as he sees fit," Bull said. "Let me see that file, I'll see if I can spot anything else." I handed over the file and he flicked through the papers. "Here you go, this one stands out. A single crate, same dimensions as the ones yesterday. Hey, to the same place. Khazar Brothers Shipping in Tabriz, six weeks ago."

Six weeks ago? That was unexpected. It didn't make sense, although a few other things were starting to.

"Tabriz," I said. I walked over to a large wall map of the region. "That's on the rail line that a lot of Lend-Lease supplies come into Russia on."

"Yes," Kaz said. "Most of the Persian Corridor supplies come in by sea, through Bandar Shahpur on the Persian Gulf. Then by rail north through Tabriz, although some supplies are sent to ports on the Caspian Sea."

"Right," I said, tapping my finger on the map. "But if Black is shipping materials to Tabriz, there has to be another destination. It makes no sense to fly them to Tehran and then send them back to Russia by train."

"Perhaps Khazar Brothers Shipping is a conduit for materials destined for the Bulgarian operation," Kaz suggested, tracing his finger along the rail line leading to Tabriz. "After all, Tabriz is near the eastern Turkish border. Bulgaria is on Turkey's western border."

"Since Turkey is neutral, they could be planning a route in that way," Bull said. "Through Istanbul. At this point in the war, Turkey might even cooperate, unofficially. The Turks wouldn't mind favoring the winning side, and they might want a claim to some Bulgarian territory once the shooting's over."

"It would be interesting to find out something about this shipping firm," Kaz said. "Who are the Khazar brothers and are they connected with the OSS or the NKVD?"

"Anybody we can ask in Tehran, Bull? Maybe outside of channels so we don't get Wild Bill Donovan too upset?" General Donovan was the head of the Office of Strategic Services and vehemently defended his organization's secrecy. He wouldn't like the army checking into his operations one damn bit.

"I have a friend in the Provost Marshal General's Office in Tehran," Bull said. "I can ask him if Army CID has any dope on them, or contacts with Iranian police who might know."

"Great," I said. We'd had a few run-ins with the Army's Criminal Investigation Division. They weren't the most cooperative bunch, but this was right up their alley. "Tell him it's about black-market smug-gling if he asks. CID will eat that up."

"I'll get a radio message out," Bull said. "But do you have any actual evidence this is connected to the murders?"

"Concrete evidence? No," I said.

"Well, I'll send the message," Bull said, heading for the door. "Make yourselves at home. I'll check on Nikolin's flight too."

"What about Big Mike?" I asked, tapping my finger against my lips and staring at the map, willing myself to make sense of all this.

"He hasn't even landed yet," Bull said, checking his watch. "Anything else, Captain Boyle?"

"Sorry, General Dawson," I said, turning and standing straight enough that it might have looked like attention. "I appreciate it, sir."

"Jesus, Billy, don't get carried away," he said, and stalked off.

CHAPTER TWENTY-SEVEN

"I UNDERSTAND WE have no actual evidence," Kaz said, still studying the wall map. "But what do you have in mind?"

"I think it's all about proximity," I said, tracing my finger on the map along a line from Poltava to Tehran to Tabriz and points beyond. "Proximity to the OSS/NKVD storeroom in the warehouse. Proximity to Tehran and Tabriz. And proximity to power, the kind that stops at nothing to achieve its goal."

"What goal?" Kaz asked, his hands akimbo, staring at the map.

"The same goal Punchy Killeen had," I said. "To fill a vacuum."

"If I had to hazard a guess, I would conjecture Punchy is from Boston," Kaz said, returning to his chair and settling in. "And you have a story about him."

"Just so happens you're right," I said, taking my seat. "Back when I was still a cop in Boston, walking the beat along the Inner Harbor, a punk named Punchy Killeen made his big move. Punchy had been part of the Gustin Gang, an Irish mob that got hit hard by the Italians and busted up."

"I recall you have mentioned them," Kaz said. "Weren't they shot under a flag of truce?"

"Not exactly, but close enough. Guy from the North End by the name of Joe Lombardo offered a sit-down to Frank Wallace and his number two man. In the crime world, that is like a flag of truce. A sit-down means no shooting and you try to talk things out. Well, Joe didn't play by the rules, and he had Frank and the other guy killed.

That broke up the Gustin Gang and put the North End Italians in the driver's seat. But guys like Punchy, they kept at their rackets and tried to not draw any attention to themselves. No one likes a gang war, it's bad for business."

"Wouldn't the police like it?" Kaz asked. "Fewer criminals all-around, I would think."

"Like I said, it's bad for business. All-around. Dead gangsters don't make payoffs. But that's not the point. Punchy had a piece of the action down at the docks. Once the war started, he noticed the supply of drugs was drying up. With the Germans sinking ships bound for the States, and the usual routes through the Mediterranean disrupted, heroin was getting harder and harder to come by."

"Ah, Marseilles," Kaz said. "The port in southern France which sees much of the drug flow from the Middle East."

"Correction. It saw drugs come through," I said. "As soon as the shooting war started, especially with the Germans and the Italians tearing up North Africa and the Mediterranean Sea, sources dried up."

"So, starting in the spring of 1940, there was a shortage of drugs, especially heroin, being brought into the United States," Kaz said.

"Right. Punchy had a connection in Mexico and started importing cocaine. Lots of it. He figured that the heroin wouldn't make a come-back until the war was over, and he could make a killing substituting coke for smack. It wasn't for everyone, since coke is a stimulant, but there was enough demand that he was riding high for a while," I said. "So to speak."

"Only for a while?" Kaz asked.

"Right. Then the North End guys tumbled to what was happening and started gunning for Punchy's boys. A few bodies were left in the streets until both sides realized they were only drawing attention to themselves. The North End gang asked for a sit-down," I said. "Punchy was smart enough not to trust them and planned to skip town with his money and his cocaine."

"Planned to? What happened?" Kaz asked.

"He had a girlfriend. Molly the Moll, they called her. Molly was pretty sharp. She saw what was coming and got out of town ahead of

Punchy," I said. "She took Punchy's stash of coke and cash with her. Neither of them was ever heard from again. People said Molly went to California. Others said Punchy's destination was the bottom of Boston Harbor. In short order the Mexican connection was reestablished, with the Italians from the North End in charge."

"Poor Punchy," Kaz said, giving a casual flick of the wrist to signify Punchy's departure. "But what does this have to do with two murders in Poltava?"

"Nature hates a vacuum, isn't that the saying?"

"Abhors," Kaz said. "Aristotle said nature abhors a vacuum."

"He knew what he was talking about. So did Punchy, and so did our killer." The random pieces of this investigation were starting to come together, but I was still flummoxed by the single shipment six weeks ago. If my suspicions were correct, that one didn't fit the pattern. I went to Bull's desk and looked at the manifest he'd found it on.

One wooden crate, three feet by two by one. Machine parts, supposedly.

Only it hadn't been signed for by Major Preston Black.

The name was Sergeant Jack Morris.

"Look," I said, handing the sheet to Kaz.

"My God, you were right," Kaz said. "Proximity. Sergeant Morris was part of this. As one of the air transport ground crew, he could sign for materials to be added to the manifest."

"He did, and a few weeks later he was killed," I said.

"Who was killed?" Sidorov asked, entering the office.

"Morris," I said quickly. "Doctor Mametova has morphine now, doesn't she?"

"Yes, she does," Sidorov said. "How did you know?"

"Indeed, Billy, how did you jump to that conclusion?" Kaz asked.

"The real question is, how did the opium harvested in the Kyrgyz province end up in a Poltava warehouse under OSS and NKVD jurisdiction? I'll admit, it is a bit of a jump, but all the pieces fit, finally. It's the only theory that works any way you look at it."

"Maiya's aircraft is inbound, with Nikolin aboard," Bull said, popping his head in. "They're about ten minutes out, and I sent the message to CID in Tehran, ought to hear back in a couple of hours."

"Let's go greet Lieutenant Nikolin," I said. "I'd like to be sure he's in one piece."

"But wait, what about your conclusion?" Kaz asked.

"Time for that later, let's get to the airstrip," I said. I wasn't sure what Nikolin would say, but I wanted to be there with Sidorov and Kaz as translators before anyone gave him the official party line. "Hurry!"

I hustled down the corridor, taking a second to glance into Black's office. No sign of him. I started the jeep as Sidorov and Kaz caught up with me, whispering to each other as they got in. It was usually the cold shoulder or veiled sarcasm between those two, so I was glad to see them kibitzing, even if it was probably about how crazy I was acting.

"Billy, are you saying Morris was involved with drug smuggling?" Kaz said, glancing back at Sidorov.

"No, not really," I said. "But he did get in over his head. Look, there's Maiya's plane."

The twin-engine Yak-6 banked overhead, lining up for its approach. I took the roadway to the hangar at the end of the runway. General Belov and Major Drozdov were already there, standing by a staff car. Two soldiers, each with a PPSh-41 slung across their chest, stood to the side. An honor guard to welcome Nikolin home, or was daddy there to threaten him?

"Have you come to welcome the prodigal son home?" Drozdov said, waving his hand in greeting. He was a lot cheerier than the last time I saw him.

"It is more like Daniel returning from the lion's den," Kaz said. "But I understand you may not be overly familiar with Bible stories. Opiate of the masses and all that." Kaz kept a straight face. I barely managed it.

"Stalin has reopened churches," Drozdov said, speaking loudly as the aircraft taxied to a halt near us. "The Russian Orthodox Church is an ally in the fight against fascism. I am a proud atheist, but I recognize the need for fairy tales to ease the burden of our times." He managed to keep a straight face himself as he spouted the party line.

Sidorov stepped forward, saluted General Belov, speaking to him in Russian. Drozdov joined in and their discussion grew heated, and louder, when the pilot cut the engines.

"Sidorov requested an immediate interview with Lieutenant Nikolin," Kaz translated for me. "Belov deferred to Drozdov, since Nikolin is NKVD. Drozdov at first objected, saying he had arranged a medical checkup for Nikolin. Then they agreed we could accompany Lieutenant Nikolin to the hospital and speak with him on the way."

"Doesn't sound like anyone's trying to keep him from us," I said.

"No. More of jurisdictional squabble," Kaz said. The aircraft door opened and Maiya stepped out, her flying goggles on her forehead and a smile on her face. She reached up to help Nikolin down. His uniform was soiled and dirty except for the white sling that held his left arm.

General Belov went forward and gave Nikolin a Russian bear hug, clapping him on the shoulders without a thought of his injury. Nikolin looked startled but managed a salute as Belov spoke. Drozdov got in his handshake as well, along with a few words. Nikolin flinched at first, then drew himself up straight and gripped the major's hand firmly. He was smart enough to know there was a certain way to act in this situation. Follow the lead of the brass and don't offend anyone.

"Belov says he is pleased Nikolin is returned to duty and tells him he should be proud of his wound. Drozdov told him the penal company was a mistake, a lazy clerk getting the paperwork wrong, and that he only demoted him to save him from a worse fate," Kaz said.

"Do you think Nikolin bought it?" I asked.

"There are worse fates than the tramplers, I am sorry to say," Sidorov said. "So yes, I think the young lieutenant believes him, because he must. After all, as an NKVD officer, he knows of other terrible fates."

As I approached Nikolin, Belov was busy chatting with Maiya, all smiles. The pilot stood by himself, and I gave Kaz a nudge. He got the message and began speaking with the pilot, pointing to the Yak-6 as if he was interested in it.

Nikolin grasped my hand and unleashed a torrent of Russian. His eyes brimmed with tears, and I could tell he was thanking me for his release. His skin was pale, grime from the battlefield still scored into his face and hands. Sidorov spoke to him in soothing tones, pointing to our jeep.

"I told him we will take him to the hospital to be checked and cleaned up," Sidorov said. "And that we have a few questions to ask on the way. He thanks you. Profusely."

"Please tell him it was Major Drozdov's order that set him free," I said, watching Nikolin's eyes. Would he express surprise? No, his reaction was flat. Nothing.

"Captain Boyle, I must thank you," Maiya said, joining us and laying a gentle hand on Nikolin's good arm. "Not only did you succeed in freeing Lieutenant Nikolin, I was able to fly the entire way back. And land! Perhaps now General Belov will let me join the Night Witches."

"I'm glad you got to fly, Maiya," I said. "But I'm surprised Major Black isn't here to welcome you home and celebrate your flight."

"I am sure the major's duties are more important than a routine flight," Maiya said, even as her eyes flitted about the hangar, looking for someone special. There were a lot of straight faces among this small group.

"Congratulations, Maiya," Sidorov said, taking Nikolin by the arm. "But we must get our friend to the hospital. Doctor Mametova is waiting for him. As is a much-needed bath."

Kaz detached himself from the pilot and helped ease Nikolin into the passenger seat.

"What happened to your shoulder?" I asked as I started the jeep, pointing to his sling. Sidorov handled the translation and reported that the penal company had been shelled last night, adding that Nikolin said he'd now paid his blood debt.

"Sad," Kaz mused from the back seat. "He had no debt to pay. He was delivered to the tramplers by error or design, but through no fault of his own. Yet he believes he must be at fault."

"Who else could it be?" Sidorov said. "The Party cannot be in error. Stalin does not make mistakes. Therefore, the burden falls on each believer who finds himself sent to a labor camp or to the NKVD cells. They search and search until they find the flaw in themselves that led them to their fate. To admit the Party was wrong would destroy the entire tissue of lies that comprises their very soul. Yes, it is very sad. But in Soviet Russia, it cannot be otherwise."

Kaz was silent. I wondered if Sidorov's words had penetrated his hatred for the Soviets, and what they'd done to his nation. In my book, Sidorov was a criminal, but also a victim. I pitied him. But I doubt Kaz did. It's hard to pity a man you hate for murdering your countrymen.

I parked in front of the hospital and turned to Nikolin.

"Tell us about the night you were sent away," I said. "About being summoned to see Belov." Sidorov rattled off the translation. As I listened to Nikolin respond, I was struck by the look on his face. It was odd, as if he didn't understand the question.

"He says he was not summoned by General Belov," Sidorov said. "He left his post to find Major Drozdov, to be asked to be relieved on account of illness. The major was angry with him and confined him to quarters. Later that night Drozdov returned and demoted him, telling him he was being transferred for his own good. He was shocked when he ended up in the penal company. He did not think Drozdov intended that."

"But that is not how it happened," Kaz said.

"It's not what he told me," I said, thinking about the order with Belov's signature still in my pocket. It wouldn't do any good to confront Nikolin with it. Somehow, he'd been told what to say. No sane man would risk a return to the minefields by changing his story. "Let's take him inside."

"You are sure?" Kaz asked. I nodded yes, smiled at Nikolin, and got out to lend him a hand. At least he had the good grace to look ashamed.

We walked Nikolin inside, where Doctor Mametova was waiting.

"One last question," I said. "Ask him if he knew the *narkoman* who overdosed."

As Sidorov translated, I saw a different look on Nikolin's face, not the feigned surprise that he showed about Belov's order, but a simple agreement.

"Yes, he knew Lieutenant Mishkin," Sidorov said. "He was troubled. There were rumors of drug use, but he never saw Mishkin take anything. Other than a good deal of vodka."

"He wasn't surprised when Mishkin died?" I asked. Nikolin shook his head.

"No," Sidorov said. "He thought he would come to a bad end, one way or the other. Mishkin's father was a high-ranking member of the *nomenklatura* and got him out of trouble several times. They were told not to speak of it, since Mishkin had brought disgrace upon himself, his father, and the NKVD. Very bad."

"Thanks," I said to Nikolin, who smiled and gave himself over to Doctor Mametova and her nurses, who were already stripping him of his filthy uniform and escorting him into a ward.

We headed back to the jeep, running into Drozdov as we left the building.

"Did you have enough time with Lieutenant Nikolin?" Drozdov asked. "You may see him again once Doctor Mametova is done. He will be kept in the hospital overnight so his wound can be tended."

"No, it's fine, Major. It was just as you said. He must have been confused before," I said.

"I am sure. The front is confusing enough, but to be in a penal detachment can be disorienting. Is that not right, Captain Sidorov?" Drozdov said as he stood square in our path.

"Indeed. I wonder why Lieutenant Mishkin was never sent to a penal company? Doctor Mametova told us he likely overdosed on heroin. There must have been signs. Is that not right, Major Drozdov?" Sidorov said, echoing Drozdov's own threatening words.

"Things are not always as they seem. You would be good to remember that. All of you. Well, except for Captain Boyle. He is well connected, as they say. Related to the great General Eisenhower. But you, Sidorov, could be returned to the camps at the snap of a finger," Drozdov said. He snapped his fingers as he turned his gaze to Kaz. "And you, *Baron* Kazimierz, any member of the degenerate aristocracy in a British uniform should tread carefully when in the Soviet Union."

"I understand it must be difficult to maintain good manners when hosting your allies," Kaz said, "especially when you have a superior officer due for an inspection. It must be trying."

"I am only giving advice," Drozdov said, inclining his head slightly as if he considered an actual apology, then decided against it. "This is not the West. There can be consequences for libeling the State. Now, I must ensure Lieutenant Nikolin receives the best of care. Good evening."

"I don't know what we learned," Kaz said. "But I do know two things. I want to hear your theory, Billy, and I want to eat. The mess hall is not the Cosmos Hotel, but it will do."

"Okay," I said. "Let's get some food, and I'll tell you both a story. And we did learn something from all this. It was important that Nikolin tell his story. The story that leaves out anything suspicious about Belov or Drozdov's actions."

"Which means, either you were lying," Sidorov said, "or someone got to Nikolin and explained what was expected of him. Sorry, but I am simply stating the facts. I do not believe you lied, at least not purposefully."

"Fair enough," I said, starting the jeep. "Kaz, what did you get from the pilot?"

"Nikolin was waiting for them at the airport, accompanied by an older fellow, one Fedor Popov, who told the pilot he was sad to see a Russian boy turned over to the imperialists. They brought him aboard and flew straight back. They were on the ground approximately ten minutes."

"Fedor was my translator," I said, driving toward the mess hall. "A former professor who survived a stint with the tramplers and was a big help to me. He was also smart enough to put on a good show once he had to associate with an American."

"A smart man," Kaz said. "What about . . .?" He nodded to my jacket pocket, remembering what I hadn't told Sidorov.

"I have the order Belov sent Nikolin," I said.

"Cunning of you to withhold it," Sidorov said. "But you know that to produce it now would sign Nikolin's death sentence."

"I do," I said, parking close to the mess hall. But not too close. "Which is why I won't use it. But now that I've come clean, it's your turn, Captain Sidorov. Tell us what you learned at the bookstore. The first time you went there."

CHAPTER TWENTY-EIGHT

I TURNED TOWARD Sidorov. My hand rested on my holstered pistol. The fading sun lit his face, the rays of western light illuminating his fear. Kaz leaned forward from the rear of the jeep, and I heard the brush of his Webley against the leather holster. Then the *clack* when he cocked it. This time he wasn't playing.

"Oh my God, Major Drozdov," Kaz said, rehearsing his sad story. "We were comparing sidearms, the Russian, English, and American models. I don't know what happened. Mine went off suddenly."

"A terrible accident," I said. "I always thought the Webley was a bit delicate."

"What are you doing?" Sidorov said. "Is this more playacting? It is not amusing."

"Keep your hands on your lap," I said as he began to slide his right hand to his side. I glanced around. Several uniformed figures strolled into the mess hall, ignoring us, anxious to get out of the cold. "We know you went to the bookstore before we made the trip together. What did you find?"

"And why the charade?" Kaz asked. "Why go again?"

"All right," Sidorov said, raising his hands carefully, as befitted a guy looking at two pistols. "Yes, I did go and ask about Kopelev's purchases. I did discover he had a keen interest in books with maps of the Black Sea. Turkey, Iran, and the surrounding area especially."

"You said maps were hard to come by. And deliberately inaccurate," I said.

"Yes. Actual maps are treated as state secrets. But those in books are not controlled in the same way, especially not the older editions. Volumes on geography and customs of other nations, for instance. That is what Kopelev was searching for."

"Why keep that from us?" Kaz asked.

"I was desperate to hide anything that would cast suspicion on a Russian," Sidorov said, turning his head to face Kaz. "As I told Billy when he first arrived, the authorities want an American to be found guilty. If not, I will be sent back to the camps."

"That is a problem entirely of your own making," Kaz said. "But you found precious little actual evidence other than Lieutenant Kopelev's interest in geography."

"Shipping and rail lines in particular," Sidorov said. "He had asked the manager to watch for any books on the subject."

"You thought this information would not be useful in bringing charges against an American?" Kaz said, thrusting his revolver between the seats and tapping Sidorov on the elbow. "The truth, for once."

"No, not what I learned at the bookstore about Kopelev," Sidorov said. "It was the information I gleaned at the Cosmos Hotel that worried me. Shall we dispense with pistols at sunset and lay all our cards on the table, as the Americans say?"

Kaz uncocked his revolver and holstered it, Sidorov letting out a sigh at the sound of metal on leather. I moved my hand off my holster.

Bull walked up to the mess hall entrance, accompanied by Major Black and a couple of other officers. I waved as they went in, as if everything was normal, while eyeing Black and figuring how to approach him.

When I was done with Sidorov.

"Okay, let's go in," I said. "We'll have a nice calm chat."

"A productive chat," Kaz said. "Otherwise I may lodge a complaint with General Belov about how unhelpful you are. Perhaps we will request a new Soviet investigator. Then what will become of you, Captain Sidorov?"

"Do that and Belov will turn to Drozdov for advice, since this is an NKVD matter," Sidorov said, getting out of the jeep and brushing off his uniform, as if getting rid of the unpleasantness clinging to it. "And we know how he feels about you, Lieutenant."

"Let's all shut up and get some food," I said, losing my patience along with my appetite as the smell of boiled cabbage wafted out of the mess hall.

We secured our food, a bottle of vodka, and a small table off in a corner. Our plates were heaped with ham, cabbage, potatoes, and carrots, but no one touched the food. Sidorov poured our drinks, took a slug, and set the glass down with a thud.

"I went to the Cosmos to ask about Lieutenant Mishkin," he said, turning the glass in his hand as he looked at us. "Is that how you knew, when I went directly to the facilities?"

"Yes," Kaz said. "And I overheard the bookstore manager talking about your previous visit. They obviously assumed I did not speak Russian."

"Ah, I see. Well, I had asked more questions about Mishkin the day you arrived, Baron. I heard he bought drugs at the hotel and thought it worthwhile to follow up. The Cosmos is not only known for prostitutes, but for illicit drugs as well, although the latter is much harder to obtain than the former."

"What kind of drugs?" I asked.

"Cannabis is the most common," Sidorov said. "It is brought up from the Caucasus and is easily available. Amphetamines, usually stolen from the military. Some heroin, which is what Mishkin wanted."

"Is that where he got it?" I asked, taking a drink. The warm glow in my stomach began to make the cabbage look good.

"No," Sidorov said. "Mishkin had purchased heroin there before, but my contact, who was also my waiter, said his source had been shut down completely."

"You are certain?" Kaz asked, trimming the fat off his slab of ham.

"Quite certain. I traded American cigarettes for information. They make an excellent and highly valued currency," Sidorov said, draining his glass.

"Okay, so why didn't you share this tidbit?" I asked.

"Because it does not implicate an American," he said. "It only highlights the fact that one NKVD officer was a *narkoman* and another was gathering what could be construed as state secrets. Hardly information Moscow wants to come out of this investigation."

"Kopelev was looking for books, for God's sake," I said. "How the hell do you get state secrets from books published in Russia?"

"Billy, I must admit Captain Sidorov has a point," Kaz said. "However illogical, Stalin's government could see these facts as disloyalty to the Soviet Union on the captain's part."

"Which by its nature, would be an illegal act," Sidorov said. "Making me an enemy of the people. Which is why I did not tell either of you. Perhaps I would have, if I thought it had any bearing on the case, but I saw none."

"In a real investigation, you don't rule anything out," I said. "Even if it doesn't seem to have any bearing on the crime. We need all the pieces of the puzzle, even the unimportant ones around the edges. Is there anything else you haven't told us?"

"Other than the meat dumplings were excellent, no," Sidorov said. "Does that satisfy you? Are we friends again? Or at least allies, I hope."

"Allies, perhaps," Kaz said, eyeing Sidorov before spearing a potato. "Which means you should explain the order you've held back, Billy."

"I'll show it to you later," I told Sidorov. "I thought it might be proof of Belov's involvement and I wanted to confront Max with it, first of all. But he's gone, and now Nikolin has been forced to change his story."

"We know what would happen to Nikolin if you produced that document," Sidorov said. "He would be an inconvenience, a pawn to be eliminated."

"I'll hold off for now," I said. I tried the ham, which was salty. "I don't really know how it would help us at this point anyway."

"Perhaps we should determine if it is a forgery or not," Kaz suggested. "That may give us a clue as to General Belov's part in all this."

"Maiya," Sidorov said, settling into his food and talking around a mouthful of ham. "She works in his office and should know his signature. You could show it to her."

"Think she can be trusted?" I said.

"To a degree, yes. She is carrying on a relationship with Major

Black. Undoubtedly, she reports to Drozdov any important information she gleans," Sidorov said. "Drozdov would have approached her once he learned of their affair and made it clear what he expected."

"You're saying I should ask without Drozdov's knowing."

"Exactly. As a Soviet soldier involved romantically with a Westerner, she needs to be careful. If it became an issue, she would be forced to denounce you. Having a military order in your possession is probably a crime, now that I think of it," Sidorov said. "So many things are."

"I agree," Kaz said. "It could be dangerous for her, but we need to know if it is a forgery or not. I am sure you can approach her quietly and get her opinion. Now, it is time for you to explain your theory."

"I will," I said, spotting someone getting up from another table. "In a minute, be right back."

It was the copilot I'd seen this morning, the shell-shocked lieutenant covered in his crewmate's blood. He looked different all cleaned up, but he was easy to recognize. Tall and thin, with thick blond hair. The only thing different was how casually he moved and how easily a smile came to his lips, as if this were a different man altogether.

"Lieutenant," I said, intercepting him as he made for the door. "We talked this morning at the airstrip. I wanted to see how you're doing."

"Sorry, Captain, I don't recall," he said, studying me with steady blue eyes. "Have we met?"

"You were watching the rest of the B-17s land," I said, checking my memory and his face. Yep, this was the guy. "Your crew had been shot up, and you told me about the apartment building in the Bronx with all the soldiers. Guys taking college classes."

"Sorry, Captain, you've got me mixed up with someone else. Have a good evening, sir." With that, he donned his crush cap and left the mess hall. Watching him, I felt a hand on my shoulder.

"Captain, he's been like that since debriefing," said a first lieutenant. "We lost three men, all shot up bad. Real bad. I sent him back to check on the waist gunners, and it did something to him. He won't even admit they're dead, says everything's just fine. I don't know what to do. I can't count on a guy in the copilot's seat if he's cracked up, ya know?"

"Yeah, I know. Get him checked out. They can fly him to Tehran if you don't want him on a mission," I said.

"His first mission. His first fucking mission," he said, wandering off, almost as rattled as his copilot. It's hard to see the horrible shredding of human flesh in battle. It's also tough to watch the human mind shut down and seal off those horrible memories, leaving a frail version of a human being where once there was a whole man. More frightening than flak.

"Someone you know?" Kaz said as I sat down.

"Someone who doesn't know himself anymore," I said, and then waved off the question forming on his lips. "Never mind." I poured myself a stiff dose, drank, and cursed this goddamn war.

"Lieutenant Mishkin," I said, getting back to the case. "I didn't know his name until today, but there was something wrong with that story. Things didn't add up."

"The Communist Party will never admit to it, but we have many *narkomen* in our nation," Sidorov said. "For those who wish to escape from the Soviet state, it may be the only route."

"Yeah, I know. There's always a way for drugs to find their way to people who have a need," I said. "There's money to be made and the customers have no one to complain to about the price."

"Capitalism," Sidorov said.

"Exactly," I said. "Supply and demand."

"Are we back to Punchy and his Boston drug enterprise?" Kaz asked.

"Not yet," I said. "At first, I was surprised that it was an NKVD officer who had overdosed. Especially one who had been assigned to a joint Soviet-American airbase."

"Ah, but we are back to Caesar's wife," Kaz said, smiling as he took a drink.

"Right. What are the chances an NKVD officer with a drug problem would be assigned to a high-profile post, especially one where he'd be expected to work with Americans?"

"If he used heroin and had a steady supply, he could have kept it a secret," Sidorov said, without a lot of enthusiasm. "He could have been using a drug dealer as an informant. Or bribing him with the threat of arrest."

"Seriously, Kiril," I said. "The way everyone in the Soviet Union watches everyone else, how realistic is that?"

"Yes, I must agree," he said. "Everyone who was posted to this base had to be thoroughly vetted. The Kremlin would take no chances when it came to working directly with our allies. Caesar's wife would be the cardinal rule. That, and total loyalty."

"We have to ask ourselves then, how did Mishkin get here, and did he have any role in the murders?" I said.

"He overdosed before the murders, Billy," Kaz said.

"Exactly," I said. "What does that tell you?"

"That he found a supply," Sidorov said. "Although my contact at the Cosmos Hotel said there had been no heroin for months."

"Okay, so let's put a few things together. Mishkin had access to heroin. There was a widespread shortage of morphine, which is now over. Sergeant Morris signed for one shipment to the Khazar Brothers in Iran. Morris was into small-time black market trading, but from everything we learned, he wasn't a real criminal type," I said.

"Everyone agreed about Morris," Sidorov said, nodding. "He was well-liked by the Russians he met because he tried to speak the language. Unusual."

"Now we have Lieutenant Kopelev," I said. "A dedicated Communist. A reader and thinker. As the officer responsible for approving flight manifests, he had routine contact with Morris."

"A reader, and a stickler for the rules," Kaz said, absentmindedly tapping his finger on his chin. "A fellow with an eye for maps, who ended up dead."

"We can assume he stumbled across something that he shouldn't have," Sidorov said. "Involving the shipment to Iran? Drugs? The black market?"

"Put it all together," I said. "The morphine drought. Mishkin's overdose. Maps of the Black Sea and Iran."

"My God," Kaz whispered as he glanced at Sidorov, whose eyes went wide.

"Heroin," Sidorov said, keeping his voice low. "Being smuggled out of the country, by Russians on American aircraft."

"Yes. Kopelev was suspicious and was trying to determine what route was being used for the drugs," I said.

"Opium is grown in the Kyrgyz province on the Chinese border," Kaz said. "The opium is processed into morphine. It sounds as if a major shipment for this region was diverted."

"Diverted, and processed into heroin," Sidorov said. "That would take resources. A secure laboratory and secrecy."

"All of which could be supplied by your former employers," I said. "My bet is Mishkin was part of the scheme and just couldn't hold back from sampling the wares."

"Yes, that makes sense," Sidorov said. "As a *narkoman*, Mishkin would be invaluable. His contacts would trust him and have access to the people to do the processing."

"Wait a moment," Kaz said. "Is it really possible for the NKVD to have stolen a large shipment of morphine?"

"Do you mean morally or logistically?" Sidorov said. "Some men might have wondered at such orders, but not everyone involved would have to know the whole story. Moving a few freight cars off a siding would not be difficult. After all, the NKVD is responsible for railway security."

"This is a decent theory, I must admit," Kaz said. "It answers the question of motive. Kopelev was killed because of his suspicions. Morris, because he declined any further involvement."

"And the double killing served as a warning to their next unwilling accomplice. Major Preston Black," I said.

"I may have an American to blame after all," Sidorov said. "But one who would likely point his finger at the guilty party, which could be a death sentence for us all."

"Who is the guilty party?" Kaz asked. "I understand how the morphine could have been hijacked. But who is behind it, and how did they plan to profit from it? Sell the heroin in Iran?"

"Those are two different questions," I said. "My guess is that it's either Drozdov or Belov. They both were perfectly placed to send me on that suicide mission, but I don't have a shred of actual evidence as to which man was behind it."

"What about the other question?" Sidorov said, raising his voice to be heard over the Russian and American officers who were doing some serious drinking at a nearby table. "Profit. Russians have little familiarity with it."

"You're forgetting the maps," I said. "They showed Black Sea ports. Ports in Turkey."

"Tabriz is not far from the Turkish border," Kaz said.

"As a neutral nation, Turkey can ship goods nearly anywhere," Sidorov said, picking up on Kaz's line of thinking. "With southern France liberated, Marseilles would be only a few day's journey by ship."

"Marseilles, the heroin smuggling capital of the world," Kaz said. "Ah, now I see. Punchy."

"Right. Punchy saw a vacuum and jumped in to fill a need. Didn't work out the way he imagined, but he had the right idea," I said. "The French mob must be desperate to reestablish supply lines. They've been disrupted by war, and I bet they'd pay top dollar for some quality heroin."

"Khazar Brothers Shipping," Sidorov said. "In Tabriz, where the rail line from Tehran goes through. From there, any halfway decent smuggler could get a few crates safely to a Turkish port. The dutiful Lieutenant Kopelev suspected as much."

"Right now, our ex-con pal Max is probably setting up delivery, courtesy of the Allied Persian Corridor," I said.

"I suggest we approach Belov and Drozdov separately in the morning," Kaz said. "We tell them we've made a connection to Max and the stolen drugs, and that we need their approval to travel to Tehran to pursue it."

"If one says yes and the other says no, we have our kingpin," I said.

"Kingpin?" Sidorov asked.

"Head honcho," I said. "Mastermind."

"Oh. The one who will have my head for revealing his role," Sidorov said. "Wonderful."

"Maybe we should speak to them without you," Kaz said. "I doubt they would allow you out of the country in any case. That may shield you to some extent."

"Why don't you go back to the Cosmos Hotel tomorrow morning?"

I said. "Confirm that there was no heroin available around the date of Mishkin's overdose and find out if any is available now."

"Good," Sidorov said. "I will claim that your request was made without my knowledge. I will be suitably outraged. Thank you, both of you."

I was about to comment how kind it was of Kaz to suggest protecting Sidorov, but I was interrupted by sirens.

Air raid sirens.

"Where's the nearest shelter?" I said as I stood, kicking the chair back. I'd never even looked for shelters, given how far behind the lines we were. Neither Kaz nor Sidorov knew, so we joined the throng headed for the exit, some of them laughing and stumbling.

"Get to the slit trenches," an officer shouted, pointing to the side of the mess hall. In the murky darkness, I could spot men running into long, narrow ditches, some of them hidden by a chest-high brick wall. We followed, huddling in the last few spots. The whirring rise and fall of the siren continued as men shouted and complained in English and Russian.

The screaming of the sirens lessened, only to be replaced by the harsh chatter of machine-gun fire as tracers lit up the night sky.

"Something's not right," a lieutenant in front of me said, arching his neck to look up at the sky. "If there were bombers to shoot at, they'd be dropping flares by now. Pathfinders, so the main force can find the target." He was right. The RAF Pathfinder units pinpointed targets at night with bright flares to increase the accuracy during the bomb run.

"Look," Kaz said, standing upright. "The tracers are everywhere. They are firing blind."

"Russians shoot as they drive," Sidorov said. "With great gusto."

The sirens faded into silence. The shooting continued. Graceful lines of tracer fire arced across the sky from every corner of the airfield, the staccato bursts heavy and harsh. But they were the only sound. No droning of aircraft engines, no detonating bombs.

"False alarm, false alarm!" voices shouted from the roadway as a jeep passed by.

"Then what the hell they shootin' at?" the lieutenant asked, a sensible question which had no answer.

"Hey Billy," Bull said, waving to us as we stepped out of the slit trench. "I've been looking for you. Big Mike's plane landed safely. My CID contact in Tehran knows of the Khazar Brothers and will have more dope in the morning."

"Good to know," I said as the throng of men dispersed, most headed to their quarters. Sudden sirens and shootings are sobering.

"General," Kaz said, "why were only machine guns firing? Are there no heavy antiaircraft weapons here?" Kaz was right. All I'd seen were the .50 machine guns mounted on trucks.

"We asked, even offered to bring in our own antiaircraft units, but the Kremlin nixed the idea. Too many Yanks for them, I guess. But they took Browning machine guns and trucks to be manned only by their troops."

"Fairly useless against He-111s flying at a height of six thousand meters," Sidorov said, casting his gaze to the stars as if the German bombers might be hiding there. "But a lot of fun to fire into the heavens, I am sure."

"If there ever is a real air raid, we'd be in trouble, no doubt about it," Bull said. "No protection, not even night fighters. The nearest Russian night-fighter base is miles east of us."

We stood as the sounds of revving vehicles and squawking men quieted under the sparkling night sky. It was too beautiful an evening to be ruined by German bombs, and I managed to drink in the grandeur of night on the steppes. Everywhere I looked, there was empty sky. For now.

"You boys need anything?" Bull asked. "Like handcuffs?"

"We're not there, Bull," I said. "But we're close. Captain Sidorov is going to interview a possible witness in town tomorrow, and we'll be talking with General Belov and Major Drozdov about developments."

"You need me there?" Bull asked.

"It would be best if you were elsewhere," Kaz said, rocking on his heels as he held his hands behind his back.

"Not a problem," Bull said. "I already wish I was."

CHAPTER TWENTY-NINE

AFTER A BREAKFAST of powdered eggs, black bread, and strong coffee, Kaz, Sidorov, and I hoofed it out of the mess hall like the three Musketeers. A Yank, a Pole, and a Russian walk into the Operations building to solve a crime. We were a joke in search of a punchline.

We figured to tackle Drozdov first, as soon as Sidorov got clear of the airbase. Talking it over, we decided he needed to cover all the bases and search out any possible drug sources in Poltava. He'd start at the hotel, then see where the trail led.

But before Drozdov, we decided to rattle Major Black's cage. If he and Drozdov were heading out on their Bulgarian mission soon, we needed to get whatever we could out of him. Without Sidorov in the room. Because, if my hunch was right, Russians would make him nervous.

First stop was Bull's office. I knocked and opened the door.

"Just in time," he said, waving us in. "I've heard from Big Mike."

"Is he well?" Kaz asked. "He is in hospital?"

"Not exactly," Bull said. "They wrapped his ankle and told him to stay off it. They had a bed for him, but when my CID pal showed up to get the details about the case, Big Mike took off with him. On crutches."

"Why the hell would he do that?" I said.

"I forgot to mention, Colonel Paul Gideon of the Criminal Investigation Division used to be a vice detective in St. Louis," Bull said. "He and Big Mike apparently hit it off."

"Jesus, I bet Big Mike couldn't wait to flash his badge," I said. Big Mike was still more blue than khaki and sending him off to Tehran to heal up had backfired. He and Gideon would be trading cop stories as they tracked down Max, dollars to doughnuts.

"Don't worry, Gideon is a good man, he'll watch out for Big Mike. Gideon's already sent news about Private Maxim Bogomozov," Bull told us. Max was already at work on the rail line, loading supplies from trucks that came up from ports in southern Iran and acting as an unofficial interpreter. He was still in Tehran, and, according to Gideon's sources, he was behaving himself and popular with the American enlisted men he worked with. A friendly Russian who spoke English, after a fashion, was a rarity to be sure. Especially one who knew how to pick up the low-hanging fruit on the supply chain. There was always petty pilferage going on, and if a guy wasn't too greedy and shared the pickings, he'd get by okay.

"I am sure Big Mike knows to stay clear of Max," Kaz said. "It wouldn't do for Max to know he's being watched."

"There's no need," Bull said. "Gideon has his own men working undercover on a black-market job, and they're keeping an eye on Max. Big Mike and Gideon are meeting today with an inspector from the Iranian Gendarmerie to find out more about the Khazar brothers."

"Good. If Big Mike has two other policemen to talk to, he may stay off his leg long enough for it to heal," Kaz said, more mother hen than crime fighter.

"What are you three up to while Big Mike is busy in Tehran?" Bull said. "I just got another message from our Military Mission in Moscow. They want answers."

"Captain Sidorov is questioning people in Poltava today," I said. "People who need a reason to flap their lips. You have anything on hand? We could use smokes and scotch if you can spare them."

"Here," Bull said, opening a desk drawer. "A carton of Luckies. And to show I want results, I'll throw in my last bottle of Jameson."

"Now that's commitment," I said, tossing the cigarettes to Sidorov and grabbing the bottle. "This oughta loosen lips."

"Just make sure they're not yours, Boyle," Bull said. "Now get to work."

On the way out, I looked for Maiya, but she wasn't at her desk. Black wasn't in his office, and I wondered if they were enjoying a last snuggle before he went off on his OSS derring-do.

"These are very effective tools of the trade," Sidorov said as we caught up with him. "The only problem will be separating the truth from the chaff of lies I will be told when the nefarious types see this bottle. Liquid gold."

"At least you've got twenty packs of Lucky Strikes to divvy up. Drop us off at Black's quarters on your way out, willya?"

"Certainly," Sidorov said as we clambered into the jeep, Kaz beating me to the passenger's seat.

"Billy," Kaz said. He nodded in the direction of the steps leading to the main entrance of Operations. It was Maiya, carrying a handful of folders. Looks like it wasn't breakfast in bed for her and Black.

"Be right back," I said, hopping out of the rear seat.

"Maiya, good morning," I said. "Do you have a minute?"

"I have many minutes, Captain Boyle. You may have one of them." She smiled, but without a lot of warmth. I was obviously keeping her from someone more important than me.

"That's all I need," I said. "You know General Belov's signature, don't you?"

"Of course, I do," she said. "I handle much of his correspondence. Why?"

"Please tell me if this is his signature," I said, withdrawing the folded, worn order from inside my Ike jacket. She opened it and scanned it, blinking her eyes in a double take.

"Where did you find this, Captain?"

"I just found it," I said, waving my hand vaguely in the direction of the roadway, as if it had fluttered by. "What do you think?"

"I think Lieutenant Nikolin is very glad to be back and to have survived," she said. "I think this document could send him back to the penal detachment, since it contradicts his most recent story. I also think you would not wish that."

"Not on anyone. I'm simply asking your opinion. Is that the general's signature, or a forgery?"

"Very well," Maiya said, glancing around to see who was watching. A trio of Russians walked down the road, all enlisted men carrying shovels and chattering away with each other. She laid the order on top of her files and smoothed it out, squinting as she studied the scrawled name on the signature line.

"Yes, I think so," she finally declared. "But the general is a busy man, and often his signature is rushed. Like this. Do you see?" I did. Belov could've had a career as a doctor.

"You're not one hundred percent sure?"

"No, not with certainty. If you are going to reveal this, it would be terrible for Vanya. Are you?" she asked as she handed it back.

"I don't think so," I said. "My main concern is whether or not General Belov signed it."

"If I had to give an answer, I would say yes. But I could be wrong. Someone could have left this for you to find with a forged signature. It is all very confusing, isn't it?"

"That it is. Do you know where Major Black is? I wanted to say goodbye before he left."

"He is in his quarters," Maiya said, with the hint of a grin, this one genuine. "No one is supposed to know he is leaving. Security is very important, Captain, even this far behind the lines. Now I must go, General Belov needs these reports."

That was my minute with Maiya. She was right about Nikolin, of course. I could use this order to shake things up, but it would only put him behind the eight ball without accomplishing anything. Belov could deny it was his, true or not.

"Nothing," I said as I got back into the jeep. "Maiya said it looked like Belov's handwriting but she couldn't be sure." I told them about her concerns for Nikolin.

"The only thing more horrifying than being sent to a penal company would be going back to a penal company," Sidorov said, starting the jeep. "She raises a valid concern, if we wish no harm to befall the young lieutenant."

Sidorov tore out into the road, passing a truck, and careening back into the right lane where he scattered another group of shovel-wielding soldiers. I wished for no harm to come to me.

"Digging more slit trenches, I've been told," Kaz shouted, holding onto his cap.

"Belov must have been embarrassed by the display last night. The false alarm, the wild firing, and the insufficient protections. I pity those poor boys, they'll be digging all day," Sidorov said, accelerating on a straightaway before skidding to a halt outside the apartment building where Black was housed.

"Good luck, Captain," Kaz said, straightening his cap and smoothing out his uniform jacket.

"And the same to you both," Sidorov said. "Do your best to get Major Black to confess, will you? He is my best hope." With that he gunned the engine and zoomed down the road.

"Are you warming up to our Russian colleague?" I asked Kaz as we took the steps to the main entrance. "You've gone from the cold shoulder to a bon voyage."

"There is no reason I should not wish him well, given he is working with us, in good faith, as far as it goes," Kaz said, opening the door.

"Meaning you don't trust him?"

"I trust he will do his best not to be sent back to the labor camps," Kaz said, "as any sane man would do. But as much as I hesitate to say it, he does have a certain charm. For a Bolshevik murderer."

"Well, let's see if an American will make a voluntary confession," I said, rapping on Black's door.

"I wonder if it will make any difference?" Kaz said, his voice low as if he was talking to himself. The way they ran this country, maybe not.

"Come in," Black shouted from inside. Pretty trusting of him, since the knock could be from one of the heavies who'd pressured him. I opened the door and saw why he hadn't been worried. Black was seated at a table, a Colt .45 in one hand. On the table in front of him was a disassembled Thompson submachine gun.

"Hello, fellas," he said. "You caught me on cleaning day. Have a seat."

"We figured you'd be on your way to parts undisclosed by now," I said, pulling out a chair and inhaling the heady aroma of gun oil.

"All I can say is I won't be here for long," Black said, wiping down the automatic and inserting the magazine. "Please don't mention Bulgaria, okay?"

"Everyone seems to know," Kaz said, dusting the seat off with his handkerchief before sitting.

"I know. Which is why I'm tired of hearing about it," Black said. "Is this a social call or what?"

"We wanted to wish you a bon voyage," Kaz said. "If you are in Sofia, be sure to visit the Boyana Church. The medieval frescoes are magnificent."

"I'll send you a postcard," Black said, setting the Colt down and beginning to assemble the Thompson. "Now cut to the chase or *amscray*."

"I do hope your Bulgarian is as fluent as your pig Latin," Kaz said.

"I never said I was going to Bulgaria, dammit," Black said, slamming down the gun's receiver. "What is it you want from me?" Now he was getting testy, just the way I liked my interrogation subjects. Mad and not thinking straight.

"I want to know what it was like, watching Kopelev and Morris get it," I said.

"It must have been horrible," Kaz said, shaking his head in sympathy.

"Did they make you clean up the blood?" I asked.

"You're nuts," Black said, rubbing down the receiver with an oily rag. "Are you accusing me?"

"Of being a patsy, yes," I said. "What was in those crates you authorized for shipment to Tehran? I thought materials came from Iran, not to it."

"Apparently you never heard of reverse Lend-Lease," Black said, sitting back and staring at me. "Chromium ore, manganese ore, tin, it all gets shipped from the Soviet Union to the States, along with other supplies."

"Are you saying those crates contained ore?" Kaz asked.

"No, I've got nothing to say about any supposed crates, except that anything sent from here under my signature is top secret OSS business," Black said, going back to assembling the tommy gun.

"I bet you don't even know," I said. "You weren't important enough to know. They used you for your signature and your top secret clearance."

"Who is *they*?" Black demanded, putting the bolt and the receiver together, each metallic *click* and *clack* bringing him closer to ramming the magazine home and facing us with a whole lot of firepower. "And what is it you think I did? Kill those two guys, or watch 'em get it?"

"I don't think you killed them," I said. "I think they were killed because they wouldn't go along with the scheme, and someone needed to pressure you. It worked, didn't it?"

"They. Someone. You keep using words that only tell me you have no idea what you're talking about. It's a fantasy, Boyle, and fantasies are dangerous. Mark my words," Black said, screwing the rear grip into place.

"Speaking of danger, watch out when you and Major Drozdov get to Bulgaria. Anything can happen there, it is a strange place," Kaz said.

"Drozdov?" Black laughed. "Why would I worry about him? Now I've got things to do. Get out and take your crazy accusations with you."

"Don't say we didn't warn you," Kaz told him as we got up to leave. "Deep in the Bulgarian forest you will come across the *lamya*, a female dragon with three dog-like heads. Quite ferocious. Be careful of her."

"Know what's even more horrifying than that? A man who pushes heroin while wearing the uniform," I said, anger overtaking me. I grabbed the edge of the table and threw it against the wall, scattering magazines and parts of the Thompson across the floor.

Black pushed his chair back, scooping up the Colt from the floor.

"Leave it," Kaz said, his Webley out in a flash and leveled at Black's head. "Or not, as you wish."

"I ought to have you court-martialed, both of you," Black snarled, his hand moving away from the pistol. "Get out."

"Our pleasure," I said. "It stinks in here."

"That was amusing," Kaz said as we exited the building, one eye on the windows in case Black got any idea about potshots. "He seems fairly confident, doesn't he?"

"He sounds like a man happy to be leaving Poltava," I said, "even if it means braving the *lamya* in the forests of Bulgaria."

"He readily dismissed the notion of Drozdov as a danger to him," Kaz said as we walked back to Operations. "His bravado may have been a front, but that was a spontaneous reaction."

"Well, I don't think it was a front. He was genuinely glad to be getting out Russia. Maybe he's just a gung ho OSS agent, or maybe he can't wait to put a threat behind him. But I agree about Drozdov," I said. "There was no hesitation, no telltale glance, no fidgeting. He went straight to the denial as if the idea was ludicrous."

"Perhaps he is simply an excellent liar," Kaz said as a column of trucks lumbered by. "An OSS agent should be, I would think."

"Even a good liar can reveal things," I said. "My dad always claimed he could spot a lie by a suspect glancing around the room, as if searching for the truth. Or if they hid their hands. Me, I find it easier to spot the truth, and that comment about Drozdov was effortless on his part. He was being honest."

"We shall see, when we present our Tehran proposal to Major Drozdov," Kaz said. "Although the paranoia of an NKVD man might prevent him from thinking straight."

"I'm counting on that paranoia," I said. "He should be happy to wave goodbye to us. Two fewer Westerners to worry about."

"Do you think he will approve Sidorov's departure with us?" Kaz asked as we hustled across the street toward Operations.

"No. Not their style. I have no idea what they'll do with him." Actually I did. It wasn't good.

We checked in with Bull to see if he had any dope on Black's mission. He didn't. The OSS played things close to the chest, although he'd heard rumors Black and Drozdov would be heading out soon. Bulgaria, unless that was a cover story. I said I didn't think Black was that crafty, and he laughed, right before he told us to get out and nail the killer before Joe Stalin got impatient.

"I thought it was our own military mission breathing down your back," I said. "The Russians too?"

"Not as bad as Major General John Deane," Bull said. "He's in charge of the US Military Mission and he's none too happy right now. About anything. This incident is making everyone nervous at a critical time."

"Please, additional pressure is so interesting," Kaz said, lounging against the door frame. "Do tell." Kaz was the only lieutenant I knew who could wax sarcastic with a general and make it sound polite.

"All this," Bull said, waving his hand in the direction of the airfield and points beyond, "it's not really about bombing Germany. It's about bombing Japan."

"You gotta explain that one, Bull," I said.

"When we first planned this operation, it all made sense. The shuttle bombing part. But since then, the Russians have moved a lot closer to Germany, but they haven't allowed us to move our bases closer."

"It did seem odd that we were this far behind the lines," I said.

"Right. It wastes fuel. But the Soviets don't want us to have freedom of movement within their country, and we're holding back on complaints because we've been angling for bases in the Far East to bomb Japan."

"But the USSR is not at war with Japan," Kaz said.

"Not yet," Bull said. "But believe me, once we get closer to defeating Japan, they'll jump on board so they can get a share of the spoils. We've been asking for a commitment for air bases in Siberia, but they've stalled so long, we don't even need them anymore. We've taken Guam, Tinian, and Saipan in the Marianas. That put our B-29 Superfortresses within range of mainland Japan."

"What's all the fuss about, then? We could just pack up and go home," I said.

"It won't be that long before we wind down here," Bull said. "But in the meantime, the brass—and by that, I mean the guys who are the bosses of my boss—want to keep things on an even keel with the Russians. Meaning you need to wrap this up, pronto."

"The closer Soviet troops get to meeting British and American forces, the greater the need for cooperation," Kaz said. "It could be a disaster."

"Bingo. The last thing we need is bad blood between allies," Bull said. "Get cracking, you two."

"I wish I had more faith in our plan," I whispered to Kaz as we went to find Drozdov.

"I wish I had more faith in those who are running this war," Kaz said. "Imagine trusting the Russians to do something simply because it will help end the war in the Pacific? Fools."

With that cheery thought in mind, I knocked at Drozdov's door. Drozdov opened it, revealing a senior officer sitting behind his desk. This had to be his Bull Dawson, but without the charming smile, and with a propensity for executions.

"Come in," Drozdov said. "I have just finished updating the colonel on your progress. Perhaps you have something new to offer?"

There was a hint of desperation in Drozdov's voice, confirmed by the look on the colonel's face, not that I could make it out through the haze of choking smoke from his Belomorkanal cigarette. Maybe we could make that work for us.

"Yes, we do," I said, as he stood aside for us to enter. The colonel was leaning back and eyeing us as he puffed away. He was a big guy, with dark hair beginning to gray at the sides where it was cropped short. He had a chest full of medals, nicotine-stained fingers, and high, pockmarked cheekbones. "If you have a moment to spare."

He did.

"May I present Colonel of State Security Aleksei Vladimirovich Aristov," Drozdov said, sounding like a butler at a society ball. He rattled off what sounded like our introductions. I nodded to Kaz, who began our report in Russian. I wanted Aristov to get the unfiltered account. Drozdov looked too nervous to say anything that might rattle the boss.

"Do you concur, Captain Boyle?" Drozdov asked.

"About going to Tehran? Yes, I do. We will need Capitan Sidorov as well. Our associate in Tehran has made contact with the Iranian Gendarmerie and they will assist," I said.

Drozdov jumped in and translated that bit, probably not wanting to look like a bystander. Aristov replied quickly in staccato bursts like a machine gun and Drozdov put his questions to us.

"Are you certain Private Maxim Bogomozov is involved?"

Yes, we were. Not the brains of the operation, but he'd been recruited for his criminal background and language skills.

"Is an American involved?"

Yes, we think a recently transferred sergeant may have been part of the scheme. He is at the Tehran base, and we intend to question him there.

"Did the American pull the trigger?"

Yes. And the Russian, I told him. As criminal partners. I figured he'd be happy to split the difference.

"Was Lieutenant Mishkin part of this plot?"

We think so, I told him, remembering that Colonel Aristov was here to investigate the death by overdose of an NKVD officer along with the killings. I said we suspected drug smuggling was part of the plan, and that Mishkin may have favored product over profit. I didn't bring up the drugs in the OSS/NKVD warehouse, since I didn't want Drozdov taken out and shot.

"Where did Mishkin get his drugs?"

In town, before the shortage. But his overdose may have come from drugs stolen from the war effort. Stolen by disorganizers of the rear, to borrow a Soviet phrase. I tread lightly on this one, knowing that any remark too critical of the USSR might get us shut down.

"Has Major Drozdov been helpful to you?" This line Drozdov managed to deliver with a straight face.

Helpful in every respect. A colleague. But strict when it came to security matters, I added, figuring being too friendly to West-erners was not exactly a job recommendation in this part of the world.

"What do you plan to do next?"

Wait to hear from our sergeant in Tehran. Wait for Captain Sidorov to finish his questioning of suspected drug dealers in town. Go to Tehran if we can secure permission. Will the colonel approve?

As Drozdov translated, Maiya appeared in the doorway. Aristov gave her an appraising glance, then returned his attention to Drozdov.

"I have a message from Captain Sidorov," Maiya said. "He asks if you would meet him at the Cosmos Hotel. He may have some important information."

"What sort of information?" Drozdov asked, pausing in his exchange with Aristov.

"He would not say, other than it was important and that Captain Boyle and Lieutenant Kazimierz should hear it for themselves," Maiya said, studiously avoiding Aristov's eyes.

"Do we have your permission to go into town, Major Drozdov?" Kaz asked. As if Drozdov was the one calling the shots in this room. The two NKVD men whispered to each other, and finally Aristov flicked his finger in Maiya's direction.

"You may go," Drozdov said. "Maiya will drive you, and you may return with Captain Sidorov. The colonel will consider your request about Tehran."

"When will he decide?" I asked.

"He has decided about Poltava. That is enough for now."

I couldn't disagree and hoped it put him in the habit of getting rid of Westerners. I thanked Colonel Aristov as we departed, tossing off a *spasibo* like I knew what I was talking about.

"Colonel Aristov is a take-charge kind of guy," I said, as Maiya fired up the jeep and backed out into the road just yards ahead of a truck carrying barrels of aviation fuel.

"State security services desire no other kind, I think," she said, jamming it into first and burning rubber to get out of the truck's path.

"We are not in an aircraft," Kaz said from the passenger's seat. "The jeep is a wonderful vehicle, but it does not fly."

"Forgive me," Maiya said, laughing as she looked at Kaz. "I am always thinking about flying. What do you think Captain Sidorov has found?"

"No idea," I said. "Maybe a connection between Mishkin and a drug dealer."

"It is sad Lieutenant Mishkin fell prey to drugs. He had so many opportunities. He came from a family with loyal Party members. It must have been a great disappointment to them," she said, slowing to speak to the guards at the gate. Slowing, not stopping.

"Is that why Colonel Aristov came to check on Drozdov? Because of Mishkin's family?" I said.

"I do not know what motivates Colonel Aristov," Maiya said, downshifting as she overtook a truck filled with soldiers. "He is from the Directorate of Border and Internal Guards, GUPVO. It is natural for him to follow up when an officer has disgraced himself."

"Has he been here before?" I asked. "I mean, after Mishkin died? It's been a while."

"I heard he was," Maiya said. "But the affair was not discussed. Major Drozdov made it clear that he would not tolerate gossip."

"Meaning he didn't want to look bad in front of his boss," I said, clapping my hand on my service cap as Maiya took a corner.

"We have no bosses in the Soviet Union," Maiya said. "Only comrades."

"And marvelous drivers," Kaz said, gripping the side of his seat.

Maiya laughed and sped up.

CHAPTER THIRTY

SIDOROV WAS WAITING for us on the steps of the Cosmos Hotel. He raised an eyebrow at our chauffer as she pulled in and slammed on the brakes.

"You got here quickly," he said as we staggered out of our seats.

"Not much choice," I said. "Maiya relayed your message while we were talking with Drozdov and Comrade Aristov."

"Comrade Colonel Aristov," Maiya said. "While we do not have bosses, we do have many colonels. You will all return together, and soon, yes?"

"Yes," Sidorov said. "It will not take long. It is a short walk to the park."

"For something useful, I hope," Maiya said, already jamming the shift into reverse.

"I will let my colleagues decide," Sidorov said. "Or should I say comrades?"

"Say whatever you wish, I only ask you because they will ask me," she said. "There are times when comrades forget they are not bosses. Especially comrade colonels. Good luck to you."

With that, she shot out backwards and barreled off.

"What have you found?" Kaz asked, brushing the dust of the road off his uniform.

"Come, let us take a walk and I will explain," Sidorov said, taking off down the sidewalk.

"Where are we going?" I asked him.

"To the park, where the Poltava chess club is meeting."

"Of course," Kaz said. "The bishop did it, I am sure."

"We are a godless country, Baron, but we do love chess," Sidorov said with a sly grin. "Even those who sell drugs love it."

"Did you break into the Jameson?" I asked. "You seem awfully chipper."

"Yes. Delightful whiskey," Sidorov said. "But it was only after Dmitri insisted that I join him in a toast. Or two."

Three, maybe, judging by Sidorov's grin. He had something juicy, and I could tell he was enjoying keeping us on tenterhooks. We followed him past ruined buildings down a side street which led to a ruined park. Flower beds were overrun with weeds, and tree trunks sat shattered by artillery or marked by saw cuts where they'd been taken for winter fuel. But the paths were clean, and a fountain at the center was being scrubbed down, offering the promise of a playful spray of water someday soon.

"Are you sure Dmitri will still be there?" I asked.

"I am. He is waiting for my last three packages of Lucky Strikes," Sidorov said, patting his uniform pocket.

An array of tables and chairs was arranged under one remaining tree, its leaves lifting and falling as a slight breeze blew through the park. Men and a few women were gathered around chessboards, some playing, some watching.

"That is Dmitri," Sidorov said, pointing to a tall, thin fellow with sparse hair the color of corn silk seated away from the others, legs crossed. He was wearing American boots.

"A chess player?" Kaz asked.

"One of the best the Poltava Chess Club has," Sidorov said. "But we are more interested in his other hobbies."

"The black market, by the looks of his footwear," I said.

"Lend-Lease is a wonderful thing," Sidorov said. "Baron, I will leave it to you to explain to Billy what we will discuss with Dmitri."

Dmitri stood as we approached, displaying the instant awareness most successful criminals possessed. Successful meaning those who hadn't yet been caught by the cops or killed by a competitor. He'd recognized Sidorov, but his eyes darted to Kaz and me, assessing our potential as a threat. I could see him relax, the tension draining from his body as he sat back down.

Sidorov tossed him one pack of Luckies and spoke with him, gesturing to us by way of introduction. He asked what sounded like a question, and Dmitri gave a whispered response.

"He says if we report him, he will denounce us as British spies," Kaz said.

"Tell him I'm an American spy, and we don't give a damn about reporting him to anybody," I said. That got a laugh, and Dmitri began to talk. I watched Kaz, nodding slowly as he listened.

Then something got his attention. Behind his steel-rimmed spectacles I could see Kaz's eyes widen as he held up a hand and interrupted Dmitri with a question. Dmitri responded with a firm nod. When Kaz finished, Sidorov tossed Dmitri the second pack of smokes.

"Interesting," Kaz said. "I can see why you called us here."

"What?" I said, watching Dmitri stow the cigarettes in a canvas bag which revealed the bottle of Jameson and a Tokarev automatic pistol. "Did he sell horse to Mishkin?"

"No," Kaz said. "Lieutenant Mishkin spoke of selling heroin to him."

"What?" I said, conscious of repeating myself. Something was off. "Dmitri's a small-time dealer, isn't he?"

"He claims to be nothing more. In Poltava, he is the king. Elsewhere, he is nothing, he tells me. But he cited the proverb that it takes cunning to pull even a small fish from a pond," Kaz said.

"Meaning not to mess with Dmitri in Poltava," I said.

"Yes. And that Dmitri knows not to anger those outside his realm," Kaz said. "He turned Mishkin down."

"How much heroin did he offer?"

"Two kilos," Kaz said. "It was enough that Dmitri knew it must be stolen, so he refused."

"When was this, exactly?"

"Two days before Mishkin was found dead," Kaz said.

"Not surprising with all that heroin at hand," I said. Sidorov quickly translated what I'd said, and Dmitri shook his head sadly as he responded.

"Dmitri says Mishkin did not overdose," Kaz said, frowning as he took in what he was being told. "He no longer was an addict. He'd gone long enough without the drug to wean himself from the habit. He was a changed man. Dmitri swears he would not have gone back."

"Do either of you think Dmitri has a reason to lie?" I asked. They shook their heads. I couldn't think of one either. "Did Mishkin show the two kilos to Dmitri?"

"*Da*," Dmitri said.

That was all I needed to hear.

WE DECIDED THAT the best place to talk over this new development was at the Cosmos Hotel. If there was a lunch rush in Poltava, it hadn't hit there yet, so we scored a table by the window. Outside, people carried on like so many in this war, with what dignity they could muster. It was worn and threadbare, like their coats and patched trousers, but they held onto it with the joy that only the recently liberated can know.

Sidorov ordered kasha with mushrooms and onions for all of us, saying it was a classic Russian dish and we had to have it before we left his country, along with a Crimean white wine which he was enthusiastic about but tasted sweet to me. Kaz made approving murmurs about it. With his nose I was surprised, but maybe he was being polite.

"Does Dmitri's story tell us anything new?" Sidorov said after we'd tasted the wine.

"It suggests that heroin cannot be a large problem in Poltava. Two kilos are a lot, but I am surprised it was too much for a man such as Dmitri," Kaz said.

"I am not," Sidorov said. "Two kilos from an NKVD man means a security force connection to smuggling. That would be enough to frighten Dmitri. He struck me as a man who pays attention to risk."

"How is heroin usually manufactured and transported here?" I asked. "Dmitri has to have a regular supply chain, although it is certainly disrupted with the war."

"Poppy farmers in Kyrgyz manage to sell small batches of their harvest to the *vor* without the authorities noticing. Or sometimes they are bribed. The *vor* set up processing in an out-of-the-way location, and then smuggle the product into cities. Sometimes the smugglers are travelers with forged papers, or the heroin is shipped with farm products from the region. But you are correct, with the war, everything is more difficult. Men are called up for service, and travel passes are scrutinized much more carefully. Which is why demand for heroin has dropped off. Users have been weaned from the drug. Or are dead."

"Which may be why Mishkin wasn't buying anymore," I said, taking another sip of wine. It was growing on me.

"Do you think he went back to his habit when he failed to sell to Dmitri?" Kaz asked. "I doubt he could have found another buyer."

"No, I don't," I said. "I think he was the first victim."

"Killed for stealing from his comrades?" Sidorov said. "That does fit with what Dmitri said about him."

"What? Did I miss something?" I asked.

"No, it was from my first talk with him. He said that after he turned down the sale, Mishkin was very afraid. Afraid of returning the product."

"Dmitri didn't ask to who?" I said.

"Dmitri is too smart to ask such questions," Sidorov said. "Which leaves the question to us. Who, besides Max, is involved in this? Who has put these wheels into motion?"

"Well, Drozdov didn't seem to mind us coming into town," I said. "But that could have been because of his boss being there."

"He would be more likely to say no in the presence of a superior officer," Sidorov said. "It would be the standard response. Any NKVD officer would know they cannot go wrong by denying any travel to foreigners. Did you ask about Tehran?"

"We did. Colonel Aristov said he'd think about it," I said.

"We plan on approaching Belov when we return," Kaz said. "We did strongly urge that you be allowed to accompany us."

"Thank you," Sidorov said as our kasha arrived. He raised his glass in a toast and we clinked. Kaz managed a decent gulp, and Sidorov dug into his meal as if it were his last.

Maybe he knew something.

We finished up and sauntered out with our stomachs full of kasha and our minds full of questions. A police car with flashing lights sped down the street, siren blaring. It turned down the side street we'd taken to the park.

"*Militsiya*," Sidorov said. "The local police."

"Going to arrest Dmitri?" Kaz said. "Perhaps we should investigate."

We did. Sidorov pulled over near where the cops had parked and told us to wait in the jeep. Foreigners would only complicate things. I watched him talk with a cop standing by a crumpled corpse as two others circulated among the chess players. In a few minutes he returned, his expression grim.

"Dmitri. Shot twice in the head," he said.

"Witnesses?" I asked.

"No one saw anything, of course," Sidorov replied. "Especially after seeing me this morning, and then you two. With the NKVD, two Westerners, and a drug dealer, suddenly everyone grows blind or fixated on their chess game. The *ment* do not seem to care very much, since they knew of Dmitri's activities."

"*Ment?*" I asked.

"The same as cop in America or bobby in England," Sidorov said. "The *ment* will not expend a lot of effort investigating."

"Which is just what the killer was counting on," I said.

As Sidorov started up the jeep, I saw the cops each pocket a pack of Luckies. I wondered who'd snatched the Jameson.

Why kill Dmitri was the topic of discussion on the way back to the base. Who'd done it? No idea. But the *why* was damn important. He'd already spoken to us. Was there something else he knew, something that he hadn't told us? Or was it revenge, punishment for speaking to Sidorov in the first place?

"Dmitri was not a *vor*," Sidorov said, hitting the accelerator. "It was not retribution for talking to the authorities."

"A competitor for the drug trade?" Kaz suggested. "You mentioned drugs were available at the hotel."

"They bought from Dmitri, that is how I got his name," Sidorov said, slowing for the guards at the gate.

"Did you tell anyone you were meeting him?" I asked. "Did you mention it when you called the base?"

"No. The desk clerk at the hotel did tell me where I could find him," Sidorov said. "And I was asking around about where drugs could be purchased. I tried the newsstand and the barbershop near the hotel, but no names were mentioned."

"You did tell Maiya we were going to the park," Kaz said, as the guards let us through with a wave. We were becoming regulars, which was kind of scary.

"It is a large park, and how would she know where to find a criminal drug dealer?"

"She could have mentioned something back at the base," I suggested.

"And someone overheard her and had enough time to get out here, find Dmitri, and plug him? Don't think so," I said.

"It is unlikely, I must admit. Perhaps you didn't need to mention names at all," Kaz said to Sidorov. "If you were asking around about drugs, people trading in the black market would know his name. And the hotel clerk told you about him."

"Yes, but why would they have their supplier killed?" Sidorov responded.

"They might not have known what was going to happen," I said, as we parked in front of Operations. "They could have been paid, or threatened, into making a call."

"How is not as important as why," Kaz said, tilting his head to the sun, which had just emerged from behind thick clouds. "Why did Dmitri need to be silenced?"

"Punishment or prevention?" I said, tilting my service cap back. "Had he told us something vital, or was someone afraid he might?"

"A warning, perhaps, to others we might speak with," Sidorov said. "Or retribution that has nothing to do with this case. Dmitri may have betrayed someone to the Germans."

"That's a long shot," I said, getting out of the jeep. "Dmitri could have been denounced to the NKVD, and they'd have taken him away."

"But then he could have revealed what he knew," Kaz said. "Better to silence him now."

"Listen," I said to Sidorov. "While we put the Tehran travel plans to Belov, why don't you head back to town? Now that the local cops have left, someone might be willing to talk."

"Good. Last time I went with cigarettes and charm. This time I shall instill fear. Harsh words are often easier for Russians to understand. Kindness can be confusing after years of listening to Comrade Stalin," Sidorov said, his voice a whisper as he glanced around to see who might have overheard him.

"If we're not in Bull's office, check the barracks when you get back," I said. "We'll try to get in to see Belov as soon as we can. You sure you don't want a resupply of smokes?"

Sidorov declined, and as we took the steps into the Operations center, Maiya stepped out. We asked if General Belov was available, and she said he had just finished meeting with Colonel Aristov. She begged off taking us in right now as she wanted to wish Major Black luck, since the rumor was he and Drozdov would be leaving tonight. I didn't want to dissuade her from a fond farewell, even if I thought Black was a bum. Whenever we managed to get out of here, I planned on letting Wild Bill Donovan know what his boy in Russia had been up to. I don't know what his thoughts on drug smuggling were, but he'd hate his agents being used. Whether Black knew what was in those crates destined for the Khazar brothers or not, he'd been a pawn and a sap, hardly the poster boy for an OSS intelligence agent.

CHAPTER THIRTY-ONE

A CLERK IN the main office told Kaz Belov would see us in thirty minutes. We went back outside, drawn by the warmth of the afternoon sun. It was early fall, but the chill in the Russian air was never far off. When would it snow? I hoped it was after we were long gone.

We exited the building in time to see Sidorov drive off with Maiya, heading in the direction of Black's quarters.

"Interesting," Kaz said. "Perhaps he wanted to ask Maiya to whom she might have mentioned our walk in the park."

"Or he's just giving a lady a lift," I said. A rough wood bench was set against the front of the building, and we sat down, stretching out our legs as if we hadn't a care in the world.

"There are no ladies in Russia," Kaz said. "Only comrade ladies."

I chuckled, but it wasn't that funny. Our predicament was a lot funnier. Our only real suspect was somewhere on the loose in Iran with a haul of heroin, our most recent witness had gotten his skull aired out, and we were dependent upon the good graces of an NKVD colonel or a Red air force general.

"Should we see if Big Mike has checked in?" Kaz asked.

"After Belov," I said. "I need to think."

"Yes, a catnap in the sun is called for."

I closed my eyes but didn't sleep. I thought about the warehouse and the murders. I thought about moving the drugs, all the way from Kyrgyz to Tehran and then to Marseilles, if my hunch was correct. Who would be able to plan and pull off that kind of scheme? My thoughts wandered back to Boston and all the thugs and drug dealers I'd run across. I thought about Punchy and his try at moving into the business.

I considered the implications of Kopelev's search for maps, and how someone had swiped the atlas from our jeep. Someone on this base.

"Billy," Kaz said, giving my shoulder a shake. Okay, maybe I dozed off at the end.

"I'm awake," I said, trying to piece together my train of thought. It had left the station.

We found Drozdov outside Belov's office, throwing on his coat. He told us the general would give us ten minutes and asked if we needed him for translating, apologizing for Maiya's absence. Kaz told him he could handle it, and Drozdov said he was needed at the warehouse.

"Do you know if Colonel Aristov has decided about our request?" I asked.

"I have not seen the comrade colonel since you left us this morning," he said. "Please excuse me."

"Loading up supplies for the Bulgarian mission?" I asked, unable to pass up the chance to needle him.

"If I were to go to Bulgaria, Captain Boyle, the one advantage would be your absence there," Drozdov said, pulling on his cap and stalking out.

"Packing for a central European voyage can be quite stressful," Kaz said, barely suppressing a smile. Belov's office door was open, and he was standing by the window, his back to us, watching Drozdov head down the road. Belov blew smoke from his cigarette against the windowpane, and I had the odd notion that he was aiming at Drozdov, blowing him a gray goodbye kiss. I guess any air force general wouldn't mind being free of the NKVD, at least for a while.

Belov's eyes blinked at the reflection in his window as he noticed us. He spoke, gesturing for us to enter.

"General Belov, we have a request," I said, nodding to Kaz. I knew he wouldn't understand, but a question coming from a captain would carry more weight than the same thing coming from a lieutenant.

Kaz spoke. I heard *Tegeran*, which I figured was how the Russkies said Tehran, along with Max's name. Belov barked a question back at Kaz, and they exchanged a few verses until Belov stubbed out his cigarette. Sidorov's name had been in there somewhere as well.

"*Nyet*," Belov said.

Kaz went back at him, not taking no for an answer.

"*Nyet, nyet*," Belov said. We were not making progress.

"No to Sidorov, or no to the whole idea?" I asked Kaz, keeping my gaze fixed on the general.

"No to taking our investigation to Tehran," Kaz said. "General Belov recommends that if we wish to be relieved, we should take the matter up with General Dawson."

"Tell him we do not. Anything else?"

"He says he may ask Colonel Aristov to take over the investigation. His superiors would not like it, and he promises we will like it much less. He claims that Aristov recently broke up a criminal gang looting trains. He gets results, but there is a price for all concerned. I think the general is afraid of him."

"Please tell him no one will need to pay such a price. Then ask him who he thinks killed Kopelev and Morris," I said.

"A disorganizer of the rear," Kaz translated. "General Belov states that it is obvious."

"Should we not follow the trail of the disorganizer wherever it leads?" I said.

"*Nyet*," was his answer, along with a few more words and a wave of his hand, dismissing us.

"What was that at the end?" I asked Kaz.

"He said that all his problems would be solved if only we went off with Black and Drozdov."

"To Bulgaria?"

"He did not mention a destination," Kaz said. "Only a heartfelt desire for our departure."

"It can't be easy having foreign investigators nosing around," I said. "Especially when you're used to the secret police handling things, no questions asked. But the question now is, did Belov deny us permission out of Soviet stubbornness or because we're getting too close?"

"Let us find Colonel Aristov and see what he's decided," Kaz said. "It is hard to judge the general's response without knowing Aristov's."

That made sense, so we asked around, but nobody in a Russian uniform wanted to talk about the whereabouts of an NKVD colonel. We checked in with Bull, who showed us a radio message from Big Mike. Max had slipped away from his duty station this morning but reappeared a few hours ago. Gideon's CID men had confirmed that the Khazar brothers were suspected smugglers. The Iranian Gendarmerie inspector had said, in so many words, that the Tabriz cops were in the pay of the Khazars and couldn't be trusted.

It was all good news, confirming our suspicions. But it wouldn't do much good if we couldn't get out of here. I told Bull about being turned down by Belov for an all-expenses paid visit to Tehran and asked if he had the authority to send us if Aristov didn't work out.

His answer was sure, if our Moscow Military Mission agreed. Which meant that the Kremlin would be consulted. Which meant *nyet*.

So, we went Aristov hunting. He wasn't in the mess hall, not anywhere in Operations, and nobody would admit to knowing where he bunked.

"The warehouse," Kaz said. Of course. He'd be overseeing Drozdov as the supplies for the Bulgarian mission were loaded onto a truck.

"Let's go," I said. "Maybe I can distract them when they get to counting the cases of morphine."

At the warehouse, a truck was backed up to the entrance, armed guards on either side. They eyed us as soldiers carried out supplies and stacked them under the tarpaulin. Drozdov stood by the door, checking off items on a clipboard.

"What do you want?" Drozdov said, barely looking up from his checklist.

"We thought Colonel Aristov might be here," I said. "Have you seen him?"

"The comrade colonel does not keep me appraised of his whereabouts," Drozdov said as a solider passed by carrying cartons of morphine. He stopped the soldier and counted. He spoke sharply to the man and motioned for him to proceed.

"It seems there is a carton of morphine syrettes missing," Kaz told me. "Major Drozdov has ordered a search of the warehouse."

"It is most likely misplaced," Drozdov said. "Inventory has been taken several times and we have had no thefts."

"Would it be theft if a carton had been directed to the base hospital?" I asked. "Hypothetically, of course. I understand your people were suffering greatly. As opposed to all those Bulgarians, of course."

"How could that happen?" Drozdov snapped. Then his eyebrows rose as he asked a silent question. Satisfied with my silent answer, he wrote on his checklist with a flourish. "How sad I have no time to arrest you, Boyle. Ah yes, they are all here. My error."

"There are occasions in every army when things happen for the best, without the benefit of onerous paperwork," Kaz said.

"On that we agree," Drozdov said, tapping his pen on the clipboard. "But I must know if there were any other occasions for avoiding paperwork."

"Onerous paperwork was avoided only once," I said.

"Good. Now I must check upstairs," Drozdov said. "And here comes the comrade colonel."

Drozdov went inside quickly, almost as if he was eager to avoid his more senior comrade. A jeep screeched to a halt in front of the truck, the newly restored Lieutenant Nikolin at the wheel. Aristov clapped him on the shoulder and vaulted out, firing off a few sentences at Kaz, who saluted and returned the volley. By Kaz's tone I could tell he was trying to confirm something, and that Aristov was being accommodating.

"*Zavtra?*" Kaz asked.

"*Zavtra,*" Aristov said with a firm nod, then hotfooted it into the building.

"He will have our travel orders tomorrow morning," Kaz said. "We can go to Tehran, all three of us."

"Sidorov too?" It was hard to believe.

"Yes. He said he insisted upon a Soviet representative with the investigation at all times," Kaz said. "He said he was too busy today, but we should see him first thing tomorrow, and he will clear the flight manifest with Belov."

"Interesting," I said. I'd wanted to know Drozdov's response but having his boss around to make the decision had gotten in the way of that.

The warehouse door opened and Drozdov stepped out. He held the door for a beefy guard who toted a crate with the money belts weighed down by gold Double Eagles and British sovereigns. Aristov was a step behind him.

"Your colonel has given us permission to go to Tehran," I said to Drozdov. He stopped, glancing at Aristov who kept his eyes on the heavy money belts.

"I am surprised," Drozdov said. "What do you expect to find there?"

"Max," I said, leaving it at that. Drozdov didn't seem worried, but I could tell the surprise was genuine. "You buying or bribing your way through Bulgaria?" I jerked my thumb in the direction of the crate being dropped into the truck.

"If I were going to Bulgaria, I would plan on doing a great deal of both," Drozdov said, signaling to the guards who jumped into the cab. As he did, I caught sight of a silvery vapor trail very high in the sky over the base.

"Would that be one of ours, so high up?" I said, craning my neck back and shielding my eyes.

"No. It is probably a German reconnaissance aircraft," Drozdov said, following the track of the contrail.

"Is that common?" Kaz asked, the blue sky reflected in his steel-rimmed glasses.

"Not common, but not unknown," Drozdov said. "The fascists are too afraid of our fighter coverage to come this far."

"Where are your fighters then?" I said, looking around at the empty sky.

"I am sure they will intercept that scout plane. Now, I must go. There is much to do."

"Isn't Major Black part of all this?" I said.

"He is busy. Language lessons, I believe. Did you know Maiya also speaks Bulgarian?" he said as he jumped up onto the truck bed. "Not that I am going there, of course."

"And not that Black's taking a language class," I said.

"There are many ways to learn, Captain Boyle. Just as long as Major Black is ready for a midnight departure. I sense he is also glad to see the last of you," Drozdov said, the hint of a smile appearing and disappearing as he spoke.

"That's me, making friends wherever I go. Good luck to you, Major," I said, surprised that I meant it and even more surprised that I gave him a salute.

"I do wish you luck in Tehran," Drozdov said, touching his cap and yelling out a command which sent the truck lurching forward in the direction of runway number three. Aristov followed in the jeep, leaving us alone in front of the warehouse.

They'd left the door open. No guards. Kaz pushed it shut and gave a little shrug.

"Things have changed dramatically, haven't they?" Kaz said. "Drozdov even seemed friendly."

"Excited about his mission?" I suggested as we walked back. "It might mean a promotion for him. Sidorov did say Drozdov was being groomed for advancement."

"What about the blind eye he turned to the missing morphine?" Kaz asked.

"I'd bet he was only half joking about not having time to arrest us," I said.

"Arrest *you*," Kaz corrected.

"Thanks for the reminder. Perhaps he didn't mind the morphine going to the base hospital, long as it couldn't be traced to him. Even an NKVD man can have a heart when it comes to the suffering of his own wounded people."

"It was convenient timing," Kaz said. "Black was otherwise engaged, and Aristov was acting like a typical senior officer. Everywhere at once, busy doing nothing."

"Ain't it the way of the world," I said, turning up my collar as the breeze kicked up. It was still sunny, but when the wind blew out of

Siberia, you could feel icicles at the back of your neck. Off the road, a couple of flatbed trucks were setting up, their mounted .50 machine guns pointed menacingly at the sky. Perfect if the Krauts came in low. Useless if they didn't. Soviet efficiency.

CHAPTER THIRTY-TWO

WE CHECKED THE barracks and the mess hall for Sidorov. No dice. Back in Operations, no one had seen him either. I wasn't worried, figuring he was following leads and frightening lower-level comrades with NKVD threats. I popped my head into Bull's office, but he was on the telephone and sounding none too happy. A couple of Army Air Force lieutenants hovered nearby, writing furiously on clipboards. Bull was saying *yes sir* a lot, which meant he was talking to some serious brass. Serious enough that I quietly backed out into the hallway.

"Let's grab some joe," I said to Kaz, who readily agreed.

"The Russians make an excellent tea, I must say."

"That's the first positive thing I've heard you say about this place," I said.

"They kill a lot of Germans," Kaz said as we strolled to the mess hall. "Now you have two positives. Although the second is cancelled out by the fact that they also kill a lot of Poles. Which brings us back to tea. Russia is very good at strong, black tea. And killing."

The mess hall was in an uproar. A huge portrait of Stalin was being carried in. Tables and chairs were moved around and a head table set up, flanked by Soviet and American flags. I got my coffee and Kaz chatted with the server as he drew his tea from a battered samovar.

"War correspondents are coming in from Moscow," Kaz said as we sat and watched the hubbub. "Several Americans and writers from *Izvestia* and *Pravda*." One was the official newspaper of the Soviet government and the other was the official paper of the Communist Party. I wasn't sure what the difference was.

"Maybe that's what Bull was getting an earful of," I said. "And probably Belov too."

"At least we can count on good food tonight," Kaz said. "And vodka. Ah, another positive, although Poland has been making vodka since the early Middle Ages."

"We should count Aristov as a positive," I said. "I didn't expect to get his permission to leave, and certainly not to take Sidorov along."

"I hope it is a positive," Kaz said. "Might not Sidorov try to escape? He faces an uncertain future here."

"Aristov doesn't seem concerned," I said. "Maybe he's satisfied with Sidorov's work."

"I don't know why he would be," Kaz said. "As a team, we have not solved much at all."

"We know how the drugs got to Tehran and where they're going. Which is where we're headed tomorrow. Could be worse," I said, watching as workers struggled with the huge portrait of Stalin.

"Indeed," Kaz said, his gaze following the dark beady eyes of Stalin as he was hung. Or was it hanged? I didn't ask Kaz, knowing which he'd prefer.

Next, they brought in a large map showing the shuttle-bombing routes. From bases in Italy, England, and the USSR, it showed targets in Germany, Poland, Romania, and Bulgaria. Rail and air traffic snaked north from Tehran, showing the flow of Lend-Lease supplies. They were really decorating the joint for the VIPs.

I got a refill and we sat and talked for a while. Not about the case, but about home. Home, meaning the Dorchester Hotel. Kaz's home in Poland was a devastated battleground, chewed up and spat out by two massive armies as the Germans and the Russians battled across it. My home in Boston was too far away to even consider, so for us it was the Dorchester. Comfortable beds, fine food, and a staff fiercely loyal to Kaz.

Kaz's family had been well-off, wealthy enough to send him to Oxford to study languages. In 1938, sensing conflict on the horizon,

Kaz's father had brought the family to England to visit for Christmas. The ostensible purpose was to see Kaz, but his real reason was to move the family to safety in Great Britain. He'd transferred his substantial fortune to Swiss banks and was searching for suitable properties for his family and business. The idea was that by the next Christmas, the Kazimierz clan would be celebrating in their new English home. But by December 1939, Poland was under the Nazi heel, and Kaz's family was wiped out, executed along with other members of the Polish intelligentsia.

All but Angelika, his younger sister who had survived, fought with the Polish Home Army, and had finally been brought out of occupied Europe.

Kaz had a small fortune at his disposal, and he used it to maintain the very suite of rooms at the Dorchester where his family had spent their last days together. It was home, if you counted as home the place where the ghosts of your loved ones gathered around you on long, lonely nights. He let me bunk with him there, and as I looked at him with his hands cupped around a mug of cooling tea, I wondered what would come next for him. A home for him and Angelika after the war? Where? Not Poland, the way things looked. And there were already mutterings in Great Britain about too many foreigners after the war. The British Empire was happy to have anyone who could bear arms, fight the Nazis and die to defeat them. Having to live next door to them after the shooting died down was another thing.

"Come," Kaz said after we'd sat at ease with the silence that bound us together. "Let us see about getting a message to Big Mike. He will need to know to expect us."

We left the mess hall as workers unfurled a long scarlet tablecloth, the lights reflecting a reddish hue across Stalin's grim and jutting jaw.

"I'VE GOT VIPS coming in from every direction," Bull said. "The Moscow Military Mission is demanding we wine and dine them and show them how well we're working with our allies."

"Journalists, we hear," I said.

"Yep. A bunch of Soviet propaganda types have been traveling around with American war correspondents. All one big happy family. So, if you run into any of these guys, keep your lips zipped about the murders," Bull said. Fine, I told him. I wouldn't mind a few hours on any other subject.

"We were able to get permission from Colonel Aristov to leave for Tehran," Kaz said. "Along with Captain Sidorov."

"Really?" Bull said, tossing down a pen and leaning back in his chair. "I'm surprised, but that's good news, right?"

"Yeah," I said, shutting his office door. "We ran a little experiment. We asked Belov and Aristov separately, figuring that the guilty party would say no. Belov was a very insistent *nyet*."

"Does that make him guilty?" Bull asked.

"All it tells me is that for all his demands, he doesn't want us to take the one step that would keep us close to the solution. Aristov had no problem, which in my book says he's not afraid of what we'll find," I said. "Drozdov was also surprised, but he didn't seem concerned."

"It will also give us a chance to squeeze Max harder," Kaz said. "Outside Russia, with few contacts, it may be easier for him to violate his *vor* principles."

"Okay. I'll have a C-47 warmed up and ready whenever you want, just give me the word," Bull said. "And I'll get a message to Big Mike."

"Aristov said he'd have the paperwork in the morning. We'll go as soon as we can. Will you need Belov's approval?"

"No. It's the responsibility of the NKVD officer to approve manifests. Be here at oh-eight-hundred, we'll get his stamp of approval, and then put you on board," Bull said as a knock sounded at the door. It was Sidorov. I explained what he'd been up to and Bull said he wanted to hear.

"I spoke to the few people who were still playing chess. Even a shooting does not stop a good game," Sidorov said, taking a seat. "I spoke to people on the street, to either side of the park. I spoke to the investigating officers. Everybody admits to seeing something, but they cannot quite remember exactly what. Some saw a couple walk by Dmitri. Some saw only a woman. Some saw a soldier, but no one agrees on his rank. One man swears it was a German who had been hiding in a basement. Another claimed it was an English agent."

"The cop's curse," I said. "Everyone wants to tell you what they think you want to hear."

"Exactly. One straightforward old man asked me what he should have seen," Sidorov said. "It was a useless afternoon."

"I saw you gave Maiya a lift," Kaz said.

"Yes. She wanted to see Major Black, and he had little time to spare, apparently."

"We saw Drozdov taking supplies from the warehouse," I said. "All of them. I was surprised Black wasn't there."

"Perhaps he had his hands full. Maiya was in quite a rush," Sidorov said. "Who can blame the man? He is going to the mountains of Bulgaria, after all."

"It can be a lovely country," Kaz said. "In the summer. But now, we have news for you, Captain. Colonel Aristov has given his permission for us to fly to Tehran tomorrow. All three of us."

"What?" Sidorov sat back in his chair as if he'd been pushed. His eyes went wide, and his mouth hung open. "Are you certain?"

"He was quite clear. He wanted the investigation to proceed and for a Soviet representative to be part of it," Kaz said. For once, Sidorov was silent.

"All right," Bull said. "If that's all you've got, get out of my hair. You might as well have one good meal before you leave, they're pulling out all the stops tonight. But get yourself cleaned up, Boyle. Put on a new shirt and look sharp. Shine your boots, for chrissakes. And you, Lieutenant Kazimierz, well, you look fine."

We got out of there before Bull could continue his critique of my military bearing. I decided a shower and shave wouldn't hurt before the shindig, since we didn't have much else to do. On the walk to the barracks, Sidorov was still in disbelief.

"What was Aristov's attitude?" he asked Kaz.

"Brusque, but helpful," Kaz said. "He was very focused on supervising the loading of the truck. There was a lot of valuable material."

"What about the morphine?" Sidorov asked me.

"I confessed to Drozdov in a hypothetical sort of way. I think he approved, although if he wasn't about to leave, he might have felt obligated to follow up. Nothing to worry about."

"When a senior NKVD officer acts in an unusual manner, it is always good to worry," Sidorov said. "But I will take him at his word. What else is there to do?"

"Return to Poltava and make your report when this is all over," Kaz said. "We shall go our way and you yours. You may put the facts, as we learn them, into whatever form Marxist dogma demands."

"Ah, yes. The corrupting materialism of the West and how the criminal classes succumbed to it," Sidorov said. "I can see a scholarly paper on the subject. Excellent idea."

"I'm taking a shower," I said.

CHAPTER THIRTY-THREE

DINNER WAS A disappointment. Fish, cabbage soup, and kasha. The American correspondents had brought along a case of bourbon, so that made them popular with officers who'd had their fill of vodka. After we'd eaten and listened to welcoming speeches in two languages—one boring in English and the other boringly Russian—we began to move around the room.

Sidorov chatted with the *Pravda* reporter while Bull introduced us to W. L. White, one of the American reporters.

"Mr. White wrote *They Were Expendable*," Bull said. "That bestseller about the PT boats in the Pacific."

"They're making a movie of it now," White told us, beaming. "John Wayne in the starring role."

"Sounds great," I said, noticing Kaz already moving away. We'd had our own encounter with PT boats in the Pacific and a troublesome sometime-pal of mine from Boston. Neither of us was interested in revisiting that memory.

I scanned the room for any sign of Drozdov or Black. No sign of them, and for all I knew, they were on their way to Bulgaria.

"What's the big deal with Bulgaria anyway?" I asked Kaz as I sipped my bourbon and watched the Russians for any more familiar faces. Belov was present, of course. But no Maiya. No Aristov.

"Bulgaria was somewhat of a reluctant German ally," Kaz said. "They declared neutrality this summer, and now various factions are urging their leaders to actively declare war on Germany."

"Switching sides before the Russians take over the whole country," I said.

"Yes. The current government wants to remain neutral, but other elements are pushing for a more active anti-German role. There are pro-Western factions and Communist factions, but all seem to want the Germans out. I imagine Black and Drozdov will be working with them and anti-fascist resistance in the mountains to cut off the German retreat. That is only my guess, though," Kaz said, with false modesty. For a lieutenant, he had an excellent diplomatic and strategic sense.

"Drozdov would be under orders to back the Communist faction, wouldn't he? And the same for Black and the pro-Western bunch," I said.

"Yes, of course. And they could be killed by either side. The riches they are carrying would tempt anyone, regardless of political affiliation. However the joint mission has the blessing of the OSS and the NKVD, so perhaps they have some protection. But they will have to be wary."

"Those fools going to Bulgaria?" Sidorov said as he joined us. "I wager they will be dead by this time tomorrow. I had a contact within the Bulgarian secret police, an agent who had Communist sympathies. She provided us with information about their methods, which were barbaric, even by our standards. But then it turned out she was a double agent. Regrettable."

I didn't ask what exactly Sidorov regretted. I didn't want to know.

I got a refill and sat down to sip my bourbon and toast this joint goodbye.

The brass and dignitaries were whooping it up at the head table under the steely gaze of Uncle Joe. I found the big map more interesting and followed the lines, starting in England and leading here, the very bomb run I'd come in on. Sofia, Bulgaria, was on the map from when they were on the Nazi side. Delivery of five-hundred-pound bombs from a squadron of B-17s probably helped them decide to give up that fight.

Someone started singing. It was in Russian, which was momentarily blocked out by "The Star-Spangled Banner." Everyone was out of tune, but it created enough noise to wipe out all the chatter and clatter going on around me. My eyes were glued to that map, and my thoughts were racing, making connections to bits and pieces we'd gathered over the last few hours and days.

Why kill Dmitri? Because he was a threat. A threat to something that was about to happen. A last-minute loose end.

Who approved the Bulgarian mission? Someone high up. Not Belov, since it wasn't a Red air force operation. Someone with clout in the NKVD.

Why was it approved now? Because the drugs were en route. I didn't have concrete proof, but the timing suggested it.

Sidorov's comment about the turncoat Bulgarian agent suggested something too. Switching sides. Hidden agendas. Nothing was as it seemed.

Hidden destinations.

Pieces clicked into place.

If I was right, no one was going to Bulgaria. They were going to Iran. Who were *they*?

I stood, looking around again. Four people were missing from this bash. Black, Drozdov, Aristov, and Maiya.

One of them was a pilot.

"Goddamn it," I muttered. "Molly the Moll."

"What is the matter, Billy?" Kaz said, giving me a concerned look. "Are you talking about Punchy again?"

"No. Not Punchy. Molly. She saw what was coming. She was a dame with a plan, and she made it work. I should have seen it. It was right there in front of me the whole time, but I didn't take her seriously."

"Who?" Sidorov asked.

"Maiya. Didn't you say a woman was spotted in the park?"

"Yes, but every witness was unreliable," Sidorov said.

"And there was also a couple seen near the killing, a woman and a man," I said, keeping at it. "You dropped Maiya off at Black's. How long would it have taken them to get into town? No time at all. That's why Black wasn't at the warehouse, don't you see?"

"But we know their mission has been approved," Kaz said. "By Moscow. Colonel Aristov confirmed it."

"However it happened, we need to find out if Maiya's been assigned to fly them, and if they've left yet. Now!"

We barreled through the carousing crowd to the head table where Bull sat with the correspondents, General Belov, and Lieutenant Nikolin, who clearly looked out of his element. Sidorov spoke quietly to Nikolin, while I beckoned Bull away from the reporters. We didn't need this scheme splashed all over the morning papers, not that the Russians would admit it ever happened.

I gave Bull the lowdown, trying to sound like I knew what I was talking about and hadn't gone off the deep end.

"Jesus, I hope you're wrong, Billy," he said as Belov made his way to us, Sidorov whispering in his ear.

Belov let loose with a long string of Russian, the words wafting over us on a cloud of vodka fumes.

"Yes, Maiya is the assigned pilot," Sidorov translated. "The general says she has proved herself a very capable pilot. Why should she not go? She deserves this honor."

"When are they leaving?" I asked, trying to hide my impatience.

"In less than an hour," Sidorov said, after Belov had checked his watch. "The general planned on going to runway three to see them off."

"Maiya, Drozdov, and Black?" I asked. The general's response was basically *who else?*

"How far is it to their destination?" I asked. It was about eleven hundred kilometers. Seven hundred miles. Belov confirmed she'd be flying a new, more powerful version of the Yak-6 on this mission. The Yak-6M model had a range of over six hundred miles, but she'd still have to refuel along the way.

But they were going even farther than Bulgaria. It was thirteen hundred miles to Tehran, somewhat less to Tabriz. Either way, they'd need two refueling stops. But they'd already planned for that, I was sure.

Kaz filled in the general on our suspicions. Belov made calming gestures, holding out his hands palm down.

"There must be a mistake," Kaz said, translating. "Maiya Akilina is a loyal Soviet officer. Are you saying she came under the corrupting influence of the American spy?"

There was no mention of Drozdov, since that would complicate Belov's one-sided view of things. But this wasn't the time for political debates, so I said yes, it was probably that. Anything to get him moving.

Then the sirens began. The low, mournful wail stopped everybody in their tracks as it wound into a higher, more insistent range.

"Another false alarm?" I asked Bull as people started for the exits, chatting with each other excitedly, showing more curiosity than fear.

"Maybe," he said. "They could still be jumpy from that recon plane this afternoon."

A Red air force officer rushed in and handed Belov a note. He read it, his eyes scanning the paper twice as if he couldn't believe it. He made a grim announcement which Sidorov repeated for the Americans.

"German aircraft were sighted crossing our front lines, on course for the Poltava area. We are on alert," Sidorov said as Belov made for the door.

"Where are the Russian night fighters?" Bull shouted. "When will they intercept the bombers?"

Sidorov spoke quickly to Belov, but the only answer was the door slamming shut behind him.

"Bull, have you ever seen a Russian night fighter?" I asked as we left the building. Outside, people stopped and scanned the skies, bright with stars.

"Never. Belov tells me they're stationed at a nearby base, but he won't say where."

A nearby machine gun fired off a few bursts, the tracers flying in bright arcs into the darkness. A few others sounded off, but it was obvious they were firing blind. The noise of the guns blended with the screaming sirens, all awaiting the oncoming fury.

"You should go to the slit trenches," Bull said. "I've got to get to Operations."

"Runway three!" I said, heading to a jeep. I let Sidorov drive. We needed to get there fast.

All the hangar lights were out, but as we turned onto the runway, I spotted a single aircraft and a couple of nearby vehicles. Sidorov saw it too, and with Kaz hanging on in the back seat he sped up, swerving as he braked to a halt alongside the twin-engine plane.

The darkness turned to light. A bright, brilliant flare burst above us. One, then another, as the Luftwaffe pathfinders dropped their parachute flares. The immediate effect was to illuminate the main runway across from us, where rows of B-17s sat like ducks in a well-lit row.

Closer to us, the face of Maiya Akilina shown like alabaster in the reflected light, her gaze raised skyward. As she turned her eyes on us, her arm rose, the dull sheen of the Tokarev automatic pistol aimed straight at Major Black, who stood next to Drozdov. Black's eyes were wide with shock and surprise, and it didn't seem like it came from the flares.

"What are you doing here?" Maiya snapped, her pistol moving in our direction. I could see Black and Drozdov had already dropped their weapons on the ground. "Get out of the vehicle. Keep your hands where I can seem them, please."

"We're about to be bombed, Maiya. You need to get to cover," I said, figuring she might think we'd come to warn her. "What's with the gun?"

"She's crazy," Black said, desperation in his voice. "I don't know what's going on."

"She says Major Black killed a drug dealer in Poltava," Drozdov said, taking one step away from Black as he edged closer to the aircraft.

"She and Black are in this together," I said. "And she's not going to Bulgaria."

"That's not true," Black said, just as the roar of engines overhead announced the arrival of the main German bomber force. "Jesus, we don't have time for this!" He turned, running for the hangar.

Maiya shot twice. Black crumpled, his faltering momentum rolling his body on his side.

Her pistol returned to me. Sidorov and Kaz stepped aside. Drozdov stood stock still, the shock evident on his face. This is not what he expected of Maiya.

The whistling sounds of falling bombs demanded our attention. The first explosions rippled along the main runway, tearing into the

Fortresses parked wingtip to wingtip. Between us and the explosions I could see ground crew running for their lives. It seemed like a damned good idea.

"There's too many of us, Maiya," I said, taking a tentative step closer to her. "You can't shoot all of us before one of us draws a bead on you."

"I don't have to," she said. Colonel Aristov stepped out of the aircraft, his PPSh-41 *papasha* trained on Drozdov. "Daddy has many bullets for you."

Aristov.

Of course.

Another cascade of bombs fell on the runway. Secondary explosions lit the sky as fuel tanks blew and sent up inky billows of yellow, smoky flames. If daddy didn't kill us, the bombs would finish us off. With a pistol and a *papasha* trained on us, running away would only buy us a patch of blood-soaked earth.

So I ran straight at Maiya, diving into a roll, hoping to distract them long enough for Kaz and Sidorov to unholster and get off a shot. Out of the corner of my eye, I saw Drozdov duck and grab for his pistol, scooping it up as shots rang out in every direction. Two bursts from daddy, then multiple single shots. Maiya screamed, but it wasn't in pain. She was mad, because Kaz and Sidorov were both behind the jeep, firing at Aristov, who was in front of the aircraft. She needed it functional, not full of holes.

I rolled under the wheels of the aircraft, getting my automatic out just as Aristov stepped in front of me and put a lethal burst into Drozdov, who'd managed to get off a couple of shots.

With Drozdov out of the way, Maiya knelt and jammed her pistol into my neck. I dropped my automatic and raised my hands as best I could.

"Stop shooting!" she yelled. There was enough light for Kaz and Sidorov to see what she was up to. Protecting the aircraft. And there was enough light for me to see the blood dripping down Aristov's leg. He'd been hit.

"Let him go," Kaz shouted as another volley of bombs hit the main runway. They were targeting the bombers, very carefully, and at their damned leisure.

"No. You come out. If you fire, Boyle dies," Maiya said, twisting the red-hot barrel against my neck. "We just want to take off."

Sidorov stood, his pistol held in his hand, but at his side.

"It was you all along, wasn't it, Maiya? You planned this. You used Black and all the others. Aristov as well," he said, frank admiration in his voice.

"Not that anyone would ever think a woman capable," Maiya said. "I wanted so much more than to be a mere interpreter. But men, they can only see what they desire. Not what is."

"This is all fine, but can I stand?" I asked as Maiya dragged me out from under the aircraft. "If I'm going to be shot or blown up, I'd prefer to do it standing." Another salvo of bombs hit the far end of the main runway, followed by the *wooshing* explosion of fuel drums.

"You may stand," Maiya said, jamming the gun into my ribs.

"There is no need of further killing," Kaz said. "Go. You have all you need."

Aristov growled something to Maiya, who nodded. He grimaced as he raised his submachine gun, blood squishing in his boots. It looked like what they needed was us dead.

"Wait," Sidorov said, holding up a hand. His eyes went to Aristov, who held a grimace of pain in check, his jaw clenched. Then Sidorov put the full force of his gaze on Maiya. "Is this man special to you in any way? A lover, perhaps? A relative?"

Why was Sidorov asking her in English? To keep Aristov in the dark?

Maiya held up her hand for Aristov to wait. He held his weapon steady but did not fire. A questioning look spread across his features as Maiya looked at his leg, the blood glistening in the reflected light of the fires all around us.

Maiya looked to Sidorov. She raised an eyebrow.

"No, he is not special," she said, turning slightly as she raised the Tokarev to Aristov's temple and fired.

His skull bloomed pink and Sidorov's pistol was suddenly in Kaz's back as he relieved him of his Webley. Maiya scooped up the submachine gun and shoved me roughly toward Kaz.

"Don't tell me this was part of your plan," I said, involuntarily hunching my shoulders as more bombs cascaded beyond us.

"One must adapt," Maiya said. "The colonel quickly became a liability. I could not tend to him while flying, and it would be inconvenient to land with a dead NKVD officer. And I know, if Captain Sidorov does not, that he will be returned to the labor camp. Whether I get away or not."

"I am sorry, gentlemen," Sidorov said, collecting the weapons left on the ground. "But it is the only option I have left. I know Maiya needs a colleague. A male colleague of some useful rank. And I need to leave the country. This outcome is not what Moscow desires."

"I hope you'll live to enjoy it," I said. "Her other male colleagues sure didn't."

Sidorov didn't respond but leaned in to whisper to Maiya. She frowned, then nodded her agreement to whatever he said, and he motioned Kaz to the plane.

"No, you're not taking him!" I said, stepping forward but halted by the muzzle of the *papasha*.

"Do not worry," Maiya said, her face glowing red. "He only wishes to make you a peace offering. It will make him more compliant if he assuages his guilt, which is why I allow it."

Kaz stood by the rear door of the aircraft as Sidorov loaded him up with the cartons of morphine.

"Stand there," Sidorov directed, moving me closer to Kaz. "Do not move, either of you."

Maiya handed him the submachine gun and got into the plane, making her way to the pilot's compartment. She switched on one engine, then the other. As they began to rev up, Sidorov hung out the rear door.

"I wish it could have turned out differently," he said. "But we did solve the case, in a manner of speaking."

"Tell it to Black and Drozdov," I said, as the prop blast hit me.

"Black was a fool and a dupe, that is obvious," Sidorov said, shouting over the increasingly loud engines. "He would have never survived in the field. As for Drozdov, well, as you well know, we men of the NKVD all have blood on our hands." With that, he gave a wry grin, flicked a salute in our direction, and pulled the door shut.

The Yak-6M rolled down the runway, flames from burning B-17s lighting the way. Maiya lifted off, went wheels up, and stayed low, snaking over the hangars to stay out of the spray of antiaircraft fire. She disappeared into the night as the Russian gunners kept up their fireworks and more columns of flame and black smoke erupted from the main runway.

"Christ on a crutch," I said. "What the hell do we do now?"

"Take this to Dr. Mametova," Kaz said, hefting the cases in his hands. "She will need it before this night is done."

CHAPTER THIRTY-FOUR

I FELT BAD leaving Drozdov and Black out in the open, but there wasn't time to move their bodies. The jeep had taken some hits in the shootout, but it started. Kaz cradled the morphine as I drove to the hospital, leaving the runways behind. The last of the flares had died away and one more salvo of explosions rippled across the ground, tearing into hangars and igniting fuel drums, sending them rocketing skyward.

We made it to the hospital on a flat tire and boiling radiator. Men were being carried in on stretchers, most of them Russian. Dr. Mametova was inside, inspecting the wounded. She saw Kaz, did a double take, and snapped out an order to a nurse, who relieved Kaz of his pain-dulling burden.

"I told her to ask no questions," Kaz said. "She told the nurse it was a gift from Stalin, which no one will question."

We got out of the way as the main lobby became jammed with walking wounded who'd made their own way in. We bumped into Bull, dragging a dazed Yank whose arm and forehead dripped blood.

"It's bad," Bull said as a nurse relieved him of his charge. "Too soon to tell, but it looks like half our B-17s have been hit."

"It's bad on our end too," I said. "Different kind of bad."

"Let's get out of here, I need to get back to Operations," Bull said, hustling outside. We followed, watching the fires along the main runway and the nearby buildings cast their eerie glow.

"We need a lift," I said, pointing to our bullet-ridden jeep.

"What the hell happened? No, never mind, I can only handle one

SNAFU at a time," Bull said, craning his neck to search the smoke-filled sky. "Looks like we have a lull. There'll be a second wave for sure, to hit everyone who comes out for damage control."

"The first thing we need to do is search Maiya's desk," Kaz said as Bull sped down the thoroughfare. "Then Black's." Kaz was already thinking along the same lines as I was. Maiya was too smart to let us live unless she had some trick up her sleeve.

"Maiya? What's she got to do with this?" Bull snarled as he braked to avoid a column of Russians with shovels hotfooting it to the hangars. A damage control party.

As if on cue, the roar of low-level aircraft sounded from the horizon, drawing closer as Bull blasted the horn and I swiveled my head trying to spot the threat. Explosions bracketed the road and machine guns spat tracer rounds in every direction. Bull pulled over, coming to a halt alongside a brick building. We took cover between the jeep and the wall, making ourselves as small as possible.

Bullets were flying in every direction. Up, down, and everywhere in between. Explosions blossomed all around us, the low-level bombers not as precise as the first wave but doing a good job of beating up the place as our B-17s burned. We stayed that way for ten minutes, until the attack abated. The Russians were still firing away with their machine guns, but the sky was empty.

"Is that it?" Kaz asked, raising his head above the jeep.

"Probably," Bull said, standing up. "I don't know where the hell the Russian night fighters have been, but those Germans have to be worried about them showing up. The Krauts are hightailing it for home if they're smart."

I walked around the jeep, cocking my ear for the sound of more approaching bombers. Flickering, rosy light danced along the roadway, shadows appearing and vanishing in an instant, smoke billowing and drifting around us. It was hell.

Then it was white-hot noon. The night sky turned white.

"Stop!" Bull yelled.

"What's that?" Kaz said.

"Don't move, dammit!" Bull shouted. "Butterfly bombs."

The intense white light was gone, and we were back to the reddish reflective glow. I could make out a small object at my feet. Butterfly? It did look like it had wings.

"Anti-personnel bomb," Bull said, working to keep his voice calm. "The Krauts drop 'em by the boatload at the end of a raid. Don't move a muscle. It'll gut you."

As my eyes adjusted, I could see it more clearly. It was about three inches long, with hinged sides that did make it look like a cast iron killer butterfly. And it was inches from my toe.

"I spotted it when that magnesium flash bomb went off," Bull said, reaching into the jeep. "Good news is the raid's over. That flash was for the recon planes to photograph the bomb damage."

"I can guess the bad news," I said, as Bull stood in the jeep and shone the flashlight around.

"How lethal are they?" Kaz asked. "At a distance, I mean."

"They can kill at thirty feet," Bull said. "We're clear except for that one. Billy, take two steps backwards. Carefully."

It was harder to do than it sounded, with a gutting death close to my boot. But I made it to the jeep. Bull set the flashlight on the grass, just as a short, sharp explosion cracked from the other side of the building.

We all jumped. The flashlight rolled. Bull's arm shot out and grabbed it, inches from the butterfly. He set the light down again, held in place by a couple of stones, the beam shining on the bomb.

"Let's go," he said. "Some of these things go off on their own, others when you touch them."

"Slowly," Kaz added. "And carefully."

I couldn't speak. I could barely breathe.

Bull drove like molasses, his headlights illuminating the road ahead. We spotted two more butterfly bombs and left gear from the jeep to mark them. At Operations, everyone was running around or yelling into field telephones. The Americans looked panicked. The Russians looked like they were about to be shot. If anyone from the NKVD above the rank of lieutenant had been here, they might have been. This was a disaster.

"Where the hell are your sidearms?" Bull asked, noticing our empty holsters for the first time.

"You've got bigger things to worry about," I said. "Right now, we need to search Maiya's desk to see if she left any clue."

"Clue? No, never mind. But first, come with me. You can't walk around disarmed. It doesn't look good," Bull said. "You've got time before the Russians come out of their shock. Half of them are waiting for Moscow to tell them what to do, and the other half are afraid to tell Moscow what happened."

Back in his office, Bull unlocked the filing cabinet and took out two Smith & Wesson .38 revolvers and a box of cartridges.

"Not a Webley, but it will do," Kaz said, loading his.

"Didn't know you had your own armory," I said, checking the weapon.

"They're from guys who were wounded. They don't need them," Bull said. It wasn't exactly a cheery thought, but I did feel better with some weight on my hip. The general pointed us to Maiya's desk and headed into a conference room where we could see Belov, sitting at a table, staring into space.

"I will never make fun of your stories again," Kaz said as he sat in Maiya's chair. "Molly the Moll had nothing on our Maiya." He began shuffling through the papers on her desk.

"That's what blinded me," I said. "*Our Maiya*. Mischievous and helpful. A pretty girl with a friendly smile. Completely disarming."

"Literally," Kaz said, opening a drawer.

"She used Aristov to set it all up. Remember she told us Aristov was from the Directorate of Border and Internal Guards?"

"GUPVO," Kaz said, flipping through a book and tossing it aside.

"Right. But Belov told us one of Aristov's recent accomplishments was breaking up a gang that was looting trains."

"You're right," Kaz said. "There is a different directorate for railway security. She lied about that to cover up Aristov's role."

"It was the only thing that fit," I said. "Once Sidorov mentioned the Bulgarian contact who switched sides, I realized there had to be someone on the inside who could get themselves clear of this place. The Bulgarian mission had to be their way out. As soon as Belov confirmed Maiya was the pilot, I knew it was true. Molly the Moll switched sides and got away with it. Maiya did the same, in spades. I think she set this whole thing in motion and recruited the people she needed."

"Like Lieutenant Mishkin, until he got greedy and struck out on his own," Kaz said.

"Yeah. That signed his death warrant," I said.

"Aristov could have arranged for Max to be brought here," Kaz said, pausing in his search of Maiya's paperwork. "We assumed it was Drozdov, but an NKVD colonel can pull many strings."

"Right. And when Kopelev started getting suspicious, and Morris refused to cooperate, she probably had Max kill them. With Black forced to witness it, which frightened him into cooperating."

"Major Black was a foolish man," Kaz said. "There was no way Maiya would have let him live. All she needed him for was to ship the heroin to Tehran under his name."

"We know the drugs went to Tehran," I said. "Now we need to figure out the next stop. Odds are it isn't Tabriz."

"We would be dead if it were," Kaz said, taking out a drawer and dumping the contents on top of the desk. I glanced at the conference room, where Russians sat stony-faced and unmoving.

Kaz was right. Khazar Brothers Shipping might still be handling the smuggling, but it wasn't going through Tabriz. Maiya's daddy would have laid us on the ground if that had been true. She knew we'd seen the cases with their destination clearly marked. Which meant they were going someplace else.

"We need to get word to Big Mike," I said as Kaz went through the last drawer. "He's got to know about Sidorov before our Russian pal shows up and pulls a fast one."

"Yes," Kaz said. "Sidorov made a gallant gesture with the morphine, but I think Maiya was right. It was to lessen the guilt he felt at betraying us. Knowing the punishment that awaits him if captured, he will do anything to avoid it. That makes him dangerous. And this desk has no clues to offer." With that, he slammed shut the drawer.

Black's office was next. There was more to search, but at least it was all in English. Kaz tried the desk and I went for the filing cabinet. Both were locked. I remembered he left a key in the top desk drawer. Kaz tried it, but it wouldn't budge.

"Stand clear," I said, and flipped the desk over. I stomped on the bottom of the center draw, the thin wood cracking beneath my heel. "There's always an alternative."

I grabbed the key as an American sergeant looked in on us.

"Redecorating," Kaz said. "We shall call if we need assistance."

"Have at it, sir," the sergeant said, and made himself scarce.

I didn't know what we were looking for exactly or how we could ever track them down, but we had to try. Maiya and her accomplices had left too many bodies in their wake.

Not to mention I'd trusted Sidorov. Maybe he'd felt he had no choice. Maybe that was true. Either way, he'd repaid my trust with betrayal, and I couldn't let that stand. I had to find him and bring him back, road of bones or no.

"Anything to do with Turkey?" I asked Kaz as he sifted through the contents of the drawers. "An alternate route?"

"No. It is not as easy as turning over a desk, since we don't know what to look for."

I flipped through the files, looking for anything out of place. Unfortunately, the OSS had a wide range of interests, so everything looked like a clue. There were thick files on Mohammad Reza Pahlavi, a kid who had taken over from his old man as king, or shah, of Iran.

Lots of stuff on Iraq too. Crown Prince Abdullah was our man there. I hadn't heard of him, but I had heard of oil. Lots of files on oil rights and possible Nazi agents, but nothing that clicked as a clue.

Then I spotted a file marked 482nd Port Battalion, US Army.

We were a long way from any port. I pulled the file and flipped through the mimeographed pages. It contained lists of officers and men, radio call signs, battalion headquarters staff, and an inventory of heavy equipment.

"Stevedores," I said, half to myself. "Longshoremen."

"Where?" Kaz asked, tossing a pile of papers aside.

"I don't know. It's a port battalion, but all it says is they're posted to Camp Gifford, wherever that is."

"Wait," Kaz said, diving into his pile of papers. "I just saw something about Camp Gifford." He came up with a folded map and laid it out on the floor. The heading read *Persian Gulf Command—Camps, Posts, Stations.*

It showed the primary road and rail routes in Iran. In the north, the routes connected to Tehran and locations marked Camp Stalingrad and Russian Check Station. Heading south through the cities of Qum and Hamadan, places named Road Camp #4 and Camp Schindler stood out. The rail line went all the way to the Persian Gulf, terminating in a place called Bandar Shapur. Right next to that port was Camp Gifford.

"Bandar Shapur," Kaz said. "It is the perfect location."

"Why?"

"There is no real town there. The rail line terminates at the wharves, and the area is frequently flooded. The port's only purpose is the unloading of supplies from ships to trains," Kaz said.

"And vice versa, in Maiya's case," I said, studying the map. It was much farther than Tabriz, which is why it was perfect.

"Yes. The trains arrive empty, so it would be a simple matter for a small party to arrive with cargo to go out on one of the neutral vessels. Then a short voyage via the Suez Canal, and they are in the Mediterranean."

"With Marseilles just a hop skip away," I said.

"Where Max has undoubtedly arranged for the sale," Kaz said. "His criminal connections make him vital to Maiya. But will Sidorov survive the journey?"

"We're not going to let them make that journey," I said. "We're getting to Bandar Shapur before them."

We found Bull in his office, surrounded by officers giving damage reports for their squadrons. We stepped back to cool our heels in the hall. From what I could hear, it was bad.

"Had you suspected Drozdov?" Kaz asked in a low voice as he leaned against the wall.

"I wasn't sure what we'd find when we got to the aircraft," I said. "I didn't buy Black as much more than a patsy. I wouldn't have been surprised if it was Drozdov. He certainly could have had the NKVD connections to make things happen. But Aristov was a shock, especially when he showed up with that submachine gun."

"Major Drozdov saved our lives," Kaz said. "If he hadn't gone for his weapon we might well have been dispatched in the next moment."

"I bet that's the first time a Pole owed his life to an NKVD man," I said.

"And the last, I would wager. Sidorov owes him a debt as well. He would not be aboard that aircraft if Drozdov hadn't wounded Aristov," Kaz said. "I hope our erstwhile colleague will have the opportunity to thank the major directly before too long."

"Sidorov's got nine lives. But this time, there's no one on his side. Maiya needs him as a front man, but once that's over with, he doesn't stand a chance," I said.

"Kiril Sidorov is not stupid," Kaz said. "He knows that. Perhaps he will eliminate Maiya first."

"Hey, Max could be the last man standing, you never know."

A half-dozen grim-looking airmen filed out of Bull's office as he yelled for us to get in there.

"I can tell you're up to something," he said. "You got ten minutes, then I'm headed out to check on the men."

"Bad as you thought?" I asked.

"Worse. Some of the B-17s I thought weren't hit were riddled with shrapnel. Small holes, but lots of them. Hydraulics and who knows what else shot to hell. Now, what do you need?"

"We need to get to Bandar Shapur," I said. "It's a port on the Persian Gulf."

"That's where they're headed?"

"Yes," Kaz said. "We found evidence in Major Black's office. We are working under the assumption that Maiya would not have let us live if they really were going to Tabriz. Either it was a change of plans, or it was a ruse all along. We know Khazar Brothers Shipping is a front for smugglers, so they may still be involved."

"From Bandar Shapur they can board a ship and be anywhere in the Mediterranean," I said. "Can you get us there, pronto?"

"That looks to be about two thousand miles," Bull said, standing to check the large wall map behind him. "What'd they fly out of here in?"

"A Yak-6M," Kaz said.

"They'll have to make several refueling stops," Bull said. "Think they're flying all the way?"

"No. Maiya will want to rendezvous with Max and the drug shipment. She's got to avoid Tehran since she knows we'll be on the lookout for her there," I said.

"There's plenty of airfields," Bull said. "They're all along the route into the Soviet Union, set up for ferrying Lend-Lease aircraft north. She could land at a Russian base outside of Tabriz and get enough fuel to land near a railway stop and hop aboard the train. Especially if she's got local smugglers working for her."

"Okay, so we need to get going. How soon can we get out of here?"

"You're in luck," Bull said. "It was a little hard going through Belov's backup interpreter, but I managed to explain that Moscow wouldn't be happy with pictures in American newspapers showing they couldn't protect their guests. I convinced the general that it would be in his interest to get the American journalists out of here before they saw the true extent of the damage."

"Meaning before dawn," Kaz said.

"Exactly," Bull said, checking his watch. "The air transport squadron wasn't hit too bad, since the Krauts really focused on the bombers. A C-47 will depart for Tehran in ninety minutes from runway one. Be there."

"Thanks, Bull. You sure Belov will approve our names on the manifest?"

"He already has. I also suggested that letting you two go would help disguise the fact that the Soviet member of this investigation went over to the other side. The story will be that all three of you went in pursuit of the killer. Undoubtedly, that killer will be Preston Black, as far as the official Russian account will go."

"But Black's dead," I said. "His body is out on runway three."

"Hell, getting killed is the most useful thing he ever did," Bull said. "The Army brass hates the OSS, so everyone's happy that the blame gets pinned on that outfit, Russians included."

"I know Black was worthless, but it doesn't seem right," I said.

"Billy, do not let facts get in the way of a satisfying story," Kaz said. "We are obviously in pursuit of Black's accomplices. The disorganizers of the rear, remember?"

"Sorry, I forgot where we were."

"You're not going to like Bandar Shapur much better. I wouldn't recommend it for the climate," Bull said. "It's usually over one hundred degrees, and the humidity is unbelievable. It's basically a low-lying mud flat covered with cranes, warehouses, wharves, and railroad cars. Nobody is happy to be there. Except the bugs."

"I shall be delighted," Kaz said, resting his hand on his holster.

CHAPTER THIRTY-FIVE

Bull had a GI drive us to our barracks and then out to the runway, headlights on to avoid lethal butterflies. Bull said he'd radio Big Mike and Gideon to expect us at Tehran, and that we'd be flying straight through to the airstrip at Camp Gifford. It almost seemed like a plan.

At the runway, trucks and jeeps were lined up with high beams illuminating the steel grating. All the hangar lights were blazing as well. We watched as a line of Russian soldiers crawled forward on their hands and knees, searching for more butterfly bombs. A few had flashlights or lanterns, but most inched forward in darkness until they came upon one of the deadly packages.

At a shout, we saw one had been discovered. The entire line crawled backwards, and one man with a long wooden pole advanced to the front. A low cart filled with stones was wheeled up and he knelt behind it, pushing the pole out to the bomb. He gave a yell and everyone within the blast range flattened themselves.

He pushed the pole and the bomb exploded, a nasty, sharp crack that left acrid smoke hanging in the air. The line moved on and another pole was brought up.

"This looks almost civilized compared to what Lieutenant Nikolin went through," I said.

"Almost civilized. I wonder when the world will return to fully civilized," Kaz said. "It has been so long."

"I'm not sure, but I think I'll pay more attention to it next time around," I said. "I'm pretty sure I took civilization for granted."

As the runway was cleared, a C-47 was towed out of its hangar and a truck brought up the war correspondents for boarding. That was our cue. I glanced around at the smoldering landscape and said goodbye to the land of Night Witches, Stalin, vodka, and betrayal. Tatyana, *Mayor* Amosova, Kolesnikov, Teddy, and a few others had been good, decent people, fighting to free their country and avenge their fallen comrades. They did it with great courage, living in a police state but managing to maintain their dignity. There were a lot like them, I was sure, and I wished them well. I was just happy to be doing it from afar.

Once aboard, I checked in with the pilot. It would be about ten hours flying time to Camp Gifford via Tehran. I figured that gave us time to get to Bandar Shapur ahead of Maiya and her band of smugglers. Her Yak-6M was slower than our C-47, but she had a good head start. Our main advantage was that we'd get closer to the port by air than she would, depending on where and how she rendezvoused with the train.

Kaz and I grabbed the rearmost bench seats, putting some distance between us and reporters. There were four wounded airmen on board, and thankfully they received most of the correspondents' attentions.

As soon as we were airborne, Kaz and I began to plan. We'd have Big Mike, bad ankle and all, Gideon from CID, and the Iranian police inspector. We'd need vehicles and drivers from Camp Gifford to get us to the port, and a few more GIs for security.

"A harbormaster," Kaz said. "They must have one for the port. Someone who knows the ships and unloading schedules."

"Good idea," I said. "The kind of ship we're looking for probably isn't one of the Liberty ships. They're all part of the Merchant Marine."

"That doesn't make their crews immune to greed," Kaz said, speaking up to be heard over the drone of the engines. Luckily there were empty seats between us and the rest of the passengers.

"No, but I'm betting on Max having contacts with someone on a neutral vessel. Some ship that works these waters," I said. "It'd be much easier to bribe the captain of some coastal rust bucket. Of course, all that goes out the window if Max has decided to go into business for himself. He could have double-crossed Maiya for all we know."

"I doubt it," Kaz said, pulling out his duffel and resting his legs on it. "The Khazars are smugglers, that is certain. But do they have the wherewithal to sell heroin to organized crime? That seems out of their league. But gold and weapons are another matter."

"Damn, you're right. All the loot from the warehouse, that must be their payment. It's a damn sight easier to sell all that than trying to move heroin."

"Exactly," Kaz said. "Which is why the Khazars are not going to let Max out of their sight. They need to make the rendezvous with Maiya to obtain their payment. And smugglers have their reputation to consider. If word got out that they lost a client's shipment, business would suffer."

If you can't trust your smuggler, who can you trust?

Knowing that Max and the drugs were in the safe, if mercenary, hands of the Khazar family, I stretched out and pulled the visor of my service cap down over my eyes. It was after midnight, and it was going to be a long flight. Not to mention a long day.

SEATS IN A C-47 aren't built for comfort. I managed to sleep off and on and, of course, deep sleep overcame me only minutes before the aircraft touched down in Tehran. A couple of jolting bumps and we were taxiing slowly toward a hangar where a line of staff cars and jeeps stood ready.

The wounded were taken off and whisked away, followed by the correspondents. As we deplaned, I spotted Big Mike on his crutches, grinning at us.

"Welcome to Tehran," he said, pumping our hands as he balanced on one crutch. "It's good to see you guys."

"Same here, Big Mike," I said, eyeing the two men standing behind him. I figured the colonel was Gideon, so I shot him a salute. He was tall, tanned, and had a solid face with gray hair showing at the temples.

"Captain William Boyle, sir," I said, and introduced Kaz.

"This is Colonel Gideon," Big Mike said. "And that's Inspector Javid Ghazi of the Iranian National Police." I shook hands with

Inspector Ghazi, a thin fellow with a dark mustache and thick black hair. He wore a dark brown khaki uniform and an expression of keen anticipation.

"Come inside," Gideon said. "We have food and coffee laid on. We'll take off as soon as they finish refueling."

Gideon led us into a brick building next to the hangar, and I could hear Kaz speaking to the inspector in a language I didn't recognize.

"Your Farsi is excellent, Lieutenant Kazimierz," Inspector Ghazi said, and they began to chat up a storm as Gideon led the way.

"How's the ankle?" I asked Big Mike.

"Better," he grunted. "As in it better get better or I'll go crazy."

"I never heard anyone complain so much in my life," Gideon said, holding the door open. I could tell another senior officer had come under the spell of the big sergeant.

"Why do you think we sent him here?" I said.

Inside, sandwiches and thermoses were set out, along with bowls of plums and apricots.

"What's the latest, Colonel?" I asked as I poured myself a mug of joe.

"Max is aboard a southbound train, headed for Bandar Shapur," he said. "The train left this morning, and we assume Max has the heroin on board."

"We decided it was safer not to watch the train too closely," Inspector Ghazi said, picking out an apricot and biting into it. "The Khazars are probably guarding it, and we wished to not show ourselves. I have men positioned along the route to watch for any unscheduled stops."

Kaz went over his theory about the gold and other valuables being the Khazars' payment.

"Yes, it is true the Khazar Brothers are skilled smugglers, with a very good reputation in certain circles. But moving a large quantity of heroin? No, that is beyond them. They would be cheated or killed. As you say, Lieutenant, gold and weapons, that is more their style," Ghazi said. "An immediate payoff."

"Bull's message said Sidorov went over to them," Big Mike said.

"There was a sudden need for a replacement," Kaz said. "Sidorov decided, quite rightly, that his days in the USSR were numbered. Suffice it to say he has nothing to lose."

"As long as they are in Iran, they will face the harshest of penalties for drug trafficking," Ghazi said. "A fact I assume they are aware of. So, we may expect a fight. There is no reason for them to surrender."

"We'll need firepower," I said.

"I've got Thompsons for all of us," Gideon said. "And an M1 for Big Mike, since we'll probably stash him somewhere with a good view of the area. He won't be much use hopping around."

"Do you know Bandar Shapur, Inspector?" Kaz asked.

"I do. It is an unpleasant place. Very hot. The air is thick and filled with insects. Before the war there was a single narrow-gauge rail line and one pier. Your engineers have laid more track and built two wharves. The boxcars are brought alongside the wharves and the cargo is off-loaded directly into them."

"That's when we make our move," Gideon said. "I want the shippers, the smugglers, and the Russians. We'll need men on each wharf."

"Is there a harbormaster?" Kaz asked.

"Yes, an officer every shift who oversees the unloading," Gideon said. "He'll be with us, plus a few GIs."

"What about native workers?" I asked Ghazi. "Can you get any of your men in there?"

"This is not your Wild West, Captain," he said. "Yes, there are Iranians who are employed on the docks, but we must assume the Khazars have their spies. Any sudden new arrivals would be suspect."

"Sorry, Inspector," I said. "No offense meant."

"Do not worry. We were once an empire ourselves, and no doubt carried our biases to the far corners of the known world," Ghazi said, with a faint smile.

"Okay," Gideon said. "My suggestion is that we split up. Each wharf will have one ship tied up at a time. When the train arrives, we should be in place. Billy and I will get on one vessel, the Inspector and Lieutenant Kazimierz on the other."

"What about me, Colonel?" Big Mike asked.

"I want to find some high ground for you and that M1. We'll figure that out once we're there."

"What about the lighters?" Ghazi asked.

"Lighters?" I said around a mouthful of a cheese sandwich.

"Barges that take loads from ships offshore," Ghazi said. "The original pier has been strengthened and is now used for lighters. When the tide is low, many of your ships cannot enter the harbor. So, cargo is taken off and brought in by lighter."

"Give me a driver and I can scout the lighters," Big Mike said. "Does the train run straight to that pier?"

"The original rail line did, so we should assume it still does," Ghazi explained. "I was last there a year ago, when we arrested a black-market ring."

"The key is to spot them at the docks," I said. "From there, they have no place to run."

"Bandar Shapur is a maze of roads, railroad tracks, brick buildings, supply dumps, and construction equipment," Ghazi said. "There are plenty of places to hide if they get spooked. There's nowhere to go, true. But they can split up and lose themselves."

"They're not going to leave their drugs and gold," I said. "It's all they have."

"Then we shall take it from them," Kaz said, taking a plum from the bowl and cutting it, twisting the flesh until it came apart in his hands, juice running between his fingers like blood.

CHAPTER THIRTY-SIX

AS WE DESCENDED at Camp Gifford, I could feel the C-47 begin to heat up. We landed on the dirt runway, the props blowing up a tornado of dust as the pilot taxied to a halt. No hangars, no tower, just a barren stretch of brown with a few jeeps waiting for us.

The rear door opened, and it felt like stepping into a furnace. We were all in shirtsleeves, and I was soaked by the time I'd taken ten steps.

"Welcome to tropical Iran," Ghazi said as he hoisted the tommy gun over his shoulder. "It is not an agreeable climate, sorry to say."

"At least the bugs like it," I said, slapping my neck. In the distance, I could see rows of tents baking under the sun. Low buildings made of mud bricks sat in a neat orderly row, their metal roofs shimmering with heat.

We had four jeeps, each with an armed driver. We helped Big Mike into one and then split up, Gideon with me and Kaz with Ghazi. We had three handheld walkie-talkies, canteens of water, and sort of a plan. Don't let them get on a boat, then don't let them get away.

"We just got word that the train is due in one hour, sir," our driver said to Gideon. He was a sergeant named Fenwick, and he told us he'd volunteered for this shindig out of boredom and a desire to see some of the shooting war before it was all over. I was about to tell him it wasn't fun and games but held back. No need to crack wise with a guy I might need for backup.

Fenwick said we had about a half-hour's drive, and Gideon told him to step on it. Our little convoy took off, raising dust as we headed for the wharves.

"How many freight cars in these trains?" I asked Fenwick, leaning forward from the rear seat.

"A hundred or more," he said. "They run these big trains double-headed so's they can pull a big load."

"Double-headed?" I asked.

"Two locomotives," he said.

"What about cargo," Gideon said. "Do these boxcars carry freight down here?"

"Oh sure," Fenwick said. "Nothing like what they haul back, but there's always some agricultural products. A load of carpets now and then. Every train brings something, since those ships don't like goin' back empty."

"They unload first, I guess," I said. "Then they take on cargo from the ships?"

"Right. They offload near the wharf. Usually the boxcars up front are the ones carrying a load. Makes it easier that way," Fenwick said.

"That's what we want to watch," Gideon said.

"From a nice shady spot, I hope."

"Not much shade on the wharves," Fenwick said. "Not much shade anywhere. Lookit, not a damn tree in sight. There's a reason no one lives around here."

Even the breeze from driving felt like being whacked with a hot blanket. I didn't know how this whole thing was going to work out, but I wanted it to be quick.

The terrain was flat, broken only by the occasional dry gulch or jumble of rocks. The road was straight, and the effect was mesmerizing as mirages danced on the horizon. As we drove on, I saw what looked like a wall dead ahead.

"What the hell is that?" I asked.

"It's an earthen berm," Fenwick said. "The port is just below sea level, so at high tide it can flood. Engineers built a five-foot berm around the whole area to keep the tidal waters out."

"It's amazing anyone can work in this heat," Gideon said.

"It ain't hard, Colonel," Fenwick said. "Long as you don't mind heat stroke. Drink your water."

We did. Fenwick slowed as we crested the incline built over the wall. I caught a quick glimpse of Bandar Shapur from what was the highest point around. It was massive—a huge, depressed, flat surface covered in supply dumps, hardpack roadways, and train tracks. Flat-roofed buildings ran along the main road, trucks parked everywhere. Cranes stood tall at the water's edge, where I could see four ships docked at the two wharves. Beyond them, on the far side of the curving shore, was a single pier with two small vessels moored up. Lighters, I guess. From there, a long stretch of flatland ran up to the berm, probably two miles from here.

In the distance I spotted a faint plume of smoke and heard the whistle from a locomotive.

"That's our train," Fenwick said, gunning the jeep once we'd gone down the other side.

"No checkpoints or sentries around the perimeter?" Gideon asked, craning his neck to track the smoke from the locomotive.

"Who the hell would want to get in here? Sir." Fenwick said. "The supply dumps are guarded, especially those that got food. But this perimeter? Ain't got enough guys to patrol it."

This place made a sieve look like a Diebold safe.

If it was possible, it was even hotter and more humid within the confines of Bandar Shapur. Acres of steel and iron held the heat in, and the waters from the gulf added their moisture to form a thick, sticky mass of air that hung heavily over us.

I drank more water.

We pulled up at the wharf, filled with sailors from the Liberty ships and GIs working the winches and unloading supplies from the ships' holds. Large crates stood along the wharf, right next to the tracks that were laid along it. Narrow-gauge stuff, which meant for smaller boxcars. No wonder they needed so many. There was a mountain of goods ready to go, and a half dozen other vessels were moored offshore, waiting their turn.

Gathering around Big Mike's jeep, Gideon began to give orders.

"Big Mike, you and your driver stand guard by the lighters. Take one of the other drivers and check them out. Call on the walkie-talkie if you spot anything. And keep your eyes peeled in our direction. They may get right off once their boxcar is close enough."

"Got it," Big Mike said, as Kaz's driver joined them. "I'll call in once we talk to the lighter crew." The three of them took off, and Gideon studied the cargo ships in front of us.

"These ships have 20mm gun mounts above the bridge," Gideon said. "A good observation point, and we can keep hidden."

"Farther for us to come down once we spot them, Colonel," I said. "Although it is the best vantage point." I'd found the best way to disagree with a senior officer was to agree with him, right after you explained why he'd been wrong.

"Colonel, allow me to suggest this," Ghazi said, with a quick glance in my direction. "If you and Lieutenant Kazimierz position yourselves in the 20mm mounts, one on each ship, you will have the observation you need. Meanwhile, Captain Boyle and I will patrol the wharf, staying out of sight. I can also speak with some of the workers, to learn if they have seen anything. In this way, we can take them as soon as they appear."

"We don't have enough walkie-talkies," Gideon said, but I could see he knew it was the better approach.

"You take one, sir, and make regular visual contact with Kaz. He can signal if he sees anything," I said. "You then radio us."

"It is a good plan, Colonel," Kaz said. "It takes advantage of Inspector Ghazi's local knowledge, and the fact that none of our quarry have ever seen him."

"You're right," Gideon said, as the sound of the train whistle drew closer. "Get into position. I'll speak with the harbormaster and then get up into this mount." The colonel ordered Fenwick and the fourth driver to remain in a jeep at the entrance to the wharf in case he needed them.

"Billy," Kaz said, pulling me aside as Gideon left. "If you encounter Sidorov, remember he is a murderer, on the large scale and small. If you stand in the way of his freedom, he will kill you. He is a charming fellow, for a Russian, but do not give him a chance. I know you, and you possess a strong streak of American sentimentality. It can be endearing, but for now, cast it out. Kill Sidorov. It will be the best thing you can do for him, believe me."

Kaz hustled up the gangway to his post, and Ghazi and I walked off the wharf and followed the train tracks.

"I could not help but overhear. Captain Sidorov, he was a friend?"

"I can't say that. He is a killer, and he betrayed me. But he's one of those people you wish could be a better person, know what I mean?"

"I do. And I understand why your friend is concerned. A moment's hesitation, and you are lost to him. Think of his loss, Captain Boyle," Ghazi said.

"Call me Billy. Everyone does."

"Very well, Billy. I am Javid. And I do not know this Sidorov fellow other than as a villain. I will kill him for you. And for Lieutenant Kazimierz. There, now we are friends."

My new friend stopped to talk with a couple of laborers who were carrying heavy burlap sacks of green beans to a platform next to the tracks. I walked on, staring down the tracks. Smoke from the engine spouted, not that far away, and as the train rounded a bend, I could see the light on the front of the locomotive.

"Learn anything?" I asked Javid as he caught up with me.

"No. They are too afraid. There has been a crackdown on petty pilferage, and they don't want trouble," he said. "But they did say the Americans take the most."

"Everybody takes a cut when it comes to the supply line," I said. "It's a matter of degree."

"Yes. Minor losses help keep everyone happy. Major losses make everyone look bad. The same the world over, eh?"

We came to another pile of heavy crates, rows of them, stacked three high, with enough space for a person to squeeze between. There was no shortage of hiding places here. How long someone could last out in this heat was another story.

I squinted my eyes, trying to keep the sweat from clouding my vision. The train didn't seem to be moving. It was coming straight at us, so maybe it had simply slowed. An optical illusion.

We circled the crates and doubled back toward the ships.

The walkie-talkie crackled. It was Big Mike. Nothing unusual at the lighters.

"Who mans them? Over," I said to Big Mike. Americans, he said. Part of the port battalion crew.

We walked parallel to the wharf, listening to the train and watching the work of the GI longshoremen. Winches hauled supplies out of the holds and lowered them to the wharf. Men swarmed over them, organizing materials for quick loading. Brutal work.

Javid came back from another chat with Iranian laborers.

"A rumor was whispered to me," he said. "Today is a good day for a blind man."

"A day not to see things," I said.

"Which tells me someone here has knowledge of the Khazar involvement, at least," Javid said as the sweat trickled down his temples. "Otherwise there would be no rumor."

"Are there any Iranian vessels in the harbor?" I asked.

"We should find out," Javid said, and I got on the walkie-talkie. Gideon said he'd check with the harbormaster.

"Where is the train?" Javid said, climbing up a pile of crates as the workers stacking them stood aside. He shielded his eyes and leaned forward. "It has stopped."

"How far?"

"A quarter mile, perhaps."

The walkie-talkie sounded. Gideon reported that there were no Iranian-flagged ships in the harbor. Mostly US Merchant Marine, with neutral ships from Portugal and Turkey. Two British vessels registered out of India, and a French ship.

"Colonel, the train seems to have stopped. Can you see anything? Over."

"Negative. Over."

"French?" Big Mike said, breaking in and forgetting to say *over*.

"Damn," Gideon said. "The *Africaine*, registered out of Madagascar." He forgot to say *over* as well.

The train whistle blew, one long blast followed by two short toots.

"A signal," Javid said, climbing down from the stacked crates.

"Colonel, can you spot the French freighter? Over."

"Yes, still at anchor. Over."

The *crack* of a small explosion sounded from the other side of the wooden crates. Flame shot up into the air and black smoke swirled around the containers as workers and GIs shouted and generally ran around in frantic circles.

"Now a distraction," Javid said, moving away from the conflagration. We stepped out into the open and onto a raised platform marked for outbound goods, products the train was delivering for export.

The train whistle blew again. Workers were lowering buckets into the water and hauling them up to douse the fire. They got a decent bucket brigade working and, of course, all eyes were on them and the fire.

Which was the idea.

"Anything?" I said into the walkie-talkie. "We have a suspicious fire here. Over."

"Nothing, over," Gideon said, followed by the same from Big Mike.

I rubbed the sweat away from my eyes again and scanned the train and the open ground around it. A siren wailed, heralding the arrival of a fire engine in olive drab, an ancient hand-pump vehicle that had seen better days. GIs drove it onto the wharf and began dousing the burning crates with a steady stream of water. Two ambulances arrived and soon the whole area was jammed with soldiers, sailors, and workers, all gathered around the vehicles.

More smoke billowed out from the fire, a thick cloud of white.

"Smoke grenade," I said, as a man screamed. A worker came out of the smoke, his ragged clothes singed and blackened. He fell on the ground, choking, as the medics rushed to his side. At the same time, the locomotive chugged on, releasing a cloud of steam as it advanced even closer. Its next whistle meant business, not a signal. Too many people were crowded on the wharf, blocking its way on the narrow tracks, and the engineer gave out a warning blast. People scattered in every direction.

"We are losing control of the situation," Javid said. "If we ever had it."

"They have to be close by," I said. Or maybe not. This could all be misdirection, getting us to focus on the train and the fire while Maiya pulled a fast one somewhere else.

"Listen," Javid said, cupping a hand around his ear. "Aircraft approaching. There!" He pointed north and I spotted it. A twin-engine plane, coming in low with wheels lowered, heading for the flat strip of land between the berm and the tracks, heading right for the pier.

Heading right for Big Mike.

I couldn't believe it. A gutsy move, but what was she thinking?

The Yak-6M put its flaps down and managed a ragged landing, sending up a plume of dust before coming to a wobbly halt about fifty yards from the pier. Big Mike's jeep raced out to the aircraft as soon as its engines cut. Three figures bolted from the rear exit, running for the train. In the shimmering heat, it was impossible to pick out faces.

"Are those Russians?" Javid asked as we moved along the side of the train, which had finally come to a halt. "I could not tell from the uniform."

"Dusty brown, about the same as everybody around here," I said. "I can't even tell if one's a woman."

My walkie-talkie squawked at me, but I ignored it, pointing my Thompson in the air. It was time for a warning shot.

I didn't have a chance to fire.

The airplane exploded, a *crack-boom* that tore the fuselage apart and sent a shockwave of heated air that almost knocked me over. Burning pieces of metal fluttered to the ground as tires burned and issued black, acrid smoke.

"Big Mike!" I yelled, my ears still ringing. I keyed the walkie-talkie, trying to clear my head and make sense of what was happening. No answer from Big Mike, but I could hear Gideon calling.

I tore my eyes away from the wreckage and glanced up the length of the train. They were gone. I looked back to where Big Mike had been and saw the jeep heading for us, one man slumped in the front.

Kaz was running toward us, his uniform soaked in sweat, hands gripping his Thompson.

"Twelve cars up," he gasped, taking in deep breaths as he watched Big Mike. "I saw them go in a boxcar."

The jeep swerved and braked close to us.

"I've got two injured," Big Mike said from the driver's seat, grimacing as he shifted gears. "Debris hit these two hard. I was in the back seat and ducked just in time. Did they get away?"

"Yeah," I said, checking the men. One was unconscious, blood seeping from his hairline. The other's face was peppered with cuts and one eye was swollen shut. "There's a couple of ambulances over by where that fire was. Go. We'll search for the Russians."

"Be careful," Big Mike said. "Tricky bastards."

As soon as Big Mike took off, Gideon pulled up with Fenwick and another GI.

"We lost them?" Gideon said.

"For the moment," Kaz said. "We shall find them."

"We need to search the train for the drugs," I said. "Find the drugs and we find them."

"That stunt with the aircraft," Javid said. "It seemed rather heavy-handed, don't you think?"

"It worked," Gideon said. "Drew our attention."

"Yes, but from what?" Kaz said. "They could have come in on the train. Why go through that entrance and explosion, only to run for the train, where they could have been all along?"

"Listen, we don't have a lot of time," I said. "Sergeant Fenwick, you patrol to the end of the train and see if you spot anyone suspicious. Then work your way back, checking each car."

We'll start at this end. No telling where they could be by now."

"Colonel, do we know when the French ship is scheduled to unload their cargo?" Javid asked.

"She's next up. They've almost finished unloading one of the Liberty ships, and as soon as the wharf is cleared, the *Africaine* will dock."

"We need armed men at the ready when she does," I said. "Sir."

"I'll get that organized. Contact me if you find anything," Gideon said, and drove off.

We began opening the boxcars, each time readying ourselves for an encounter. But there was just a lot of nothing.

I tried to see this through Maiya's eyes. Even though there was little chance, in her mind, that we'd discover her true destination, she'd planned everything in case we did, distractions and all.

Kaz and Javid had a point about the airplane. What was the real purpose?

Misdirection.

Like a magician. They make you look up and to the right while the trick is being played low and to the left. The only question was, what was the trick?

Misdirection.

"Damn," I said, stopping in my tracks as Javid was about to unlatch another boxcar.

"What?" Kaz asked.

"That wasn't them. The three people. It had to be the Khazar crew. It's not impossible for a smuggler to have a pilot in his gang, right?"

"Not at all," Javid said. "It would explain how the Khazars evaded our border patrols so easily."

"The explosion was meant to distract us," Kaz said. "But from what?"

"The drugs. They must have off-loaded them," I said. "And they wanted us to waste our time searching the train for three Russians."

As we walked back, I called Gideon and told him to have the ambulances checked and to detain anyone who couldn't be vouched for. I told Fenwick and his buddy to keep searching the train, in case I was wrong.

But I knew I wasn't.

The fire. The smoke grenade. The ambulance. The airplane landing, the explosion.

Brilliant.

The platform for export materials was already filling up as workers unloaded cargo from the boxcars at the head of the train.

Javid opened the door, and as if the train itself was granting me a reward for my deduction, we were greeted by the sight of five disassembled and empty cases. Cases marked for delivery to Khazar Brothers shipping. Next to them were discarded Russian uniforms.

"The men from the plane are now mixed in with the laborers," Javid said. "Impossible to find."

"But not the drugs," I said. "I think I know right where to find them."

The export cargo platform was filling up. Crates and canvas sacks of all sorts were piled up, some of it had writing in Farsi and some in English.

"What exactly are we looking for, Billy?" Kaz asked.

"Packaging roughly the same volume as five cases, each five by two by two feet," I said, eyeing the laborers all around us. Any one of them could be in the pay of the Khazar brothers, with knives hidden in the folds of their clothes.

"This may be helpful," Javid said. He tapped his finger on a wooden crate. Unpainted, new wood. If it hadn't been so muggy, the paint might have dried in the heat. Instead, when I ran my finger across the destination, the black paint stuck to my finger.

Africaine. Destination Marseilles, France.

I had them. Without the drugs, they were dead.

"Ten crates of pistachio nuts, if the label is to be believed," Javid said. I got Gideon on the walkie-talkie and told him where we were. And that we needed a truck and armed guard.

He pulled up a few minutes later, Big Mike in the rear seat, his bum leg stretched out.

"Guards and a truck are on the way," he said. "Is this it?" He pointed to the pistachios.

"Probably, but I don't want to open them here. Too public. Once we get them into the truck we can check," I said.

"How did they manage it?" Big Mike asked.

"Distracted us with the airplane. While that was going on, they put the heroin into these crates aboard the train, then had them unloaded here," I said, working it out as best I could.

"Not sure about that," Gideon said. "There's a manifest for the unloading from the train. It's all double-checked."

"Jesus," I said, cursing my stupidity. "Did you find those two ambulances?"

"There was only one," Big Mike said. "They took my two guys away. Oh, damn, I see."

"The second ambulance," Javid said. "They must have caused that stoppage on the line we saw. Then loaded the new crates into the ambulance."

"And put them on this platform which the fire started," Kaz said. "No need for a manifest. Anything here will be loaded according to the labels. Ingenious."

"But where are they now?" Big Mike said.

"There's only one place. They think they're safe, and the drugs are going to be loaded aboard the *Africaine*. That's where they must be headed," I said.

Kaz and I raced to the wharf. We left Gideon and Javid to guard the heroin, with Big Mike in his jeep watching the crowd, M1 at the ready.

I held my hand over my eyes, shielding them from the sun. The water glittered, each wave reflecting pinpoints of bright, dazzling light.

"There!" I said, pointing to a rowboat just leaving the far shore beyond the pier. A lifeboat, probably from the *Africaine*. It was too far to tell for sure, but it looked like four rowers and three passengers.

I prayed this wasn't another of Maiya's tricks. If it was, she was just too damn smart for me. I ran, Kaz hard on my heels, off the wharf and onto the roadway that led to the pier, where one lighter stood at the ready. A jeep was parked next to a loading crane, and I jumped in, the GI who was taking a smoke break in the shade too startled to speak. With Kaz hanging on, I sped down the road, wondering if Maiya would spot the racing jeep.

And what Sidorov would do.

What I would do.

I slammed on the brakes right at the edge of the pier. We both vaulted out of the jeep and found two sailors lounging in the partial shade of a makeshift wall built along the pier.

"What's all the fireworks, Captain?" one of them asked.

"We need to intercept that rowboat," I said. "Too complicated to explain. Let's go."

"Is it dangerous, sir?" the other guy asked.

"Very," Kaz said. "Which is why we are so heavily armed. Now go."

Something in Kaz's tone convinced them to shove off without delay. The engine rumbled to life and as we cast off, I eyed the distance between us and the rowboat. I couldn't tell which ship was the *Africaine*, but I didn't want them getting close. I didn't know if the crew was in on it and might take exception to our collaring their clients. Or if we'd get mixed up in some sort of Iranian, French, and Russian jurisdictional issue.

No. We were going to settle this now.

Empty, the lighter wallowed in the water, even in the gentle rolling swells. It wasn't designed for speed, but slowly we drew closer. Close enough to make out Maiya standing at the bow, with a pair of binoculars aimed our way. I waved and aimed my Thompson her way.

I could see her yelling at the rowers, and damned if they didn't pick up the pace.

"Billy, we can't let them get to the ship," Kaz said over the rumbling roar of the engine. "There she is, the *Africaine*." He pointed to a small ship that had just become visible as it moved out from behind a larger Liberty ship.

"Their ship still has to dock," I said. "Gideon can handle that end. We've got to stop them from boarding."

"They may have willing accomplices on the *Africaine*," Kaz said. "The ship could be crewed by *Le Milieu*."

Damn. Kaz was right. The French mob might well operate a small coastal freighter like this shallow-hulled one-stacker. Just the thing for smuggling. Not that they'd be happy about abandoning their drug shipment on shore, but maybe they'd take out their frustrations on us. Then Maiya and company, but we'd be dead.

"Can you go any faster?" I asked.

"Some," the sailor answered. "Hang on."

We grabbed the rail on the starboard side as the craft thumped over the waves, water splashing us and swirling over the deck.

"If they have any firepower at all on the *Africaine,* it'll be like shooting ducks in a barrel," I said, looking at the wide-open steel deck of the lighter. "Literally."

"I for one refuse to quack," Kaz said, and fired off a burst at the rowboat, kicking up splashes of water short of it. The Thompson had great stopping power up close, but lousy range.

"You're not going to hit anything yet," I said.

"I know. But I want the rowers to think about what will happen when we get closer. If they are not *Milieu,* it may give them pause."

Apparently Sidorov and Max had the same idea. They stood and quickly unleashed a couple of bursts from their PPSh-41s. We ducked, but their rounds fell short.

"How soon can you close the range?" I shouted to the sailor at the wheel.

"About one minute, sir. Those fellas are pulling hard, but they can't keep it up. We can."

I counted to thirty, and then let loose a few rounds in front of their bow. They fell about ten yards short. We'd be within a hundred and fifty yards, the Thompson's effective range, in half a minute.

"Aim for the oars," I told Kaz. "Shake up the rowers."

We both fired, raising some serious spouts along the port side of the boat. The rowers ducked, losing their rhythm, leaving some oars dead in the water. The starboard rowers maintained their pace, but that only caused the rowboat to swerve closer to us.

"Maiya, give up!" I shouted, cupping my hands around my mouth.

She raised her PPSh-41. Not at me, but at the head of the rower closest to her.

Sidorov fired, then Max. A few rounds *zinged* against our steel hull. The message was clear. Back off or the rower dies.

I wasn't buying it.

"Straight at 'em!" I shouted.

"Again, at the oars," I said to Kaz. We fired, emptying our clips and reloading. This time, it looked like we struck a couple of the wooden oars. It was mass confusion on their port side as the starboard rowers looked around for instructions, slowing their pace. The rowboat wallowed, Maiya waving her weapon and yelling at the crew.

Max and Sidorov fired at us, rounds ricocheting inside the lighter as they targeted the coxswain.

"Son of a bitch," he shouted as a bullet grazed his arm. His pal went to help but he waved him off, his mouth clenched in fury. He bent low, grasping the wheel, and kept straight and true on an interception course.

The rowboat was hardly moving. Two rowers jumped over the side and began swimming away. Maiya aimed her *papasha* and fired at their bobbing heads, sending up sprays of foamy blood. She quickly turned her weapon on the remaining men. Smoke curled from the barrel. Sidorov joined in and manned an oar. The boat got going again. But too much time had been lost. We were nearly on them, coming in at an angle to ram. More rowers abandoned ship, and Max stood, leveling his daddy at us as the boat rocked beneath him. His burst went high.

Mine didn't.

It caught him dead center and knocked him down.

Maiya fired, her aim better than Max's. She peppered the wheelhouse, causing the coxswain to dive for cover.

Which was a mistake, since he couldn't slow or swerve to avoid the rowboat. The lighter crashed into the boat, splintering wood and tossing Maiya overboard. We churned over the wreckage, Maiya disappearing under our hull.

The coxswain regained control, bringing the lighter about. The remaining rowers had all given up and were making for the *Africaine*, a hardy swim away. The smashed rowboat was afloat, with Max sprawled in the stern, one arm moving enough to show he was alive.

Sidorov managed to stand, maintaining his balance as the boat slowly sank.

"Not the ending I wished," Sidorov said, gesturing at the waves lapping at his feet. "But at least it is not the road of bones."

He drew his pistol and aimed it at Kaz. His hand shook, just for an instant. But he didn't fire.

"*Smert' shpionam*," Sidorov said, his voice loud and clear.

Kaz shot him. Two rounds in the chest and Sidorov tumbled into the water, a river of red trailing him as he floated away.

"What did he say?" I asked Kaz, as we watched Sidorov's sinking corpse.

"Death to spies," Kaz said. "It was the motto of the original Soviet secret police. I took it as his death sentence."

"Self-proclaimed," I said. "I don't think he was going to shoot you."

"I agree," Kaz said. "I gave him what he wanted. A warm grave."

"Captain," the coxswain's buddy said. "There's the woman we ran over."

Maiya was face down, her dark hair a bloody halo around her ruined neck, mangled by the propellers.

"Leave them for the fishes," I said. "But we should help Max."

"He should be dead," Kaz said. "But, if you insist."

CHAPTER THIRTY-SEVEN

MAX WAS MOANING as we hoisted him onto the lighter. I'd gotten into the rowboat as it was about to go under and lifted him, surprised at how little blood there was. Kaz took him and the sailor helped me aboard.

We laid him out. Blood soaked his shirt where I'd hit him, low and on his left side. It looked like only one bullet, but a .45 slug at that range should've done a world of damage.

I opened his shirt, just as Max's eyelids fluttered open.

I almost laughed out loud.

Wrapped around his skinny waist were two money belts filled with gold coins. It was like wearing armor. My slug had smashed into one gold piece, nearly flattening it. There was another underneath it, and it had broken through his skin and gave him a thickening bruise.

"Once a *vor*, always a *vor*," Kaz said. "After all the lies and betrayals, it is refreshing to find a man who is at least consistent."

"It saved his life," I said. "But what good does that do him? He may come to regret it."

"Look," Kaz said, pointing out to sea as we neared the pier. "The *Africaine*. She's weighed anchor."

"And she's not headed for the wharves," I said. "I wonder if Gideon can call on a warship to intercept her?"

"For what crime?" Kaz said. "Leaving without unloading cargo? There may be something to that, but the captain can claim to have been under attack. Or they might just take the cargo and scuttle the ship. With *Le Milieu*, it may be just a business loss."

AN HOUR LATER, Max was in the base infirmary, bandaged and sitting up. Big Mike was off getting his ankle taped. Inspector Ghazi stood at the end of Max's bed, Kaz and I on either side. A ceiling fan moved the hot air around as my saltwater-soaked clothes clung to my skin. Colonel Gideon joined us, first having gone to the radio room.

"Thank you for saving me," Max said. "Maiya forced me, you know."

"Max, you tried to kill us," I said. "I think you killed Morris and Kopelev in the warehouse as well."

"No, no, never would Max kill Boris Morris. I like him."

"Kopelev?" Kaz asked.

"No one like Kopelev, boss. But Max no kill him either."

Of course not.

"Then help us Max. How did the Khazar brothers do it?" Gideon said. "Was it Maiya's scheme or theirs?" That was smart. He was letting Max off the hook.

"Oh, they come up with plan. They use the ambulance before, at other ports. Good trick, yes? And the airplane, they have pilot. Smart boys. They put drugs in new containers. Make train stop, load ambulance. Then boom!"

"You must have been afraid for your life," Javid said. "To fire on these officers."

"Yes, yes, very afraid. Afraid Maiya will kill me. But I did not hit you, boss, did I?"

Not for lack of trying, but I let that slide.

"You stole the map back in Poltava, didn't you?" I asked.

"Sure. Maiya tell me to watch what you do, take what I can. Or she denounce me, which means no more Max."

"Was Black working for Maiya?" Kaz asked.

"Black is a fool. He prays at the church of Maiya, but she uses him," Max said. "Maiya good at using people. Bend them around finger, yes?"

Yes.

"So Max, just answer me this," I said. "How did Maiya and the Khazars communicate?"

"What? Oh, pain is bad. Please, drugs."

"How droll," Kaz said. "No drugs, Max. Answer the question."

"Bad pain," Max said, moaning and squeezing his eyes, not to mention his mouth, shut.

MAX WAS SMART enough not to incriminate himself. He had a story and he'd stick to it. Maiya the evil temptress who called all the shots. Well, good for him. The only question was, would he end up back in the Soviet labor camps or in an Iranian prison? Neither was a pleasant option, which was fine with me.

We left the room to the groans and protestations of Max's innocence.

Big Mike came down the hall, crutches swinging.

"What now?" he asked.

"I guess we have to report back to Poltava?" I asked.

"No. I've taken care of that," he said. "I sent a radio message to General Dawson, informing him that Major Kiril Sidorov and Lieutenant Maiya Akilina died while in pursuit of drug smugglers. I fingered Max as being in league with Iranian smugglers. Bull said he'd throw a Major Black into the mix as one of the culprits. Convenient because he's dead."

"Why?" I asked, even though I knew the answer.

"Allied unity," Gideon said. "It's all-important. We still want the Russians to come into the war against Japan. We want them to be cooperative when our armies meet in Germany. This way, we give them two dead heroes and a plausible story of a Russian thief and a renegade OSS officer."

It made sense. I also knew that this fairy tale would spare Maiya's family from any retribution Uncle Joe might hand out. The Soviets, like the Nazis, practiced wholesale family punishment on anyone accused of anti-state behavior. Sidorov's wife as well, although he'd said she was protected by a well-placed father.

"Okay," I said. "I buy it. What's next?"

"A flight to Tehran," Gideon said. "You three have travel orders to head to Cairo within forty-eight hours."

We drove back to the airstrip, and Javid promised a lavish meal at his favorite restaurant tomorrow night before we left. That sounded fine. But what I really wanted to do was put this part of the world behind me. I wanted to go to a place where motives were straightforward, where lies and betrayals were not standard issue, and where I knew who the enemy was.

If I could find it.

HISTORICAL NOTE

THE SHUTTLE-BOMBING CAMPAIGN known as Operation Frantic carried on from June to October 1944. After that, the airbase at Poltava was maintained on a skeleton basis until the end of the war.

While there were early successful bombing raids, the enterprise was marred by a lack of Soviet cooperation. The absence of antiaircraft and night-fighter support as described in this story were two of the major factors that resulted in a disastrous raid by the Luftwaffe. The actual bombing took place in June 1944, with German aircraft targeting the Poltava base just as described in chapter thirty-three. Forty-seven of the seventy-three American bombers at the airfield were destroyed, laying bare the inadequacies of the Soviet defenses. Wanting to limit the presence of foreigners within the Soviet Union, Stalin would not allow more Americans to enter with antiaircraft or night-fighter units. But neither did he provide them for the defense of the three airbases.

Tensions increased in the summer of 1944 when the Russians would not allow American bombers and fighters operating from bases in Ukraine to bomb targets in support of the Polish Home Army's uprising in Warsaw. Stalin wanted the Poles to be defeated by the Nazis to facilitate his take-over of Poland.

After the war, Soviet officers who had worked well with the Americans were punished for their cooperation with Westerners. One Air Marshal, who had been awarded the US Legion of Merit by the Americans, was tortured and jailed for his helpfulness.

The Night Witches, officially known as the 46th Guards Night Bomber Aviation Regiment, was one of three all-female air force units. The night bombers specialized in idling the engines of their wood-and-canvas biplanes and gliding to the target, with only wind noise between the struts to reveal their presence. German soldiers likened the sound to broomsticks and named the pilots *Nachthexen*, or Night Witches. They were so hated and feared by the Germans that any airman who shot one down was automatically awarded the Iron Cross. Even though the Night Witches were the most highly decorated Soviet air force unit of the war, they were disbanded six months after the end of hostilities and were not invited to participate in the victory parade held in Moscow.

Shtrafniki were Soviet penal units made up of troops convicted of political or military wrongdoing. Although mine-clearing was one of the duties often imposed on the *shtrafniki*, they were also used in suicidal attacks. During the battle of Stalingrad, one penal battalion made up entirely of nine hundred disgraced officers who had been demoted in rank to private, was reduced to only three hundred survivors after three days. During the war, about 423,000 soldiers served in these penal units, very few of them surviving.

In researching this novel, I wanted to gain a better understanding of the experience of bomber crews over occupied Europe. The 2018 documentary film *The Cold Blue* was invaluable in that regard. Put together from footage found in the National Archives, it utilized materials originally filmed by director William Wyler for his well-known *The Memphis Belle*. The film prints were found in pristine condition, and when matched with narration from surviving flyers and sounds recorded from the few remaining B-17 bombers, it is an astounding account of what it was like to fly, fight, and die in the cold blue skies over the Third Reich.

ACKNOWLEDGMENTS

FIRST READERS LIZA Mandel and Michael Gordon once again provided superb feedback and offered helpful commentary as the story was finalized. My wife, Deborah Mandel, listened to chapter readings throughout the writing process, offered valuable critiques, and edited the manuscript to bring it into sharper focus. I am also indebted to Miriam Kalman for her childhood recollection of soldiers attending NYU in the Bronx and clambering up the fire escapes, as described in Chapter 25.

I am also grateful to Abe Seidman, WWII Army Air Force veteran and my wife's cousin, whose stories of bomber missions in the skies above Europe led me to write of that terrible, cold struggle in tribute to all those who flew.

Finally, kudos to Paula Munier and the entire team at Talcott Notch Literary Services for their brilliant guidance in bringing this and other stories to fruition.